Love Finds You™

Lake Geneva
WISCONSIN

Love Finds You™

in Lake Geneva

WISCONSIN

PAMELA S. MEYERS

summerside
PRESS™

New York

Love Finds You in Lake Geneva, Wisconsin

ISBN-10: 1-60936-769-3
ISBN-13: 978-1-60936-769-5

Published by Summerside Press, an imprint of Guideposts
16 East 34th Street
New York, New York 10016
SummersidePress.com
Guideposts.org

*Summerside Press™ is an inspirational publisher offering fresh,
irresistible books to uplift the heart and engage the mind.*

Distributed by Ideals Publications, a Guideposts company
2630 Elm Hill Pike, Suite 100
Nashville, TN 37214

The town depicted in this book is a real place. References to actual
people or events are either coincidental or are used with permission.

All Scripture quotations are taken from The Holy Bible,
King James Version.

Cover design by Lookout Design, Inc., LookoutDesign.com
Interior design by Müllerhaus Publishing Group, Mullerhaus.net

Printed and bound in the United States of America
10 9 8 7 6 5 4 3 2 1

Dedication

....

Dedicated to the memory of my parents, Roger and Peg Meyers, and all the special times we had together during my growing-up years in Lake Geneva. Although they are not here to read my story, there is a bit of both of them in Meg and Jack.

Acknowledgments

....

I thank God Almighty for blessing me with the opportunity to write this story. I've always wanted to set a story in Lake Geneva, and God has granted my desire in a huge way.

I am very grateful to the Lake Geneva Public Library and particularly to staff member Alisha Benson, who graciously bent over backwards assisting me with the microfilms of the *Lake Geneva News-Tribune* from that period. She also helped me by uncovering several different resources when I needed to make sure Flat Iron Park was called by that name in 1933.

Thank you to Doug Elliott, retired editor of the *Lake Geneva Regional News*, the current Lake Geneva weekly newspaper that succeeded the *News-Tribune*. I thoroughly enjoyed our long conversations, Doug, as you enlightened me on the culture of the news biz back in the thirties. I couldn't have made my story true to that era without your input.

Thanks also to the Geneva Lake Museum and to museum volunteer Linda West for your encouragement and help with learning historical facts about the town during my visit there.

Thank you to Sandi Rothengass. I appreciate your friendship so much, which goes back to when we both worked at Citizens Bank in Lake Geneva. Your help and encouragement with this project is so appreciated. It was because of you that I learned that Violette Smith, a key person in my story, was still living, and I was able to visit with her.

And I thank Diane Smith Krapfel, daughter of Violette Smith, for allowing me to visit Violette in the nursing home. Little did we know that she would pass away a week and a half later.

Thank you to Chuck Gray, Lake Geneva harbormaster, for taking time out of your day to allow me into the Riviera ballroom for photographs and notes. Although I'd been in the ballroom many times, I'd never looked at the details through an author's eyes. You were very helpful!

Thanks to American Christian Fiction Writers (ACFW) and all there who have mentored me, taught me the craft of writing, and encouraged me with prayer over these many years. I've said it before and continue to say it: you guys rock!

Many thanks to my Penwrights critique group, which critiqued this story from beginning to end. Thanks also to Ane Mulligan, who, in addition to critiquing my story, brainstormed much of the plot with me. And thanks to Andrea Boeshaar for her support, especially during the time of waiting to see it published.

Thank you to my editor, Rachel Meisel, who encouraged me to write this story from the moment I mentioned I had grown up in Lake Geneva. Who knew when you came to my ACFW chapter meeting that long ago May evening that this would result! I appreciate your input on this story so much.

Also thank you to my wonderful copyeditor, Connie Troyer, for the time she took on this story. You moved my writing to the next level.

I would be remiss to not mention my agent, Terry Burns, who goes above and beyond. Thanks, Terry, for all you have done to enhance my writing career.

Last but not least, I want to thank my Life Group members, past and present—Catherine, Nancy, Judy, and Betty for their ongoing prayer support. Girlfriends, you prayed this book into existence. I love you all!

Trust in the Lord with all thine heart;
and lean not unto thine own understanding.
In all thy ways acknowledge him,
and he shall direct thy paths.

PROVERBS 3:5–6

Lake Geneva, Wisconsin

AT THE CLOSE OF THE CIVIL WAR, MILLIONAIRES FLOCKED TO THE Lake Geneva, Wisconsin, area and built magnificent mansions in which to escape the summer heat. The locals became accustomed to seeing their wealthy neighbors about town, and many found employment as caretakers or household help on their estates.

Today, excursion boats carry tourists past the many remaining mansions on Geneva Lake's shoreline, while an announcer relates their fascinating histories. Other tourists take advantage of the public shore path for up-close views of the estates. Back in town, the Riviera Beach is a perfect place to cool off after browsing the many unique gift shops along Main and Broad Streets. Visitors can also cap off the afternoon with a horse-drawn carriage ride through the town's historical neighborhoods or enjoy a meal in one of the many restaurants.

As summer eases in to fall, ancient oak and maple trees turn to brilliant oranges and golds, offering an ideal time to catch a final boat ride of the season. If visitors are in town during the first weekend of February, they'll be able to catch the annual snow-sculpturing contest, which takes place on the front lawn of the Riviera with the frozen lake as a backdrop.

The Riviera, a beautiful Italian Renaissance Revival structure on the shore of the lake, with thirty-two Doric columns, parquet dance floor, and sparkling mirror ball, is a focal point of this story.

No matter the season, the time is always right to visit Lake Geneva.

—*Pamela S. Meyers*

Chapter One

....

March 1933

Meg Alden closed the notepad and stuffed it into her handbag. A whole hour spent on what would amount to a single paragraph on the society page. Maybe by the next Garden Club meeting, her beat would be hard news about the new building and not about which flowers should grace its grounds.

She stood from the dining room chair the hostess had provided and picked up the brown envelope that hadn't left her sight all morning. She grabbed her coat and gave a tiny wave to her mother before she slipped out the front door. She had less than an hour to give what she considered her best work to Mr. Zimmer.

This afternoon might be too late.

With quick strides, she arrived at the town's main intersection and peered down the street toward the lake. Thanks to the meeting, she'd missed her daily check on the new building's progress.

Even though the outside work was completed, she still loved her regular walks past the brown brick structure, as she imagined tourists and bathers enjoying its new bathhouses and food counters during the day and energetic dancers kicking up their heels in its beautiful ballroom at night.

Meg shifted her attention to the traffic light suspended over where Main and Broad intersected. In the stiff March wind, the thing bobbed precariously. Pressing the envelope to her chest, she shifted her weight from one foot to the other. A gust smacked her in the face, and she grabbed for her hat as the envelope slipped from her grasp and spiraled upward.

It twisted and tumbled, lifted and dropped to the pavement inches from a muddy puddle.

Meg darted into the intersection.

A horn blared.

She froze.

Fred Newman glared at her through the windscreen of his Model A pickup truck, his lips pursed as if he'd just sucked on a lemon.

She snatched up the envelope.

He leaned out the window, his leathery face looking as though it would crack if he smiled. "You'd better watch where you're going."

Meg tossed him a wave and puddle-hopped to the curb. The old busybody would have it all over town by lunchtime that Meg Alden had nearly caused him to run her over in the middle of the street. Well, let him. She had other things on her mind. Meg lifted the flap of Dad's thick legal envelope, and her spine relaxed. No water had seeped through.

She raced down Main Street, her two-inch heels clacking on the sidewalk. Mr. Zimmer would have the front page laid out already, but he always left room on the second and third pages for last-minute items. Meg turned on Center and stepped through the *News-Tribune*'s entrance. The rat-tat-tatting of typewriter keys, a ringing phone, and cigarette smoke as thick as ground fog assaulted her: deadline day, and she loved every minute of it.

Next to her, the switchboard lights flashed. Meg dropped her things to the floor and pressed the headset to her ear. She grabbed a back cord from a column of cords on the desktop and plugged its end into a flashing socket. "*Lake Geneva News-Tribune.*"

"This is Jim Olson. Is Oscar there?"

"One moment." She pulled the front end of the cord from its position on the desk and plugged its other end in the socket assigned to Mr. Zimmer. Then she pulled a small lever in front of the cords to cause her boss's phone to ring.

Why was the new building's construction manager calling? A last-minute update for tomorrow's edition? If things went as she hoped, she'd be the one to take such calls and Mr. Zimmer wouldn't need to be bothered.

The outside door opened. "That's some wind. Morning, Meg." Emily Johnson glanced at the board. "I only ran to the post office. Where's Dotty?"

Meg glanced into the newsroom and looked for the part-time typist who helped on deadline day. "Over there typing. She probably got called away to do a rush job."

Emily scurried to the closet and removed her coat. "Thanks for stepping in." She plucked out her hat pin and removed her hat. Her topknot had already begun losing its battle against her naturally curly hair. "Have there been many calls?"

A pair of tiny lights flashed, and Meg released the cords. "Only one. But now that you're here, I need to talk to Mr. Zimmer."

She stepped to the closet and reached for her hat. Her heart sank. The stylish new cloche was probably lying in front of Cobb Hardware. If not already trampled on, it soon would be. Such a pretty color too.

Meg peeked into the mottled mirror hanging on the back of the closet door and rearranged what was left of her finger waves. At least taking want ads over the phone had its benefits. No one could see her. The lost hat forgotten, she picked up the envelope and hurried toward her desk on the far side of the newsroom.

Thelma Brown, Mr. Zimmer's middle-aged secretary, looked up from her typing as Meg passed and nodded at her. Always the picture of perfection with her iron-gray bun and crisply starched blouses, the woman gave Meg a critical look and returned to her work.

Meg dropped her purse into her bottom desk drawer and then slipped the single sheet of paper from the envelope. She skimmed her words for the umpteenth time. Not a single mistake. She peered into the corner office, thankful for the unobstructed view of her boss as he sat at his desk.

Oscar Zimmer, his sleeves rolled to his elbows and his unruly thatch of white hair looking as though it hadn't seen a comb in days, pressed the telephone to his ear. Another call must have come in. She needed to talk to him right away. Meg tiptoed across the newsroom, hoping to catch him before he received another call or took the layout to Composing.

Mr. Zimmer hung up the phone, and she rapped on the door frame.

He looked up, his eyes wide behind his thick wire-framed lenses. A smile erupted on his wizened face. "Miss Alden, come in."

Meg gulped against the dryness in her throat and stepped closer. "Mr. Zimmer, would you please read this article I wrote on the lakefront building? My friend Gloria's husband is one of the bricklayers, and he gave me wonderful insights from a worker's perspective. With Mr. Bowman's departure, you'll need additional articles this week." Castigating herself for talking too fast, she held out the paper.

He stared at the article as his mouth made a slight downturn at the corners. Wasn't he going to take it?

Finally Mr. Zimmer drew in a breath. "The article sounds interesting, but we won't need filler pieces this week."

Pressure built behind her eyes. *Not now.* She had to remain composed. "Perhaps. . .if you read it—"

"I've got a man taking over Bowman's position." Mr. Zimmer's gaze shifted to a spot behind her right shoulder as his lips lifted into a smile. "Ah, here he is now. Miss Alden, meet Jack Wallace, our new reporter."

Meg's heart squeezed. Mr. Bowman had left so suddenly, she thought she'd at least have a chance—the only chance she'd had in three years.

Gone.

She turned slowly. The tall, broad-shouldered man was about as good looking as Clark Gable. Actually, better. She always did dislike mustaches. His blond, short-trimmed hair glistened. Never had she seen eyes such a deep blue. His impeccable suit and polished wingtip shoes were of far better quality than—

"Miss Alden?"

At Mr. Zimmer's voice, Meg dragged her gaze away from the man's footwear and up to his chin. "Pleased to meet you."

Mr. Wallace flashed a smile that could have lit up a dark alley on a moon-less night. "Nice to meet you, Miss Alden. And you are a reporter as well?"

She met his eyes, and their warmth drew her in.

"No."

At Mr. Zimmer's strong tone, she snapped her head his direction. "Miss Alden is our want-ad taker and occasionally does society news—who's visiting whom or garden-club doings. She also fetches me coffee when I ask." He held up a dirty coffee mug.

Dregs from yesterday's brew adhered to its insides like glue. Meg frowned as she took the cup. Unlike most people, Mr. Zimmer didn't drink coffee until afternoon. She recognized a brush-off when she saw it. "Welcome to the *News-Trib*, Mr. Wallace." Without waiting for a response, she spun and dashed toward the door.

What a dolt she'd been, acting as if she'd never seen a good-looking man before. A man who came out of nowhere, taking something that wasn't his. She plopped onto her desk chair, crumpled the article, and tossed it into her wastebasket. She heaved a breath and removed the typewriter cover.

Where had he come from? Judging by the cut of his suit and the shine of his shoes, not from any food line. Maybe he'd had a good job and lost it. News from the city was filled with hard-luck stories. If that were the case, could she blame him for taking the position? But she'd spent hours last night at Dad's typewriter. She at least deserved a chance. She rolled paper into her typewriter and then pushed a stack of forms aside to make room for her notes.

Her phone rang, and she yanked the receiver to her ear.

"Isn't he a looker?"

Meg turned. Emily wore her headset cocked at an angle, and her playful grin filled her round face.

"I didn't notice."

"Come on, Meg. You may be older than me, but you're not dead. Any woman would give her silk stockings to go out with the likes of him. I say he's a needed distraction around here, with only Mr. Zimmer and Lester to cast a shadow."

"You're forgetting Hank and the guys in Composing."

A loud sigh came through the connection. "All Hank cares about is sports or selling an ad, and Leo and Gus in Composing are as old as Moses. I hear Mr. Wallace is single. Oops. Got a call." Emily waggled her fingers and yanked the cord connecting them.

Meg slammed the receiver onto its cradle. Mr. Jack Wallace might have the good looks of a leading man, but until she became a reporter, romance would have to wait.

She faced Mr. Zimmer's open door. Mr. Wallace nodded his head as the older man held open last week's edition. The interloper had taken the first opportunity she'd had to move up in three years, but she wasn't quitting yet.

* * * * *

"Thanks, Oscar." Jack held up his notebook. "I'll get on this lakefront-building story. Bowman's articles make me wish I'd not missed all the excitement over the past year. Getting the bond issue passed and the building built was a swell way to put some men to work and, at the same time, provide good entertainment for the town."

Oscar hitched up his pants. "And add some beauty to the place. That old pavilion they called a ballroom had to go. Now with the expanded beach and new bathhouse, we'll draw more tourists from Illinois—and that means money for the merchants." A shrill ring filled the air, and he grabbed the candlestick phone. Lifting the earpiece to his ear, he barked, "Zimmer."

Jack edged toward the open door. Miss Alden sat hunched over the desk adjacent to his, her telephone tucked under her chin, writing on a form. Her tousled hair, the color of dark chocolate, fell over her forehead. He couldn't help but smile. Like his twin sister, Kate, she pursed her lips when she concentrated. All determination. . .like a few minutes ago when she'd burst into Oscar's office.

What was it she'd said? Had he taken away her hope for a promotion? A burning sensation singed his insides. Only one job filled his need, and it wasn't here. Too bad he couldn't pass on this one and move on.

"Sorry for the interruption."

Jack faced his new boss.

Oscar came around his desk. "I need to head over to Composing. The guys have a question."

"We were done anyway."

By the time Jack crossed to Miss Alden's desk, she'd finished her call. She looked up, her smile not reaching her golden-brown eyes. She pushed back a lock of hair from her forehead.

Jack smiled. "The article you described earlier sounded interesting."

"Doesn't matter, if he won't consider it." She brushed something off her skirt and shrugged. "Funny how women can vote now, but we're not allowed to report on the politicians we're voting for."

Vote? Weren't they just talking about her article? He allowed his eyes to linger on her heart-shaped face as she fluffed her loose waves. Not the type he normally went for, but the woman was definitely appealing. "Maybe we could work together on something."

She leaned forward as her eyes widened. "What do you mean?"

Jack pushed aside a stack of papers and perched on a corner of her desk. He folded his arms. "I'm to report on progress at the new building. The piece you wrote could be a tie-in."

As though someone flicked a switch, the twinkle left her eyes. "That's kind of you, Mr. Wallace, but I don't think Mr. Zimmer would appreciate us working behind his back. He's already. . ." She clamped her mouth shut, and her red lips compressed into a thin line.

"Please call me Jack. Who said our story would be without Oscar's knowledge?"

She tapped her pencil on the desk. "It's the only way what you're proposing can be done. It's tempting, Mr. Wallace, but I can't take the risk."

What kind of man was Zimmer that he wouldn't even read her piece and see if it was any good? Jack already knew. The kind of man most editors Oscar's age were. Men who believed that news reporting was for men only. It wasn't like she wanted to interview Baby Face Nelson at his current hideout. Now her comment about voting made sense. Someday women would snag reporter jobs and do well. Nothing to say he couldn't help move progress along.

"Anyone who helps me gets credit. No secrets from me." Jack swallowed the invitation to lunch poised on the tip of his tongue. He had to focus on one thing only, and that didn't include women. Besides, she didn't seem very interested in him.

She stood and picked up a stack of forms. "Thanks for the offer, but no. I need to get these to Composing."

She disappeared around the corner, her hips moving in a delightful sway as her skirt pleat lifted and revealed a pair of shapely calves. He might have to rethink swearing off women.

* * * * *

Meg opened the closet, grateful the day was over. A man's black wool coat, with a plaid scarf looped around its lapels, hung next to her winter wrap. Mr. Zimmer's threadbare overcoat and his son Lester's old flight jacket, which he claimed a war hero gave him, hung nearby. The black one must belong to Mr. Wallace.

She ran her fingers down the sleeve. Cashmere? What else would feel so smooth and soft? She yanked her hand back. *What am I doing?* Heat traveled to her face, and she peeked into the Composing area. Mr. Zimmer sat bent over the Linotype keyboard. Mr. Wallace stood beside him, his dark blond hair in contrast to the older man's white tangle.

Meg grabbed her coat, and the plaid scarf slipped to the floor. She stepped away then stopped. She couldn't leave it there. Her heart racing, she picked up the muffler and caught a whiff of pine soap. A warm sensation filled her. She needed to leave. Now. She draped the scarf over the black coat then called out, "Night, Mr. Zimmer."

He looked up and waved. But it was Mr. Wallace's grin and "Good night, Miss Alden" that sent her scurrying to the door before he could notice the flush on her cheeks.

Chapter Two

. . . .

Meg charged up Broad Street, head bent against the wind. Whatever had happened back there at the coat closet, she had to ignore it. The man was a thief and a flirt. She'd watched him charm Emily with his lopsided grin, saying how perfect she was for her job. Meg thought the girl would swoon right there at the switchboard.

All day she'd endured the sound of him pecking on his typewriter and asking questions over the phone to which she already had answers. He'd probably never even seen the town or the lake until he arrived for the job. Didn't Mr. Zimmer realize she could put heart into those articles that Mr. Wallace couldn't?

Meg opened the door to the Powder Puff Beauty Shop and scrunched her nose. Helen was using that new permanent wave machine again. How could anyone allow such harsh chemicals on their hair for the sake of a few curls?

A woman giggled from behind a curtain. "Helen, I never dreamed I could look like this. You are wonderful."

"Not me, Mrs. Schroder, my magic machine here."

Meg hung her coat on a wall hook. "I'm here, Helen."

Helen McArdle stuck her head out from behind a drape drawn across one of the workstations, a pink-and-black scarf tied around her head, her face made up as if she were about to step onto a movie set. "I'll be done in a minute. Wait over there." She gestured toward another workstation.

Meg nodded. "Okay. I sure need your touch today." She sauntered to an open door that led into Helen's living quarters and waved at Helen's mom, who sat in an upholstered chair with her legs stretched out on an ottoman. "Hi, Mrs. McArdle. How are you feeling?"

"Pretty good, 'cept for my one appointment today taking three hours. Too much standing on these bad legs."

Meg stepped into the bungalow's small living room. "Maybe you need to cut back and leave the longer appointments to Helen."

Mrs. McArdle waved off the comment. "I'm not ready to let a few aches and pains get me down. Only take one or two long-time customers a day now anyway." She offered a smile. "I'm fine. God's gifted my girl and she's doing a good job, but I don't want her to wear herself out." She went back to reading her *Good Housekeeping* magazine.

Meg turned and stepped into what had once been the home's enclosed sunporch to wait. Her own mother was one of those ladies Mrs. McArdle kept as customers, but how much longer would that last? The lady had seemed to go downhill a lot since Christmas.

Helen fantasized about becoming a hairstylist to movie stars, but would she ever be able to leave Lake Geneva to follow her dream if her mom didn't improve? Even if she were free to move away, a person probably needed connections for a position like that.

A sudden thought caught Meg up short. Did her own dream of being a reporter garner a similar reaction? Her father didn't give the idea much weight. But then, he hadn't given much credit to anything she'd set out to do after her grammar school teacher said she'd never amount to anything.

She moved to the workstation and stared at her sorry reflection in the mirror. Not only did her hair look terrible, but the tightness around her eyes made her look old.

"You aren't kidding you need help. Today's wind got you good. No hat?" Helen came up behind Meg and caught her gaze in the mirror.

"A gust stole my cloche when I chased an envelope into the middle of Broad Street. Nearly got run over by Fred Newman in his old truck." Meg raked her hand through what used to be wavy hair. "Guess I'll take a shingle cut again."

"Longer styles are returning. Want to grow it out?"

Hours of crimping with a hot iron filled Meg's thoughts, and she grimaced. "Too much work. No thanks."

"I don't mean real long. That's passé. Just a bit longer—like mine." Helen untied her scarf and fluffs of soft platinum waves tumbled to a couple of inches above her shoulders.

Meg almost laughed out loud. If she had luminous skin and features like Helen's full mouth and turned-up nose, she'd even consider going blond. "I have enough trouble with finger waves."

"Don't you want to catch the attention of the new reporter?" Helen's hazel eyes twinkled in the mirror.

Meg flinched and spoke her next words at a measured pace. "How did you hear about him?"

"I saw Emily Johnson at Arnold's lunch counter. We shared tuna sandwiches, Cokes, and gossip."

"Emily is a little man-crazy, if you ask me. I'm not surprised she gushed, after the way he flirted with her. He's good-looking, I suppose, but I have other fish to fry."

Helen scrunched a handful of Meg's hair in her fist then let it fall loose. "Some Marcel waves would turn Jack's head."

"Jack?"

"Isn't Jack Wallace his name? That's what Emily told me." She ran a comb through Meg's tousled locks.

"That's the man. Why would I want to attract a scoundrel?"

"Did I hear you right?" She fluffed Meg's hair as if visualizing the finished style in her head.

Meg faced Helen. "Mr. Zimmer hired him not two days after George Bowman left."

The hairdresser's eyes widened. "His job is the same one you were writing that article for?"

"It took all last night to write the story. Mr. Zimmer never read it, just introduced me to Mr. Wallace, the new reporter." Meg bit down on her quivering lip. The last thing she wanted was to get the weepies.

Helen leaned in. "You're always saying that God has a plan. Maybe it's His plan for you to meet a nice guy and forget being a reporter. Or maybe Mr. Wallace is going to help you with your dream."

Meg hated the penetrating look in Helen's eyes. Why did she have to bring God into this? She picked a hair off her skirt. "Mr. Wallace did ask me to help him on a piece about the new building."

Helen's eyes crinkled at the corners as she smiled. "Good. When you do that and Mr. Zimmer finds out—"

"I told him no."

Helen's penciled blond brows lifted. "What?"

Meg squirmed. "I already got in trouble for over-editing Lester's stories."

"What kind of trouble?"

"This is just between us, but Lester's work requires more than a proof job for grammar and typos. I felt bad for him, being that he's the boss's son, so I rewrote some lines as examples. All he did was copy my work. Mr. Zimmer saw him doing that and laid down the law." She let out a deep breath. "Other than getting Mr. Zimmer's coffee and doing regular office duties, as long as I'm at the paper, I'll only be a want-ad taker and sometime-gatherer of society news."

A stab of guilt pierced Meg's conscience. Every time Lester begged her to look at his latest article, she couldn't resist the opportunity to see her work in print, even if she wasn't recognized as the writer. Bowing to guilt, last week she'd told Lester he was on his own in hopes that he'd learned enough to get by. Now the new man was tempting her. The very charming and handsome new man.

"But working on an article with Jack is different than editing or proofing, isn't it?" Helen asked.

"Yes. But no woman has yet to write a front-page article for the *News-Trib*. It would have to be done on the sly."

Helen tipped her head. "Maybe Jack could convince Oscar to give you a shot."

"Ha! You don't know Mr. Zimmer very well. He'll go to his grave before letting a woman write news for his paper."

Helen draped a white cape over Meg's shoulders. "You can tell Mother Helen all about your woes while I give you a wave. You never know, maybe Oscar likes waves better than straight hair."

Before Meg could protest, Helen disappeared out of the cubicle. She returned a moment later, pushing the permanent wave machine she'd showed off last time Meg visited the shop.

Meg eyed the tiny metal curlers dangling like crystals on a chandelier. Did she really want all those stinky chemicals on her hair?

"Here's the look we're going for." Helen held up a *Photoplay* magazine, open to a profile view of Jean Harlow. "Those Marcel waves will be perfect. When your hair grows, I'll be able to give you a softer look."

"Helen, I'll be going now, but I need to pay."

Meg turned.

Tiny springlike coils framed Edith Schroder's puffy face like a helmet. Not a Marcel wave in sight.

"I can't wait for Howard to see my new hairdo." Mrs. Schroder patted her graying spirals. They sprang back like a coil-spring mattress.

While Helen walked her customer to the door, Meg worked her fingers through her limp hair. Her reflection seemed to mock her.

Helen returned and pushed the machine closer to Meg. "Now, let's get a permanent going on you."

She shook her head. "Not doing it. Coils aren't for me."

"Who said anything about coils?"

"I saw that woman's hair."

Helen's throaty laugh filled the space. "Edith wanted those things. You think I like them?"

Meg shrugged. "You gave them to her."

"You should've been here when I tried to talk her into waves. Yours will be like mine after it grows." She turned to give Meg a back view of her head.

Meg studied the soft yellow-white waves. Last year Helen had taken some criticism for bleaching her hair, but every time a stranger did a double take, thinking she was Jean Harlow, she thrilled at being compared to her favorite movie star.

Maybe a change would be good. Besides, hair always grew out. "How much?"

"Normally ten dollars, but for you, five."

Meg had only allotted a dollar for a trim. "If you want to see *State Fair* tomorrow night, I can't get a perm until after payday."

Helen rested a fist on her hip. "When is payday?"

"Friday."

"We can go then. If Harlow isn't in a movie, I don't need to see it that bad."

* * * * *

Jack rolled down his shirtsleeves while the large rollers spun and spit out the front page. He soaked in the wave of pleasure washing over him. How many times as a boy in knee pants had he trailed behind Dad when they visited the Composing room, then later watched the huge printing presses churn out the *Chicago Beacon*?

He had nothing but admiration for his father, the owner and publisher of Chicago's second largest daily. But unlike Oscar Zimmer, who wasn't afraid to get his hands dirty, Dad probably didn't know how to run a Linotype machine. Jack had learned more today than in five years of journalism school.

When he'd opted to head to DC after college graduation, things had become strained between him and Dad. His sister had dreamed for years of running the *Beacon* and he'd hoped Dad would train her for the job in his absence, but it never happened.

His stomach rumbled, and he checked his pocket watch. Seven o'clock. No wonder. Fastening his shirt cuffs as he came down the stairs from the second floor, he entered the newsroom and strode to Oscar's office.

The older man was working his way into his suit coat.

"I don't suppose I could interest you in grabbing some chow."

Oscar flicked off the desk light. "Thanks, but if I don't come home, Doris will have something to say. She always keeps my supper warm on Wednesday nights."

Jack nodded as he scanned the deserted office. "Guess Lester left too."

"Had some kind of gathering for Great War veterans." Oscar plodded to the closet and pulled a gray overcoat off a hanger.

Jack came up behind him and reached for his own coat. "Lester was in the war? I didn't realize he was old enough."

"He isn't, but he can't seem to get enough of it. Drives me and my wife crazy." Oscar set a checkered fedora on his snowy mound of hair. "The Gargoyle has a special on Wednesdays. Not sure what 'tis, though."

Jack buttoned his coat and draped his scarf under the lapels. "I've been there a couple of times. Grand restaurant. But I think I'll find a diner and get some soup."

"Try the Utopia Café down the street. They make a new soup every day."

Jack set his fedora on his head, thanked Oscar for the tip, and stepped into the brisk evening air. The Utopia occupied a building two blocks to the east. He turned that direction then stopped suddenly. A table for one held little appeal. He was going home.

By the time Jack steered his Ford toward the Elgin Club to begin the mile-long drive to the lakefront, he felt as if he could eat anything, cooked or raw. A bologna sandwich would have to do. It was the only thing, except for a carton of eggs, in the icebox.

* * * * *

Jack stretched out his legs, sitting sideways on one of the living room davenports, and bit into his sandwich. Taking a swallow of ginger ale, a memory of an excited Meg Alden bursting into Oscar's office popped unbidden into his thoughts. It quickly became apparent that she had no idea he was to start the job that day. Not the way he would have handled things.

When Meg wasn't working, how did she spend her evenings? Did she enjoy reading? Taking a walk? Listening to the radio? He wouldn't mind finding out while looking into those eyes over a good meal. He gave himself a mental shake. *Thoughts on work, Wallace.*

He turned back around and set his plate on the coffee table then sauntered into the hall. Knowing Dad, he'd still be at his massive desk, studying the latest distribution statistics. Jack settled onto the telephone stand's navy-and-red-striped upholstered seat and picked up the receiver.

"What number, please?" A familiar voice came through the wire.

"Peggy? Jack Wallace. You still working those cords?"

The operator giggled. "I'll never leave, Mr. Wallace. How may I help you?"

A few moments later, John Wallace answered.

"Dad, it's Jack."

"Hey, I was about to call. How was your first day?"

"Good. I'm assigned a story on the new recreational building next to the beach and got my hands dirty in the Composing room. Even used the Linotype."

"Good, good. It's been awhile since I've used a Linotype, but I never forget that setting up the story is as important as writing it. If it's not laid out correctly, it's not going to have the same impact."

Jack frowned. "I didn't realize you ran a Linotype."

Dad coughed. "When I worked at the Terre Haute paper before you were born, I did a lot of assisting in the Composing room."

A new respect for his father came over Jack. What else didn't he know about him? Plenty, but he couldn't let it distract him from the reason for his call. "Dad, I think I may be standing in the way of a long-time employee getting the position. Maybe it would be better—"

"What makes you think so? Excuse me. . ." Several sharp coughs exploded into Jack's ear. "Something got in my throat. Now, what were we saying?"

"Sounded more like something got into your toes. Those were deep coughs. You okay?"

"Yes, yes. I'm getting over a cold. Why do you think you're in someone's way?"

"I only became aware of the situation this morning, and it's rubbed against my conscience ever since."

"Oscar only has two full-time reporters, and one is his son. Do you mean the sports man he told us about who also sells ads?"

"It's. . .one of the society writers. . . ."

"Jack, I know you're all for women moving up in the paper business, thanks to Kate. But after what happened with that girl at the university paper. . .what was her name?"

Jack winced. "Virginia. But Meg is. . ."

"She attractive?"

"Sure, but this isn't about her looks. She has a swell idea for an article about the building. I'd like to see her be able to write it."

"You know as well as I do you're not blocking her way. I don't allow women reporters here, and I'm certain Oscar doesn't allow them there. If you're going to get ahead in newspaper management, your view will have to change."

Jack rubbed his stubbled cheek. Dad's disappointment that Jack didn't come to the *Beacon* after graduation still showed. "But I don't—"

"I'll give your mother your love. I need to go."

They said their good-byes, and the line went dead. Jack shook his head. His father hated conflict and avoided it by not talking. But was Dad right about his motives? Meg's pretty face popped into his thoughts, and a warm feeling came over him. He just wanted to help her get her dream.

* * * * *

Meg skulked into the office on Thursday morning later than she'd intended. Despite numerous spritzes of Mom's rose-scented perfume, she still smelled like chemicals. She removed her hat and scrunched up her nose at the aroma.

Taking the long way to her desk to avoid stares, she dropped into her seat and smiled at the sight of Mr. Wallace's empty chair. Lester whished past her without a glance. Hopefully the others would react the same. She picked up a note from Mr. Zimmer.

"Meg! Your hair. I adore it."

At Emily's squeal, Meg slunk deeper into her chair. She should have kept her hat on.

"Marcel waves are so fashionable now. I've been wanting them ever since I saw a picture in *McCall's Magazine*." Emily now stood inches away.

Meg rolled her eyes. "Don't you think it's a bit much?"

Emily patted her topknot. "If I didn't have to live with my father, this would be gone in a day. I'm still working on getting a bob, and now that's passé." She frowned. "Guess till I'm married I'll always be behind the times."

"Fathers can be difficult, can't they?"

Emily's gaze went over Meg's head, and her face lit up like a spotlight. "Good morning, Mr. Wallace." She dragged out his name as if it were a chocolate bar melting on her tongue.

Meg eyed the inviting space under her desk. Could she take her typewriter and phone down there with her?

"Morning, ladies."

She held her breath. If Emily said one word about her hair. . .

"What do you think about Meg's new hairdo?"

Her cheeks warmed. The next time she and Emily were alone, the girl would get an earful. Meg glanced toward the front door. "Seems the board is lit up like a theater marquee on opening night."

"Oh! I forgot all about it." Emily scurried to her post.

Feeling Mr. Wallace's penetrating stare, Meg froze. If she had his job, she'd be pounding on the typewriter or, better yet, visiting the construction site. Not standing there, mocking someone's hair.

"I like the curls, Miss Alden. Very nice."

Was he just saying that to be polite? She faced him, and her eyes unintentionally zeroed in on his full lips and clean-shaven jaw. She raised her gaze to eyes as blue as the sky outside, and he grinned. How did he always manage to make her feel as if she were the only person in the room? Heat filled her cheeks. "Thank you."

She pulled her eyes away. The heel didn't deserve such politeness. Her chest tightened. It wasn't like the position was really hers to take, though. And what if her thoughts about his being out of work were true? He might have needed the job more than she.

She stared at Mr. Zimmer's note and attempted to read the scrawl.

"So much has changed since I last spent summers in Lake Geneva. I'd love a tour of the town. Maybe someday soon we could arrange one."

She jerked her gaze away from the note. "Summers?"

"Yes. I've been coming up here since first grade. The lake house was my second home until I headed to college."

She glared at him. Summers and a house on Geneva Lake meant something else. Did the man's chauffeur drop him off each morning? Did the cook have his dinner prepared each evening? What was Mr. Zimmer thinking, hiring a rich guy? Hadn't he heard? They were in the middle of a depression.

She straightened and patted her new waves. "Sorry. I'm going to be busy for the next few days. I'm sure Emily would love to show you around."

He shrugged. "But I'd rather see the town through your eyes. . .hear about it from a fellow writer's perspective." He edged toward his desk.

Meg studied Mr. Zimmer's note.

Miss Alden,

For next week's "Town Talk," find out what people have planned for this weekend. We've got some space to fill. I don't care if someone is just thinking about having visitors—print it.
OZ

Why not something with meat? From her desk drawer, Meg pulled the article she'd rescued from her wastebasket yesterday afternoon and smoothed its crumpled edges. She'd have an even better story for next week.

Chapter Three

....

That evening, Meg settled into her dad's Chevrolet sedan, and he put the car in gear and backed onto Geneva Street.

He shifted gears. "I suppose you've heard the rumors flying around town."

She shrugged. "Only about a new contest to name the building." Unless she counted what she'd overheard him telling Mom last night.

He turned the vehicle toward the high school, where the evening's town meeting was to be held.

"What rumors are you talking about?" she asked.

"Never mind. It's likely much ado about nothing."

Meg peered out her window. "I don't know why anyone would cause problems. The building is beautiful, and I've heard they've booked some wonderful bands for the summer."

"Do you think we should keep the name as is?"

She shrugged. "It's okay. But since we called the rickety building it's replacing the Northport, a new name would be nice." And a different name would remove any reminders of the worst night of her life.

Dad turned onto Madison Street and pulled into a parking place alongside the school.

Inside the filling auditorium, a sizable group sat in the two front-center rows. It included Fred Newman, the man who'd almost run over Meg the day before. Considering their frowns and choppy hand gestures, they didn't appear to be pleased. Her father said he'd see her later and strode toward the stage, his form as straight as a pole. He stopped halfway down the aisle to greet the Arnolds, proprietors of one of the drugstores. As he spoke to the couple, he glanced several times toward the front rows.

Meg slid into an aisle seat at the back then pulled her notebook from her handbag, training her eyes on the crowd at the front. She jotted down their names. Interesting. . . They all farmed in Linn Township on the lake's south shore.

On the stage, her dad shared a joke with the committee chairman as if he hadn't a concern in the world—except, of course, the naming of the new building, which had been his responsibility since last fall.

Raised voices came from the center section, and Meg looked over as Fred pointed toward the door. She followed his gaze to a young couple in the second row. Fred and another man crowded in to speak to them. The woman, Violette Fenner, had sort of won last summer's Name the New Building Contest. The committee didn't like any of the names submitted to the contest, however, and decided to keep Northport for the time being. They awarded the prize money to the best one of the lot, Miss Fenner's entry. The whole thing seemed odd to Meg, but she'd known better than to question Dad.

Almost bouncing on her seat, Meg scribbled on the notepad. She'd figured out the rumor, and Jack Wallace had just missed out on his big story. So what if she'd told Lester she was through ghosting for him. Just seeing her story printed next to whatever drivel Mr. Wallace hammered out was enough gratification to make the risk worthwhile.

* * * * *

Jack parked the Ford V-8 and leaped out. Every curb closer to the school had been filled with cars. In Chicago or DC, he expected parking problems, but not in Lake Geneva. The two-block walk was going to make him late.

Jack took off in a sprint, and his left heel connected with ice. His feet went up and his posterior hit the hard cement. His entire body shuddered as though he'd been walloped with a billy club.

He scrambled to his feet and rubbed his backside. He scanned the ground for his notebook. Up ahead a car turned the corner, and its headlights landed on the tablet in the middle of the street. A second later, its left front tire ground the pad into the road. Jack stepped into the street, picked up the tablet, and shook dirt and sand from the torn pages. Swell. His first assignment, and he arrives late *and* has the tools of his trade run over.

Stepping into the lobby, Jack brushed dirt from his coat then opened the doors to the auditorium and slipped inside. A gray-haired man stood at the podium spouting statistics. He surveyed the crowded room. Something must be afoot. A few rows down, his eyes landed on a familiar head of wavy brown curls. And the seat next to her was empty. Maybe this was his lucky day after all. Grinning, he made a beeline to Meg's side and whispered, "Is that seat taken?"

* * * * *

Meg jumped and turned. As much as she wanted to say there were at least a half dozen other seats he could choose, she knew there weren't. She shifted her body so he could slide by.

"Parking was terrible. You'd think I was back in Chicago. Did I miss anything?" With his sheepish grin, he looked like a boy late for school.

She shook her head and glanced away before his grin caused tingles in her stomach once more. "They just started. He's reviewing what the committee discussed last time."

He bundled his overcoat and stuffed it under his seat then held up his notepad. "I don't suppose I could borrow a few sheets from you?"

Was that a tire mark on the cover? Meg hid a smirk and pulled a couple of blank pages from her notebook.

On the stage, the committee chairman shuffled papers in his hands and cleared his throat. "And the widening of the beach should be completed by the grand opening. A new contest to name the lakefront building begins tomorrow. Mr. Louis Alden, the contest chairman, will speak about that now."

A few men in the front row whispered among themselves, and then a hand shot up. "We have a question."

The committee chairman sent a pointed stare to the questioner. "Can it wait until the end of the meeting?"

"I think it should be addressed now."

Dad stood from his seat at the table. A twitch in his upper lip caused his mustache to bounce—an affliction that occurred whenever something annoyed him. "We will entertain all questions at the end. This is an informational meeting only."

"And that's exactly why we're here." Fred Newman stood. "Last summer, Miss Fenner already won a contest to name the building. But you people decided to keep Northport. Now you want another contest. Miss Fenner's choice of Harborlight should be the official name."

Everyone in the first two rows clapped. The young brown-haired man with Miss Fenner patted her hand, and she turned to him, her cheeks tinged red. Her engagement had been announced last Christmas. He had to be her intended. Meg frowned and jotted a note.

Dad grabbed the chairman's gavel and pounded the table. "Order, order."

"He sounds like a judge." Mr. Wallace's whisper was more of a shout, with the noise in the room.

Meg nodded. "He is a judge in the municipal court. My father is an attorney."

His brows shot up. "He's your dad?" He looked to the stage with new respect written on his face.

"This new contest is illegal," Fred shouted over raised voices, some telling him to sit while others urged him on.

"Sir, the rules of the first contest stated the winning name would be the one judged most appropriate, not necessarily the actual name." Dad faced the audience, his dark eyes finding Meg. "The committee didn't feel that any of the suggestions made earlier contained a name with enduring quality. To that end, we are announcing a new contest. The prize for the best name will be twenty-five dollars. We encourage all of you to come up with a name worthy of this beautiful new facility."

Mr. Wallace nudged Meg with his elbow. "You still don't want to work with me on this?" He held up his notes.

Only three or four written lines took up a third of his sheet, while she'd filled several pages. Would it hurt? He wasn't Lester. With him as a buffer, maybe it would work. She shook her head slowly. "Mr. Zimmer would have a conniption."

"But, Miss Alden, you know these people, why they're upset. You'd bring life to a pretty dull story. How could Zimmer say no? What do you say?"

"And what makes you think it's more than what you just heard?"

"There's usually something going on beyond what's said in public."

"This is small-town Wisconsin politics. You're too used to playing with the big boys."

"The way I figure it, people are the same. It's just the size of their area of influence that's different."

She fingered a corner of her tablet. He had implied that he would credit her on the piece. But the paper's stories didn't use bylines. He'd likely use her information and take all the glory. She shook her head. "Sorry. I'm sure you'll do fine. You heard the same words I did."

Meg continued to take notes, through a report that Wayne King and his Orchestra were booked for the grand opening; they were hoping to contract with Tommy Dorsey over the summer. A wave of excitement bubbled beneath her breastbone as she wrote.

Mr. Wallace nudged her during a lull. "I didn't realize they were looking to get such big names. Wayne King, Tommy Dorsey. . ." He paused. "You like to dance?"

His question, asked so softly that it seemed he was asking her for a date, pushed against the fortress around her heart. She turned, and their gazes connected. The platform speaker's voice faded as a zillion butterflies took flight in her stomach. If she'd met him anywhere but at work, she wouldn't have minded going out with him.

"Yes. I dance."

He responded with a crooked smile. "Good."

His voice, so low she barely heard it, threatened to disarm her. She had to keep her head. Meg turned her attention back to the speaker. No man was going to distract her.

"Whatever's behind your smile is what I want to convey in this article, not humdrum contractor numbers and an anticipated finish date. You show me what almost every person here must be feeling—pride, joy, anticipation. . . . I'm catching the fever, but it's not the same as feeling it like you are."

She drew in a breath and let it out slowly. He made a good argument, but how could she trust her wounded heart to resist working with such an attractive man? She'd seen how he was with women. Even Thelma. No one got that lady to smile, but Jack had when he complimented her on her "Town Talk" article. He'd probably left a trail of broken hearts from DC to Chicago. She shook her head. "Sorry. I can't."

He answered with a downturned mouth and hands raised in surrender. "On another subject, you'll love Tommy Dorsey." He launched into a story about a time when he'd met Mr. Dorsey. Now it seemed he would have opportunity to see the famous bandleader again.

Meg's thoughts conjured up an image of the two of them spinning around the new dance floor beneath a mirror ball. She hadn't danced much lately. . .

"Ready to go, Meg?" Dad stood in the aisle beside them, his coat on. Had the meeting ended? How long had she and Mr. Wallace been talking?

She jumped to her feet and grabbed her coat by its collar. It slipped out of her hand and fell to the floor. As she reached for it, Mr. Wallace's hand landed on top of hers. Electric-like sparks zinged up her arm. She gave a nervous giggle and straightened. Mr. Wallace gathered her coat and held it while she slipped her arms into the sleeves.

Dad frowned, his eyes on Mr. Wallace until the coat was in place. "I don't think we've had the pleasure." He stuck out his hand. "Louis Alden."

"Jack Wallace."

The men shook hands.

"I'm a new reporter at the paper," Mr. Wallace said. "Can I get a quote from you on that little disturbance?"

Sandwiched between the men, Meg's thoughts spun. She'd have to work fast.

"Give me a call at my office in the morning," Dad said. "Ready, daughter?"

"Yes, sir." Careful to avoid his eyes, Meg whispered a good-bye to Mr. Wallace and followed Dad to the door. He'd said at dinner that he had to be in court first thing in the morning. She'd get her own quote on the way home and have her notes ready for typing before Mr. Wallace had a chance to talk to her father.

* * * * *

When Meg arrived at work the next morning, Lester sat in front of his typewriter, staring at it as if words would magically start typing themselves onto the paper.

She stuffed her coat and hat into the closet then patted her hair. She had to admit, she liked her new hairdo. Even Dad, who at first had had a fit over such frivolous fussing, admitted at breakfast that it suited her.

She sidled up to Lester's desk, waving his smoke away. "Morning, Lester. I'm surprised you weren't at the town meeting last night."

Lester mashed his cigarette butt into a glass ashtray, sending still-burning embers flying. He looked up through dark-framed oval glasses then rubbed the scruff on his narrow chin. "I met the war vets at the bowling alley. Why would I go to the meeting when the building is Jack's story?"

"You never know when an article idea might leap out. A good reporter is always digging, always looking for a story."

"Oh." He looked at his typewriter and the blank page. "You've said that before. I've been here the last ten minutes, waiting for an idea. Dad asked me to report on new construction happening around the area besides the lakefront building. With the economy, not much is going on except for a house on Dodge Street and a barn on Highway 50." He handed her a typewritten page. A brown burn mark marred one corner. "He wants more than this, I'm sure."

Meg read the article. Except for a few grammatical mistakes, it looked to be acceptable. When Lester did pieces citing facts and figures, he usually did okay.

"This is good, but you need to give your dad more than what he assigns." She handed him the three pages of meeting notes she'd taken. "I know we talked last week about my not helping you anymore, but a group from Linn Township is rankled that a second contest to name the new building has been announced. Fred Newman seems to be the ringleader. Here's a list of who was there and the reason for their protest. Be sure to use the quote from my father at the bottom of the third page." Meg gave him a moment to skim. "Any questions?"

He frowned. "Dad didn't assign this to me. Won't he wonder why I'm writing the piece?"

She worked her lower lip. He had a good point. Until now she'd only ghosted his assigned articles. "It will impress him that you're always looking for interesting stories, like I said."

He shook his head. "He knows I didn't attend the meeting."

She forced her voice over the massive lump in her throat. "Maybe someone tipped you off."

He cast her a skeptical look. "You're the one excited about the building. Why don't you write it yourself?"

Meg bit back her words and took a deep breath.

"Hello, this is Jack Wallace from the *News-Trib*." Mr. Wallace's voice carried across the two desks between him and Lester. "I'm calling Mr. Alden for a quote on last night's lakefront building meeting. Is he there?"

A wry smile played on Lester's lips. "Now I get it." He reached into his breast pocket and pulled out a pack of Camels. Meg sent him a hard stare, and he tossed them onto the desktop displaying more burns marks than Helen had lipsticks. "I found out last night the war vets want to march on Washington again to demand their bonus money." His brows knit together. "That should be making news."

She was losing ground. Meg forced a chuckle. "Lester, you'd think you'd fought in the war, the way you carry on."

"I would've, if I'd been old enough. At least now I can support them." He turned to his typewriter and set Meg's notes beside it. "How about tit for tat? I'll do this article for you and you use your magic on a second article about the war vets for me."

Meg's chest constricted, and she pressed a palm over the spot. Although she'd not been on good terms with God lately, she hadn't forgotten what the Bible said about dishonesty and disrespecting those in authority. If Mr. Zimmer heard of any of this, she'd be the one out on the street, not Lester. "I'll rewrite your article on the war vets. But then we'll need to stop. What we're doing is wrong." She turned, and her knees almost gave out.

Mr. Wallace stood within earshot, his arms folded across his chest.

Chapter Four

....

Meg raised her chin. "Good morning, Mr. Wallace."

He opened his mouth, but she didn't wait to hear his words. By the time she hurried into the restroom, her knees felt as if they would buckle. She gripped the sink on both sides and leaned forward, studying her reflection in the mirror. Was Mr. Wallace telling Mr. Zimmer what he'd overheard? How could she be so daft?

She wet a pinky finger and smoothed down her left brow—it tended to have a mind of its own—checked her seams, took a steadying breath, then opened the door.

Back in the newsroom, Mr. Wallace hunted and pecked on his type-writer, Emily plugged and unplugged cords at the switchboard, and Thelma drummed up news for "Town Talk" on the phone. Grabbing a want-ad form from her desk, Meg went to Mr. Zimmer's door and peeked in.

"Oscar is out until three."

She faced Mr. Wallace.

He leaned back in his chair. His tie was slightly loosened at the collar, and his mischievous grin seemed to say, "I've got the goods on you."

She pushed out a smile. "Thanks. I'll see him later." She returned to her seat, certain his gaze followed her with every step.

He cleared his throat. "Change your mind about collaborating?"

"No. How's your report on last night's meeting coming?"

He rolled a paper out of his typewriter. "See for yourself. Short and to the point. The contest chairman was out, so no quote from him yet." He handed her the article.

She skimmed his work. His report had all the facts, but it lacked depth. She handed it back and inserted a blank sheet into her typewriter. Maybe he hadn't overheard the conversation after all.

* * * * *

On Sunday after church, Meg took the stairs with her sister nipping at her heels. "What's the hurry, Laura? You can't be in such a rush to get out of your church clothes to help Mom with dinner. If you were, it would be a first."

"I got out of helping because I have a huge English test tomorrow. Yesterday's play practice took up all my study time. I'm surprised Mom didn't ask you to help."

They reached the second floor, and Meg stopped and rested her fists on her hips. "Wish I'd thought of that excuse when I was in high school."

Laura tipped her blond head. "Maybe if you had, you'd have gotten better grades and finished college."

Meg stepped toward her bedroom door. "You know my leaving college had nothing to do with my grades."

"You weren't here listening to Dad before he pulled you out. If you'd been doing better, he'd have left you there." Laura raised her chin. "The depression was only an excuse. He has an education fund for both of us and made sure the money was protected."

Meg bolted into her room and flung the door shut. The sound of wood hitting wood cracked the air, and she flinched. How did Laura always manage to get her acting like a child? Dad didn't tolerate tension between them any day of the week, but especially not on Sunday. Hopefully he was still in the basement adding coal to the furnace and hadn't heard the commotion.

She removed her gloves then unbuttoned her dress and stepped out of it, letting the flowered print garment puddle on the floor. Without bothering to put on the more casual wool skirt and blouse she'd planned, Meg plopped onto the chintz-upholstered chair. Through the window, her dad leaned against the old oak tree, puffing on his pipe. Above his head, remnants of a rope that once held a swing lifted in the breeze.

Meg couldn't help but smile. Dad laid down the law in many ways, but when it came to smoking, Mom ruled her roost. If she'd hoped that banishing him to the backyard when he got the urge to puff would convince him to quit, it hadn't worked.

Meg's thoughts went to her sister. Until a couple of years ago, the girl had been tolerable, but since then Laura had become snippy and sarcastic. Meg had chalked it up to growing pains, but now the girl was eighteen and graduating soon. Time to grow up.

A knock came. "Meg, it's Mom. Can I come in?"

"Sure."

The door opened and her mother stepped in, still wearing the jersey knit she'd worn for church. She gaped at Meg. "What are you doing by the window in only your slip?"

"I'm back far enough, and no one can see in during the day."

Mom crossed over the green rug and picked up Meg's dress, giving the garment a shake. "The wrinkles have already set. Now come away from the window."

Meg stood and took the dress from her. She pulled a hanger from the closet. "Maybe the wrinkles will hang out."

"I heard you girls fighting again. I'd hoped that with age you two would grow to like each other. I know she goads you, but can't you turn the other cheek and give her a good example?"

A million answers raced through Meg's mind, but they all made her sound younger than Laura. She faced Mom, noticing for the first time wisps of gray marring her dark brown hair at the temples. "It's just because of habit that we squabble. I'll work at it. She said you gave her permission to study and not help with dinner. I guess we won't be playing games today either."

"Your father isn't going to like the change in schedule, but homework comes first. We'll play something anyway."

"Laura already gets straight A's. How much better can she do?" Meg took the wool skirt and blouse from the closet and slipped into the top. "Dad took me out of college because of the cost, right?"

Mom stared at her with a start. "What brought that up?"

"It wasn't because I'd been on probation the second semester of my sophomore year, was it? I'd buckled down and was getting better grades." She stepped into her skirt and worked it up around her hips. "Laura said he has education funds for both of us."

Mom worried her lower lip. "He does. But when your tuition went up, he thought it better to have you come home and finish college later, after the economy righted itself. He wasn't sure he'd be able to protect the funds he'd set aside for you girls. Fortunately, he was able to do that. I didn't think you wanted to return to school."

Meg plopped on her bed. "I would, but Dad probably wouldn't approve of the college I want to attend."

"Which one is that?"

"Northwestern, down in Evanston. They have a great journalism school."

Mom's mouth tightened into a flat line. "It's also one of the most expensive schools in the Midwest. What about a state college like Whitewater?"

"Whitewater is for teachers. I don't want to be a teacher. I need to go to a journalism school." Meg grabbed her mother's hand. "Don't you see, Mom? I'm meant to write. I'm no teacher."

"I do see, Meg, more than you know. Let's get Laura settled up at Whitewater next fall, and then we can find a good school for you." Mom jumped to her feet. "I need to get the meat into the oven if we're to eat by three. Can I count on you to set the table?"

"Sure. I'll be down in a minute."

Mom left, and Meg returned to the window and pushed the priscilla curtain back with her hand. A bird fluttered past and perched on the bare branch of a crab apple tree. He let out a tweet. "Okay, Mr. Robin, if you can be happy, I can too. At least while I was at college I worked hard for my grades. Jack Wallace didn't have to work to get that job, but I'll get it away from him by proving to Mr. Zimmer that I deserve it. And when I get the job, I won't need any journalism school."

After setting the table, Meg joined her parents in the living room.

Dad looked up from his paper. "Ready to begin our game? Your mother and I thought the three of us could play Landlord's and Prosperity."

Meg fought rolling her eyes. That game made her brain hurt. Numbers were not her strength, and the game centered around buying and selling properties and counting money.

"Dad, can't we have a Sunday off from games?"

He closed the newspaper and set it on the ottoman in front of him. "Maybe if you played it more often, arithmetic would come easier for you."

She shrugged. "You know words come easier to me than numbers."

"I heard about a new game coming out called Monopoly. It sounds similar to Landlord's, but maybe it will be easier for you."

Meg glanced toward the front window. "It's a beautiful day. If you don't mind, I'd like to walk to the lake with my Bible. I'll be back in time to help Mom with dinner."

Dad rubbed his back against the wingback chair as though he had an itch. "This is Sunday—"

"Louis, why not let Meg go?" Mom asked. "She is planning to take her Bible. I'd like to work on my knitting. A break from games this week might be nice."

"Okay, go." He gave a wave. "Before I change my mind."

Meg dashed to the hall for her coat and the red beret she'd worn to church. She collected her Bible from the side table and called out a good-bye.

Outside, she lifted her face to the sun's welcome warmth. She should thank Laura for having homework, since it got them out of playing Dad's boring board game. Ever since Prosperity came out last year, the new version of The Landlord's Game, he hadn't wanted to play any of the card games they used to play. The new Monopoly game didn't sound much better.

At least she didn't have to play anything today. Hopefully she'd find a spot to sit and be able to think over the reverend's sermon. She crossed Main Street and ambled through Elm Park to the lake, claiming the first empty bench she came to.

A distance out, past the ice, open water sparkled in the sun. Down the shore, the windows encasing the new building's second-floor ballroom glistened. Soon warm breezes would float through those windows on the night of the grand opening, cooling dancers as they kicked up their heels. She and Helen would have to start scouting for new dresses.

Meg opened her Bible. Reverend Hellman had mentioned that he planned to preach on Proverbs 3:5–6 over the next month or so. Today he'd said trusting meant knowing that God had your best interests in mind. Meg worked her lower lip. Lately that didn't seem to be true for her. Every time an opportunity beckoned, He slammed the door in her face. Why, when she'd followed Him faithfully?

She randomly flipped to Isaiah, one of her favorite books of the Bible, and read: *"For my thoughts are not your thoughts, neither are your ways my ways, saith the Lord. For as the heavens are higher than the earth, so are my ways higher than your ways, and my thoughts than your thoughts."*

God had made it clear that He didn't agree with her. No wonder going to church was becoming a chore, the Scriptures seeming stale and the hymns even dryer. Maybe next weekend she'd stay home even if she had to feign an upset stomach.

She crossed her arms and focused on Geneva Bay's eastern shore. Without leaves on the trees to shield it, the huge Younglands estate with its rumored gold doorknobs and private bowling alley ruled the bay. The other lakeshore mansions, no doubt including Mr. Wallace's, paled in comparison to the gargantuan building.

Whatever the size of his estate, Jack Wallace was probably reclining on one of his half dozen davenports, enjoying an unmatched lake view. He mentioned the other day that he was living in the house without any family. Well, it served him right to spend Sunday alone in his ritzy home.

"Miss Alden? Fancy meeting you here."

Meg turned. "Mr. Wallace. What a surprise."

Chapter Five

. . . .

Trapped in the woman's mesmerizing gaze, Jack forced himself to move his eyes away from Miss Alden's face. Problem was, the rest of her looked just as appealing. Especially with that red beret perched on top of her wavy hair.

"Nice day." He should get moving, but she was the first person he'd recognized all day. It felt good to speak to someone. . .someone as attractive as she.

"It's such a pretty afternoon, I thought I'd come here and read." She held up a Bible with her gloved hand.

How had he missed the black leather-covered book? This was obviously a private moment. "And I'm interrupting. I'll see you tomorrow." He stepped back.

"That's okay. I was finished."

"Do you read by the lake often?" He edged closer.

"When the weather is nice. I only live a block away."

As if drawn by an invisible magnet, he stepped off the path onto the grass. "Since I'm not interrupting, do you mind if I sit?"

She fanned the Bible's pages with her thumb. He should continue on to the building site. After all, that was where he was headed, and she appeared to want privacy.

"Mr. Wallace, I thought you wanted to sit."

Her comment jolted him to attention. "I do. But only for a moment." He settled next to her and clasped his hands. The Bible sat in her lap, unopened. "What's God saying to you? Anything good?"

Miss Alden shrugged. "It's called the Good Book, isn't it?"

She stared at the lake, giving him opportunity to take in her profile. Upturned lashes, creamy skin, cherry-red lips. . .

"With this warm breeze, the ice should be out by tomorrow." She suddenly faced him.

He jerked his eyes away as if to study the thinning ice. He had to, or else drown in those golden-brown eyes. "It already is, by my place."

"I suppose from your home you have a good view of the water without having to go outside."

"I can't argue there." He looked at her. "Have you always lived in Lake Geneva?"

"Other than two and a half years at Ripon College, yes."

Jack leaned her direction. "What did you study?"

"Journalism."

The guilt he'd managed to bottle and stuff away reappeared, pressing against his rib cage. "So you transferred elsewhere?"

She shook her head. "Because of the depression, I had to come home." Her eyes grew cold despite her smile. "My contribution to easing the economic crisis. But God was good, and I found a job at the *News-Trib*."

And I just took away your chance to move up.

"Do you have the time?"

He pulled out his watch. "Two thirty."

"I didn't realize it was so late." She gathered her Bible and stood. "See you tomorrow."

He pushed to his feet, not ready to be alone again. "Let me walk with you."

"Not necessary. It's only a block." She took off down the path with determined steps.

He caught up to her. "Dad taught me to never let a lady walk home alone."

* * * * *

Meg pressed her lips together to stop the rejoinder on her tongue. The man was persistent. "Really, it's only a block away. I came here alone. I'm fine."

"What you did before I arrived can't be helped. But now that I know you're walking home by yourself, it's the right thing to do."

He continued in step beside her. They approached Lake Geneva Ice Company, shut down until next winter's harvest of ice blocks could be cut from the lake. Meg turned up the path that wound through the trees toward Main Street. He came with her.

She stifled a sigh as her traitorous heart leaped in glee.

"A merry heart doeth good like a medicine."

She inwardly groaned at the verse from Proverbs. Not so good if she stared too long into those startling eyes so blue they rivaled her mother's morning glories. It was only a block's walk, and then he'd be out of her life until tomorrow.

"I presume by your Bible reading that you attended church today."

She gave him a sideways glance. "Yes. And you?"

"No. I went to church as a child, but once I escaped the clutches of my parents, I never felt the need."

They came to Main Street and waited for several vehicles to pass.

Meg cast about for something to say. "Where did you attend college?"

"University of Missouri. Dad encouraged me to apply to Yale, his alma mater, but I wanted a good journalism school." They crossed the road, Mr. Wallace keeping a respectful distance between them. She knew all about the University of Missouri—ahead of its time in journalism. She didn't dare suggest a school so far away. Even Mom hadn't been favorable to Northwestern. "Sounds like you won the battle I couldn't win."

They headed up Warren Street until they reached the end of the block. Meg pointed at the white two-story house she'd called home for as long as she could remember. "We have to cross here. I live over there on the corner. Or we can say good-bye right here."

Mr. Wallace's eyes danced with mischief. "If I didn't know better, I'd think you're afraid your family will see the riffraff you brought home." He shot her a crooked grin. "I'm a gentleman, remember? Always see to it that a lady gets home safe."

Meg worked to stifle a grin without success. "Your dad must be quite the man. Your mother is a lucky lady."

His mouth twisted as though fighting a grimace. "Yes. She is."

She frowned as they crossed the street. Perhaps things weren't so hunky-dory in the lakeshore crowd.

On her front stoop, Meg paused beside a stone pot that awaited its summer crown of red geraniums. She tipped her head and sank hopelessly into the sway of his gaze. "Thanks for escorting me home. I'll see you—"

The door swung open, and Mom stuck her head out. "There you are, Meg. I need your help with dinner." Her eyes rounded as she noted Mr. Wallace. "Oh. I didn't realize you had someone with you."

"Mom, this is Jack Wallace, the new reporter at the paper. We bumped into each other at the park, and he walked me home."

Mr. Wallace gripped the brim of his fedora. "Mrs. Alden, it's a pleasure. Now I'll leave you ladies to your meal preparation and be on my way."

Mom slipped through the slightly open door, her apron bow catching on the knob. She backstepped and pulled it free. "Mr. Wallace, if you haven't yet eaten, you're welcome to join us."

Meg stared at her mother. "I'm sure his cook has already prepared his meal."

Mr. Wallace gave her a quizzical look. "As a matter of fact, other than a couple eggs I fried up this morning, I haven't eaten." He sniffed the air. "And if what I smell is any indication of what you're fixing, I'd be pleased to stay."

Reconciled to her mother's belief that the family table was always open to unexpected guests, Meg led him inside and left him with her father in the living room while she hurried down the center hallway to the kitchen.

Meg tied an apron around her waist, then lifted the potatoes from the stove and drained the hot water into the sink. After slamming the pot onto the kitchen table, she went to a drawer and yanked out a can opener, an eggbeater, and a small strainer, tossing them onto the counter one by one. Voices drifted in from the living room as Jack related a story to Dad about working for Senator Glenn.

"Goodness, Meg, who got your pantaloons in a knot?" Mom picked up a platter heavy with beef roast.

Meg grabbed the potato masher then returned the other items to the drawer and banged it closed. "I wish you'd have asked me before inviting him to dinner."

Her mother disappeared with the roast through the swinging door to the dining room.

A second later, the door flew open and Mom stepped back into the kitchen. "You've never objected before when I've invited your friends to eat with us. I just assumed he was alone. No one should be without company for Sunday dinner."

Meg took milk from the icebox along with the butter dish and set them next to the pot. "He's hardly alone. He has his servants."

"Servants?"

"Couldn't you tell by his cashmere coat and sweater vest? He lives on the lakeshore in one of those mansions."

"Meg, I'm surprised at you. You've never shunned anyone because of his status. Even well-to-do people can be lonely. Maybe more so than those who have less." Mom picked up a plate and silverware. "I'll put this extra setting on the table."

After her mother left, Meg added milk and a large pat of butter to the potatoes before grabbing the masher and pushing it into the steaming pot. Mr. Wallace, lonely? Not possible. She drew out the masher and attacked another area. With servants around, how could he be?

She flicked another pat of butter into the pot. He did say he'd made his own breakfast that morning. Maybe the cook took Sundays off. She gave the masher a couple more thrusts as her mom's last words seeped into her heart. She'd let the man get under her skin all because of a job she stood little chance of getting anyway. Having Mr. Wallace to dinner didn't mean she had to be his best friend.

"How are the potatoes coming?" Mom picked up a bowl of green beans.

Meg lifted the pot and scraped the contents into a serving bowl. "Guess you can call everyone."

She arrived at the table as Mom was instructing people where to sit. "I put you and Meg over here, Jack. Laura will be on the other side." She peered in the direction of the stairs. "Louis, did you call Laura?"

"Yes. Twice. She's probably got her nose in a book."

Mom looked at Meg. "Sweetie, would you mind?"

Meg nodded as the sound of footfalls tumbling down the stairs came from the hallway. Laura bounded into the room. "Sorry I'm late. I wanted to reread *Romeo and Juliet* and make sure I didn't miss anything the—" Laura stopped and flashed Mr. Wallace a smile. "I didn't realize we had company. Hello, Mr. . . ."

"Wallace. Jack Wallace. I work at the paper with M—your sister."

Laura gave Meg a knowing look. "Keeping secrets from me, big sister?"

Meg's face warmed. "No secrets. Mr. Wallace only started this past week."

Laura returned her attention to their guest. "Well, I'm glad to know about you now, Jack. Welcome." She slid onto her chair.

"Thank you. You'll have to tell me later what you're learning from *Romeo and Juliet.*"

Meg flashed a pointed stare at Laura then sat.

"Now that we're all here, let's say the blessing." Dad took Meg's left hand. She reached across the table with her right then shrank back. Already her mother had grasped Mr. Wallace's other hand. They were waiting on her. She touched the tips of his fingers, and he gripped her hand. An electric-like charge zinged up her arm, and she wanted to yank her hand back. The tingles reached her stomach, and she felt like she was about to swoon. How could she have such a reaction to a man she disliked?

". . .for these blessings, we thank You, Lord. In Your Son's name we pray, amen."

Mr. Wallace gave Meg's fingers a little squeeze that almost sent her over the edge. She snapped her hand back as though it had been released from a trap. If Dad had said anything different in his routine guest prayer, she'd missed it.

The next several minutes were spent passing the roast, potatoes, and beans. Once plates were full, everyone dug in to the meal. Meg forked some green beans and lifted them to her mouth. Maybe they'd get through the dinner with Mr. Wallace leaving afterward. It could all be over in one tiny hour.

"So tell me, Jack, how is it you came to work at the *News-Trib*?" Mom cut her meat as she talked.

He wiped his mouth with his napkin. "My dad thought it would be good for me to work for a small-town weekly in preparation for taking over the family business. He and Oscar Zimmer are friends."

"Your father is in the news biz?" Dad asked.

"You could say so." Jack speared a piece of meat and shoved it into his mouth on top of the potatoes he'd just eaten. He reached for a slice of bread.

"What does he do, Jack? I've been fascinated with the newspaper business ever since Meg started working at the *News-Trib*." Laura kept her eyes on Mr. Wallace as if he were the only person in the room.

Dad pinned a stare on Laura, his mustache twitching. "Mr. Wallace to you, young lady."

Mr. Wallace's Adam's apple bobbed. "He. . .owns a. . .paper."

Dad leaned in. "What paper?"

"The. . .*Chicago Beacon*."

Meg gripped the sides of her chair and squeezed. Her stomach burned hot.

The man was a charlatan, plain and simple. And Mr. Zimmer had gone along with it. She had no future in Lake Geneva if she wanted more than reporting on garden-club doings. As soon as Mr. Wallace took his leave, she'd have to convince her father that Northwestern was the right school for her.

"That's why Wallace sounded so familiar." Dad's voice broke into her thoughts. "I met your father at the country club last year. Nice fella. Didn't he say you have a house over in the Elgin Club?"

Mr. Wallace nodded. "That's where I'm staying." He cast a glance at Meg. "Alone. No servants."

By the time Mom took the dishes into the kitchen, Meg had managed to rearrange the food on her plate to appear as if she'd eaten most of it. Everyone was so caught up in Jack's story about the time his father had interviewed President Coolidge that no one noticed she wasn't eating.

When Mom returned with spice cake on a glass platter, Meg declined a piece, saying she was full.

Over the next half hour, Mr. Wallace's stories continued to captivate everyone as they ate cake and sipped coffee. How could they be so mesmerized by the pretender? Only when Dad urged Laura upstairs to study, along with the command to take the books she'd left on the steps, did the conversation break up.

Meg stood. "Mom, you and Dad go relax. I'll do the dishes." She faced Mr. Wallace. "Please don't feel that you need to stay. Weren't you on your way to see the new building?"

He nodded. "I was, but I'm enjoying the company here." His face brightened. "Unless you want to come with me."

Meg gathered the water glasses. A walk to the new building she always enjoyed, but never with him. "I already promised I'd do the dishes."

"Nonsense. You can help with those any other day." Mom pried the glasses out of Meg's hands. "What better person to show off the building than you? You haven't missed the addition of a brick since they laid the foundation." She stepped through the kitchen door.

Dad ran his thumbs up and down his suspenders. "Good idea. Show Jack around. Make sure he writes up a good story."

"My car is parked on Main near the library. I'll drive you back."

Mom came from the hall and handed Meg her wool coat. "Take this. Temperatures drop fast this time of year once the sun goes down."

Before Meg could protest, Mr. Wallace took the coat and draped it over his arm, along with his overcoat.

He held the door as she traipsed outside. As soon as they got to the building, she'd insist he bring her home. She'd be back in less than an hour.

Chapter Six

. . . .

A few minutes later, they crossed Main Street and headed down the same path they'd traveled earlier. Meg kept her arms folded across her chest, her mouth clamped shut against the words she itched to say. It appeared he'd run out of words himself. Fine with her.

They reached the two-story frame house that served as the town's library, and he glanced over. "Do you like to read for pleasure?"

"Yes. I was on the wait-list at the library for *Magnificent Obsession*. It was worth the wait."

"I liked it too, but I enjoyed *Maid in Waiting* more. It's a bit older, but I'm just catching up on my reading since returning to Chicago."

Meg stared at him. A man who took pleasure in a good story as much as she did was a rarity. Getting news over the Teletype at work, she had no desire to listen to the radio in the evening, instead devouring almost every novel the library acquired, using the time to build up her ability to read faster. A vision popped into her thoughts of her and Jack sitting in front of a roaring fire, both reading, and she mentally recoiled from the image.

"Did you attend last fall's informal opening of the ballroom?" Mr. Wallace asked.

"Oh, yes. We had to walk over planks to get inside and the woodwork still needed painting, but it was a lot of fun." She picked up her pace, her excitement mounting as it always did when she neared the construction site.

"Tell me about the building this one replaced."

Bad memories of last summer's final dance crowded out her enthusiasm, and she slowed her pace. Matthew's coming for the weekend let her think he planned to ask Dad for her hand. Instead, he picked the middle of the Northport's dance floor to tell her he'd fallen in love with someone else.

"It was a sorry place by the time they tore it down," she said, "with pathetic changing rooms and a minuscule dance floor. I'll miss the water slide, though. It stood near where the west terrace is now."

"You go to many of the dances?"

Her breath hitched. "Some."

"I'll bet you turned some heads. Let's have a closer look."

He thought her attractive? She lifted her face to the sun and let his words seep in. Words he probably said to all women. She shook off the euphoric feeling. Other women might fall under this man's spell, but not her.

They headed down a freshly laid cement walk to the building's front staircases that circled up to the ballroom's entrance from either side. Jack grinned. "Think we can peek in?"

Meg laughed. "Sure. Why not? Race you to the top." She scrambled up the stairs as fast as her heels would allow. Jack passed her, taking two steps at a time, then waited at the top, his arms akimbo.

"I'd have beaten you if I had flat shoes like yours." She cupped her hands around her eyes and looked through the glass. She let out a gasp and bounced on her toes. "The sunlight is shining off the mirror ball, making it look like a fairyland. Jack, you've got to see this."

He peeked through the window next to hers and let out a low whistle. "I didn't expect the ballroom to be this beautiful. They've put a lot of work into this place."

"Gloria's husband told me about the touch-ups they've made over the winter, but seeing it in person is so much better."

"Isn't he the worker you said inspired your article?"

An ache pressed against Meg's heart, and she stood back. Why did he have to bring the article up now? "Yes."

He straightened and caught her gaze. "So what did he say?"

"It's not important. Let's go around to the lake." She started down the stairs.

Jack came behind her. "It *is* important. Oscar should have printed your story."

At the bottom, she faced him. "Jack, you haven't even read it."

He held up his hands in surrender. "True, but I'm sure you're a good writer."

She rolled her eyes. "You can forget about buttering me up. The answer is still no."

They headed under an arch then passed the spot where the gigantic water slide once stood.

"So what's behind these?" Jack pointed with his thumb at three yet-to-be stained doors.

She stepped over and ran a hand across the raw, smooth wood. "Bathhouses complete with lockers. So much better than before." She tilted her head. "Don't you want to take notes?"

He pulled a pad and pencil from his coat pocket. "Good idea. I've been distracted by the view."

She turned away from his irresistible smile and continued walking toward where the new docks jutted out from the back of the building, reminding herself that charm was often deceptive.

"So when did construction actually begin?"

Meg faced him. Jack held his pencil over his notepad.

"Shortly after the bond vote passed." *May as well answer and make sure he gets his facts straight.* "Men worked twelve-hour days for most months, but the area looked nothing like it does now."

He glanced up. "This is good. Go on."

"Jack Wallace, surely you can't mean that after working for a US senator, a little recreational building in Lake Geneva is exciting news? I know we don't have much action around here, but don't mock me." She turned on her heels and marched around the east side of the structure. He was wasting her time.

Hurried footsteps slapped the pavement behind her.

"I did read the archives, but hearing the history from you makes it come alive, Meg. And yes, I find it exciting because I love this lake and town and want to see it prosper."

She stopped in front of where a pier for small boats was planned and stared at him. "I didn't agree to a first-name basis."

The left corner of his mouth twitched. "You've been calling me 'Jack' for the past half hour."

She flushed, scrambling to remember. "I have not."

He threw his head back and guffawed. "Yes, you have. Once I thought it was a slip of the tongue, but after the third time, I took it to mean I could call you 'Meg.' Away from the office, of course. But the last time, you used both my names together, so maybe that didn't count."

He hadn't given one hint that she'd called him "Jack," but somehow between dinner and now, he'd stopped being "Mr. Wallace." She allowed him a small smile. "It came out so naturally, I never noticed. But I still don't think you're going to learn anything new here."

He held up his hands in surrender. "No more questions. Want to stop somewhere for coffee?"

She raised a brow. "Where do you think you'll find a café open on a Sunday?"

He took her elbow as they meandered under an arch toward the street. "Shows you how long I've been living in the big city. There's always something open there. I owe you a rain check."

Somehow she'd gone from being upset to a first-name basis. Now he held her arm as though they were a couple. If she were smart, she'd pull away. But it had been a long time since a man had treated her like a lady. Maybe Mom still had coffee in the pot at home.

Chapter Seven
....

On Monday night, Meg folded her arms against the stiff breeze as she and Helen walked to the Geneva Theatre. "Are you sure your mom will be okay while we go to the picture show? It looked like her legs were giving her more pain than usual."

Helen flicked her wrist, her blond waves bouncing. "She was on her feet for three hours with Mrs. Whiting this afternoon. No one's hair takes as long as hers, and she won't let anyone but Mom work on her. I offered to stay home, but Mom shooed me away. Said I need some fun in my life." She picked up the pace. "I can't wait to see Dick Powell and Ginger Rogers dancing their shoes off." She twirled with an imaginary partner in the middle of the sidewalk.

While Helen spun, Meg's thoughts whirled back to yesterday and her unexpected afternoon with Jack. Since then, she'd tried to see things from his point of view. He said his position at the *News-Trib* had been arranged and it wasn't his decision. But his taking the job still didn't seem fair when he had a position waiting for him in Chicago.

Helen fell in step beside Meg. "A girl can dream about dancing with someone like Dick Powell, but I'd be satisfied just styling Ginger's hair."

Meg loved her friend's drive to never give up on her dreams. If Meg had stayed in school, maybe she'd be working for a large paper like *The Chicago Tribune* or the *Beacon*, ready to break ground into the reporting pool. They turned the corner, and the flashing marquee came into view. Several people stood in line, including Jack. Meg's heart quickened.

"Isn't that Jack Wallace?"

Meg stared at Helen. "How do you know what he looks like?"

"I told you, I was introduced to him at the Utopia Café the other night." Helen grabbed Meg's arm and tugged her the last fifty feet. "Hi, Jack. So you like musicals too?"

Jack turned, and his gaze flicked from Helen to Meg and settled there as a grin took over his face. "Hello, ladies. To be honest, I prefer an old who-dunit. But a movie beats sitting at home and listening to the icebox run."

Helen laughed. "That sounds better than listening to my mother's radio programs."

A memory of Mom's comment about well-to-do people being lonely popped into Meg's thoughts. Would she enjoy rambling around in a mansion alone? Most times, someone else was at home with her. She checked her watch. Jack and Helen's conversation had moved on to movies they'd seen. She waited for him to end his sentence.

"Helen, if we're going to catch the newsreel, we'd better get inside."

Jack looked at Meg with a start. "I'm sorry. Didn't mean to horn in." He held up his ticket. "I'm all set here."

Helen flashed him one of her playful smiles. Her clear complexion seemed to glow beneath the marquee's bright lights. "Jack, why don't you join us?"

Meg's eyes widened. She did not want the man sitting next to her in a darkened theater, their arms sharing a narrow piece of wood. Nor did she want her friend sitting next to him. Stunned at her last thought, Meg flushed and scurried over to the ticket booth.

She shoved her dollar under the window. It was a free world and he could see whomever he wanted, which he probably did anyway. She gathered her change and ticket then turned and caught Jack's eye. Feeling as if he had read every thought in her head, she looked away.

Helen stuffed her change into her handbag. "What do you say, Jack? Sit with us?" She clasped the purse shut.

"I like the balcony, but thanks for asking." Jack opened the door and waited for the women to enter.

"If you prefer sitting next to strangers over our scintillating company, so be it." Helen laughed as Jack headed for the stairs. "That's one good-looking man." She turned to Meg. "Here I'm trying to help you out, and you clam up."

"Help me how? I'm not looking for romance. And if I were, I wouldn't look for it at work or with him."

"I don't see why not. Seems to me you and Jack might be destined for something more than coworkers. If you let yourself."

"What do you mean?"

"In this small town, you can't let office protocol block the road to love. The way the man looked at you back there, if I were you, I'd get my claws in him before another gal steals him away and just like that"—she snapped her fingers—"he's gone."

Helen made it sound like every single woman in town was after Jack. Even if he wasn't a big flirt and handsome beyond words, the truth remained. He was lakeshore and ran in a different crowd than the townies. Meg opened the door to the auditorium. "Let's get inside." Someday Helen would learn that life wasn't a movie script.

They found seats on the aisle halfway down. On the screen, black-and-white images of President Roosevelt's recent inauguration flickered. Meg had wanted to see the newsreel, but her thoughts drifted. Had Jack really looked at her the way Helen said? All she saw was his eyes fixed on Helen. How could he not stare at her friend? The woman was gorgeous. Meg twisted in her seat and studied the balcony, but no face was visible in the dark theater.

She turned as the newsreel ended and a Popeye cartoon began. Another reason to avoid Jack was that he'd probably overheard her conversation with Lester. Any attention he gave her would likely hold a price she wasn't willing to pay.

Since that day, a Bible verse kept popping into her thoughts: *Ye have sinned against the Lord: and be sure your sin will find you out.* The same verse that had convinced her to stop helping Lester. Not only were her actions against God, but despite Mr. Zimmer's old-fashioned views, he was a nice man and she hated going behind his back. She'd stop for sure after Lester turned in the meeting article and she fulfilled her part of their agreement.

The movie began, and Meg escaped into a world where women's career dreams were realized instead of snuffed out by the men around them. All too quickly, the film ended and the lights went up. Blinking, Meg turned and scanned the balcony. A man stood in the aisle with his back to her. It could be him. The build was similar.

Helen poked her. "For someone who doesn't care to be involved with the man, you're sure interested in his whereabouts." She snickered. "Are we going to get to Franzoni's before all the booths are taken?"

"I was just noticing how full the theater is tonight." Meg stood and started up the aisle.

"Especially the balcony. Hey, if I worked with a good-looking man like Jack, I'd search for him too. But right now I'm more interested in a chocolate soda."

The women managed to snag the last available booth in the packed soda fountain next to the theater. They gave their orders to the waitress then slipped out of their coats.

"Wasn't that a marvelous picture?" Helen set her pocketbook on the seat beside her. "There's my customer, Mrs. Crumple." She waved at a woman sitting at a nearby table then continued to scan the crowd. "Jack must have gone home to his icebox."

Meg rolled her eyes. "I loved the movie. A good picture helps to get one's mind off her troubles."

Helen faced Meg. A frown creased her forehead. "Other than 'the man,' what kind of troubles?"

"I wish you'd stop. My only man trouble is how Mr. Zimmer refuses to consider me for a reporter job. I'll never be able to break in if I stay around here."

"Didn't you say Jack's family owns the *Chicago Beacon*? Maybe he can put in a good word for you."

"I doubt his dad would agree to hiring a woman because she's a friend of his son's. Especially a woman with no known experience."

"Why is it so important you become a reporter now?"

Meg drew in a breath. "I've told you before. I feel it's my calling in life."

The waitress burst upon them with their chocolate sodas. After she left, Meg scooped ice cream and whipped topping onto her spoon. She closed her mouth around the concoction, enjoying the feel of the carbonated mixture on her tongue.

"Come on, Meg. Out with it."

Meg tilted her head. "Out with what?"

"What's the real reason you want to be a reporter?"

Meg raised her shoulders and let them drop. "That is the reason, the same way you feel called to be a hairstylist to the stars."

Helen flipped a platinum wave away from her face and sipped her drink. She stared off to the side for a moment. "I may have a solution to your problem."

Meg's eyes widened. "What?"

Helen rested her elbows on the worn tabletop and leaned forward. "It's obvious that as long as Mr. Zimmer is the boss, you aren't going to become a reporter in this town. Right?"

Meg stared into her soda and studied the swirls of whipped cream floating midway in the chocolaty drink. "Right."

"Your best chance is to work your way up at a large daily paper. Right?" She nodded.

"Then move to Hollywood with me."

Chapter Eight

....

Meg gaped at Helen. "You can't be serious. We're in the middle of a depression. And what about your mother?"

A grin split Helen's face. "Mom is the one encouraging me to give Hollywood a shot. We have a beautician friend who's interested in coming on board with us. She can take my place. And Mom will be better soon. Until then, what she does lightens the load enough."

Meg tilted her head. "Your mom can hardly walk after being on her feet. There's been times you've had to assist her to bed."

"Beatrice, our friend, will be living with her. She'll be fine. Mom says it's time I chase my dream while I'm young. It's something she never did herself and she doesn't want me to have regrets." Helen waved a hand, almost whacking her glass. "I bet those LA papers have lots of women reporters. Not to mention warm breezes all year, palm trees, and the Pacific at our doorstep." Her eyes widened. "Maybe we'll even have an orange tree in our backyard."

Meg pushed her glass away and leaned across the table. "Why haven't you told me about this before? It sounds like you've been planning for weeks."

"I have, in my head mostly. Beatrice spent the weekend with us. We just decided yesterday."

Meg drew in a long breath. In less than an hour she'd gone from expecting to spend her entire life in Lake Geneva stuck in a dead-end job to considering a move to California, of all places. "I don't know, Helen. If you don't find a job at a studio, you can always work in a beauty shop, but getting my foot in the door of a large daily may not be so easy."

Helen's eyes twinkled. "I know you'd find something. Maybe you can take want-ads like you do here and work your way up."

Meg sat back. Doubt swirled in her chest, but Helen had a point. "Mattie Nordman, who used to proofread for the *News-Trib*, now works for the *Los Angeles Examiner*. I could write and ask her how jobs are there."

"Do I know her?"

"Maybe. Her husband was hired to work on the tunnel related to that big dam project on the Colorado River. He died last year on the site. She moved to Los Angeles to be with her mom and sister."

Helen's eyes dulled. "I remember. That was so sad. Good idea to write her." She slurped up the last of her soda. "Maybe you should pray about it."

Meg started. "Since when have I known you to pray about anything?"

Helen looked away. "I wasn't suggesting that *I* pray. You're the one who is always preaching to me about God's will and praying over things." She faced Meg. "Come to think of it, I haven't heard you say much about God recently."

Meg jabbed her straw against the bottom of the glass, willing away the swelling guilt. "That's because I haven't said much. God hasn't been answering my prayers lately."

"I can't believe I'm hearing you right. You've always said sometimes His answers come in ways we don't expect. Maybe my idea is your answer." Helen wiped her mouth with her napkin. "Are you game to at least think about it?"

Meg squirmed. She'd need traveling money, not to mention cash to live on, until she got a job. At the moment, her savings would barely take her past St. Louis. "Not so fast. I can't move without assurance of a job or money." She hated the disappointment etched on Helen's face, but she needed time to process everything.

Helen wiped her mouth then checked the wall clock. "Do you mind if we call it a night this early? All the talk about Mom and her aching legs makes me want to get home and check on her."

Meg tipped her glass and drank the last of the melted concoction, letting the chocolaty flavor linger in her mouth for an extra second. She swallowed and set the empty glass on the table. "I'm ready."

She followed Helen out into the chilly night air. Her friend had to be joshing about moving. If Helen couldn't be away from her mother more than two hours without checking on her, how would she be able to move anywhere else, let alone California?

* * * * *

Jack entered his house and tossed the keys onto the kitchen counter. Behind the round oak table, the new gleaming icebox stood like an armed sentry. He stared at the thing. "Hi, icebox. Miss me? Can't say I missed you." The machine's motor kicked on as if to say, "I'm new and sleek and have a new name." He chuckled. One of these days he'd get used to calling it a refrigerator.

He wandered through the dining room, where he shed his suit coat and draped it over the back of a chair, then pushed on to the living room and sank onto a sofa. As much as he loved the old house, he hated living here alone. His days passed quickly, but the nights were murder. He loosened his tie and pulled off his sweater vest, tossing it aside. What he needed was some noise. He stood and crossed the room to the radio console and flicked it on.

"Today in Washington, President Roosevelt—" Jack turned the dial. The tune "I've Told Ev'ry Little Star" blasted from the speaker. Satisfied, he returned to the sofa and stretched out his legs.

His thoughts shifted to that evening's encounter with the girls. He hated balconies, so why did he say he preferred them? Probably because he hadn't figured out whether Meg even liked him; she seemed so hot and then cold. The expression on her face when he'd revealed at the dinner table that his father owned the *Beacon* was enough to sour milk. He'd been working up to apologize during their walk later, but when her mood changed as she raced him up those steps, he refrained. She'd been like Cinderella wanting to go to the ball, peering through the window. He'd be her Prince Charming if she let him, but after tonight's frosty reception, he doubted she was interested. At least she was calling him Jack. He liked that much better.

He should have told her he needed to be in Chicago tomorrow, but with his doing interviews away from the office for most of the day, he hadn't gotten a chance. Maybe after his visit with Dad, life would be a bit easier for her.

He let out an audible sigh. Probably a good thing he wasn't going into the office tomorrow. He needed a breather.

* * * * *

At midmorning the next day, Jack entered the *Chicago Beacon*'s tenth-floor office suite. Millie, Dad's secretary, looked up from her typewriter and flashed him a smile that caused the laugh lines around her eyes to deepen. "About time you got here." She pushed her wire-framed glasses farther up the bridge of her nose and stood. "Come closer so I can get a better look at you."

Since he'd been a boy, Millie had always greeted him as the son she never had.

Jack closed the space between them, and she ran her eyes over his face. "How's life in the country?"

"Less hectic than here. It's been a nice change." He shrugged off his overcoat and hung it on a coat tree in a corner of the spacious room.

She laughed. "I imagine a weekly is less hectic. I bet the editor's secretary makes it home most nights before five."

"I believe you're right, except for Wednesdays. Then she stays until at least six."

Millie shook her head as deep dimples appeared on her plump cheeks. "Maybe I should retire to Wisconsin."

Jack chuckled. No way would she leave Dad. She lived alone in a walk-up apartment, and other than her cat, the *Beacon* was her life.

The door to his father's office swung open and Dad stepped through it, impeccably dressed—but his three-piece suit hung loose over what used to be a sizable paunch. He pulled a watch from his vest pocket and flipped it open. "The Northwestern Railroad is on time as usual." He returned the timepiece to his vest and held out his hand. "Son, good to see you."

The men shook. Dad hung on to Jack's hand a bit longer than usual, giving him a moment to study his father's face. Decidedly thinner since he last saw him. They released their grips, and Jack stepped into his dad's wood-paneled inner sanctum. He headed for the upholstered armchair situated in front of the desk.

"Let's sit on the davenport. No need to be formal."

Puzzled, Jack paused then went to the leather sofa and sat while Dad took his place at the other end. What was going on? Was he thinner because of sickness, or had he finally listened to Mom's chiding that he needed to lose weight?

Dad reached for a wood box decorated with inlaid leaf shapes sitting on the coffee table, opening the lid. He selected a cigarette and, with shaking hands, stuck it between his lips. "I take it you still don't indulge."

"No, I don't." Jack picked up the sterling silver lighter from the table and flicked a flame to life. He held it against the cigarette's tip.

Dad took a long draw and exhaled the smoke through his nose, an old ritual designed to give him time to think. "So, how are things in Lake Geneva?" He ran his hand over thinning gray hair.

"Good. The town is excited about the new recreation building and ballroom. May twenty-second is the grand opening. They've booked Wayne King and his Orchestra."

"Must be quite a place, to get someone like King."

"I've not yet been inside, but on Sunday I had a look through the windows. The ballroom is a dandy. They've already got Tommy Dorsey coming this summer."

"Seems they'd want a reporter inside to keep everyone excited about the opening."

"I was planning to interview the building contractor today, but when you called, I canceled the appointment."

With a flick of Dad's wrist, an ash dropped into a crystal ashtray. "You still have misgivings about taking away the job from that gal?"

Jack picked up the lighter and worked the lever several times. "Yes, but I guess Oscar wouldn't offer her the position anyway."

"You sure there aren't other feelings going on with her? You've got the same faraway look on your face you used to get whenever Natalie Higgins was mentioned."

He flicked the lighter and held the flame. Natalie hadn't invaded his thoughts in at least two years. She'd married a congressman from Arizona, dropping Jack like a hot potato when the politician showed interest. He extinguished the flame. "Nothing like that." Whatever feelings he had for Meg, they were unlike anything he'd experienced before, but he wasn't about to admit it to anyone.

Jack set the lighter on the table and crossed his arms. "You know I can't afford to get involved with a woman right now. No distractions for me. Just learn the biz and get back here. In fact I wanted to sug—"

Dad hacked into his free hand, the same kind of cough that came over the phone the other day. He stubbed out the cigarette then settled back into the couch cushion, his face pale against the dark brown leather. Color slowly returned to his cheeks.

Stunned, Jack shifted his weight, causing the cushions to rustle. "What's wrong?"

"Wrong?"

"You've lost weight, and your cough sounds bad."

Dad gave an eye roll and shook his head. "At your mother's insistence, I cut out starchy food. Picked up the cough a few weeks ago with a nasty cold. You know how it is. The barking is always the last to go. Your mother made me a doctor's appointment for next week. In the meantime, I want to hear how things are going with you and Oscar."

"Are you sure you called me down here to talk about a job I've only had a bit more than a week?"

Dad sat up, his soft expression dissolving into a rigid mask. "That, and your mother is coming into the city to have lunch with us."

As usual, his father was holding a figurative arm out, keeping Jack at bay. Was it no wonder he always felt like an exile? If his father wanted to deny his motives, so be it.

"Dad, I don't understand how working for a small-town weekly will help me run the *Beacon*. Once the new lakefront building opens, the hottest news to hit the area in years will dry up. You're the one I should be learning from. Not Oscar, who's done nothing but run weeklies for the past thirty years."

Dad pushed to his feet and walked to the window overlooking Madison Street. "I had a feeling you'd want to back out of our agreement." He jammed his hands into his pockets and jingled his coins. "Back in Terre Haute, when I started in the business, my desk looked out onto the sidewalk, much like yours must today. From this height, the people look like ants.

"A lot has happened in my rise to this lofty place. If I'd come here directly, I wouldn't know what it takes to work a Linotype or put a paper together from beginning to end. Learning how to do everything on a weekly made it easier to take over for your grandfather twenty-five years ago." He turned. "You've only been there a week. You've got to give the year we agreed upon."

Jack blew out a breath. Twelve months of sitting within feet of one very distracting lady. But none of that mattered. Not with the way his father looked. Jack leaned forward and rested his elbows on his knees. "Be honest, Dad. You have to be dragged kicking and screaming to the doctor. Do you know something you're not telling?"

A shadow of uncertainty registered on Dad's face before he faced the window once more. "This cough needs some medication, is all."

"I hope you're right. Have you talked to Kate lately?"

"Just last night. Paul got the promotion he'd hoped for, and they're moving to Chicago this coming summer."

Jack grinned. "That's swell news. I hope they settle in time to spend some of the summer up at the lake." With his sister back in the area, his plan would work even better. "When is the doctor's appointment?"

"Next Monday at ten." Dad walked back to his end of the couch. "Your mother should be here soon. She's been wanting to eat at the Tip Top Inn's Dickens Room ever since your aunt Emma mentioned it."

"Sounds good." He'd pull Mom aside and ask her to call him later. That was the only way he'd get any answers.

Later that night back at the Elgin Club, Jack asked the central operator to connect him to Detroit and his sister's telephone. Kate's husband answered and called her to the phone.

"Hey, sis, I heard today that you and Paul are moving to Chicago."

"Jack," she squealed. "Your voice sounds so good. We'll be in the Windy City by this summer. We thought we'd look for an apartment near Lincoln Park. How are you doing?"

Jack drew in a breath and held it. "I'm doing fine. It's Dad I'm worried about. You have a few minutes?"

Chapter Nine

....

When Jack arrived at work the next morning, Meg was already at her desk, frowning at whatever she'd just typed. He stopped by the coffeepot then strolled up to her, filled cup in one hand and briefcase in the other. "Morning, Miss Alden. I see I'm not the only early riser, even for deadline day." He glanced at the empty desks, pretending to not notice her arm placed strategically over her typing.

"The early bird gets the worm, they say." Her weak smile didn't match the fear in her eyes.

He wanted to tell her that her ghosting secret was safe with him but thought better of it. Best to apologize for his appearing to hide his own secret first. But it needed to be done away from work. He moved to his desk and set down the piping hot brew. "Then I'd better get busy if I'm going to get a worm at all."

"I suppose you were out yesterday getting information for your story."

"Actually, no." He rolled a clean sheet of paper into his typewriter. "If you're free for lunch—and we both get our work to Composing by then— would you care to join me?"

She bit her apple-red lower lip. "I have to run to Helen's shop and drop off something for her mother. She lives close to the Geneva Grill. We could meet there."

"Sounds good. We'd best get to work, then, so we don't have to change plans." Jack tossed her a wink then opened a drawer and took out his notebook. Outside of the quote from Meg's father, his notes were not enough to bring the story up to snuff. What he needed was likely on the paper in Meg's typewriter.

* * * * *

Meg rolled the article from the platen of the typewriter then slid it between two sheets of unused paper. Across the room, Thelma and Emily chatted. She glanced at Jack. His handsome face was set in concentration as he two-finger typed. If it weren't for him, she would have finished the article before Thelma and Emily arrived. It was bad enough he sat next to her, but with that wink, her concentration seemed to fly out the window. Twice, she had to retype the article after she left out a word.

She placed the papers on a corner of her desk then stood and strolled through Composing and into the tiny restroom, where she leaned against the wall. Pressing her palm against her chest as if the gesture would still her heart, she forced herself to take a deep breath. Maybe she should have taken Jack up on his offer of collaboration. At least she wouldn't have to sneak around.

Her face freshened with splashes of cold water, she returned to her work area. Her eyes went to the empty corner of her desk and then to Lester. He acknowledged her with a nod before ambling toward Mr. Zimmer's office, Meg's article in hand.

Meg went back to writing "Town Talk" with its usual litany of social doings. She'd spent a good portion of yesterday calling her usual sources, but all she'd picked up was someone's sister visiting from Indianapolis and a bridal shower. She'd have to go with the usual filler of garden-club activities and birth announcements. She counted back the days to Saturday morning when she'd mailed her letter to Mattie Nordman. The post should arrive there by the weekend.

God, if this is not the right direction, please give me a reason to stay here.

"Miss Alden, my work is done. What about yours?"

Meg opened her eyes and found herself staring into Jack's blue-eyed gaze. No. . .God wouldn't answer like that, would He? She managed a smile. "Almost done."

* * * * *

Meg scurried the short distance from the Powder Puff Beauty Shop to the Geneva Grill, her thoughts remaining on her previous conversation with Helen. Both Helen and her mother had customers at their workstations when Meg entered, and Helen had insisted Meg wait until she finished giving a trim so they could talk about California. Meg told her she was still thinking about it and had written to Mattie. Until she heard from her, Meg would have no decision.

She entered the crowded restaurant, and the aroma of their signature chicken noodle soup tickled her nose. Jack sat at a table toward the back, frowning at his open pocket watch. She cringed. Why hadn't she told Helen she couldn't wait? She scurried past the lunch counter and up to his table. "Sorry I was delayed. Helen insisted I wait until she finished with a customer. I guess we should have made it another day."

Jack stood. "I was afraid you'd changed your mind. I hope soup is okay with you since we don't have much time." He pushed out the chair to his right and waited for her to sit before he retook his seat.

She sat and removed her gloves. "Yes, the soup here is wonderful."

A waitress appeared, notepad in hand. "Ready to order now, Mr. Wallace?"

Jack grinned. "Yes, Alice. Thanks for your patience."

The brunette's face lit up. "No problem at all."

Meg's chest constricted. He was even on a first-name basis with the waitress. It was bad enough watching women almost eat out of his hand at the office, but the stabs of jealousy surging through her now were worse.

Jack ordered two chicken soups and coffee. The server closed her pad. "If you need anything else, just holler."

After the waitress left, Jack inched his chair closer to the table and leaned on his elbows. "You deserve an apology."

"For what?"

His right brow rose a half inch. "You don't think I owe you one?"

"Depends on which offense you're apologizing for." She sent him a smile.

A V-shaped crease appeared between his eyes. "Here I'd hoped you hadn't noticed all the other ones. Have you kept track?"

She feigned flipping open a notebook and running a finger down an imaginary list. "Where should I start?"

He laughed. "That bad, huh?"

She leaned her elbow on the table and rested her chin in her hand. "Depends on what you call bad."

He rewarded her with a wry smile, and her stomach dipped and fluttered. Who needed soup? She gave herself a mental shake. What she needed was a dose of reality. The man may as well have *Heartbreaker* written across his forehead.

His face turned serious. "Joking aside, I should have told you first how I came to be at the *News-Trib*, not spring it on you at your family's dinner table. The news must have stunned you." His mouth turned down at the corners. "I'm sorry."

The waitress brought Meg coffee and added more to Jack's cup. Thankful for the time to calm her nerves, Meg stirred a couple of sugars into her brew. She had to give him credit for compassion. "I was surprised."

Jack looked her in the eyes. "If it's any consolation, it was Oscar's idea to not tell the staff of my connections. The other day when your father asked about my family, I answered truthfully. I should have declined your mother's invitation to avoid disclosing myself, but. . ." He flashed her a lopsided smile that threatened to melt any defenses she had left. "After living on bologna sandwiches all week and then smelling your mother's marvelous roast, I couldn't refuse."

She regarded her lap as regret took over. "I really thought you had a cook."

"Why would you think that?"

She shrugged. "Families who live on the lakeshore have servants. Even in these times."

"I suppose my parents could afford domestic help, but my mother's family never had much, and she prefers taking care of things herself."

Meg sipped her coffee and set it down. "Keeping up a mansion must be hard without servants."

A smile played on his lips. "Have you ever seen the Elgin Club?"

Meg shook her head.

"The houses there are nice, but they hardly qualify as mansions."

Okay, so he hadn't been spoiled growing up, and he drove a regular car. Albeit a brand-new one. She caught his eye. "Looks like I misjudged you. I'm sorry, but you still haven't said why the heir apparent of the *Beacon* is working at the *News-Trib*."

"My dad feels the experience he received on a weekly paper—before he took over from my grandfather—was invaluable. He insists I do the same. Dad has known Oscar for years and asked him if he knew of anyone looking for reporters. Turned out Oscar had an opening." He picked up the saltshaker and studied it. "The deal is, I'll work here for a year. You'll have your opportunity back next spring."

"Here you go." The waitress placed steaming bowls of soup in front of them and looked at Jack. "Anything else?"

Jack shook his head, and she left. He and Meg ate in silence for several minutes. Then he took a slice of bread from a stack on a plate and buttered it while he spoke. "If it helps, Oscar planned to advertise the job in Chicago and Milwaukee, hoping to lure someone with experience who might have been laid off."

Meg lifted a spoonful of fragrant hot broth to her lips and blew on it. "It doesn't matter. By the time you're gone, I'll likely be living where women have a chance to advan—" She clamped her mouth shut and rested her spoon on the table. It clattered to the floor.

She bent and peeked under the tablecloth. The utensil lay a few inches from his wingtip-covered right foot. She straightened, and the brim of her hat caught on the table ledge. The hat dropped over her right eye.

Jack's mouth twisted into a smirk. "I'll ask Alice to bring you another spoon."

She adjusted her hat. "Don't bother. . . ."

Jack raised his hand and waved toward the girl. "Too late."

The waitress hurried over, all smiles, and he asked for a new spoon for the lady. They waited in silence until Jack spoke. "That's what I like about you, Meg. You're a fighter."

Relief washed over her. Apparently he'd missed her allusion to moving away. "How so?"

"A lot of women probably feel stifled by a tradition that says certain jobs are for men only. Maybe some positions should stay that way, but God gave writing ability to both men and women. If a gal wants to write fluff, so be it. But if she wants to write hard news, she should be allowed."

Meg stared at him. Maybe he really wanted to help her. But if she wasn't careful, he'd become a distraction, same as Matthew had been— a distraction that cost her the grades she'd worked so hard to attain and gave Dad more reason to pull her out of school. The only answer was to see Jack at work only. At least she'd have the weekends to gather herself for the next five days.

Meg looked at his empty bowl and then at her half-full one. She'd lost her appetite. "If we don't get back to the office, neither of us will have a job. But then, I suppose you're safe, having an in with the boss."

He scowled. "But you've not finished eating."

"All this rushing took my hunger away. I've had plenty." She picked up her handbag.

Jack stood and grabbed the check. He came around the table and waited for her to stand. "By the way, can you tell your mother that I accept her invitation to join your family for services this Sunday? You'll have to tell me where to find your church."

Chapter Ten

Meg remained seated as though glued to her chair. Mom invited people to church all the time, but it never occurred to Meg that the practice would include Jack.

"Meg?"

She snapped her thoughts to attention and stood. "We'd better hurry."

Outside, as they headed past the movie theater toward Main Street, Meg resolved to adopt the positive view her mother heard recently on the radio: *When fate hands you a lemon, make lemonade.* She couldn't help Jack's arrival or the fact that he had gotten the job she wanted. She had to make the best of the situation. She supposed she could always use a friend. But what was she to do when her heart did flip-flops at his lopsided smile?

"From the surprised look on your face, I presume you didn't hear your mother invite me."

Meg stared at the cement under her feet and stuffed her hands into her coat pockets. "No, I didn't."

"She asked me over dessert."

She forced a chuckle. "Maybe I dozed off."

"You okay with it?"

"Of course. It'll be fun to have you visit."

"Good. It's probably best I meet you there. . .wherever *there* is."

Meg relaxed. He didn't suggest he call for her like it was a date. This friend-only status would work fine. "It's Faith Community Church on Madison Street, just before you come to the tracks. The service starts at ten thirty."

"Sounds easy enough. It's been a long while since I've been to church. I'm looking forward to it."

They arrived at the office and stepped inside. Emily pulled her head-set away from her mouth, the movement causing a strand of hair to fall from her bun. "Meg, your mother wants you to call home immediately."

Meg hurried out of her coat and hat and handed them to Jack, who offered to put them into the closet. Mom never called her at work unless she needed something from the grocery. That was probably all it was, but the "immediately" part had her on edge. Emily put her through.

"Hi, Mom. I heard you called."

"Will you be home by five thirty?"

"I can. Is something wrong?"

"Your father called. You know how he likes his girls home for supper."

With their neighbor Mrs. Branigan, who shared their party line, likely listening in, Mom used the coded language she'd developed. Meg got the message. Dad planned a family meeting at five thirty. Probably his usual "Let's pull up our bootstraps and support our merchants speech."

She agreed and hung up, and Jack came up to her desk. "Everything okay?"

"She just had a question. Mom's looking forward to your joining us on Sunday."

Jack answered with a grin and moved to his seat, while she took a want-ad call. Not exactly political intrigue, but for the first time in a long while, she was content to do her job no matter the task.

*   *   *   *   *

Refreshed by her walk home, Meg stepped into the house and passed by the living room. She waved at Dad, who had his nose in the *Beacon*. In the kitchen, Laura stood at the counter mashing potatoes, while Mom spread tomato sauce on top of a meatloaf.

Meg went to the sink and washed her hands. "How can I help?"

"This needs a few more minutes in the oven. Can you set the table?" Mom opened the oven door and slid the meat inside.

Meg gathered silverware, plates, and napkins and went through the swinging door. She gave the table a glance then returned to the kitchen. "The table is already set."

Mom wiped her brow with the bottom of her apron. "Oh. How silly of me. Just fill glasses with water."

Meg stared at Mom. "Is this meeting something more than the usual rally-around-the-storekeepers mantra?

Mom shrugged. "I have no idea what's on your father's mind."

Ten minutes later, the family gathered at the table. Dad's brown brows knit together as he peered at Laura. "Young lady, did you cut your hair?"

Laura patted the waves framing her face. "I just used the curling iron a bit. But don't be surprised if one day I get it waved."

He narrowed his eyes. "Not while you're still in school, you won't."

"I'll pay with my own money." Her lower lip protruded into a pout.

Meg picked up the bowl of mashed potatoes and slapped a mound onto her plate. After a couple of minutes Dad would give in and Laura would get her way—again.

Mom frowned. "Louis, you know you never get anywhere with the girls when you start discussing their hairdos." She handed Meg the carrots. "Would you start these, dear?"

The family was occupied for the next few minutes as food bowls were passed around the table and plates were filled.

Meg dug into her meal, extra hungry since she hadn't eaten much lunch. She glanced at Dad. He appeared to be relaxed, eating and sipping on his water. If what he had to say was crisis-ridden, he didn't seem rattled. Maybe he just wanted his family around the dinner table. She speared a carrot and popped it into her mouth.

Dad cleared his throat. "I have an announcement."

Meg drew in a deep breath and set her fork on her plate.

Her father scanned everyone's faces with a penetrating stare. "I'm losing my secretary. Kathleen announced today that she and Richard are expecting a child."

Meg relaxed. Was that all? "They've been married three or four years already. I bet they're happy."

"She was beaming. The baby is due in October, so I'll be replacing her by the first of the month."

"She's the best secretary you've had, Louis." Mom kept her eyes trained on Dad. "Where are you going to find such a person?"

He cast her a knowing smile. "I don't need to look far, Margaret. She's sitting right here."

"But Laura is going to college in the fall," Meg said.

Color rose on Dad's neck as he turned toward her. "I didn't mean Laura. I meant you, Meg."

She flinched. His words didn't make sense. "I'm not a secretary. I'm a reporter."

"You're a want-ad taker who also writes society news. I can pay more than what Oscar's giving you."

She sat up straight and glared at him. "More money doesn't matter. I don't know the first thing about law. I know newspapers."

The flush had risen past his twitching moustache and into his cheeks. "You'll know as much about law within a few weeks. You type at the paper, and you'll type for me. You'll start on the first. That'll enable you to give Oscar three weeks' notice."

Meg looked at Mom, sending an unspoken plea for help.

Her mother peered at Dad. "Louis, Meg adores working for the newspaper. Why are you doing this?"

"If you must know, Margaret, I'm not pulling in clients like in the past, and I've had to grant pro bono to more people than before. I can pay Meg more than she makes now, but it will be a lot less than what I give Kathleen." He picked up his fork. "It's an economy move." Stabbing a carrot, he lifted it to his mouth.

Meg's stomach lurched, and she threw her napkin next to her plate. "I am not a secretary." She pushed back her chair and stood, keeping her eyes on Dad, who stared at his plate.

He raised his gaze to meet hers. "You should be grateful. In this day and age, many girls would love to have such a job."

"Then you'll have no trouble finding someone else." Her hardened tone echoing in her ears, Meg stormed out of the room and scrambled up the stairs, nearly stumbling over Laura's purse halfway up. She picked up the bag and slammed it onto her sister's bed before going to her own room. Was this the sign from God she was looking for? What she needed now was a positive answer from Mattie.

* * * * *

The sun flashed in Meg's eyes the next morning as she turned and headed down Main, her heels clacking on the cement. After tossing during most of the night, she'd crawled out of bed at four AM and opened her Bible, hoping for answers. But all she encountered were more questions. God said He had a plan for her, yet her life was unraveling.

With His help, she'd gotten through high school. Then, later at college, after seeing her grades drop—thanks to a six-foot-tall distraction— she'd raised her average to a B before Dad insisted she come home. When Mr. Zimmer offered her a job at the *News-Trib*, she was sure God had provided for her.

Working at the paper at least kept her in journalism, and she had no intention of working anywhere else as long as she lived in Lake Geneva. She quickened her pace. Dad wasn't going to determine her future.

By the time she reached the center of town, her stomach gnawed against her insides. Too upset to eat, she'd left home without her usual cereal. She checked her watch then crossed the street and stepped into the café next to the Hotel Clair. People filled the four tables next to the wall, smoking and drinking coffee. She slid onto an empty stool at the counter.

"Morning, Miss Alden." Lester Zimmer plopped onto the neighboring seat. "I've never seen you in here this early."

"I've never come here for breakfast. I couldn't sleep."

"What can I get you folks?" Joe Schenk, the café owner, rested his burly fists on the counter.

Meg ignored the menu clipped to the napkin holder in front of her. "Dry toast and coffee, for me."

"Two soft-boiled eggs, toast, and coffee." Lester pulled a pack of cigarettes from his breast pocket.

Meg scrunched her nose. "Would you mind waiting until later to smoke? The fumes don't go well with my empty stomach."

He frowned but returned the cigarettes to his pocket. "If you're not feeling well, maybe you should have stayed home."

She let out a soft sigh. "I'm fine." If feeling like a forgotten corpse in the county morgue was normal, she was fine.

"Dad liked the article."

"Good." Meg dropped sugar cubes into the coffee Joe set in front of her. She waited until Lester stirred cream into his brew. "After you do the war-vet piece, you'll be on your own."

He heaved a sigh. "Dad wants me to write an article next week on Wayne King and the other bands they're booking for the summer."

Meg's chest constricted. She could write that story in a wink. But she wouldn't give him her file on the big bands. Best she cut all ties, even in sharing research.

Her toast arrived, and she spread grape jelly over one of the slices. "Sounds like a fun article."

"For you, yes, but not for me. I don't know the first thing about the music."

"Wayne King must have a booking agent in Chicago. Find out who it is and call him with your questions. There's a file at the office." She bit into her toast. She'd given him a morsel of help. No more.

"Would you at least read the piece?" Lester's soft-boiled eggs arrived. He turned them out into a bowl then broke pieces of toast into the yellow mixture.

Meg gathered her thoughts. She wanted to say yes, but she shouldn't.

Some people might be able to skim it and hand it back, but not her. "I'm sorry. I can't. Before we know it, we'll be back to my rewriting the whole article."

He grew quiet as he ate. By the time she shoved the last of her toast into her mouth and washed it down with her coffee, he'd finished and was reaching into his pocket for his smokes. A good time for her to exit. She opened her purse and pulled out several coins. After leaving them on the counter, she stood. "See you later."

She headed for the door. She'd probably just cut herself off from any newswriting as long as she was at the *News-Trib*. It was time to go.

* * * * *

When Meg arrived home that evening, she felt ill-prepared to face Dad. She went directly to the kitchen and grabbed an apron. "Hi, Mom. Need help?"

Mom turned from the sink. "Not tonight. I'm keeping it simple. How was work?"

Meg replaced the apron on its peg. "Okay."

"Did you talk to Mr. Zimmer?"

"Not about quitting. And I don't intend to."

"Did I say anything about your quitting the paper?"

Meg shook her head and worked her lower lip between her teeth.

Mom turned off the water and scurried over. She pulled Meg into a hug. "Did I ever tell you how I told your father I intended to keep working at the library after our wedding?"

Meg stepped back. "You worked at the library?"

"My dream was to write a novel, but my parents scoffed at the idea. Your grandmother was educated at the seminary that used to be on Baker Street. Practicing the refinements of painting on china and other ladylike aspirations was her idea of appropriateness for a young woman. Fortunately, my interest in reading got me a job at the library." She smiled. "I have yet to use my china-painting skills." She let out a sigh. "Your father was just out of law school and not making much money when we planned on marrying. Still, he insisted I stay home. My last day at the library was two days before the wedding."

"And you never wrote a story." Meg brushed back a stray lock from her mother's face.

Mom's face brightened. "I'll tell you a secret. I've been working on a novel whenever I have a few minutes. Maybe someday I'll finish it."

"Where is it?"

"In my underwear drawer." She went to the stove and stirred a pot. "Meg, if your dream is God's plan for you, it will happen in His timing."

Meg stared at her feet. "All God seems to want for me is typing boring society news or briefs for Dad."

"Just because your father wants you to work for him doesn't mean it's God's choice for you. Don't give your notice just yet."

Meg stepped to the sink and stared out the window at the orange-and-yellow sunset. "But what will Dad think if I don't do as he said? The last thing I want is to cause a problem between you and him." She forced a smile. "I'll be upstairs if you need me."

* * * * *

At Mom's call, Meg followed Laura downstairs to the dining room.

Dad already sat in his chair, staring into his bowl. "Margaret, what on earth is this?"

"Tomato soup, dear."

Meg took her seat and inspected her serving. The red liquid looked nothing like the cream of tomato soup Mom usually made. She spooned some and brought it to her nose. Familiar aroma—but what was it?

"Let's pray." Dad held out his hands to Meg and Laura.

His prayer was the usual short version he used when they didn't have guests. As soon as he uttered "Amen," he released Meg and Laura's hands then lifted a spoonful of soup to his mouth and sipped. "This tastes like hot, watery ketchup." He stared at the platter in the center of the table. "Are those sandwiches? This isn't lunch."

"Since you had to cut back at the office, I thought we should do so at home. We'll only have meat on Sundays now." Mom selected a sandwich then passed the platter to Laura. "We had some cheese in the icebox, so I thought we'd better use it up."

Dad shifted in his chair. "We're not that bad off, Margaret. It's an exercise in good budgeting, that's all. Couldn't the sandwiches have been grilled like they're doing at some of the restaurants now?"

"Not enough butter, Louis. I don't get my food allowance until Friday. I'll get some then."

Meg hid a smile as Dad harrumphed and passed her the sandwich plate. She took the last one and bit into it. At least the mustard made it palatable even if the American cheese was a little dry. She looked at her father. "I think this is a good reminder of what so many are going through every day."

The family ate in silence. When Meg finished her sandwich, she glanced at Mom's bowl, then Laura's and Dad's. None had been touched. She still had her own ketchup soup to eat, but by then it'd grown cold.

"I'm going to thank God for His blessings when we go back to normal." Laura finished her sandwich and pushed her chair back. "I have play practice tonight. I'll take my dishes to the kitchen." She picked up her empty plate, soup, and water glass.

Dad frowned. "I almost fell over your schoolbooks while coming down the steps, Laura. You've got to take things all the way upstairs, not partway."

The girl dropped her gaze. "I'm sorry, Dad. It's just that I'm always so busy."

Mom looked from Dad to Laura. "We know, dear, but you could cause an accident if you don't keep the stairs clear. Go ahead to practice. We'll be having a similar meal tomorrow night. Remember, I don't get the week's food money until Friday."

Dad leaned forward and pulled a leather billfold from his back pocket. He flipped it open and drew out a couple of dollars.

"Louis, put that back. You need money for your practice. We'll be fine until Friday."

Meg collected the empty dishes and took them to the kitchen, leaving her parents' escalating voices behind.

Laura stood in front of the open icebox. She pulled out a plate and peeked under the waxed paper.

"I thought you had to leave for play practice."

"Not for another fifteen minutes. I'm sure there's leftover meat loaf. It has to be in here."

Meg stepped closer and ran her eyes over the icebox's contents. "It was there this morning, but I don't see it now. It won't kill you to be a little hungry."

Laura slammed the icebox door. "I need energy for tonight. If you'd told Dad you'd take that secretary job, we wouldn't be starving now and Mom and Dad wouldn't be arguing." She marched out of the room, her skirt swirling around her legs.

Meg set her dishes on the counter and ran the water. Raised voices still filtered in from the other room, and her chest tightened. Laura was right. If she'd agreed to take her father's job, none of this would have happened.

She swished her hand through the hot water and dropped in soap powder. Mom had become an expert at softening Dad when he became too dictatorial, but her methods hadn't worked tonight.

The voices quieted, and Mom came through the swinging door carrying a pair of untouched soup bowls. "You go ahead, Meg. I'll do the cleanup. I need some time to think, and I do it best with my hands in sudsy water.

Meg's stomach growled. Maybe if she went to bed early, she'd manage until breakfast.

As she climbed the stairs, Jack popped into her mind. He might be at home eating alone, but at least he had food. If he hadn't taken that reporter job, maybe she'd have been given a chance to write at least a couple of articles. And maybe after Mr. Zimmer saw how well she did, he would've given her the job. She reached her room and flopped onto the bed. She might as well stop thinking that way. Jack was there and nothing was going to change.

* * * * *

The next morning, Meg stepped into the kitchen with her stomach growling. Mom stood at the stove, wearing a dress she usually reserved for Sundays. "I'll have the oatmeal ready momentarily. We only have enough bread for you three to carry in your lunches, so there's no toast."

"All of us are carrying lunches?"

"Since our budget is tight, I don't see how your father can eat out today." She held up a jar of Skippy peanut butter. "This is all we have." Mom scooped up a small portion of oatmeal and dropped it into a bowl. She added a dollop of milk then placed the serving in front of Meg.

Meg studied the lump of cereal. "What happened to the food we had in the icebox and cupboard before today?"

"I gave it to the food pantry at church. If you have time, I'd appreciate your rinsing your dishes. I have an appointment in a half hour."

"An appointment, this early?"

"I'm applying at the library for a job."

Meg twisted to face her. "Why?"

"Why not?" Her mother removed her apron and hung it on a wall peg. "No reason I can't go to work. See you tonight." She left through the door leading to the hall. Meg stared at her food. If there were fireworks at last evening's dinner, tonight's should be like a bomb going off. She picked up her spoon and shoveled the hot cereal into her mouth. She had a few dollars in her purse to last till payday. Maybe she'd spend some on supper elsewhere.

Chapter Eleven
. . . .

"That looks like a pathetic lunch." Jack stood next to Meg wearing his hat and coat.

Meg glanced up from unwrapping the waxed paper from what looked like a peanut butter sandwich and shrugged. "It's enough for me."

He'd believe her except for her forlorn expression. If he could take her into his arms and comfort her right there, he would, but not only was it inappropriate, he doubted she'd let him. At least he was there to save the day for a hungry damsel, and he couldn't think of anyone with whom he'd rather dine. "I hear the Utopia has Boston Bean on special today. Join me?"

She placed a palm over her stomach. "I can't let this good food go to waste."

He chuckled. "Food it may be, but I'd be willing to debate its value. Besides, I wanted to talk to you about something." Where did that come from? At least he had the five-minute walk to think of a topic.

She pursed her lips as if in deep thought, and then the smile he loved filled her face. "Well, all right. Bean soup sounds fine, so long as it's served with a side of pie."

At the luncheonette, Jack led the way to an oilcloth-covered table in the back. He ordered two bean soups, two slices of apple pie, and two coffees from the waitress, whose name he'd learned on his last visit was Ruby.

When the young woman left with their orders, he focused on Meg and held her brown-eyed gaze. Eyes that he could lose himself in for days. But that was something he needed to avoid—at least for now. "I'm looking forward to church on Sunday. I'm glad your mother invited me."

She offered a smile that stopped at her eyes. "That's Mom. Always inviting people to church."

"And you don't?"

She lifted her shoulders and let them drop. "Now and again. She beat me to it this time."

For a girl who carried her Bible to the lakeshore, she didn't sound very enthused. He picked up his knife and tapped it on the table. "Do you have a strong faith in God?"

Ruby brought their soups, placing a steaming and fragrant bowl first in front of Meg and then Jack. He waited while she tasted hers.

She looked up and grinned. "This is much better than my sandwich."

"And you still need to answer my question."

"What question?"

He filled his spoon. "I asked about your faith. Since I'm to attend your church on Sunday, I wondered what to expect."

She set the spoon in her bowl. "My family believes in God's saving grace. That without His Son dying on the cross and taking the punishment for our sins, we would have no standing before God." She returned to her soup.

Jack took a yeast roll from a basket and buttered it. He'd had no idea the Aldens were so religious. They seemed like the usual family the other day. Well, he'd go this Sunday. If it wasn't to his liking, he'd make his excuses if they invited him back.

She took a roll. "Did you see many breadlines in Chicago and DC?"

Relieved that she didn't continue the discussion about faith, he lifted a spoonful of soup to his mouth and swallowed. "I think either city has as many breadlines. Do they have them around here?"

Meg shook her head. "People have had to tighten their belts, but overall, it's not been as bad as in the large cities. We have a food pantry at my church, which is used a lot."

Jack sipped his coffee. "I'm not a millionaire, but I can't say I've suffered. I volunteered at a breadline in DC. It was a very sobering experience."

The conversation flowed to whether there were any breadlines in

Walworth County. Jack decided he'd check into it. She suggested the food pantry at her church as a good place to volunteer, but he avoided the statement. Better wait to see how religious her church was before he committed.

Meg finished her soup then dug into her dessert. Her appetite caused him to chuckle. He'd had several meals with her, and she'd never seemed like a voracious eater until today.

A movement across the way caught his eye, and he glanced over. "Isn't that your father?"

Meg turned then jerked back around, ducking her head. "Yes."

He eyed her curiously. "Don't you want to say hello?"

"I'd rather not." Meg forked another bite of pie and directed it to her mouth.

He waited for her to swallow then said, "It's none of my business, but—"

"The other night, he told us his secretary is expecting. She's quitting to stay home, and he thinks he's already found her replacement." She kept her focus on her plate.

If he hadn't been watching her so closely, he'd have never noticed the slight tremble in her lower lip. "Anyone you know?"

She looked up at him and blinked. "Yes. Me."

* * * * *

Jack held Meg's coat while she slipped her arms into its sleeves. He wanted to march over to Louis Alden's table and ask him why he was insisting his adult daughter quit a job she loved to work for him instead. Good thing the man sat out of earshot on the other side of the café, because Jack had about split his sides laughing over Mrs. Alden's ketchup soup and cheese sandwiches for supper and how she'd sent them all off with peanut butter sandwiches this morning.

He suggested Meg wait outside while he paid the bill, careful to turn his face away from Mr. Alden's table. Meeting her on the sidewalk, they started toward the office. He only had about five minutes to convince her not to quit the *News-Trib*. "You haven't said whether you're going to give in to your father's orders."

She emitted a long sigh. "Last night the tension between my parents was awful, and I was ready to say yes. But this morning I realized how courageous Mom is. Sometimes Dad forgets that his family isn't a courtroom." She raised her chin. "Quite a few people in town have rooms to let to help with expenses. There are usually no vacancies during the summer, but during the rest of the year, many are available. I'm thinking of taking one myself."

"What would you do for food and other expenses?"

"Some of the rooms include a light breakfast and supper at night. What stops me is that I'd not be able to save any money."

"Saving for something in particular?"

She opened her mouth then shut it.

"You don't have to tell me. That was a rather personal question."

She stared at the sidewalk. "It's okay. It would help me to talk about it, but you mustn't breathe a word. Truth is, I might move out of town with Helen. Before I decide for sure, I'm waiting to hear from a friend about a possible position." She faced him, and a smile danced across her lips. "Why, Jack, by the expression on your face, I believe I pulled the rug out from under *your* feet for a change."

He pushed his fedora back on his head. She could say that. But what surprised him most was his response to her moving away. He didn't like the idea one bit. "You did startle me."

They came to the corner, and he took her elbow and guided her to the opposite curb. At the office entrance, he faced her instead of gripping the door handle. "Where are you girls planning to land? Milwaukee? Chicago?"

"Hollywood." She averted her eyes.

"Hollywood? As in California?"

She smiled. "That's the place. I'm hoping to get my foot in the door at the *Los Angeles Examiner*."

He yanked at the door handle, and they entered the office. At the closet they both reached for a hanger, and their hands landed on the same one, his on top of hers. A warm tingle shot up his forearm, and he wanted to hang on for dear life.

He released his grip and took a different hanger. "So when's this big move?"

"I'll thank you not to say a word," she whispered. "Nothing is settled."

He hung his coat on the rod, making sure it wasn't anywhere near her wool wrap, the one that made the gold flecks in her eyes pop. He stuffed his right hand into his pocket and crossed his fingers. "My lips are sealed."

Chapter Twelve
. . . .

Jack approached Faith Community Church's white clapboard building. Since waking up that morning, he'd wrestled with canceling his plans—thanks to Louis Alden. What kind of Christian would treat his adult daughter like a child? He didn't want to disappoint Meg's mom, so he'd decided to endure. Meg waved from the church steps. Unable to ignore her infectious smile or the pull she had on him, he picked up his pace.

Meg led the way to a pew halfway down and slid in, leaving Jack room to sit on the end. He nodded a greeting to the rest of the family then assisted Meg out of her coat, the movement causing a pleasant lilac scent to waft over. He studied her as she read the bulletin then dragged his eyes away. If he wanted to get anything out of the service, he'd have to move to the other side of the room.

The background organ music switched to a different melody, and a balding man in a dark suit came to the front and raised his arms. Everyone stood.

"Good morning. Our opening hymn on page 355 is one we all know and love: 'Great Is Thy Faithfulness.'"

Instead of singing the unfamiliar hymn, Jack read along in the hymnal Meg shared with him. Was God really faithful? Had He provided all Jack ever needed? Around him, robust voices sang out as though their owners really believed the words. They were already on the last verse, singing about bright hope and assurance of God's blessings. Could he trust God for his future?

Tomorrow, Dad had a doctor's appointment. Last night, Mom had said the cough was as bad as before. Her voice sounded thin and unnatural. If it turned out to be bad news, how could Jack trust God? Kate's dream to run the *Beacon* had become his dream for her. Could he trust God enough to let Him have it?

The sound of rustling pages drew him back to the present. Meg slipped her open Bible in front of him and pointed at the page. Jack started at seeing penciled lines under several verses. His family's large Bible stayed on a fancy table in the main hall except for maybe when Dad read from it on Christmas. He supposed there were smaller Bibles around the house, maybe on the shelf in the library. But no one had a personal Bible they carried to church the times they'd attended.

He followed along as the reverend read the words.

"Trust in the Lord with all thine heart; and lean not unto thine own understanding. In all thy ways acknowledge him, and he shall direct thy paths."

Kate had said she knew nothing about their father being sick and reminded him that Dad did have a flair for the dramatic. But, still, why had he asked Jack into the city unless it was serious?

An hour later, Jack held the door for Meg and her family then followed them into the bright sunshine. The temperature had risen, and he decided to keep his coat over his arm.

Mrs. Alden glanced at him. "Jack, I hope you haven't made plans for later. We're having roast chicken for dinner. Will you join us?"

He caught Meg's gaze and received no indication that she was uncomfortable with the invitation. "I'd like to."

"Dinner is in two hours. You're welcome to come anytime."

"Would it be okay if Meg and I took a ride? It's a beautiful day, and I'd like to discuss the sermon with her."

Meg's eyes grew large as half-dollars. Louis Alden appeared as if he were about to protest, but Mrs. Alden gave him a look and the man pressed his lips together and nodded.

"I think that's a lovely idea. We'll see you kids later." Mrs. Alden turned her eyes to Laura. "Let's go. I have a meal to prepare."

* * * * *

Meg sat beside Jack as he headed his Ford V-8 down Madison Street. The sun's rays streamed through the window, and she regretted not shedding her coat. Crazy as it sounded, she'd much rather spend the next couple of hours playing Landlord's and Prosperity with Dad than be alone with the handsome man at the wheel. A proverb from the Bible popped into her mind. She truly needed to keep her heart with all diligence.

"Cat got your tongue?"

She glanced his direction. "Where did such an odd phrase come from?"

An appealing chuckle rumbled from deep in his throat. "I have no idea, but the lady evades my question. So, I'll start the conversation. I enjoyed the service."

The last thing Meg wanted was to reveal her misgivings about God. She needed to get him onto another subject. They reached Main Street and Jack waited for a car to pass. Ahead, the lake sparkled in the sun. "Looks like the last of the ice is gone."

He turned the wheel and headed west. "Before you know it, the building's new name will be announced and we'll be dancing to Wayne King."

We?

A mental picture of her and Jack spinning around the new dance floor invaded her thoughts as a delicious sensation washed over her. Of course, he meant the royal "we."

"Ready for a little drive?"

"How far?"

"Just a few miles." He downshifted and maneuvered the vehicle past Snake Road and up Dummer's Hill. At the crest, the car picked up speed, and Jack cracked his window. "The air feels wonderful. Too bad we don't have a convertible."

Meg gripped her hat brim. Permanent or not, her waves would never survive the stiff wind of a convertible. Off to her right, cows grazed in a meadow. It had been too long since she'd ventured outside of town. Now, here she was, planning a possible move halfway across the country.

"Keep hold of your hat. I have to signal that I'm turning." Jack cranked his window down and stuck his left arm out straight as warm air caressed Meg's face.

He turned onto a gravel road then closed his window. Meg glanced at him. "Where are we going?"

"I thought since we had time, I'd prove I don't live in a mansion." He tossed her a wink. "Just the outside. We'll have to wait until the family is here to show you the interior. Not that it's anything fancy."

Meg let out the breath she'd been holding. She might want to challenge the archaic notion that women couldn't be newspaper reporters, but she wasn't ready to sully her reputation by being in a man's home without others present. "I'm glad you clarified yourself."

Jack let out a hearty laugh. "What does the lady take me for? I wouldn't think of such a thing."

They continued down the gently sloped road under a canopy of trees still bare from winter. At a sharp bend, he stopped the car and pointed at a large home.

"That's the Mitchells' house. They're the only ones who live here year-round." He drove at a slow pace past several homes, then turned onto a cement apron and parked. "We're here."

Ahead, except for a cupola that seemed to soar upward into the surrounding trees, the two-story wood-frame house appeared almost plain, its front door having no more than a small roof overhead for protection. *Why would someone build a home on the water and make it so basic?* "Okay. You win. No mansion. But you have to admit, Jack, it is larger than my house, and we don't have the lake as part of our backyard."

"The lake is our front yard. We're sitting in the back. With such a beautiful view, why would the front of a house face away from the water?"

She chuckled. "How silly of me not to know that."

"But view and size have nothing over what your home has."

"What?"

"People."

Meg laughed. Right about then, she'd take an empty house. "But, come summer, your family will be here."

"Dad's usually busy with the *Beacon*, and my sister is married now. Mom won't come up with just me here. She has her charity work, and Dad needs her to grace his arm at social events." He opened his car door. "Shall we get out? I want to show you the front."

Meg nodded. "That's a marvelous idea."

Basking in the grin Jack flashed, Meg waited for him to circle around and assist her out of the sedan.

He offered his arm, and she gripped it just above his elbow. The silky feel of his wool suit stirred her senses, reminding her of the day they met, when she touched his overcoat. They followed a flagstone path along the north side of the house and came to a wide stone porch that curved around the width of the home. Tucked into a corner of the porch, a swing bobbled in the breeze, as though waiting for its occupants to return. A perfect place to sip lemonade and write or read a book.

Jack indicated tiny nubs of green poking out of the ground in front of the porch. "The daffodils are growing. Soon this spot will be ablaze in yellow. Then, later, red tulips will join them. Mom keeps this place colorful all summer long."

She grinned. "My mother likes gardening too. This is wonderful. I have to admit I've not come this far along the shore. I didn't realize there were places like this."

"When our boat comes out of storage, I'll take you around all twenty-one miles of shoreline. You'll see plenty besides those mansions."

She glanced down the shore path that traveled beneath tall, over-arching trees and past other houses of similar size. "Has your family lived here long?"

"Ever since Granddad bought the lot, when it was first parceled out. The deed will eventually pass to me and my sister."

At the catch in Jack's voice Meg's heart squeezed.

He waved at a stack of white pilings. "The dock is still dismantled for winter, but we can sit on the porch swing. I'll head inside and get something to sit on. Do you want anything to drink while I'm. . ." He chuckled. "Guess I'd better check and see if I have anything to offer. I think there's some ginger ale in the icebox. Or there's water."

Meg laughed. "Whatever you find is fine."

Jack ran up the stairs at the far end of the porch and let himself through the front door. Overhead, white cumulus clouds drifted across a deep blue sky, and Meg relaxed for the first time in days. She'd always considered her family privileged to live a block from the water, but to have a home this close was heaven.

A door clicked shut behind her and she turned. Jack carried two glasses of water and a dark green blanket. She met him at the top of the stairs and took the drinks. He spread the blanket over the swing and they sat side by side. Jack started the swing moving in a gentle sway.

Meg sipped her water and tipped her head back. She closed her eyes, enjoying the companionable silence.

"What did you think about the sermon?"

Meg opened her eyes and drew in a deep breath. "What do you mean?"

"That verse about trusting God makes sense. Sometimes it's difficult to understand why things happen the way they do, but then later I look back and realize it was all for the best."

She gulped. "So now you think it's been God all along who worked things out?"

"I've always called it luck, but I wonder if it was God. You've been going to church all your life. This is nothing new to you. Right?"

Meg worked her lower lip. "I've heard it all my life, but sometimes. . ."

"Sometimes what?"

She shrugged. "God doesn't always give us what we want."

Jack swirled the water in his glass. "Like the reporter position?"

She snapped her eyes away from him and stared at the lake. "Yes. But realistically, my chances of getting the job were small. The Bible says that God has thoughts toward us of peace and not evil, to give us an expected end. Whose expectations? Mine or God's?"

"What your preacher said about trusting God even when our anticipated answers don't come right away seems to cover that."

A kernel of hope welled up in Meg's chest. She focused on the distant shore and blinked hard. God surely was still on His throne, but lately it felt like He was too busy with others needier than her. Jack apparently thought she had a lifesaver to offer, but she was drowning herself. "I suppose you're right, but you seem to have had a good life so far."

He stopped the swing with his foot. "Life's not so rosy with me. My dad has a terrible cough. He says it's left over from a cold, but he's going to the doctor this week. I've never thought much about him not always being here."

Meg chided herself for her selfishness. What kind of louse was she, thinking of herself and her job while Jack's dad might be seriously ill? "That must be scary, not knowing what's wrong with him. Has he been ill before?"

Jack shook his head. "Other than the occasional cold, no."

"If he thought his condition was serious, wouldn't he want you back in Chicago?"

"I keep telling myself that." He offered a smile that seemed forced. "Enough of the serious talk. Doesn't the lake look marvelous today?"

Meg glanced at the lake and then looked back in Jack's direction. He stretched out his legs, crossing them at the ankles as if what he'd just revealed about his father no longer bothered him. He was probably one of those people who could easily distract himself from the worries on his mind. Meg envied him that.

His eyes closed, she studied his profile. Square jaw, chiseled features, full lips. . . What would it be like to kiss him? He probably had a lot of experience in that department. Meg drew her head out of her not-so-lofty thoughts and looked at her watch. She hated to disturb the tranquility, but if they were late for dinner, Mom wouldn't be happy. "We should get going."

Jack scrambled to his feet. "There isn't a single Bible in this house. I'm going to have to buy one. Maybe next Sunday's sermon will help shed more light."

Meg accepted his proffered hand and stood.

He kept his grip as he regarded her face and then her mouth.

She felt heat tinge her cheeks.

"Thanks for helping me sort out my thoughts. For listening. I've enjoyed this." He gave her hand a quick squeeze, and a tingle shot up her arm.

She bobbed her head. "Me too."

He released his grip then gathered the blanket and empty glasses. "I'll put these inside before we go."

Back on the state road, the memory of Jack's palm against hers teased Meg's thoughts. Something had sparked back there, and sparks like that meant danger. They came from different worlds, didn't they? She'd heard the stories about rich men from the shore showing interest in girls from town, only to take up suddenly with women of their own class and leave broken hearts behind.

She peeked his direction. "How did your dad come to run the *Beacon*?" Her voice sounded shaky. Hopefully he wouldn't notice.

"Like the house, he had the paper willed to him. My grandfather had worked his way up from a small-town paper to the *Beacon*, and he eventually bought it."

"A position you didn't have to apply for, a house you never bought. . . I can't imagine having one's entire life handed down like a commodity." A sigh slipped out. "I suppose you didn't purchase this car either."

Jack changed gears as they headed downhill into town. "It was a belated graduation gift. In DC, I didn't need a car. Look, Meg, I probably am a little spoiled by not having to grapple for privileges." His expression became somber. "Nothing humbles a man like working a breadline and handing a plate of beans to a former business executive who used to be your neighbor."

Meg fingered the strap of her handbag. "That really happened?"

"Yes, and I realized in the wink of an eye that I could be that man. That's why I asked if you knew of any breadlines around here."

Why couldn't she appreciate how blessed she was, living in a town like

Lake Geneva? She had a job, a home, food in her stomach—and yet she felt so restless.

By the time they entered the house, Mom's chicken was out of the oven and Laura had set the table. Like the week before, Meg and Jack joined hands for Dad's prayer, only this time she didn't shy away from the pleasing sensation his touch caused. After dinner, Laura was excused to study and Dad suggested they play Landlord's and Prosperity, with Meg's parents teaming up against her and Jack.

Jack was unfamiliar with the game, and it seemed Dad was on his way to winning as usual. But Meg surprised herself. She helped Jack strategize, and soon they began to overtake her parents, buying up most of the properties on the board.

Dad threw up his hands. "We should know better than to play with a couple of whizzes."

Jack grinned at Meg. "Looks like we're going to trounce them—thanks to your help."

Meg grinned. It had been a long while since such laughter had filled her house, and she loved it.

Later, when Jack said good night at the door, it seemed with his leaving the joy went too. She wanted to make him stay longer. . .but she didn't try.

Chapter Thirteen

The following morning, a gust of wind whipped off the lake, causing Meg to fasten the top button on her coat. Yesterday's warm promises of summer— gone in an instant. Maybe the sharp breeze would awaken her, since she'd tossed and turned for most of the night, trying to discover when she and Jack had progressed from acquaintance and coworker to something more.

Was it when they held hands for a second, or when they laughed through the game? Maybe while they sat at the kitchen table over coffee and second servings of Mom's apple crisp. Pinning down the moment was like trying to grasp a fistful of wind. . .maybe because the moment was only a figment of her imagination and hadn't really happened at all.

Her mother had capped off the day by bringing a brown leather book into the kitchen and handing it to Jack, saying, "No need to buy one. Here's an extra we have."

His face lit up like a light bulb as he flipped through pages so new they wanted to stick together. Mom's generosity wasn't a surprise. She always had a Bible handy for moments when she sensed the Spirit's leading to give one away.

God's Word used to give Meg the same joy she'd seen Jack display, and she'd have wanted nothing more than to know a man who felt the same. An ache pressed against her heart, and she slowed her steps. Now every time she opened the Bible, the words seemed dry and lifeless. The last thing Jack needed was to be involved with someone on the outs with God.

"Trust Me."

Meg stopped and gasped. The voice seemed to come from within her. Mom would say she'd heard God. But why would He speak to her now?

Dad had changed his mind about her becoming his secretary since Mom took the library job. Was that God encouraging her to trust Him again?

When Meg arrived at the office, Jack sat at his desk typing. She nodded hello then sat and pulled a stack of want-ad forms from a drawer. As much as she wanted to peek at him, she stayed strong. She didn't need his crooked smile discombobulating her. Her phone rang, and she answered it.

"I heard you were in church with Mr. Wallace yesterday."

Meg's face warmed, and she turned toward the switchboard. Emily wore an impish grin, and nut-brown ringlets escaped her topknot. Meg cupped the mouthpiece with her hand before speaking into it. "If you'd been there, you'd know he was with my family."

"I was under the weather, but my sister gushed about the handsome man with you. I just knew it was Mr. Wallace. You lucky girl."

Meg sensed someone standing nearby. She turned and looked up at Jack. A lock of hair had fallen over his forehead, giving him an appealing boyish look. Heat surged up her neck and into her cheeks. "I have to go." She hung up the phone.

"Oscar asked me to find out whether Fred Newman and the protesters plan to raise another stink when they announce the contest winner." He kept his gaze pinned on her. "I still think there's more to the story than their caring about a young woman's contest entry. Want to help?"

Temptation dangled before her like a bag of Hershey's Kisses, but if Mr. Zimmer heard of her working with Jack. . . "I'm sure you'll learn what's there if you dig."

He opened his mouth then snapped it shut and went back to his desk.

Meg pushed aside her completed want-ad orders. Composing required them soon, but she needed to think. Working with an experienced reporter like Jack might give her an advantage when she moved. Maybe if she made sure Mr. Zimmer saw it as assisting Jack. . .

"I'm looking for Jack Wallace. Am I in the right place?"

Meg turned toward the melodious voice. A slender woman stood near Emily. Her red cupid's-bow mouth and pink spots of rouge stood out against her alabaster complexion. She patted the fawn-colored turban that framed her auburn curls and blended perfectly with her brown tweed suit.

Probably one of the lakeshore people Jack knew. Meg returned to her work.

"Ginny?" Jack rushed past Meg, nearly falling over a chair.

He pulled Ginny into a hug and whirled her around. A hint of gardenia tickled Meg's nose with each spin. "I can't believe you're here."

Meg forced her mouth shut before he noticed it gaping. Not that it mattered. He only had eyes for *her* at the moment.

He set Ginny down, and she smoothed her skirt. "It's me in the flesh, Jack. I thought you were still in Washington and come to find out you're here. Fancy that. How've you been?"

Jack dropped his arms to his side. "Boss got voted out, and it was time to leave." He stepped back and appraised her as a smile filled his face. "You look marvelous. New York agrees with you. On a little vacation from the *Times*?"

"I wish. They brought Denise Swanson home from the London office. I'm looking for a job." She scanned the room like a queen surveying her domain. Her lips pursed. "What are you doing *here*?"

Meg's spine stiffened. Who did Ginny think she was? She gripped the edge of her desk and forced herself to stay seated.

"What better place to learn the biz than on a weekly? I highly recommend it."

"But why not learn from your da—"

"Let me introduce you." Jack faced the double row of desks and laughed. "I guess everyone already knows you're here. Lost myself for a minute."

Meg surveyed the room. Even Gus and Leo from Composing had stepped over to see what the commotion was about. Served Jack right to be embarrassed.

"Everyone, I'd like you to meet an old college friend of mine, Virginia Colson." He gave her an admiring look. "Ginny has been working at the *New York Times*—since when?"

Ginny flicked her wrist. "Just under a year. But that's over now. I'm back in the Midwest."

"She'd been a feature writer." He grinned. "Loved your piece last week on the innovative ways people are using to make extra money."

Mr. Zimmer walked over. "Jack, why don't you bring your friend into my office?"

"Sure." Jack nodded. "Come on, Ginny. Oscar might be able to help your job search."

Ginny faced Mr. Zimmer, who had found a moment to slip on his suit jacket and tame his cowlick with some pomade. She tipped her head back and laughed. "Love to. Maybe you have a job right here for me."

She pranced into Mr. Zimmer's office with the men following her like a pair of ducklings. The door shut and Meg glanced at Emily, who waved a cord and stuck it into the switchboard. Meg's phone rang.

"You've got your work cut out, Meg Alden."

She caught Emily's gaze before whispering into the mouthpiece, "The only work I have is taking the next want-ad order."

"I've seen the way Mr. Wallace looks at you. Or did until Miss *New York Times* strutted through the door. She turned this place upside down faster than a tornado. Do you suppose the men are falling over each other, creating a job just for her? . . .Got a call." The line went dead.

Meg hung up and stared at Mr. Zimmer's door. The faint tinkle of a woman's laugh filtered out. Her phone rang, and she jumped. If Emily wanted to continue their conversation, she wasn't going to find a very willing participant.

Relieved that the call was for a want-ad, Meg reached for a form.

An hour later, Mr. Zimmer's door swung open and he stepped out, followed by Jack and Ginny. Jack whispered into Ginny's ear and she approached Meg's desk, her ruby-red lips forming a smile as fake as a Kewpie doll's. "It's Peg, right? Jack said you can show me to the restroom."

Meg pasted on her own smile, ignoring the pull to lead the woman to the outhouse next door. "Sure. And the name is Meg with an *M*." She led Ginny to the other side of the Composing area. "It's there. Be sure to lock the door. There's no separate one for men."

Ginny arched a penciled brow. "At the *Times*, the ladies' room was smaller than the men's, but it was all ours." She breezed into the compact space.

"You're welcome," Meg said to the closed door. She returned to her desk.

Jack and Mr. Zimmer stood at the switchboard chatting with Emily, both with their coats on. Mr. Zimmer beckoned Meg over. "We're taking Ginny to lunch at the Gargoyle. Be sure to get the want-ad orders to Composing by this afternoon."

Meg nodded. "Sure thing." She and Helen were going to the movies later, but she couldn't wait until then to talk to her. Humming "California, Here I Come," she picked up the phone.

* * * * *

"There's a booth." Helen sashayed past the tables filling Franzoni's, her platinum waves glistening like spun gold in the soda fountain's overhead lamps.

Meg trailed behind and slid onto the seat.

"Well, the only redeeming thing in that movie was the strong woman lead. Imagine taking on the government like she did." Helen slipped off her coat and let it puddle around her.

"It was okay."

"Okay? Where's the movie critic who's always ready to point out plot flaws?" She tilted her head and studied Meg. "What's with you tonight?"

Meg shrugged. She couldn't admit she had no opinion about the movie because she'd been distracted by visions of Jack whirling Ginny around the office and having a fancy lunch with her. Mr. Zimmer returned after lunch alone, and Jack never did come back. He was likely enjoying another meal, this time at a table for two. All the more reason not to get involved with the man.

The waitress appeared and took their orders.

When the girl left, Helen leaned across the table. "How did yesterday go?"

Meg shrugged. Yesterday felt like a million hours away. "He came to church and then showed me his house. Have you ever been to the Elgin Club?"

Helen shook her head. "No. What kind of home does he have? Pretty fancy, I bet."

"I only saw the outside. It's big and comfortable, but not a mansion." She focused on a young couple sharing sodas and lovesick stares and then glanced back at her friend. "We sat on the porch swing and talked a bit. Later we had dinner at my house. It was a good time."

"And then came today." Helen touched Meg's arm. "Sorry I couldn't stay on the phone earlier. I'm dying to hear the rest of the details about the mystery woman."

Their sodas arrived, and they attacked the frosty drinks.

Helen looked up. "I'm still waiting."

Meg launched into a full description of Virginia Colson's grand entrance, including her snotty comment about the bathroom. "I saw neither hide nor hair of either of them for the rest of the day."

"Didn't he say she was an old college friend?"

"No one hugs an 'old college friend' of the opposite sex like that unless they have a history. And the way Mr. Zimmer practically rolled over at her feet at the mention of her working for the *New York Times*. . ." Some of the soda she'd just swallowed rose into her throat, and she pushed the glass away. "If Mr. Zimmer changes his mind about women reporters, it's obvious Ginny would benefit. If I want to get ahead, I need to move. I wish I'd hear from Mattie."

Helen grinned. "I have news you'll love. Mom's been feeling a lot better, and Beatrice, our beautician friend, was over yesterday. To tell you the truth, I was leery of leaving Mom, the way she's been feeling, but since she's better now and Beatrice is eager to start working, I see no reason not to plan the move."

Meg wiped her palms on her skirt and forced herself to breathe. "I thought we weren't making definite arrangements until I could secure a job."

"Well, Beatrice can't do anything until summer. I feel it in my gut that you'll receive good news from Mattie. Besides, I want to be here for the new building's grand opening, and I know you do too."

Excitement coursed through Meg's veins. "Of course I do."

Helen grinned. "The dance will be our going-away party."

Helen was moving ahead like a steam locomotive. Even if there were openings at the *Examiner*, the pay had to be enough to live on. "Moving is going to cost money. If we want to save enough by summer, it may mean foregoing our weekly movie date."

Helen bobbed her head. "That's okay unless it's a Harlow picture."

Meg stabbed her straw against the bottom of her glass. It folded like an accordion. "You sure are anxious to go all of a sudden."

"I've been dreaming about this for years. You know that. Mom's all for it and I don't want to wait too long. She may change her mind."

Meg stared into her friend's dreamy expression. How could she back out and disappoint Helen? Mattie's letter had to hold a positive answer.

Chapter Fourteen

Jack's stomach rumbled as he pulled the Ford into a parking place near the *News-Trib* on Tuesday morning. The toast he'd eaten earlier would never hold him. Served him right for spending most of Saturday at the typewriter instead of going to the market. He checked his watch. If he hurried, he had time to grab some breakfast.

Leaving his briefcase in the car, he set out for the café, whistling "I've Told Ev'ry Little Star" as he strolled. The lyrics ran through his mind, followed by the memory of a conversation he'd had with Ginny. It *was* high time he stopped keeping his feelings to himself.

He reached the intersection at Main and Broad, and his heart raced. Meg stood on the opposite corner, wearing the same red beret she'd worn that Sunday they'd bumped into each other in the park. Was this a coincidence? The traffic light changed, and she stepped off the curb.

His gaze locked with hers, and he grinned. "Morning. I was just heading to the café for a quick bite. Care to join me?"

She blinked as though in a trance. "No thanks. I already ate."

He ignored the itch to ask what was troubling her. "Not even a cup of coffee?"

She shook her head as her eyes sparked. "*I* have a deadline. 'Town Talk' is due for proofing by tomorrow."

His spirit sagged. Did she think him a slacker? Hadn't he mentioned on Sunday how he'd spent most of Saturday roughing out this week's story? "Suit yourself. I'll see you at the salt mines."

One fried egg and two pieces of bacon later, Jack arrived at work.

Meg looked up from her typing as he passed her desk, and a corner of her mouth curved up. At least she'd thawed some—but he kept walking.

Oscar walked up. "Jack, good morning. Can I see you for a minute?"

In the boss's office, the men sat and Oscar leaned back, his old wood chair creaking. He linked his hands behind his head. "I enjoyed meeting Ginny. Accomplished young woman. Did you help her see the light of working for a weekly?"

Jack shook his head. "It's hard to convince her that a weekly can have the same excitement as the *Times*. She wants me to put in a good word with my father."

"How does he feel about women reporters?"

"He doesn't think it's right."

"Nor do I, as you may have gathered." Oscar stared out the window. "I talked to the editor of the paper over in Burlington. He's not against women reporters, and there's a spot open there." He scribbled on a piece of paper and handed it to Jack.

Jack frowned as he skimmed the information. "I take it this is for Ginny?"

Oscar nodded.

"I'll give her a call." At least Oscar didn't say the information couldn't be passed on to Meg after Ginny declined. He crossed his legs. "Oscar, if you've known all along that the editor in Burlington is willing to give women a chance, why didn't you tell Meg about this position?"

Oscar ran his hand down one of his suspenders. "It has nothing to do with her ability to write, but I prefer to keep my reasons to myself."

* * * * *

After delivering the want-ads to Composing, Meg returned to her desk. Next to her, Jack laughed into his phone. Ever since she saw him on the sidewalk that morning, she'd regretted her abruptness. The surprising strong feelings she'd felt at Ginny's sudden appearance yesterday had thrown her off guard.

"I think it's a great opportunity for you to look into, Gin," Jack said. "And you would love living here. I'll see you later."

Despite emotions with more ups and downs than a yo-yo, Meg finished her "Town Talk" article an hour later. She skimmed the words, pleased that she'd managed no typos on her first try.

"Hello, Meg. Good to see you again."

Meg looked up. Ginny's eyes seemed even bluer than yesterday, thanks to her periwinkle coat. No turban today. Just a simple hat, placed at a jaunty angle on top of her curls. "Nice seeing you too. Are you enjoying your visit to Lake Geneva?"

Next to Meg, Jack hurried through a rushed good-bye on the phone.

Ginny's eyes sparkled. "I may soon be more than visiting. I'm about to find out." She winked. "Wish me luck."

The sound of Jack's receiver hitting its cradle interrupted them. "Ginny. Good timing. Oscar's free. Let's go see him." Jack came up beside her. "Better get your coat off, or you'll roast to death."

Meg feigned interest in her work as the rustle of Ginny's removing her coat, no doubt with Jack's assistance, grated against her ears. The words blurred. She should have accepted his offer to co-write that story. Stubbornness had gotten in her way again.

Across the room, a door clicked shut. Without them nearby she'd have some peace. If she blocked out the trills of laughter coming through the walls. Memories of enjoying laughs with Jack last Sunday flowed into her thoughts. She supposed Ginny and Jack had had their share of laughs too. Maybe more.

By the time Meg left for lunch, Mr. Zimmer's door still hadn't opened. She slid onto a stool at Arnold's Drugstore fountain and studied the menu scratched onto a blackboard above the back counter. The choices hadn't changed in days, but she always checked. She ordered a tuna fish sandwich and settled in to wait.

Jack plopped onto the next stool.

She jumped. "What are you doing here?"

"Looking for you."

A wave of electricity ran down her spine. "Where's Ginny?"

"On her way to Burlington. I lent her the Ford." He grinned. "Hope she drives better now than she did in college."

"I thought she had a car."

"She'd borrowed her friend's, but Ellie needed it today. Oscar arranged an interview for her at the Burlington paper."

Meg tensed. "For what kind of job?"

Jack stared at the counter. "Seems the editor over there is more forward thinking than our boss."

The soda jerk brought Meg a Coke then asked Jack for his order. When the man left, Meg glanced at Jack. He'd leaned both elbows on the counter, using his clasped hands as a prop for his chin. He stared straight ahead.

"I want to apologize for my touchy behavior this morning."

He faced her, his eyes full of concern. "That's okay. I figured you had a lot on your mind. I did defend you to Oscar this morning, but he shot me down."

Pressure built at the back of Meg's eyes, and she turned away.

The soda jerk brought Jack's Coke then looked from Jack to Meg. "Anything else?"

Yes, please go away and don't come back. Meg shook her head

Jack took a sip. "Is your father still insisting you work for him?"

"Mom got a part-time job at the library, and that took the strength out of his argument. But I wouldn't have done it anyway."

The sandwiches arrived, and their attention went to their lunches. Meg relished the silence.

"I wish you'd rethink moving away."

Meg stared at him, touched at the sudden expression of caring. It also frightened her. She picked up her Coke and sipped. "I have to move."

"Why the urgency?"

"To get ahead. You know that."

"Nothing to do with those secret rewrites for Lester?"

The syrupy drink lodged in her throat as though she'd swallowed molasses. She picked up her napkin, wadding it into a ball. "I thought you didn't know."

"Didn't you realize I'd overheard you and Lester that day?"

"At the time I thought you had, but when you never mentioned. . ."

He looked away. "Didn't think it was my business."

"And now it is?"

His Adam's apple bobbed. "No. I'm just concerned."

"The article I'm working on is my last with Lester."

"How did it start?" He took a bite of his sandwich.

Her tongue felt as if it were glued to the roof of her mouth. "I was Lester's proofreader, and I ended up rewriting a lot. Mr. Zimmer didn't like that it was more my work than Lester's and ordered me to stop helping him.

"Later, Lester asked for help, and we agreed I'd tutor him after work. I rewrote paragraphs as examples, but he copied them verbatim. When Mr. Zimmer praised his work, Lester asked for more help. It's been going on for almost a year."

"And Oscar never found out?"

She shook her head. "If he did, I'd probably be out of a job."

"I don't know. He seems quite taken with you in a fatherly way."

She huffed. "Between him and my real father, I'd do better as an orphan."

"I came across a statement in the Bible that says He's always thinking about us and doesn't wish us evil. It sounds like God always has our best interests at heart."

She picked up her half-eaten sandwich and studied it. "I've been trying to trust God, but it's not always easy."

"I've been working to apply that verse to my situation with my dad. Maybe—"

"Your circumstances are different. You'll eventually have a large fancy office at the *Beacon*." She set her uneaten sandwich on her plate.

He stared at his lap. "True. But with my dad's health problems. . ."

"You haven't heard anything since his doctor's appointment?"

"I plan to call tomorrow if I don't hear." He shoved the rest of his sandwich into his mouth then reached into his pocket and pulled out some coins. He dropped them on the counter next to the bill.

She gathered her belongings. "Thanks for the lunch."

He glanced at her plate. "You've hardly touched your food."

"I've had enough. If you'd rather I'd pay. . ."

"Hush. We'd better get back to the office."

Sadness washed over her as she let Jack help her with her coat. If his dad were seriously ill, in a couple months' time, he might be working in Chicago while she and Helen apartment hunted on the West Coast. Would he notice her absence, or would Ginny occupy his thoughts so much that he'd scarcely notice?

Outside, they passed First National Bank with its imposing gray edifice; then at Moore Hardware, she waved at Mr. Moore through the store window. As they passed the bakery, Mrs. Blackwood, the florist's wife, stepped out, and Meg greeted her. In California, she wouldn't know anyone except Mattie and Helen. But if she were honest with herself, the one she'd miss the most was Jack.

Chapter Fifteen
....

Jack stepped through his back door, and the telephone jangled. He tossed his keys onto the counter and dodged around the table, catching a chair with his thigh. He rubbed his upper leg as he ran toward the phone. It had to be Dad. "Don't hang up."

The ringing stopped. He grabbed the receiver and jabbed at the switch hook.

"Operator."

"Who was calling 5550?"

"Oscar Zimmer. Do you want me to ring him?"

Jack frowned and rubbed his thigh. "Yes. Put me through."

Zimmer answered with a weak "Hello."

"Oscar, it's Jack. You called?"

"I've got a nasty flu bug, and I'm not going to make it in tomorrow. This week's layout needs to be done. Lots to do. . ."

Jack dropped to the seat. "Don't worry about a thing. I've done layouts be—"

"I've assigned Lester. No time like the present to see if he's a chip off the old block. But can you stick around the office?"

Jack's throat felt as if he'd swallowed a cotton ball. He slumped against the wall. They could only hope Les had a knack for laying out other people's words. "You can count on me."

"Good. I have a feeling there's some ink in my boy's blood. I need to get back to bed."

A *click* sounded. Jack moved to hang up then poised his hand over the switch hook. Should he call Meg? After their lunch conversation that day, hearing that she'd be needed would boost her confidence. He returned the receiver to its cradle. Tomorrow was soon enough. She'd need her sleep tonight.

* * * * *

Meg shrugged out of her coat. She had at least a half hour before people would arrive for the day. Time enough to finish Lester's article. Pressure pushed against her chest wall until a sour taste rose in her throat. This had to be the last time. Period.

Across the room, light from Mr. Zimmer's office caught her eye. Why wasn't he at his weekly breakfast meeting with the mayor? If she started typing, he'd probably step out to see who was there. She went to her desk and slid the folder containing the edited article into a drawer then went to the open door.

"What are you doing in here?"

Lester looked up and stared at her with eyes that seemed to have sunk deeper into his head. "Dad's sick and he asked me to take over. I barely slept last night, and the layout must be done today." He waved his hand over the papers strewn across his dad's desk. "I've already messed this up, and I don't remember what was to be on the front page." He rubbed his eyes with the heels of his hands then put on his glasses.

Meg stepped closer. "What's wrong with your father?"

Lester shrugged. "Influenza, I guess. Hopefully the twenty-four-hour kind." He stubbed out a cigarette then pulled a pack of Camels from his breast pocket. Tapping it against his index finger, he shook out a smoke and stuck it into his mouth. Letting the cigarette dangle from his lips, he looked at Meg. "I don't think I can do this."

Her eyes ranged over the disarray strewn about the desktop. "Of course you can." If only she could believe her words.

He struck a match and lit the cigarette. Streams of smoke emerged from his nostrils while he extinguished the flame with a flick of his wrist.

Meg pulled a chair over to Lester's side, blinking against the sting in her eyes. "He starts by assessing the stories he has and those he knows are coming, then develops the layout." She reached for an article. Lester pushed her hand away. A glowing ash flew onto a stack of papers.

She grabbed a dictionary and dropped it onto the ember. "Maybe you should refrain from smoking while you're doing this."

His face reddened. "What I need is to work alone. Dad's counting on me. Besides, you said you didn't want to help me anymore."

Meg lifted the book. At least the article underneath was still readable enough for Composing. "That was about writing articles. No one can do a layout for the first time without direction."

Lester pushed his chair back and stood, waving his lit cigarette like a conductor's baton. "Well, I have to. Ask Emily to hold my calls."

Meg closed the door tightly behind her, praying the man didn't torch the place. She let out a heavy sigh. If she hadn't been helping Lester in secret, Mr. Zimmer would know his son's limitations.

"Sighing already? Not a good sign. I presume Lester's working on the layout." Jack came across the room. With dark circles underscoring his eyes, he didn't look much better than Lester.

"You know about Mr. Zimmer?"

"He called last night. He's adamant about Lester taking over." He tossed a bundle of mail onto his desk.

Meg moved to her chair and sat. "Lester sent me away after nearly setting the place on fire with his cigarette." She wiped a speck of ash from her skirt. "Do you think Mr. Zimmer's fever has affected his reasoning?"

Jack narrowed his eyes. "He mentioned the other day how proud he is that Les's writing has improved. Why wouldn't he have hope in his son's abilities?"

Despite his gentle tone, Meg felt the color drain from her face, and she looked away. "Being a good writer doesn't make one a good editor."

"And the reverse is also true."

Jack picked up his phone, and Meg pulled out the folder containing Lester's article. She could bang out a copy in twenty minutes as long as Jack stayed busy over there. She rolled a clean sheet of paper into the type-writer and typed the first line. Then her fingers froze. Wouldn't move. She yanked out the paper and crumpled it into a ball.

The telephone rang, and she tossed the wad into the waste can before she answered. "Meg Alden. How may I help you?"

"Thelma got halfway here and went back home sick." The usual happy-go-lucky Emily sounded flustered. "You know how many calls come in on Tuesdays. Everyone wants his or her bit of news on the front page. What should I do?"

To Meg's right, Jack sorted through the mail. "Send them to Mr. Wallace."

Emily giggled. "I thought you liked him."

"That's why I suggested it. He needs the experience."

* * * * *

Jack had finally gotten a moment from all the phone inquiries to call his father. When Millie answered, he asked her to connect him to Dad.

"He went to the doctor's from home." Millie let out a sigh. "His cough hasn't improved, and I'm worried."

"I thought the appointment was yesterday."

"The doctor had to reschedule. I'll have him call you."

His insides twisted into knots. "Thanks, Millie." A soft *click* sounded. He slammed the receiver down and faced the window.

God, if both Oscar and Dad are sick, I can't be in two places at once. If You are there, I need Your help.

"Jack, can you help me?"

He swung around.

Lester's wild-eyed stare bore into him. "I laid out all the front-page stories and set them to the side, but now they're mixed with ads and filler. I don't know how Dad keeps everything organized."

"Okay, Lester." Jack stood. "Let's get you straightened out."

* * * * *

A half hour later, Meg looked up as Jack emerged from Mr. Zimmer's office. He approached her, bringing the acrid smell of smoke with him.

"What's going on?" Meg kept her voice low.

"I suggested he use last week's paper as an example. Then we sifted through articles in the hold file, weighing the pros and cons." He leaned down and whispered, "Lester's very reluctant to use one he wrote on the meeting we attended. He says it's because it's old news by now, but I have a feeling his reason goes deeper than that. Can we talk?" He glanced around. "Maybe we should go elsewhere."

She stiffened. Jack didn't have the authority to fire her, did he? "We can't leave when everything is about to explode."

"Grab your coat and come with me."

At the back door, Jack held it open for her. Across the alley, men readying the new funeral parlor paused their hammering and looked over.

She forced a chuckle. "Not very private."

"We'll keep our voices low. You should be grateful Les doesn't want to run that article you wrote."

Meg stared at her shoes. "He wrote it. I edited it."

"He must have gotten the information from someone else, since he didn't attend the meeting." Jack crossed his arms and stood stone-still, his face expressionless. "Why did you turn down my suggestion that we collaborate and then use Lester as a front to write your own article?"

She folded her arms around herself and stared at the ground. "It was childish and unprofessional. I apologize."

"I understand that you want to be a reporter. But, Meg, writing other people's work without getting credit isn't going to get you ahead. And it isn't honest."

She grimaced. What he must think of her? She wanted to disappear. "I was upset and wanted to show Mr. Zimmer that I could do better than you. Are you going to tell him, or should I?"

"I have a feeling—"

The door flew open, and Emily stuck her head out. "They're taking Mr. Zimmer to County Hospital in Wightman's ambulance. He's burst his appendix."

Chapter Sixteen
....

Meg followed Jack inside and detoured into the restroom. Mr. Zimmer could die from a burst appendix. She slouched against the closed door and jammed a fist into her mouth.

What had she become, going behind Mr. Zimmer's back and justifying it as helping Lester when it was for her own gain. Why? All for a moment's satisfaction at seeing her words published even though no one knew? Since her first day, Mr. Zimmer had treated her with kindness, and she'd betrayed him.

"God, forgive me."

She turned on the faucet and splashed cold water on her face. The least they could do for Mr. Zimmer was get the paper out on time. Drawing in a breath, she opened the door and headed toward the buzz of conversation.

"I'm taking Mom to the hospital. The paper is all yours." Lester flew past, tie waving and suit coat over his arm. He stopped at the closet and grabbed his flight coat then flung the door open. A loud *slam* reverberated through the office as he left.

No one moved.

Jack's gaze flicked from one person to the next. "We need to keep Mr. Zimmer in our prayers. He asked me to be available if Lester needed help, so I'll complete the layout. Please don't leave for the day without checking with me."

Meg crumpled into her seat. "Town Talk" had already been turned in. Except for want-ads, she had nothing to contribute. Her phone rang and she answered, surprised to hear Jack's voice.

"I need your help."

Curious, she picked up a notepad and slipped into Mr. Zimmer's office. Two stacks of folders rested on the desk in front of Jack. He handed her the ghosted article on the protesters. "Lester didn't do half bad with the layout, but there are some holes. I want to run this."

Meg's mouth fell open. "I don't understand."

His Adam's apple bobbed. "There's no time for a rewrite. Besides, I couldn't improve upon it. It may not be up-to-the-minute news, but it's good to let those protesters know that people are watching. This doesn't change what I said before. We're in a unique circumstance."

She nodded, hating the wave of excitement racing up her spine. "Are you going to tell Mr. Zimmer who wrote the piece?"

"Later. Telling him now might do more harm than good. It goes below the fold, left side." His brows knit together. "Looks like you got what you wanted."

"I don't want it. Not this way. Put an ad there instead."

"We're obligated to print news that's relevant. This is relevant, given the current contest."

An ache filled Meg's gut. "I suppose."

"Tomorrow we'll add tonight's basketball score, and then we'll be set except for Oscar's editorial." He handed her a folder. "Here are his ideas. Work them into a column without diverting from his position. I'll include a statement saying the article was composed from his notes."

She took the file with a shaking hand. How had she moved so quickly to editorial writing? "I'd love to."

"You may not when you see the topic."

Meg opened the folder and skimmed the first handwritten page. A bitter taste filled her mouth.

"I need it before you leave tonight."

She closed the folder. "You should ask someone else."

"Who? Lester is gone, and even if he weren't, it's over his head. Hank does okay with sports scores, but his forte is selling advertising." Jack held her gaze in a hard stare. "We have to filter out our personal feelings in this business. Best you decide if you have what it takes before moving."

Meg stood. "You'll have it in an hour."

At her desk she sifted through the familiar scrawls. She had no idea her boss felt so strongly, and worse, so must Jack, or he would have chosen something else.

She rolled paper into the typewriter. Jack probably didn't think she could do this. Well, she could. After all, they weren't her words. Her fingers moved over the keys as she typed the opening sentence.

> *We live in unstable times and have had to adjust to many changes, including more women in the workplace than ever before. That does well for some organizations, but not the news business....*

By the time Meg handed Jack the article, they were the only two people in the office. As he read, the creases around his eyes deepened. "Good job. I knew you could do it justice."

Struggling against the way his grin made her light-headed, she shrugged and stared at her lap. "I almost didn't write it because I disagreed. Then I realized that I am paid to type the words. It doesn't mean I have to feel the same way."

Jack stuck the article inside the thickening folder. "I think we can end the day on this good note."

The phone rang, and he pressed the earpiece to his ear. "Jack Wallace."

At his scowl, an uneasy feeling came over Meg. She didn't think she could take more bad news.

"I see," Jack said. "Glad they got all the infection out. How long?" His jaw pulsed. "That's quite awhile. Can I count on you, Les?" He pursed his lips. "Just a few weekly articles. We can handle the rest."

He hung up and rubbed his temples. "Oscar is fine, but he won't be back to work for at least two months. Pray that my dad is okay. I can't be in two places at once."

Meg started to reach across the desk for his hand but then pulled back. "We'll just have to take it one day at a time. I'm here to help."

* * * * *

After a hot bath, Meg donned her flannel robe and stepped toward the darkened staircase in search of the soup Mom had promised her.

Several steps down, her foot rammed into something hard.

She fell forward and grabbed for the banister, but her fingertips only grazed the smooth wood as she tumbled to the landing. Pain sliced through her left arm.

"Meg! Are you okay?" Mom sat beside her.

Meg pushed to an upright position. The pain worsened. She winced and rubbed her arm, fighting tears. Several steps up, Laura's clarinet case lay on its side. Her sister had really done it this time. "I think my arm is broken."

Chapter Seventeen

. . . .

Dad knelt next to Meg. "Laura, get down here now!" Deep lines formed on his forehead as he gently touched Meg's arm.

She yelped, and he snapped his hand away.

Laura appeared at the top of the stairs. "What's going on?"

Dad spoke through clenched teeth. "You left your music case on the stairs. It's by God's grace your sister only hurt her arm." He stood and headed to the phone. "I'll call Dr. Jeffers."

"I'm sorry. I didn't leave it there on purpose." Laura scrambled down the stairs and sat on the step next to Meg.

"Of course you didn't leave the case there on purpose, Laura," Mom said. "But it was careless. And after the many times you've been asked to not clutter the stairs too." She gripped Meg's right elbow. "Come on, Meg. Let's get you to a chair."

Meg struggled to her feet. "I need to be at work tomorrow. How can I type?"

Dad rushed up, his mustache twitching. "The doctor wants us to come to his office. If it's broken, he can cast it there."

After some debate about whether Meg should dress, it was decided that she would wear her robe. Mom threw a coat over Meg's shoulders, and they sat in the backseat while Dad drove the four blocks to Dr. Jeffers's office. An hour later, they returned home, with Meg's arm in a cast. Against her parents' protests, she insisted on calling Jack.

He answered with a sleepy voice.

"Jack, it's Meg. I'm sorry to call so late. Did I wake you?"

"I fell asleep on the davenport. Everything okay?"

"I just broke my arm." She bit her trembling lower lip.

"Holy cow. How'd that happen?"

"I tripped over something on the stairs. I have five or six weeks in this cast." She sat in a nearby chair. "What are we going to do?"

"It must be painful."

"A little," she hedged. "The doctor said the discomfort should ebb in a couple days."

"Which arm?"

"My left, but I need both to type."

"You can handwrite your work and someone else can type it."

She grinned despite the pain. "That's brilliant. I'll be there in the morning."

"Stay home until the pain stops. We've got all the articles ready for Composing. I'll have Emily take whatever want-ads come in."

"Maybe Ginny can help." Had she really said that?

"Ginny got the Burlington job. We'll get by."

"I'll be in. Maybe not on time, but I will."

Meg hung up and padded toward the stairs.

"I heated some milk for you." Mom approached her, carrying a cup of the tepid liquid on a small tray.

Meg offered a closed-lip smile. As many times as she'd said she loathed warm milk, it was always Mom's remedy. A few moments later, having forced down the liquid, Meg lay on her bed with her throbbing arm resting across her chest. She blinked back tears. "God, how am I supposed to trust You when every time I turn around, something bad happens?"

* * * * *

Jack flicked on the bedside lamp and studied the clock. Three thirty. How could he sleep when people at work were dropping like clay pigeons? He threw back the covers, and his bare feet hit the cold floor. In the kitchen, he got strong coffee going in the dripolator then sat at the table with his Bible. The book fell open to Proverbs 3:5–6. He read the words, and the same question plagued him now more than ever. How could he acknowl-edge God in all his ways?

It wasn't only the staff's health issues troubling him. Was his inten-tion to have Meg write articles without Oscar's consent really okay? Was it any different than her secretly helping Lester? But if he didn't use Meg, the paper wouldn't print. Was her accident a sign that he needed to find another approach to get the paper out? Could he trust God in this like the words said?

The coffee finished dripping. He grabbed a cup from the cupboard and stared at the pink flowers bordering its rim. He should shop for a more masculine design. But with Dad's health issues, how much longer would he be here?

He filled the cup, and then with the coffee's nutty aroma tickling his nose, he bowed his head. "God, I'm trying hard to trust You despite every-thing, but it's difficult. If You want me to understand, I need Your help."

An hour later, Jack arrived at work and started some coffee with the old percolator and hot plate kept in Composing. At this rate, he'd have his daily caffeine quota by seven.

If no one else called in, he should have Emily, Hank, and Gus and Leo in Composing. Thelma was questionable. He took a file from Oscar's desk with the names and numbers of the two women who came in to type on deadline day. He'd call them later to check on their availability over the next several weeks.

Satisfied that things were under control, he checked the advertisement folder Hank had left late yesterday. Several grocery-store ads and one for a new restaurant. Feeling a smile tugging at the corners of his mouth, he relaxed a bit. More revenue. For that, they could always add an extra page.

* * * * *

Meg's eyes fluttered open, and she pulled the covers over her face. It was too bright for so early in the morning. Why hadn't her alarm gone off? Downstairs, Mom's cuckoo clock chirped the time. One, two, three, four, five, six, seven, eight.

Eight!

She flung back the covers with her free arm then moved to swing her legs over the side of the bed. Pain shot through her limbs, her torso, her shoulders. She plopped onto the pillow. Wasn't it enough that she'd broken her arm?

The door opened, and Mom stepped in, her face all smiles and flour smudges. "I thought I heard you stir. How did you sleep?"

"Okay, but I feel like I've been run over by a bus."

Mom sat on the edge of the bed. "I figured that would happen. We use muscles we didn't know existed to brace for a fall. Are you hungry?"

Meg shook her head. "Don't you need to be at work?"

"I called and told them I wouldn't be in. You can't be alone."

"I don't plan to stay home. We're shorthanded at work."

"Didn't you say Jack said not to come in?"

She looked away. "Lester's with his dad, Thelma has the flu, and—"

"—you're missing out on your chance to show Mr. Zimmer what you can do."

Meg pressed her lips together.

"How do you plan to type?"

"Jack suggested I write out my assignments and have someone else type them."

"You can write out your work and Laura can use your father's typewriter."

Meg rolled her eyes. "I can already hear her complaining."

"It's the least she can do for having left her case on the steps. And she'll do it without pay." Mom stood. "Let's see if we can get you up. Moving will do more good for those muscles than lying here."

* * * * *

The phone rang and Jack cringed. If anyone else was sick. . . He lifted the earpiece. "Jack Wallace."

"Son? I just called the house and got no answer. Thought you must have gone to work—" A sharp cough ended his father's greeting.

"Oscar had a ruptured appendix, and I'm suddenly the temporary editor. What did the doctor say?"

Silence filled the connection, and Jack hit the switch hook. "Hello? Hello?"

"I'm still here. Is Oscar okay?"

"Yes, but he's out for a couple months. You have good news for me?"

"Wish I did. I. . .have TB."

Jack tensed. He'd feared cancer, but TB was just as bad. Dad could be sent away to a sanitarium. Maybe the doctor was wrong.

"Jack, you there?"

He wiped the sweat off his free hand onto his pants. "Don't you need a second opinion?"

"I got one yesterday. I'm leaving for Colorado the day after tomorrow."

"Colorado?" Jack surveyed the piles on Oscar's desk. The guys in Composing would soon fire up the Linotype and need direction. His calendar showed a lunch appointment with the mayor and, tomorrow, breakfast with the rec building's contractor. His chest tightened. He should be heading to Chicago.

"There's a wonderful sanitarium in Colorado Springs. The mountain air does wonders, and most patients return home within six months to a year. Your mother can even stay in a guest residence on the property."

Jack drummed his fingers on the desk. He'd been ready to throttle Lester for walking out on his dad's paper. He wasn't about to do the same to his own father. "I need to decide how, Dad, but I'll be in Chicago by tomorrow."

"Oscar needs you worse than me. I've got Will Snow, the managing editor, primed and ready. I left everything in order. Will's a good man."

Jack's thoughts spun. He couldn't accomplish his plan while stuck in Lake Geneva. "How can you turn the *Beacon* over to me as we planned unless I get some time working there instead of here?"

"I intend to return. I'm not going to let a little thing like TB—" The sound of his covering the mouthpiece muted a sharp cough.

Jack swallowed back the vinegar-like taste in his mouth. So what if Snow was a good man? The *Beacon* had to stay in the family, to go to Kate like she wanted. Yet he couldn't leave Oscar in the lurch. He had to trust God.

Sunday couldn't come soon enough to hear what Reverend Hellman had to say about acknowledging God in all one's ways. Maybe he took personal appointments? Did Jack even have time for another meeting?

"I'll call from Colorado. I've hired a driver to take us in the Buick. That way your mother will have the means to get around."

"Aren't you afraid of her catching TB from you?"

"She hasn't yet." The connection went quiet. "But you should get yourself tested. I was coughing up a storm the last time you were here."

"I will as soon as I find a minute."

"Mr. Wallace, you got work for Gus and me?"

Jack faced Leo Kelly, the other Linotype operator.

Leo studied his shoes. "Sorry. Didn't notice you were on the phone."

"I need to go, Dad. I'll pray for you. Keep me posted, or have Mom call me." He hung up and stood. "Okay, Leo, let's get the show on the road."

* * * * *

"This is not how I expected to spend Saturday." Laura hit a key on Dad's typewriter and shot Meg a hard stare.

"Nor did I." Meg squirmed in an attempt to find a comfortable position on the dining room chair. "Maybe you should have thought of that when you left your clarinet case on the stairs. It won't kill you to type two handwritten pages."

"Why do you get so excited about who visited whom or what child had a birthday? Who reads this?"

"You'd be surprised." Ever since Mom had informed Laura that she was to type Meg's work, the girl had complained. Meg wanted to turn her sister over her knee.

Laura huffed and began typing.

With the sound of the typewriter keys smacking the platen, Meg stood and moved to the window. Across the street, Mrs. Branigan kneeled in front of her flower bed, her fleshy arms jiggling as she turned over the dirt with a trowel. Was it warm enough to go without a sweater? Three days inside had Meg feeling like a caged animal. A walk to the lake later might help.

"This scribble of yours is atrocious, Meg. I don't know how you expect me to read it."

She stepped over to the table. "Recital. Edna O'Leary's students will be giving a piano recital on Monday."

The telephone rang. Relieved to escape, Meg went to answer it.

Jack's bright "Hello" lifted her spirits. "So how's 'Town Talk' coming with your assistant?"

"Don't ever hire her. She has a terrible attitude. Not that she'd ever apply for a job. I think I've heard a dozen times how boring it must be."

Jack chuckled. "Still think you'll come in for a while on Monday? Thelma says she plans to be here. Maybe she can help with your typing or we can call one of the other typists."

"Anything would be better than my grumpy sister. I'll see you at eight on Monday."

"Not at church tomorrow?"

Staying home, she'd lost track of the days. "I'll have to see how I feel."

"Physically or spiritually?"

How could he see into her heart so easily? "Physically, of course."

"A walk by the lake with a pretty companion suits me. What do you say?"

Butterflies took flight in her stomach. "How soon?"

"Give me ten minutes."

A short time later, Meg greeted Jack at the door, unable to stifle a grin. "You're a minute early."

"Caught the light when it was green. You sound in better spirits than you did on the phone."

"Knowing I'm going outside for a bit is better than medicine." She took him into the dining room.

Laura had her back to them, still pounding the typewriter. "I'm almost done, and I hope this is the last. I don't even read this stuff if I read the paper."

Jack chuckled. "Sorry you feel that way about our content, Laura."

She jerked around, a smile pasted on her face. "Jack. I didn't hear you come in. I was only kidding."

Meg chose to ignore the comment. "We need to proof your work before we can say you're done."

Laura rolled her eyes. "You mean, if you find mistakes I need to start over?"

"Maybe. Let me see it." Meg held out her free hand.

"This better be okay." Laura pulled a pout and wheeled the paper out of the machine. "I have homework."

Meg read through each line. Like everything else she tackled, Laura was a good typist. "I only see a missed period at the end of a sentence. We can pencil that in for Composing." She handed it to Jack. "You want to double-check it?"

He held up his hands in surrender. "I've seen enough copy this past week to last until Monday." He pulled out his wallet. "Laura, let me pay you for your work."

Laura gave Meg a smug look as she held out her hand.

"She's not supposed to be paid, Jack. Typing for me was an agreement between Mom and Laura in payment for something else."

Jack's eyes ricocheted between Laura's outstretched palm and Meg. He put his wallet away.

Ignoring Laura's glare, Meg went to the front hall. "Do I need a wrap?" At that point she'd take a walk to the city dump over listening to more of Laura's complaints.

"I'd bring one," Jack said. "It might be cooler next to the water."

As they headed down Warren Street, Jack walked beside Meg, carrying her coat. "Does Laura always have such an attitude?"

"My sister has been insolent since the day she came to live with us."

Chapter Eighteen

....

Meg's step lightened. "It's a beautiful day, isn't it?" She glanced at Jack. Not seeing him beside her, she turned.

He stood several paces back, staring at her as if she'd sprouted an extra head. "Is Laura adopted?"

She frowned. "Why do you ask?"

He caught up to her. "You said she came to live with your family. I take it to mean she's adopted."

She drew in her lower lip. "I said that?"

"Yes."

She must have. Was she losing her mind? "She doesn't know."

They came to Main Street, and Jack took her elbow. "Maybe she suspects she is and that's the reason for her attitude." They crossed to the park and strolled between the budding trees. "How old was she when she joined the family?"

"Six months. Her parents died in a car crash."

"And how old were you?"

"Almost seven. Mom and Dad left the house one morning and were gone most of the day while my grandmother stayed with me. When they returned, Mom had Laura in her arms and announced that she was my new sister." A chill ran down Meg's spine as memories flowed into her thoughts.

"When is she leaving, Momma?" Meg asked after three days of watching her parents dote on Laura as if she'd been dropped by special delivery from heaven. If Momma wasn't diapering or feeding the little charmer,

Daddy was walking her in the straw baby buggy that came with her, stopping for the neighbors to chuck the baby's chin. By the fourth night, Meg stood before the bathroom mirror wondering if laundry bleach would make her brown, straight hair blond and wavy.

She'd only managed to bleach her bangs and was unplaiting her braids when Momma's curdling scream interrupted her.

"You had no warning of Laura's coming?"

Meg pulled herself out of her recollection. "Not one hint. At first, I thought she was the answer to my prayers for a brother or sister, but I hadn't realized that another child meant sharing my parents. When I turned ten, I told Mom it felt like they'd found a prettier daughter to replace me. Even though she assured me that their hearts had room enough to love both of us, I didn't believe her. Now I know better, but Dad still favors Laura. She gets away with murder."

Jack gestured toward a bench. "Want to sit?"

Meg sank onto the hard seat, suddenly feeling naked for having admitted so much. What must he think? She blinked her watery eyes.

He settled beside her. "Most kids think their siblings get away with murder. My sister always thought I got away with stuff because I was a boy, and I watched my dad practically eat out of her hand because she was a girl. Maybe most of what you felt was misperceived."

"I don't want to talk about it anymore."

"The warm breeze sure feels good, doesn't it?"

She faced him. "Warm? I was just thinking about how chilly it's gotten."

He held her coat open. "We'd better get this on you."

With Jack's assistance, Meg pushed her free arm into the coat sleeve. After he arranged the other half of the wrap over her sling, he fastened the top button, his fingertips grazing her skin and setting off a swarm of tingles racing down her spine.

Jack gave his handiwork a look of satisfaction then raised his gaze to her mouth.

An ache to feel his kiss pressed against her breastbone. He inched closer, and her world closed in. She lifted her chin and her eyes slid shut, anticipating his lips touching hers.

"My dad is on his way to Colorado."

Her eyes popped open. He'd settled against the bench, facing the lake. Certain her burning cheeks must be as red as her lipstick, she averted her gaze. What must he think of her, begging for a kiss in broad daylight?

"The doctor must have given him a good bill of health," she said. "Is he going there on business?"

His lips settled into a tight line as he stared ahead. Several moments passed before he faced her. "He has tuberculosis. He's on his way to a sanitarium."

Biting her lower lip, she looked away. Had she been so focused on her own problems that she'd not noticed the sorrow in his eyes? She turned back and lifted her good hand to touch his arm but withdrew it before making contact. "Jack, I'm so sorry. Why are you here? Don't you need to be helping at the *Beacon*?"

He leaned his elbows on his knees and stared at the grass. "I can't. Oscar's laid up and no one else can take over. Besides, Dad's already trained the managing editor to step in."

"And Lester left you in the lurch." Heat filled her stomach. She wanted to go and find Lester and give him a piece of her mind.

"Don't get mad at Les. His mom needs him now as much as Oscar. What's more, he's been caught between pleasing his dad and what he's really cut out to do." Jack straightened and draped his arm across the back of the bench.

"And what is he cut out to do?"

"Not newspaper reporting, as much as Oscar would like it." He stretched out his legs and crossed them at the ankles. "Funny, I'm aching to get to the *Beacon* and help my dad, but he doesn't seem to want me there. Meanwhile, Oscar wants to hand the *News-Trib* over to Lester, but Lester doesn't want it."

She wanted to comfort him with a hug but instead studied the shimmering lake. Hugging would only give him the wrong idea.

Funny how they both had father problems. She a dad who didn't think she could be a reporter, and Jack a dad who didn't seem to think he could run the family business.

Would Dad ever be proud of her like he was of her sister? Everything Meg wasn't, Laura was. Smart, pretty, talented. . . Seemed that way with most people in her life. Dad favored Laura, Matthew favored tall, willowy Betty Watkins, and Jack favored Ginny.

"Dare I ask a penny for your thoughts?"

Meg's face warmed, and she turned to him.

Jack held out a penny.

She couldn't help but chuckle. "Keep it. I wasn't thinking about anything in particular."

"Judging by the expression on your face for the past several minutes, you've got a lot more on your mind than a broken arm or a troublesome little sister."

Meg let her shoulders rise and fall in a shrug. "Nothing you care to hear about."

He cupped her good shoulder with his hand, giving a gentle squeeze. "Try me."

Her breath caught in her throat. How was a girl supposed to carry on a decent conversation when the guy beside her kept causing her stomach to dip and flutter when she didn't want it to—or did she?

He nudged her shoulder and tugged her closer. "Is it the move?"

She straightened and put some space between them. She was falling for this man, and if she knew better, she'd head for California even if she had to hitchhike. "The move isn't firm as yet. We're still working out the logistics."

"Well, I have another question for you, then."

She tensed. "Okay."

"Are you seeing anyone?"

Meg nearly jumped. That was the last thing she'd expected him to ask. She ached to say there was no one, but she needed to keep her distance. Twisting to look him in the eyes, she nearly crumpled at his lopsided grin.

"There has been someone special, but we're, um, taking a break right now." Not exactly a lie, was it?

His smile slackened as a large cumulus cloud covered the sun.

Goose bumps rose on Meg's neck.

"It's getting chilly. We'd better get you back home." Jack pushed to his feet, and she took his proffered hand as she stood. He kept hold as they walked. Even through her gloves, the sensation of their touching palms caused a fluttery feeling in her stomach.

She glanced over her shoulder. The last thing she needed was for word to get out that she was holding hands in the park with the lady-killer reporter. If Emily heard, Meg would never hear the last of it. But then, if Ginny happened by, it would be deliciously wonderful. Meg's spirits sagged. For a moment there she'd managed to forget about Miss *New York Times*. Ginny was probably busy this afternoon, or he'd have been with her.

"After all this craziness calms down, I'd like to take you out for dinner. Would you be interested?"

Her breath caught. "You mean as a date?"

"Yeah. I presume I'm not stepping on anyone's toes, since you and that other fella are taking a break from each other. Or did I misunderstand?"

She looked up at him. "You understood right."

He flashed her another breathtaking grin. "Good. Then the answer is yes to a nice evening over dinner. And, just so you know, there's no work talk allowed."

A bubble of joy filled her chest. They came to the crosswalk, and he gave her hand a squeeze before cupping her elbow. "I don't know what I would have done without your support this past week, Meg. You've been a good sport, taking on all that work despite your broken arm."

A prick of disappointment burst the bubble. Was the dinner invitation a gesture of thanks for being a good sport? But if he only thought of her as a chum, would he hold her hand or make sure that she was available? They reached the far curb, and he took her hand again. She should pull her hand away. She was entering dangerous territory. As if reading her thoughts, he tightened his grip. She'd let herself enjoy the sensations for a few minutes more.

Chapter Nineteen

....

Jack pointed the Ford toward the Elgin Club. A quick glance in the rearview mirror told him he still wore the same smile that had plastered itself onto his face since Meg had agreed to a dinner date. Before that, he'd managed to catch himself before he kissed her. But after finding out that she wasn't officially seeing anyone, it was all he could do not to plant one on those pretty lips right then and there. So much for not getting involved with a woman. He'd fallen for a lot of girls over the years, but Meg was different than the others. A special kind of different.

What did she mean by taking a break with the other guy? How long had they been apart? A month? Two months? An ache filled his gut. Maybe the man had moved out West for a job and was now asking her to join him.

Time to prioritize. He had his own problems to think about. Sometimes people didn't recover from TB. Snow could manage the paper temporarily, but the *Beacon* had to stay in the family. If God didn't answer his prayers, he might have to run his endgame quicker than planned.

He'd go back to Chicago and, after a few months at the helm, turn the reins over to Kate. Then he'd figure out what he was to do with his life. Political reporting in DC held excitement, and he'd dreamed of the White House as his beat. But then Senator Glenn had lost the election, and he was out of a job.

Now he was filling Oscar's shoes and loving every minute. Maybe after leaving the *Beacon* in Kate's hands, he'd head to California and find a small paper to run—and then lure a certain brunette from the big city. If she wasn't already taken. He laughed out loud at himself, spinning daydreams like a schoolboy with a big crush.

He couldn't wait for tomorrow to hear Reverend Hellman's next installment. Besides Meg, another ingredient had been added to his life. God. God, Meg, and printer's ink on his hands. He'd never expected any of it. Now he wondered if he could live without them.

* * * * *

The following morning, as they were preparing to leave the house, the telephone rang, sending a tingle of foreboding up Meg's spine. No one called early on Sunday unless it was an emergency. She answered.

"Meg, I need to cancel church. Ginny called a few minutes ago. . ."

Jack's voice faded as *"Ginny called"* echoed in her head.

"Meg, you still there?"

"I'm here. Thanks for calling. I'll tell Mom."

Her mother entered the hall, a curious expression on her face.

"I hope she didn't plan extra food just for me."

"She always makes a big meal on Sunday, not knowing who may end up at the table."

Mom's brows shot up, and she frowned.

"Have a nice time, Jack. See you at work." Meg replaced the receiver.

"What did you mean by all that?" Mom moved to the hall mirror and patted her hair into place.

"Jack had to cancel today." Meg stepped over to the closet. "He said he hoped you hadn't fixed more because of him. I didn't want him to feel bad, and what I said is true."

Mom set her brown felt hat on her head and studied her reflection. "It must be important, to change plans so late."

An ache the size of Wisconsin filled Meg's chest. "A friend called this morning, and he changed his mind." She gave Mom a tight smile and reached for her coat. "Dad's beating the horn. We'd better go."

* * * * *

On Sunday afternoon, Meg helped Laura box up the Landlord's and Prosperity game. She'd made it through church, dinner, and a rather sub-dued match with her parents and Laura. Just a few more hours before she could say good riddance to the day.

Her mother stood in the arched doorway. "Meg, Jack's on the phone."

Her heart quickened, but the thought of his choosing to be with Ginny quenched the sensation. "Tell him I'll call him back."

"Meg Alden, I'm surprised at you." Mom rested her fists on her hips. "It was quite honorable what Jack did for his friend."

"What Jack did?" Meg handed the box to Laura and headed to the phone. She lifted the receiver and said a quiet hello.

"Hi, Meg. I'm sorry for the change in plans this morning. If I hadn't gone to help, Ginny's friend would be a very sick lady."

"What do you mean?"

"Ellie woke up with a huge stomachache. Ginny remembered what had happened with Oscar and they decided to go to the hospital, but then the car wouldn't start. She called me in a panic."

"You didn't say all that."

"Granted, I spoke pretty fast." He paused. "Actually, your response was odd. You told me to have a nice time."

Meg strained to remember. "I don't recall."

He let out a loud breath. "I wouldn't cancel plans for any other reason but an emergency. Ellie did have appendicitis, but they got to it before it ruptured. Since Ellie was to take Ginny to Burlington later, I took her after we knew Ellie was okay."

Meg's shoulders sagged. "You did all that?"

"So much for a day of rest. How was the sermon?"

She couldn't admit that her mind had been full of not-so-nice thoughts toward Jack all service long. "Good."

"Maybe I can read your notes."

"Sure." Mom was the note taker. She'd borrow hers for him. "Get some rest, and I'll see you tomorrow."

Mom looked up from her knitting as Meg entered the living room.

"Jack's day went right along with Reverend Hellman's sermon—dying to self and doing for others."

"Yes, I suppose so. I'm going upstairs to read. Maybe I'll turn in early."

Mom's grin lit up the room. "Is there something more between you and Jack than friendship? Yesterday when he was here, he had that look in his eyes. He's such a nice—"

"What look?"

"The same kind your father gave me when we were courting." She set her knitting in her lap. "I noticed your Bible stayed closed the entire service. You know, it was hard for me to concentrate on church when I was first taken with your father."

Meg pressed her lips together. "We're only friends. That's all. Coworkers shouldn't be romantically involved." She turned toward the stairs.

"Methinks thou doth protest too much."

Mom's comment rang in Meg's ears as she climbed the steps. Reaching her room, she plopped onto her bed and studied a crack in the ceiling. Like it or not, she found Jack attractive. But so did a lot of women. Ginny's call this morning did her a favor by reminding her that Jack had Ginny in his life and Ginny was much more suited to him than Meg. Besides, she'd likely move to California soon, and Jack would be at the *Beacon*. If he weren't still seeing Ginny by then, he'd probably end up with a debutante.

She changed into her nightgown and crawled under the covers. Jack had probably forgotten about the dinner date. But if he mentioned it, she'd say she changed her mind. The last thing she needed was to let a man gum up her plans just as they were falling into place.

Chapter Twenty

....

Meg entered the office, marveling over how, in the three weeks she'd been back at work since her accident, things had calmed down. Emily pushed her headset away from her mouth. "Morning, Meg. Mr. Wallace wants to see you right away."

Meg's effort to stifle a smile failed. "I hope he can wait until I remove my coat. Thankfully, I only have a few more weeks in this cast."

"I can wait, but let me help you."

At Jack's voice, a trail of goose bumps snaked up her spine. The same ones that happened whenever he was nearby, despite her determination to not react to him. A difficult task, with church, followed by Sunday dinner, board games, and walks to the lake filling their Sundays.

She let him take her coat, and he gently maneuvered it around her sling with a practiced hand. Trying hard to ignore her stomach flutters, she handed him her hat. He placed her garments in the closet. Grateful as she was for his help, the process held a level of familiarity that unsettled her.

He turned, and Meg glimpsed a fresh knick on his jaw, likely from his morning shave.

"What did you need to talk about?" she asked.

"Probably best discussed in there." He tipped his head toward his temporary office. "Meet you in five minutes?"

* * * * *

Meg sat across from Jack. "A town meeting is scheduled next week to announce the winning name for the building." Jack rested his elbows on the desk and steepled his fingers. "We'll both attend, but I'd like you to find out whether the protest group has influenced the selection."

It was one thing to write articles for which she was able to gather facts through research, but an investigation with possible interviews was different. A vision of Mr. Zimmer calling her to his hospital bedside and waving a copy of the *News-Trib*, saying, "I told you *no* reporting. You're fired," erupted in her thoughts. "Jack, I appreciate your help, but if Mr. Zimmer—"

"You know these people. If they swayed the committee at all, that's news." He leveled his gaze on her, so intense she felt its heat. "I intend to tell Oscar how you're assisting me. He'll be okay. Without you, we'd only be printing half a paper."

Fear crept up her spine. "You don't know him like I do." She shifted in her seat. "He won't be okay. As for the protesters, I doubt they influenced anything, especially with my father heading the committee. He's proud to a fault about his involvements being aboveboard."

Jack frowned. "What if another committee member isn't concerned about integrity? Maybe willing to accept a little bribe?"

Meg chuckled. "What would the protesters use for a bribe? A bushel of corn?" She stared at her clasped hands. *Why, when I have the chance to do an investigative story, does Dad need to be involved with the topic?*

"Just see what you can find."

She nodded and prepared to stand.

"This letter came for you."

She took the white envelope he held out and read the return address. Resisting the urge to whoop, she worked to stay calm. "It's from Mattie in California."

He sat up a little straighter. "You already know someone out there?"

Meg reread the return address. Was Santa Monica near Hollywood? Helen wanted to live near the studios. "Yes. I have a friend who works for the *Examiner.*"

"Swell connection. Is your friend a reporter?"

Was it her imagination, or had some of Jack's enthusiasm vanished? "Research assistant. No doubt I'll have to start at the bottom and work my way up."

Meg studied the envelope. Mattie's backhanded scrawl showed through the thin paper. Would her words hold the answer to Meg's dreams?

"We haven't yet set our dinner date."

She snapped her head up. "I thought you'd forgotten."

"Hardly. What about this Friday?"

To save money, she and Helen had replaced their Friday night movie dates with coffee at one of the cafés. But, knowing Helen, she'd insist Meg have dinner with Jack. If Meg declined, she'd always wonder what she missed. But accepting could set her up for another hurt. Still, she always enjoyed Jack's company and his riveting stories about life in DC or discussing a novel they'd both read.

Meg fixated on a pencil cup. Canceling was the safe choice. She looked up, and his gaze melted into hers. If she kept the guard on her heart firmly in place, she'd be fine. "I have nothing scheduled."

Jack stood as she basked in the effects of his grin. "We can talk later about when and where."

Enjoying the lingering warmth flooding her insides, she didn't want to leave. His phone rang, and she stood. What was wrong with her? Earlier, it was all she could do to not dash off with Mattie's letter. Now, all she wanted was for Friday to arrive.

Meg gave a small wave and left Jack to his call while she headed straight for the restroom. Behind the locked door, she managed to one-hand-wrestle the letter from the envelope and shake open the single sheet of paper.

Dear Meg,

I'm sorry to respond so late. The postman delivered your letter only yesterday. I'm delighted you want to move to LA! What a needed tonic for my poor old heart. We're going to have

so much fun after you get here. As luck would have it, a lady in
the typing pool is leaving on June fifteenth. I spoke to my boss,
Henry Gibbons, and if you write him directly to apply, he'll wait
to hire until he meets with you in person. His address. . ."

Meg lowered herself to the edge of the commode and continued reading. Mattie hadn't had much to be excited about since her husband's death. Now Meg not only had Helen depending on her to make the move, but Mattie too. She'd write Mr. Gibbons tonight. For now, she had research to do.

Her notepad in front of her, she called Edna Bingham first, one of the three women sitting with the protesters during the meeting.

Mrs. Bingham answered with a loud "Yes," followed by, "You can hang up now, Bess." A *click* came through the connection. "Now we can talk. Go ahead."

Meg stifled a chuckle. "Mrs. Bingham, this is Meg Alden from the *News-Trib*. I wanted to get your reaction to the Lakefront Building Committee's announcement that a winning name has been selected."

"Sorry, but I have no idea what you mean."

Meg lowered her voice. "You were part of the group who defended Violette Fenner at the town meeting and demanded that her winning name from the previous contest be used."

"I felt sorry for Violette. Her entry was chosen as the best and then they announced a new contest. Kind of like a slap in the face."

Meg scribbled on her notepad. "Do you think Miss Fenner is upset by the outcome?"

"She seemed embarrassed about all the fuss. She married the weekend after the meeting. I expect she has different things on her mind now."

"Do you know if the others have tried to influence the committee members?"

"You mean getting them to change their minds?"

"Perhaps."

"When I saw how embarrassed Violette was, I stopped being involved. If you want to know more, call Fred Newman. He's the ringleader."

Meg thanked her, hung up, and tapped her pencil on the desk. She didn't blame the woman. If it weren't for Miss Fenner's fiancé offering comfort that night, she might have left the meeting early. Why hadn't she asked Mrs. Bingham for Violette's new name? She pushed back her chair and walked to the archive shelf. Finding out shouldn't be too hard.

* * * * *

Meg closed the one-week-old paper and returned it to its place on the shelf. She'd gone through the past month's editions without finding a marriage announcement for Violette Fenner. Most girls published their wedding details the week following the nuptials. The newlyweds probably preferred to enjoy their new life without the intrusive attention brought on at the meeting.

But Fred Newman never let a little controversy stop him. Maybe if she spoke with him first, she wouldn't have to bother Violette. Never before had she wished for a driver's license or a car of her own, but right then she wanted both. She glanced up. The answer was right in front of her.

* * * * *

Jack waited for several minutes after Meg told him Lester was driving her out to the south shore to interview some of the protesters. The letter she'd received only had a street address and no name, and ever since their conversation, the possibility niggled at him that the friend in California and the on-again-off-again boyfriend were one and the same. The handwriting was more like printing—could have been written by a man or a woman. One person might be able to clear it up. He stood and headed for the newsroom.

Jack meandered up to Emily's desk and stood back while she took a want-ad over the switchboard. She pulled the cord on the connection, and he stepped up. "Did Meg leave?"

"Yes. Lester drove her to the south shore for an interview. They left about ten minutes ago." The corners of her lips tipped up. "I'm sure if you'd offered to drive her, she would have liked that a lot better than riding with Lester." She giggled and dropped her gaze to her lap. "There I go, sticking my nose where it doesn't belong. It's just that I'd love to see Meg have some fun in her life again. Ever since Matthew moved away. . ." She gasped and covered her mouth with her fingertips. "You never heard me say that."

Jack crossed his arms and leaned in. "Don't worry. I won't say a word about old what's-his-name."

The board lit up and Emily plugged the cord into the socket and gave her usual friendly greeting. She covered the mouthpiece with her hand and looked up at Jack. "This is for you. I think it's your friend Ginny."

He nodded. "I'm heading for my office." He walked toward his open door. At least he had a name. Friday night, he'd get Meg talking.

Chapter Twenty-One
. . . .

Meg could think of any number of things she'd rather be doing than riding with Lester to interview the town crank. If he drove his Model A any slower, they'd be standing still. They rumbled past a field of freshly turned dirt and then Fred's white barn came into view.

Lester glanced at Meg. "I don't understand why you couldn't call him. He had a phone put in last year."

"Fred doesn't usually answer. Besides, it's better to look a difficult interviewee in the eyes."

They reached Fred's property, and Lester turned the vehicle into a rutted drive. Meg swayed and bounced on the seat, her head almost grazing the ceiling. She gripped her casted arm. "Someone ought to speak to him about his driveway. A person could be killed just trying to visit him."

"Maybe that's why he keeps it this way."

"All the better, then, to surprise him."

Lester brought the car to a halt on the only level ground in view. Fred stepped out of the barn carrying a slop pail, his eyes never leaving their automobile. Meg opened her door. Suppressing the impulse to gag at the stench of fresh manure, she gingerly set her foot on the driest patch of dirt she found then gathered her notepad and pencil. Breathing through her mouth, she toe-picked across the mud toward Fred.

He furrowed his leathery brow, his wary gaze never leaving her face. "What on earth are you doing out here, Meg Alden?"

"Came to see you, Fred."

He pushed back his cap and scratched behind his ear. "Well, seein' how you and I aren't exactly on visiting terms, I have a hunch you're not checking on my welfare."

She didn't flinch. "Can we go somewhere to talk?"

"What's the matter? You don't like a little dirt?" His lip curled into a sneer. "I should make you stay here for practically causing me to run ya over that morning. No paper is worth losing your life over."

Meg resisted the urge to roll her eyes. "The incident was over a month ago. I'm surprised you even remember."

"When you almost hit someone, you remember." He turned toward the two-story house sitting across the yard. "We can talk in the kitchen." He glanced at Lester's Model A. "He want to come too?"

Lester sat slumped against the driver's seat, his newsboy cap pulled over his eyes. A cigarette dangled from his lips.

"He's fine. I don't intend to be long."

She followed the farmer across the dirt and up some steps into a closed-in porch. Fred removed his work boots and pushed open a door. "After you."

Meg followed him into the kitchen. Fred gestured to a wood table placed in the middle of the large room. "I'd offer ya some coffee, but I drank the last cupful."

Meg slid onto a mismatched chair. "Not a problem." She brushed some crumbs off a spot on the tabletop and opened her pad to a blank page.

Fred hitched up his overalls by the straps before plopping into a blue chair across from her. He stared at her notebook. "So what do you want with me?"

Meg poised her pencil. "I'm looking for your reaction to the news that the winning name for the new building has been chosen. Since you were so adamant about Miss Fenner getting her due after winning the first competition, I wondered what your thoughts were now."

His forehead creased. "Violette got cheated. What's wrong with calling the place Harborlight like she suggested?"

"I guess none of the entries impressed the committee. That's why they had a second contest."

His white bushy brows shot up. "Do you know what the winning name is?"

"No. They'll announce it next week."

"Why don't you ask your daddy? He's on the committee."

Meg pressed her lips together. "What brought on your interest in Miss Fenner's cause?"

"You sure ask a lot of questions."

"That's what a reporter does if she's going to get a story."

He narrowed his eyes. "Since when have you been a reporter, and what makes you think there's a story?"

"You and your friends' strong defense of the young woman piqued my curiosity." She doodled a design on the pad. "I'd like to make this a human-interest item."

Fred jumped to his feet, his face suddenly crimson. "Violette was cheated. It's as simple as that." He stabbed his index finger toward the door. "Now I'll ask you to leave so I can get back to my chores." A vein in his neck pulsed.

Afraid he'd drop dead of a heart attack, Meg gathered her things. "If you change your mind, give me a call at the *News-Trib*."

"There's nothing to change my mind about."

Meg crossed the muddy yard to the Model A and yanked the passenger door open. "Let's get out of here."

Lester started. "Get what you needed?"

"Hardly." She slid onto the seat. While Lester stepped out to crank the engine, Meg jotted a note on the pad. *Source, Fred Newman. Refuses to talk. Seems to be hiding something.*

Lester climbed into the car and put it in gear. "Where to next?"

"Do you know Violette Fenner's married name?"

"She married Hobart Smith. They live on County Road B. That's where we're going?" At Meg's nod, he drove toward the gate and turned right onto the highway.

The Smith farm was well-kept with a gravel drive. After Lester stopped the car behind the house, Meg climbed out and made her way past what looked like a large lilac bush to a side porch and knocked. The door swung open. Violette Fenner Smith wore a simple dress and flour-sack apron that looped over her head and tied around the waist. A smudge of flour graced one of her cheeks. "May I help you?"

A whiff of baking bread teased Meg's nose, and her stomach rumbled. "Mrs. Smith, I'm Meg Alden from the *News-Trib*. Do you have a minute to answer a question?"

The young woman nodded. "Sure, if it's fast. I'm baking."

"Seeing as how last fall your entry won first place in the contest to name the new building, I wanted your reaction to the news that a winner of the new contest has been selected."

Violette grinned. "When are they going to announce the winner?"

"Next week during a meeting at the high school. How do you feel about it?"

Her eyes twinkled. "Do you know when, exactly?"

"I can find out and let you know. Doesn't it upset you that they opted not to use the name you won with earlier?"

"Not really. The important thing is, I won the fifteen dollars. And this time the prize is twenty-five dollars. We can sure use the money."

Meg's jaw dropped. "Are you saying you entered the contest again?"

"Why not? They didn't say I couldn't."

The woman had spunk, and she liked that. "Care to share the name you suggested?"

"I entered several times." Lines around her sparkling eyes deepened. "To tell you before the announcement might jinx me."

"If you win, I want to interview you for a story." Meg held her pencil over her pad. "For now, what's your reaction to the protest group that defended you?"

Violette's face pinked. "I don't want to talk about that night. If Hobart hadn't been with me, I'd have walked out."

"Do you know why Fred took such an interest in your plight?" Meg shifted her weight from one foot to the other, wishing Violette would invite her in for a slice of bread.

"Maybe because he's got a bone to pick with your father."

The pencil slid through Meg's fingers and bounced off the step. She drew her gaze back to Mrs. Smith. "My father?"

"Fred claims that, a number of years ago, he was pulled over by a policeman for a reason he won't disclose, and that your father secretly kept him in jail during harvesttime, causing him to lose nearly all his crop. He wants your dad to pay."

Chapter Twenty-Two

....

Outside the *News-Trib* office Meg said good-bye to Lester, and he went on to County Hospital to see his dad. She headed down Main Street and climbed the stairs to the second-floor offices over Kohn & Jennings Men's Store. She paused in front of the first door in the long hallway that ran the length of the building and studied the stenciled gold lettering on the bubbled glass window.

> LOUIS P. ALDEN
> ATTORNEY AT LAW

If she tore up her notes, no one would be the wiser. But a reporter must be ready to tell the truth at all times. *Does that count when it involves family?* Meg gripped the doorknob and turned.

Sally Drummond, Dad's new secretary, glanced up from studying her steno pad. "Meg." A sunny smile emerged. "It's been a long time."

Meg regarded her with a wary eye. During eighth grade, Sally and her girlfriends had relentlessly teased Meg because she couldn't stay focused during class. She'd kept her distance from Sally and her friends during high school. "It's been awhile. I was surprised to hear you were back in town."

The brunette nodded. "When Charles was laid off, we had to move in with my parents." She ran her hand over her typewriter as if it were solid gold. "With this job and Charles working at the National Tea, things are looking up. The Lord has blessed us."

The Sally Meg remembered had scoffed at her for believing in God.

She liked this Sally a whole lot better. "That's wonderful." She glanced at the closed door leading to Dad's office. "Is my father free?"

"I'll check." Sally stood and went through the door, her full skirt making a swishing sound as she walked. Meg wandered to the window. Across the street, Jack emerged from the bank and headed toward the office, nodding a greeting at old Mrs. Fitzsimmons as she stepped out of the bakery. He stopped and said something more. Mrs. Fitzsimmons jiggled with laughter. The man could even charm the old ladies.

"You can go in."

Meg turned. Sally stood by her desk.

"Thanks." Meg whooshed past her and stepped into her father's wood-paneled office. A faint hint of his pipe tobacco tickled her nose.

He leaned back, his leather chair creaking under his shifting weight. "Well, Meg, to what do I owe this honor in the middle of a workday?"

She shut the door and sat in front of his mahogany desk. Her tongue felt as dry as day-old bread. "I need to ask you something." She scanned the rows of law books filling the shelves behind him. She was right to come here, wasn't she? "About Fred Newman."

His iron-gray brows knit together. "Fred?"

Meg nodded and studied the swirls of green and yellow in her print skirt.

"I have an appointment in ten minutes. If this isn't important, maybe it can—"

She lifted her gaze.

Dad sat as straight as a pole, his face stoic but pale.

Meg clasped her shaking hands. "Did you send Fred Newman to jail and keep it off the record?"

He snapped his head back in surprise. "I have no idea what you're talking about."

"According to a source, Fred says it happened."

His jaw clenched. "If it's not from Fred, it's only hearsay."

His answer slammed into her heart. He hadn't denied it, so it must be true. Dad never lied. "Why does Fred carry a grudge against you?"

Meg flipped open her notepad. "It seems when he questioned the integrity of the contest at the meeting, he wanted to humiliate you. Unfortunately, it was Miss Fenner who ended up being embarrassed."

"You're not putting what those people told you in the paper, are you?" She looked up. "Why not?"

"You'll start rumors that will have a terrible backlash."

"Meaning?"

"My reputation will be tarnished, which will result in lost clients and lower income. That would affect our family. I might have to let Sally go, which would affect her and her family." He pulled his pipe from his pocket and took the lid off the humidor sitting on the corner of his desk.

"Is it rumor or truth?" Meg scanned her father's taut features. "Just tell me it's not true and I'll stop investigating."

The pipe clattered onto the desk. Dad pushed to his feet. "If the type of material you aspire to write depends on half-truths and innuendos, then I understand Oscar's reluctance to allow it. The discussion is over. And not one word of this at the dinner table."

Pressure pushed at the back of her eyes as she closed her notepad. "I'll see myself out."

* * * * *

At the office, without first removing her wrap, Meg scurried to Jack's open office door. He sat bent over the desk, his shirtsleeves rolled up, scribbling notes. She coughed and he looked up, offering her a disarming grin. "Hey there. Any luck with the interviews?"

"I have a dilemma."

He set down his pen and waved at the visitor's chair. "Let's hear it."

Meg shut the door with a soft *click*. "I know why Fred Newman was so vocal at the meeting, and it had nothing to do with Miss Fenner." She plopped into the chair. "He wanted to embarrass my father because some time ago Dad had Fred thrown into jail off the record." Meg shook her head. "I don't know why or any details."

Jack's eyes widened. "Do you have any proof other than what Fred said to you?"

She took out her notebook. "Mrs. Smith told me."

"Who's Mrs. Smith?"

Meg worked herself out of her coat and let it fall over the back of the chair. "The winner of the first contest. She's married now. I interviewed Fred before I spoke to her. He acted as if he was hiding something. This frightens me, Jack. If my father—"

"We can't run the story on conjecture only. Do you want to drop it?"

Meg ran her palms over her skirt. What would it hurt? Let life go on as it had been. "Yes. . .I mean, no." She let out a groan. "I don't know."

"What would you do if it didn't involve your dad?"

"Keep investigating."

Jack steepled his fingers to a point in front of his mouth. "Having a loved one as part of the story makes a difference, doesn't it?"

"Yes." Meg studied a knothole in the floorboard then looked up into Jack's solemn face. "It's not in Dad's character to go against the law. There must be more to the story. I have to find out what really happened. And then clear my dad's name."

"That's the answer I was hoping for." Jack picked up his fountain pen and scribbled a note. "If Fred spent several days in jail off the record, the sheriff would have been in on it. When did this supposedly occur?"

"All I know is that it was several years ago. I'll see what I can learn." Meg jumped to her feet and gathered her belongings. "Just pray I don't find anything I don't want to know."

"Off the subject. Was that letter from California the answer you were waiting for?"

She forced a smile. "Yes. Mattie is putting in a good word for me at the *Examiner*. It looks like I have a favorable chance at a job in the typing pool." She turned to leave. "Would you like the door left open or closed?"

"Closed."

* * * * *

The door shut, and Jack let out a long whoosh of air. Had she said *Maddie* or *Mattie*? *Mattie* could be a pet name for *Matthew*. Something a woman might call her sweetheart. Pain sliced through his heart. He rested his elbows on his desk and put his face in his hands. What was going on? Was he falling in love with her, or was it because he wasn't used to being on the losing end? He stood and paced a circle. He was jumping to conclusions. Either one could be a woman's name. He turned and headed back to his chair. He needed to focus on the paper, not his personal life, which was becoming more tangled by the moment. And he needed to talk to Oscar.

* * * * *

At County Hospital, Jack parked under a maple tree and cut the motor. He gripped the door handle and paused.

God, You said You'd make the way straight if I acknowledged You. Here's another thing to add to the list. For Meg's sake, let this rumor about her father and Fred be hot air and nothing more.

He almost added another request, asking God to stop Meg from moving, but thought better of it and climbed out of the Ford instead. Despite the cool temperatures, the sun warmed his neck as he approached the main door. Even if Oscar was well enough for a visitor, Jack still needed to gauge the man's strength. The last thing he wanted to do was upset Oscar and cause him to have a setback.

He reached the entrance and a nurse rushed up, her navy cape lifting in the breeze. He held the door open for her, and she nodded her thanks. Jack removed his fedora then followed her inside, his nose twitching at the antiseptic smells. "Would you be able to direct me to Oscar Zimmer's room?"

She waved down the first-floor hallway. "He's in Room 110. Maybe some company will cheer him up, because he's crankier than usual today."

Chuckling, Jack approached Oscar's door and tapped.

"Don't just knock. Come in and do what you need to do."

Jack pushed the door open. "I don't know who you're expecting, Oscar, but I'm only here to say hello and get the cobwebs out of your brain."

A broad grin stretched across Zimmer's face. "Well, if you aren't a sight for sore eyes. Figured you were too busy getting the paper out on time to pay me a visit." Oscar scooted up higher on the angled mattress.

It seemed odd to see him in a faded hospital gown instead of the ever-present starched shirt and tie. At least his white thatch of hair still looked as if it had been styled with an eggbeater.

Jack snagged a straight-backed chair and dragged it next to the bed. He plopped down. "It was a rough first week, but the last couple have been okay. The way Lester talked, I thought it better to not disturb you."

"Outside of a few days, I've been ready for some visitors besides the missus and Lester. I hope my boy's been helpful. It seems like he's been here more than there. I guess it didn't work out, having him take my place."

Jack cast about for words. "We're all cut out for different things. He's been a great help."

"I heard Meg broke her left arm, but at least she can still write the want-ads and Thelma can do 'Town Talk.' You been able to keep up with your reporting?"

Jack's pulse quickened. "It's taken some overtime on the part of Meg and Thelma, but we're managing." He swallowed hard. "In the interest of getting out the paper, I've had to tap into Meg's talents."

Oscar scowled. "What do you mean by that? She's not reporting, is she?"

"I've had to use her to write up some pieces. If I didn't, we'd have half a paper."

Zimmer stared straight ahead, his frown deepening. "You've probably opened a Pandora's box, but as long as she understands that it's only till I get on my feet."

Jack squirmed. "I'll make sure she's aware."

"That was a good story on the meeting protesters. You following up? Finding out what's going on?"

"Actually, that's why I'm here." Jack crossed his legs. "Do you know anything about Fred Newman being jailed several years ago?"

Oscar pushed his glasses farther up his nose. "Where did you get that notion?"

"The story goes that Fred was unofficially jailed and the public never knew."

Oscar's face blanched. "You think I was paid not to publish the news?"

Jack raised a hand. "If a cover-up happened, you wouldn't have known. I've got half a mind to drive into Elkhorn while I'm here and see what the sheriff remembers."

Oscar picked up a glass of water from the bedside table and sipped on its bent straw. "Did the source mention names?"

"Only one." Jack stared toward the window, wishing he didn't have to say the words. "Louis Alden."

Chapter Twenty-Three

....

The County Sheriff's headquarters sat at the north side of Elkhorn's town square, next to the courthouse. Jack parked in front of the two-story brick structure. Within minutes, a deputy ushered him into Sheriff O'Brien's office.

The round-faced man stood behind his wooden desk. His rectangular toothbrush-like mustache seemed out of place under his broad nose. The man's smile welcomed, but his hazel eyes held wariness. He stuck out his hand. "Good to meet you. I didn't realize that Oscar Zimmer had left the *News-Trib*."

Jack shook the man's hand, impressed by the strong grip. "He's still there, but he's been laid up with appendicitis. He suggested I ask you to help solve a mystery."

"Sit." O'Brien waved toward a wooden straight-back chair then sat on his battered and scratched desk chair. "I've only been in this position a short while. I'm not sure I'm your man."

"Oscar said you were a deputy before this job." Jack studied a crack that trailed down the wall behind the sheriff. He drew in a breath and caught the man's gaze. "It's come to my attention that a few years ago, a Linn Township resident was possibly jailed off the record. Would you recall anything like that?"

O'Brien frowned and rubbed the gray scruff on his chin. "You're asking whether a serious breach of protocol took place."

"Our source is reliable, but we won't run the story without confirming documentation."

A woman's voice filtered in from the outer room, and the door behind Jack creaked open. "Sheriff, I got a lady out here from the *News-Trib* wanting to talk to you. Thought since your visitor is also from there, it'd be okay to send her in." Jack turned.

Meg peeked around the secretary's shoulder and pinned a wide-eyed stare on Jack. "Mr. Wallace. What are you doing here?"

A sinking feeling sent his spirits on a nosedive, and he popped to his feet. "Sheriff O'Brien, this is Meg Alden, our reporter who first stumbled onto this possible cover-up." He glanced around the austere room then indicated his chair. "I can stand."

As Meg sat, the sheriff's eyes ricocheted from her to Jack then back to Meg. "I'm not liking the odds. First there was one of ya, and now there's two. The incident likely happened when Sheriff Mason was in charge."

Meg moved to the edge of her seat. "Can we speak to him?"

The sheriff pursed his lips. "Not unless you've got a connection to heaven. He died six months ago. You two wait here. I want to ask the jailer if he recalls anything. He's been here a lot longer. It won't take me long."

The sheriff shut the door as he left, and Meg pierced Jack with a hard stare. "Did you not think I had the gumption to do this?"

Jack stepped to the window. Was that why he was here? He hadn't given her much of a chance. He turned and leaned against the windowsill. "Without a car, I didn't expect—"

"I managed to get a ride." She lifted her chin and crossed her arms. "If you care to leave now, you can."

He stuck his hands into his pockets. "I visited Oscar earlier and asked whether he recalled the incident. He sent me here."

"I was going to the hospital next."

"Would you have felt comfortable seeing him in a hospital gown?"

She dropped her arms, and her face relaxed to the natural softness he found so attractive. "I guess not. What did he say?"

Jack's insides settled. "He didn't know anything about a cover-up."

She faced the wall on the other side of the sheriff's cluttered desk as if trying to decide whether to drop the subject.

"He paid a high compliment to the story you wrote last week."

She faced him, eyes riddled with alarm. "You told him?"

Jack's stomach tightened. He wanted to support her, but if he weren't careful, she'd see him as another adversary. "Not about that story, but I did mention you were helping on minor pieces. He was a bit troubled but agreed that need had to come before philosophy." He let go of a loud breath. "I'll tell him about the bigger stuff, but not till he's stronger."

The door flew open and Sheriff O'Brien exploded into the room, bringing the distinct scent of cigar smoke with him. "The jailer says he'd remember something as screwball as what you describe. Sounds like your rumor mill is alive and well but the sources are bad."

Jack held out his hand. "Thanks anyway. If the jailer recalls anything, please have him call us at the *News-Trib*." The men shook hands and then Jack escorted Meg to the outer office.

Outside in the warm sun, he glanced around at the parked vehicles. "How did you get here?"

Meg regarded her feet. "I caught a ride with Gus, who was coming this way on an errand. He's supposed to come back in five minutes."

Jack pushed his fedora back on his head and grimaced. "I shouldn't have meddled. I apologize."

She dropped her gaze. "That's okay. I'm sorry I got so upset. You didn't know I was coming here."

"Why don't you ride with me? We can talk about the story on the way." *And I can enjoy your company.*

Meg's face brightened, and she started toward his Ford. "Okay. You're always after me to collaborate with you. Maybe I should."

Women would never stop confusing him. Jack moved past her and opened the passenger door. "I have no idea what brought about the change of heart, but it sounds like a grand plan."

"You know the saying, 'Two heads are better than one.' It's time to join forces." She slid onto the seat.

He moved to close the door then leaned over the top of it and caught her gaze. "What do you think about Sheriff O'Brien saying the jailer didn't recall the incident? I sensed the guy was lying to save his hide."

"It crossed my mind." She took her notebook and pencil from her handbag and jotted a note. "Another unanswered question."

Jack shut the door and rounded the rear of the vehicle, relieved that they were back on good terms. Gus's car pulled up, and Jack told him Meg was riding back to Lake Geneva with him.

Jack climbed behind the wheel of the Ford and started the car. In the past hour, he'd visited Oscar, interviewed the sheriff with Meg, and seen the Linotype operator. He loved the personal feel he could never have at the *Beacon*. He glanced at Meg. "What do you think about fate as far as God is concerned?"

She kept her eyes on the windshield. "The Bible says that God determines where we live and what we do, but our independent decisions also have a role."

He backed out of the parking spot. "But what if our decisions aren't what God wills for us? What if we go off on our own?"

"Reverend Hellman says that God didn't make us like puppets with Him as the puppeteer. He gives us our free will, but if we seek God through prayer and reading the Bible, our decisions will mesh with His."

"Running the *Beacon* is Dad's dream for me, not mine. There's a lot more out there than sitting in a fancy office. I thought I wanted to be a reporter on a large daily, but these weeks at the *News-Trib* have me thinking that maybe owning a small paper like Oscar's is the ticket." He paused and swallowed back a wad of emotion that had built up in his throat. "Even if that's God's plan for me, I can't do it."

"Why not?"

"It's a long story."

"Funny, I want to work for a large daily, and you want to own a weekly. Yet we're stuck where we are."

"You're not stuck." He briefly glanced at her, expecting to see joy on her face. Instead, he was greeted with something akin to sadness. "The proverb Reverend Hellman is preaching about got me to thinking. Even though Dad's health and the *Beacon* take precedence right now, I can trust God to fulfill the desires of my heart in His timing."

They were halfway to Lake Geneva when he glanced at her again. He loved how her nose tipped up and her long lashes framed her eyes. He wasn't ready to go home to an empty house and call it a day. "What do you say we have our dinner date this evening?" He waited through the silence, keeping his eyes on the road.

"I plan to be at work extra early tomorrow since it's deadline day. Best we keep our plans for Friday."

He gritted his teeth. He'd been so distracted that he'd forgotten the work schedule. But somehow he doubted it was the real reason she declined. Nevertheless, by Friday, the week's paper would be out and they could relax, making a longer evening of it. "Then Friday it is."

She expelled a loud sigh. "If I'm still alive by then."

* * * * *

Meg watched the houses on Dodge Street go past. They'd soon come to the cemetery and turn on to Warren Street. Then two more blocks and she'd be home. Ever since she first saw Jack in the sheriff's office, her emotions had acted like an out-of-control roller coaster. How could she be so angry at a person and at the same time have such strong feelings for him?

Jack lowered his window, and the moving air brought a pleasing, citrusy scent to her nose. She'd seen men's cologne advertised recently but hadn't noticed anyone wearing it. She sniffed again, and her thoughts drifted to a nighttime stroll along the lake and putting her head on Jack's shoulder. Maybe she should change her mind about dinner.

Jack pulled up in front of her house. Home meant dinner, and dinner meant facing Dad. If she invited Jack to stay, she might get through the meal unscathed, but what if Dad told Jack off?

"Thanks for the lift. No need to walk me to the door." Meg gripped the handle.

"I won't feel right if I don't." He climbed out before she could issue a retort.

They arrived at the stoop and faced each other. Why did he have to look at her as though he could see straight into her soul? She averted her gaze and began breathing through her mouth. The scent of his cologne was making her crazy.

He pushed a lock of hair off her forehead, and his blue-eyed gaze went to her mouth. She needed to move, not get more entangled than she already was. But her black pumps felt glued to the concrete.

He lowered his head, his eyelids at half-mast. Her lips tingled. How many other women had he kissed in his lifetime? In the past year? In the past week? She took a deep breath through her nose and the intoxicating aroma of lime and oranges awakened her senses. She rose to her toes and closed her eyes.

The storm door whooshed open and connected with Meg's backside. She tumbled against Jack's chest, and his arms went around her.

"Looks like I interrupted something cozy." Laura gave them the once-over with her eyes. "Sorry. I didn't see you two." She tossed her blond tresses over her shoulder and pranced down the walk. "Mom needs your help with dinner. I have an extra play practice."

Meg stared after Laura's retreating figure.

Jack uttered a sardonic chuckle. "Looks like I'm not on her favored list anymore."

"My sister does have a fickle heart." Suddenly aware of Jack's arms still around her, she attempted to wriggle away, but he tightened his hold and said in an almost-whisper, "Maybe we should finish what we started."

The door opened, and Meg scrambled out of Jack's embrace.

Mom stepped out, wearing a flower-print apron and smelling like onions. "I thought I heard voices." She cocked her head at Jack. "There's plenty, if you'd like to stay for supper."

He searched Meg's face, and she shot him a warning look.

"Thanks, Mrs. Alden, but I'd best go." He offered Meg a lopsided smile before turning away. "See you tomorrow."

Meg followed his car with her gaze until it turned the corner. She touched her fingers to her lips. He'd been about to kiss her, and she would have let him. She'd have to be on her guard on Friday night. One slip and she'd be over the moon.

She stepped inside the house and sniffed. Meat loaf.

In the kitchen, she collected dishes, balancing the stack on her free arm. Things seemed normal enough. Maybe she'd been too cautious. Maybe she should have encouraged Jack to stay.

The front door slammed. "Is Meg home?" Dad's bellow sent a shudder through the house.

A plate slipped from the stack Meg balanced and shattered on the floor.

Mom scurried into the hall. "Louis, what on earth? She's right here in the kitchen."

Dad appeared in the doorway, his scowl deep enough to plant seed in the furrows. "To my study. Now."

Meg set the remaining plates on the counter. "I have to clean up the mess." She stepped toward the broom closet.

"Now."

Meg followed him to the book-lined study, feeling more like fifteen than twenty-five.

"Shut the door and sit."

Meg sat in an upholstered armchair as he took a seat behind the desk, looking as though someone had starched his backbone. "Are you going to print this Fred Newman rumor?"

She raised her chin. "I don't decide what runs, but Jack won't print anything without documentation."

"And what do you think happened?"

"It appears that you put Fred in jail and covered it up. I know it's not like you to do something like that, and I'm trying to learn the truth." Sounds of banging pots and pans filtered in from the kitchen as the hair on her neck rose in the electrified air.

"If one word of this is printed, I'm likely to lose my license."

Visions of Mom shopping in the food pantry, her father sitting on the street corner with a cup in his hand, Laura working as a waitress at the Utopia, and Meg living somewhere far from Lake Geneva filled her thoughts. Her throat closed. "I already told you, the decision isn't mine."

Dad slapped both palms on the desk and shot to his feet. "You demand that Jack not print the story, for the sake of your family and for Fred."

Meg flinched and ran her gaze over her dad's pinched face. She worked to keep her voice even. "Fred embarrassed you in that meeting. Why do you want to protect him? If he broke a law, it should be on his record. And the public has a right to know."

He moved to the window overlooking the backyard and stared out into the dusk-filled night. "If the story runs, you can plan on moving out immediately. Please close the door on your way out."

Chapter Twenty-Four
....

Meg banged on the beauty-shop door then hurried across the porch to the home's main entrance and rapped her knuckles against the glass windowpane.

The shop door opened and Helen poked her head out, her face covered with white cream. "It's only six thirty." She hid her yawn with a hand. "What's wrong?"

"I'm sorry to wake you, but I need to talk before work."

Helen grabbed Meg's elbow and pulled her inside. "Come in out of the chill. Let me put coffee on."

Meg waited for Helen to shut the door. "No time for coffee. I'm in a fix and may need to leave town sooner than planned."

Helen tightened the sash on her pink robe. "I thought you said the man at the *Examiner* wouldn't need you until mid-June."

"That's what Mattie said. I have my inquiry letter to him in my purse. If he can assure me of a position, I'll try to move now, since I may be kicked out of the house any day."

Helen sat in front of a mirror and plucked a tissue from a nearby box of Kleenex. She began wiping the lotion from her face. "Your parents aren't going to kick you out. Some might, but not yours."

Meg caught Helen's eye in the mirror. "My father threatened to."

Helen faced Meg, half of her face still covered with cream. "Why?"

"I can't say."

"Must be serious if you can't tell me why." Helen stood and came to Meg, drawing her into a hug. "You poor thing. I'd say you could move in here, but as it is, it's a tiny house."

Meg stepped back. "Truth is, unless Dad gives me my school fund, I can't move anywhere. And after our argument, it's unlikely he'll give me so much as a dollar." She stared at a glop of white lotion resting on her coat lapel. "I should have left things as they were."

"Now I've messed you up good." Helen grabbed the tissue box. "I have one question." She dabbed at the face cream on Meg's coat.

Right now Meg didn't care about her old cloth coat. "What's your question?"

"How do you account for God watching out for you like you always say He does? Doesn't sound like He's doing such a good job." She stood back and examined her handiwork. "Got it all."

How was Meg to answer that when she didn't know herself? "Forget what I said. I need to get to work."

As she headed down Main Street, Meg pulled her coat tightly against a wind that felt more wintry than springlike. The past few weeks she'd looked forward to work, knowing she'd see Jack, and today was no different. Their almost-kiss had popped into her mind at least a thousand times since yesterday—a welcome respite from all that was going on with Dad. But she couldn't let her feelings for Jack distract her. At least she wouldn't be alone with him this morning. On deadline day, everyone came in early.

She rounded the corner to the office entrance and entered a frenzy of hazy smoke, clacking typewriters, and jangling phones. Dotty, the substitute typist, occupied Lester's desk, while Louise, the other sub, pounded on Meg's typewriter. After hanging up her coat, she headed for Mr. Zimmer's office and stood in the open doorway.

"Meg, good morning." Jack stood from behind the desk, the top button on his shirt undone and his tie loosened. His mouth twitched as if he wasn't sure whether he should smile or not. "Come in."

She sat, relieved that it was business as usual.

His smile faded. "From your expression, I take it things didn't go well with your father last night."

"If anything is published about Fred's jail time, I'll have to move out."

Jack tossed his pencil onto the desk. "He should blame me if we run the story, not you."

"I explained that it was out of my control, but he thinks I have influence over you." She bit down on her lip. "The article could take away his livelihood and affect my family. I feel like a rope in a tug-of-war."

"Who's winning?"

Meg took a hankie from her skirt pocket and twisted it around her index finger. As demanding as her father was, she loved him. But she had a job to do. She raised her head. "I still don't believe my father has it in him to do anything illegal, but if we find documentation to prove otherwise, the story should run. Even if I end up on a breadline."

Jack's concerned gaze ran over her face. "I won't allow that to happen. Remember the proverb. We need to trust God."

Meg rolled her eyes. A few weeks ago he didn't even own a Bible and now he was reminding her of its words. "What should I work on?"

Jack handed her a file. "I need you to call store owners and then write a report on how recent merchant sales and the banks' reopening have affected business. I sent Hank out to gather the latest news on the high school baseball season. Use his phone since I've got one of the subs at your typewriter."

Relieved to be working on something unrelated to her family or the contest, Meg stopped at her desk for her notepad then went to Hank's station. She'd think about the mess with Dad later. Right now she had a story to research and a letter to mail to California.

* * * * *

On Thursday morning, the crisp, hot-off-the-press edition of the *News-Trib* waited for Meg on the polished wood surface of her desk. Her article on the increase in merchants' sales had been placed on the left above the fold. Feeling like a giddy teenager, she read the story as if she'd never seen it before.

"I thought you'd like to see the piece as it published."

Certain she was glowing like a lightbulb, she faced Jack. "I didn't realize you'd given it a premium location."

"It's a good story." He tilted his head. "You're building quite a portfolio. Have you written to the man at the *Examiner*?"

Feeling her smile dissolve, she nodded. "I sent it yesterday."

"So why the sad-sack expression?" Jack sat on a corner of her desk. Although they were the only two in the office, Meg lowered her voice. "I was counting on asking Dad for my education fund for my move. Now he's not speaking to me."

He gently touched her arm, sending a warm feeling through her body. "Meg, you don't have to be a part of the investigation."

She grimaced. Even if Jack conducted all the research, it wouldn't stop Dad from kicking her out. "I appreciate your concern, but it's too late. Dad will forever associate me with the matter."

"But it might help if he knows you've stepped back."

Dad had taught her that the truth had to prevail, no matter the cost. "If I don't, I'll never find out what really happened, nor will I clear Dad's name."

He gave her a soft smile. "Only if you're sure."

"I am."

"Okay. How about a visit with the jailer when the sheriff isn't around to influence his answers?"

Was he asking her to go there alone? How would they feel about a woman coming into the jail unescorted? "Lester's not back until Monday. I have no way to get there."

"I could give you some quick driving lessons." Jack chuckled and rested his hand on her shoulder. "Don't look so shocked. I was only kidding. It's just as well Les isn't here. The fewer who know about this rabbit trail, the better. I'll give the jailer a call and see if he's open to us stopping by this afternoon."

The outside door opened, and Emily stepped inside. "What a beautiful day. I think I'll take my lunch to Flat Iron Park." She reached for her hat then stared at Jack and Meg. Jack's hand still rested on Meg's shoulder. Emily's eyes gleamed. "Am I interrupting something?"

Jack pushed off the desk and stood. "Just getting a head start on next week's edition." He strode to Mr. Zimmer's office and closed the door.

Emily scooted over to Meg, her open coat flapping. "If I'd known you two were here alone, I'd have lingered outside a few more minutes."

Meg turned her attention to her article. "There's nothing between us, so wipe that goofy look off your face." If only she could convince herself of it.

"The way his gaze lingers on you whenever you pass by or yours stays with him when his back is turned, you're not fooling anyone."

Heat rushed up Meg's neck as a memory of the almost-kiss flashed in her mind. She faced Emily's smug expression. "That's preposterous. We only work together."

The door to Mr. Zimmer's office opened, and Jack stuck his head out. "Miss Alden, tomorrow morning we have an appointment with the man we spoke about."

She inwardly cringed. "Okay."

His head disappeared behind his door, and she looked at Emily.

Emily giggled. "If you ask me, you two aren't the only ones working early." She mimed shooting an arrow from a bow. "Sly man, making an interview appointment for both of you, together, alone for a good part of the day. *Zing.* Cupid strikes again."

Meg waved toward the switchboard. "You forget, there's a third person involved—the interviewee. Get to your station and hush your mouth."

"Just don't forget to invite me to the wedding. Remember what I told you before, when you and Matthew parted ways." Emily wended her way around the desks.

"You are a hopeless romantic." Meg opened her top drawer. She remembered Emily's words—that someday God would bring her a better man than Matthew. Someone who would be faithful and love only her. Behind Meg, a door clicked shut. She spun toward Jack's closed door. Had he heard that silly conversation? Heat spread up her neck. If he had, he was probably trying to find a way to wiggle out of that dinner date.

Chapter Twenty-Five

....

Jack skulked back to his desk. Out the window, Fred Newman's pickup truck rumbled past with bags of grain loaded in the back.

Emily's words rang in his hears. *"Invite me to the wedding." "You and Matthew."* Was Matthew this Mattie person Meg always talked about? Was he the real reason she wanted to move to California? Jack had heard it with his own ears. He should be focusing on the investigation, but how could he, when his heart felt as if it had been run over by a locomotive?

An image of Meg's face, full of excitement over anything involved with news reporting, tumbled into his thoughts, followed by memories of the dreamy expression on her pretty face when they almost kissed. The moment her mom went back in the house, he should have followed through and planted one on those gorgeous red lips of hers—make her think twice about returning to the cad who'd left her for California.

He dropped into his chair. How serious was she about the guy, anyway? Maybe she was going merely on the hope that he'd welcome her back into his life. If he had already proposed, she wouldn't be so indecisive. If she really loved the guy, would she be holding Jack's hand or acting like she wanted him to kiss her?

None of her family had mentioned a wedding, but if her intent was to reconcile with Matthew, maybe she hadn't told them. They probably didn't think so highly of the man after he broke off the relationship. Now there was a presumption. Maybe *she* had broken it off and was now having second thoughts.

Well, it was a good thing Jack had learned this before getting more involved with her. He'd sworn off women before coming here. Too bad he hadn't stuck to the plan.

* * * * *

The following morning, Meg shifted against the cloth seat of Jack's Ford and stared at the plowed fields whizzing past the window. Next to her, Jack gripped the wheel, his jaw set and lips pressed together as though they'd been sewn shut.

He hadn't stopped by her desk for their usual chat that morning, but she'd presumed he wanted to clear his desk before they left for the interview. Was she ever wrong.

Another mile passed. "Got your questions ready for the jailer?" he asked evenly.

"Of course." Meg opened her notebook and skimmed her notes. "Do you think we can do this without the sheriff knowing?"

Silence passed as they entered Elkhorn's city limits. Jack shifted into a lower gear as they came to a stop sign. "The jailer told me to come to the back entrance. Let's hope we're not seen."

At the jail, a woman wearing a starched blouse, a navy skirt, and a severe bun in her hair led them to a dank room in the basement.

Meg sat on one of the four wooden chairs around a small table, the only furniture in the cell-like space. She rubbed her arms against the chill. "This must be the jailer's idea of keeping out of the sheriff's sight."

Jack leaned against the stone wall. "I wonder if they use this for interrogations. An hour in here, and the most innocent man might be led to confess." He sniffed. "It smells like something is rotting. Did you notice those two cells we passed?"

Meg nodded, relieved that Jack's bad mood seemed to have lifted. "Easy places to secretly jail someone and forget they're here."

The door creaked open and a jowly man stepped in, his uniform shirt straining at the buttons. He held out a pudgy hand to Jack. "Deputy Munson."

"Jack Wallace." The men shook, and Jack nodded at Meg. "This is Meg Alden."

The deputy stared at her, his eyes so dark she couldn't discern his pupils. His brown brows lifted. "Don't get many lady reporters in here. I hope this isn't gonna take long." He pulled out a chair and sat across from Meg.

Jack took a seat and flipped his notebook open. "I don't think it will. Sheriff O'Brien asked you a few days ago whether you recalled a man being jailed several years back without going through the proper channels. Have you had any new recollections?"

The man's face reddened. "Our office clerk seemed to think this was a report on how we need a new jailhouse. I brought you down here so you can see where we bring overflow prisoners. If something that crazy ever happened in the twenty-five years I've been here, I'd remember."

Meg tapped her pencil on her pad. "Perhaps the imprisonment was done without your knowledge. Maybe in one of those cells out there." She indicated the door with her thumb.

The deputy narrowed his eyes. "Nothing happens here without my knowing. Now, if you two don't have any other questions, I have work to do." He pushed back his chair on the dirt floor and stood. His trousers caught on a splinter and he yanked his leg away, sending the chair to the floor. He uttered an oath and glared at Jack. "There's a reason I don't come down to this dungeon." He set the chair upright.

Jack exchanged a look with Meg. "Thank you for your time, Deputy. We'll find our way out." He caught her eye and nodded toward the door.

She gathered her belongings and scrambled to her feet. As she passed in front of Jack, relief and frustration stirred in her gut. If Munson wasn't talking, they couldn't print the article. But if he never went into the basement, Fred could have been held there on the sly.

* * * * *

Jack got the car started and faced Meg. "Fred could have been in that dungeon a couple of days without Munson's knowledge. Maybe the sheriff tended to Fred's needs and then let him go in the dark of night." He backed up and pointed the car toward Lake Geneva. "If we never get proof of this incident happening and can't run the story, maybe things will calm for you at home and you'll have the money to move."

Meg nodded. "I thought of that. Mattie is already searching for the perfect apartment for us." She peered out the window at the rolling hills occasionally broken up by a barn or herd of grazing cattle.

As they neared Lake Geneva, Meg stole a glance Jack's way. The sewn-shut lips were back. Maybe over tonight's dinner date he'd become the talkative Jack she enjoyed being around.

"About tonight," he said. "I should have said something earlier, but something has come up. Do you mind a rain check?"

Chapter Twenty-Six

....

Meg scanned the clusters of people greeting each other at the front of the church before Sunday's service. Her lackluster spirits nosedived. But did she really expect Jack to be standing in his usual place after his stony attitude on Friday? She trudged toward the steps. Let Mom and Laura wait for Dad. He wasn't speaking to her either. Maybe before the others came she'd have a moment of quiet prayer and reacquaint herself with the One who'd promised to never leave her or forsake her.

She stepped into the sanctuary and peered down the aisle at the family pew. Someone sat there, hunched over as if in prayer. Likely a visitor unaware of the "unofficial" seating arrangements. She approached, taking care to not let her heels clack on the wood floor. "Excuse me."

Jack raised his head and grinned. "Morning. I arrived early and decided I'd wait here."

She gaped at him. So he now took for granted that he could sit with her family? Meg chided herself. Wasn't that what she'd done earlier, expecting him to be waiting at the curb? Why wouldn't he presume to sit in their pew? "Slide over. The others will be here soon."

The family arrived a few minutes later, and Meg and Jack moved down. She turned her attention to the bulletin, trying unsuccessfully to ignore his citrusy scent—the same fragrance that had nearly caused her to let him kiss her. She glanced past her sister and mother to her father. Good thing the three Alden women sat between the men, given Dad's hard-hearted expression. She flipped open her Bible to Proverbs and silently prayed that God would unlock His voice.

By the time the Reverend Hellman began his sermon, Meg had ceased waiting for God to speak to her, and her thoughts drifted to California. Would their apartment be near the ocean? Hollywood appeared to be a distance from the Pacific, but Santa Monica, where Mattie lived, was near the beach. The large daily papers were probably located downtown. If they wanted to live near their jobs, she supposed they could take a bus to the beach on weekends. The beaches were probably twice the size of Lake—

"We all need to trust God with our whole hearts."

At the preacher's raised voice, Meg looked to the pulpit.

Reverend Hellman stood in front of the lectern with a wide grin on his face. "We'll conclude our series on trusting God by issuing a challenge. Ask yourself what parts of your life you have not wholeheartedly trusted God for and pray about surrendering those areas to Him. The last sermon in this series will occur on Mother's Day. What an appropriate time to rededicate your whole life to God."

Meg traced a ketchup stain on her cast with her finger. It didn't take a college degree to figure out her problem areas, but how could she trust God when He had turned His back on her? She shut her eyes.

Lord, I want to trust You, but You stopped listening to me.

She set aside her Bible and stood with the congregation. Maybe in her new home she'd hear God's voice again.

* * * * *

Mom shielded her eyes to block the late-morning sun. "Are you joining us for Sunday dinner this afternoon, Jack?"

Meg stared at Mom. Dad hadn't acknowledged Jack all morning. How could the man feel welcome with the head of the household holding him in disdain?

Jack stuck his hands into his pockets and studied the ground. "I hate to decline one of your good meals, Mrs. Alden, but I think I'll head to the office and then grab something later." He shifted his eyes to Meg. "See you tomorrow." His hands still in his trouser pockets, he headed down the sidewalk.

"I hope all the rumor business hasn't affected your friendship with Jack." Mom came alongside Meg and touched her elbow. "I'd hoped his joining us today would return some normalcy to our lives."

"We're okay. We've both got other things on our minds." Meg stepped over to the curb to wait for her father. It felt like nothing would ever be normal again.

* * * * *

"Hey, are you tied up with Jack?" Helen asked when she called later that afternoon.

Meg curled the phone cord around her index finger. "He decided to work after church."

"I know how your father feels about Sundays being family days, but I have a yearning for pie à la mode, and I heard the Geneva Grill is now open on Sundays from four to nine."

Meg checked her watch. "I doubt Dad will miss me, since we aren't speaking. Laura is at another play practice, and my father's been in his study since dinner. I'll meet you there at four fifteen."

* * * * *

Meg stabbed her fork into a cherry and dragged it through the melting vanilla ice cream. She lifted it to her mouth, and the sweet frozen dessert mingled on her tongue with the tart cherry filling. She closed her eyes. A little piece of heaven.

"Are you ready to talk moving plans?"

Meg's eyes popped open. No, she wasn't ready. She wanted to savor her dessert a moment longer, not think about her lack of moving money. "Sure."

Helen set her coffee cup on the checked tablecloth. "Beatrice spent yesterday with Mom and me and finally agreed to take my place in the shop." A broad grin split her face. "She'll live with Mom, and that settled it for me."

"What about your mom's health setback?"

"She's fine now, but her arthritis does have a nasty habit of coming and going. I was leery of moving so far away, but with Mom's encouragement and Beatrice's moving in, there's nothing to keep me here. How does boarding the California Express on May thirty-first sound?"

Meg scrunched her nose. "Something is nagging me about that day. And I haven't yet heard from Mr. Gibbons about the job at the *Examiner.* As for the funds—"

The outside door at the front of the restaurant opened, and Meg glanced over. Her nerves snapped to attention. *Where is all that work he had to do?* She ducked her head and forked a large piece of pie, stuffing it into her mouth.

"Well, fancy meeting you ladies here."

At Jack's comment, Meg lifted her head and ran her eyes over Ginny's pale-green knit dress and matching cardigan. Meg caught Jack's gaze then swallowed her half-chewed pie and forced a smile. With a shaking voice, she said, "Long time no see."

He frowned. "I guess it was just a few hours ago."

Ginny's red lips formed a perfect O. "And what were you two doing together on a Sunday morning? I hope not working."

"We attended church." Jack glanced at the half-eaten desserts. "Looks like you're at the end of your meal, or we'd join you."

Helen pushed out one of the two empty chairs and offered a smile that would have stopped cameras from rolling, if there'd been any around. "Forgive our manners. We should have asked. We'd love to visit while you eat."

Meg glared at Helen. Wasn't it obvious that the couple was on a date? Helen ignored her.

Ginny slid into the offered seat and smiled at Helen. "I don't think we've had the pleasure. I'm Ginny Colson. Are you part of this churchgoing activity too?"

Jack settled into the remaining chair and cast Meg an apologetic look.

"Church? Me?" Helen waved her hand. "Not hardly. Meg and Jack are the churchgoers."

"That's news." Ginny lifted one of the menus the waitress had dropped off. "So," she said, without lifting her eyes from the bill of fare, "what kind of magic power do you have over Jack, Meg, that he's going to church with you?" She flipped over the coffee-stained menu and checked the back then laid it on the table.

Meg sipped her lukewarm coffee. "He did it all on his own."

"Really?" Ginny looked at Jack. "Praying for your boss's speedy recovery, no doubt."

Jack picked up a menu. "You should try church, Ginny. I'm learning a lot about trusting God—something I haven't been doing much of until now."

"And all this trusting has you running a weekly when you should be helping your dad. Wouldn't God want *that* for you?" She looked at the waitress, who had returned. "I'll have the turkey and gravy over mashed potatoes. And a coffee."

The woman scribbled the order then peered at Jack, her pencil poised over her pad. She broke out in a wide smile. "Hello, Jack. What can I get you?"

"Just coffee. Strong and black." He handed her his menu.

Ginny eyed him across the table. "I thought you were starving."

"I was, until a few minutes ago." His jaw muscle pulsed.

Hating the judgmental tone in Ginny's voice, Meg's insides twisted. She glanced at the waitress's puzzled face. "Can I have a refill on my coffee?" She wasn't going anywhere.

The waitress returned with cups and a carafe. While she splashed hot coffee into everyone's mugs, Helen's fork clinked against her plate as she scraped up the last of her dessert.

Meg turned to Ginny. "How is your new job?"

"Well, the Burlington rag isn't the *Times*." She gave a shrug. "But then what is? At least I'm a reporter. More than your boss would allow a woman."

Meg chuckled. "The lake will freeze over in July before Mr. Zimmer allows a woman on his reporting staff."

Ginny put her coffee cup to her lips and sipped. "If it makes you feel any better, he told me that if he were to allow such a thing, he already had a talented woman on staff."

"Oh?" Meg picked up her spoon and absently stirred sugar into her brew. "Who's that?"

"You, of course."

She jerked her attention to Jack's beaming face then to Ginny. "You must have misunderstood."

"He definitely said, 'Meg Alden would get the job if there was one available.'"

Meg set her spoon down. "I wish he'd tell me that."

"Well, you know how it is," Ginny said. "Sometimes men tell everyone else their true feelings instead of the person who should hear them. Give him time. He'll change his mind in a year or two."

"By then I won't be here. Helen and I are moving to California on May thirty-first."

Jack straightened. "That's *News-Tribune* night at the. . .the. . .whatever the building will be called. You need to be there."

"That's what I forgot about the date." Meg glanced at Helen. "Looks like June first is the day."

Helen's brows arched, and she tipped her head. "So be it. Seems like a *News-Trib* affair is a fitting way for you to say farewell."

Meg shrugged as a pall settled over her. Their plans were becoming more real by the minute, money or no money. "I guess so."

Jack inched his chair closer to her, his face serious. "Meg, I need to ask—"

"Here are your orders. Turkey and mashed potatoes for the lady and more coffee for the gentleman." The waitress set Ginny's order in front of her then sloshed coffee into Jack's mug. After adding to Meg's and Helen's cups, she left.

"Jack," Meg picked up a sugar cube with her spoon, "you wanted to ask me something?"

He avoided her gaze. "We'll need a moment at the event to send you off. You know, wishing you congratulations, best wishes, and all that. And don't be surprised if we throw in a gift or two for you to set up housekeeping out there."

He might as well have picked up his knife and stabbed her in the chest. The way he talked, he couldn't care less about her departure or the fact that they'd probably never see each other again. The message was clear. Moving away couldn't happen any faster.

Chapter Twenty-Seven

....

Meg's distorted reflection stared back from the tiny mirror hung on the office's coat closet door. She angled her bell-shaped purple hat to the right then made a face. After adjusting it to the left, she fastened it with an amethyst hat pin. Could she wear the hat till tomorrow's hair appointment?

"Meg, I'm glad you're still here."

She turned as Jack rushed up. "The building committee plans to reveal the winning name tomorrow night."

A shiver shimmied down Meg's spine. Would Fred Newman and his gang show up? If so, there was no telling what might happen. Managing the fragile tension between her and Dad over the last few days was like tiptoeing around broken glass. It could all be over soon. "I'll be there." Maybe Helen could squeeze her in tonight. At least when she asked Dad about the money later, she'd look good doing it.

* * * * *

"That fund is for one purpose only: education. The answer is no." Dad's mustache twitched as he shook out his napkin and placed it on his lap.

Meg gulped. At least it sounded like the funds had survived last March's bank holiday. "It *is* for my education."

He fastened a hard stare on her. "And what school do you plan to attend?"

She held his gaze, determined not to be the one who blinked. "The school of hard knocks."

He picked up his soupspoon. "Very funny. Answer my question."

She drew her lower lip between her teeth. Despite having rehearsed her answers on the way home from Helen's, the words escaped her.

"Do you want to take some correspondence courses?" Mom picked up the bread basket and passed it to Laura.

Meg shook her head. "If I'm to become a reporter, I must work for a large daily and claw my way up. I need the money to move."

Dad's spoon dropped into his soup and brown droplets sprayed onto his white shirt. "No woman is going to become a reporter in this day and age."

Meg raised her chin. "Ginny Colson did."

"Who's she?" Dad dipped his napkin into his water glass and dabbed at the soup spots.

"Jack's friend. She was a feature reporter for the *New York Times*."

He narrowed his eyes. "Why the past tense?"

She plunged her spoon into her soup, lifted it, then let the hot liquid trickle back into the bowl before she answered. "They laid her off."

"Another reason not to pursue a large paper. The first to go would be a woman."

"Ginny's working for the Burlington paper now as a reporter."

"So when do you expect to move to Chicago?"

"I never mentioned Chicago."

"Then where? Milwaukee?"

"Hollywood."

"Hollywood?" Three voices bombarded Meg as Dad's knife clattered onto the table.

"Helen expects to get a beautician job at one of the—"

"I should have known Helen McArdle was behind this." Dad stood. "First she has you getting those permanent waves, and now it's moving to Hollywood."

"But I have a good chance for a job at the *Los Angeles Examiner*. I've been—"

"In my study. Now." Dad marched out of the room.

Meg threw her napkin into a crumpled heap on the table and pushed back her chair. "Laura, you can wipe that gleeful grin off your face and return the suitcase you borrowed. I may be needing it soon." She stood and headed for the kitchen door.

"Meg, wait."

She faced her mother. "What else can he do but kick me out? I'm not a child."

Mom's face fell. "If he refuses your school fund, how can you move?"

"We're supposed to trust God and not lean on our own understanding. If He comes through, I'll have quite a testimony, won't I?"

"If you act according to God's will. I don't sense that's what you're doing."

With Mom's words still ringing in her ears, Meg approached her father's study. She felt in her pocket for a slip of paper she'd tucked there earlier and then knocked.

"Enter." Dad's barked command reverberated through the oak slab. She hauled in a breath and pushed the door open.

From behind his desk, Dad peered at her with reddened eyes. He yanked at his tie and loosened it. "Don't just stand there." He pulled the short end of the tie from the knot and tossed the neckwear on the desk while Meg sat.

"I presume that with the request for your education fund, the story is running this week."

Meg stiffened. "Since I'm not able to use the funds for college, I'd hoped you'd support my aspirations by letting me use the money to move."

"Seems to me Wallace is giving you reporting opportunities right here."

Meg shrugged. "It's only while Mr. Zimmer recuperates."

"Does Oscar know how you're contributing?"

Meg focused on a paperweight in the shape of a judge's gavel. "He knows I'm helping, but he thinks Lester is writing most of the stories. Jack plans to tell him how much I'm involved when he's better. He doesn't want to cause him to have a setback."

"So a good portion of what I've been reading the past couple of weeks has been your work?"

Buoyed by the hint of pride in his voice, Meg nodded. "About half the paper."

"Why isn't Lester helping?"

Meg cringed. "Because he can't write."

"And I presume Oscar thinks he can." Dad narrowed his eyes to tiny, dark slits. "I'm almost afraid to ask the next question."

"Then don't."

His fist pounded the desk. "Meg, if you've done something deceitful, I want to know."

A bitter taste erupted in her throbbing throat. She looked him in the eyes. "I don't think I'm the only one here who's holding back the truth."

Eyes sparking, he jabbed a finger at the door. "Get out."

"I'll be gone by tonight." She stood on wobbling legs.

His face fell. "Where will you stay?"

She raised her shoulders and let them drop. "Maybe God will lead me to a nice room where I'll have peace and quiet." She turned and opened the door.

"Meg, I didn't mean—"

The door slammed behind her.

The leather suitcase Laura borrowed sat on top of Meg's pink chenille bedspread. She unbuckled the straps in an awkward one-handed way and then flipped open the top. Letting go of a sigh, she walked to the closet and tugged several dresses and skirts off their hangers. *Is this really happening?* It was one thing to decide to move in search of her dream, but to be asked to leave the house seemed unreal.

She tossed the clothing on the bed then went downstairs to the phone and lifted the receiver to her ear.

"What number, please?"

She tucked the phone under her chin then pulled the scrap from her pocket and held it up. "Give me 5551."

A gravelly woman's voice came through the connection. "Barkers'."

"I'm answering your ad for a room to rent."

"It's a small room on the third floor. No pets. Two dollars a week. We don't serve meals, but you can use a hot plate if you bring your own."

"Can I see it tonight?"

An arm came around her from behind and depressed the switch hook. Meg faced her father.

"Your mother is upstairs crying." He ran his bloodshot gaze over her face. "Please rethink this. I never said you had to move out."

"That's not how I heard it. It's best if I go."

He averted his eyes. "Your mother will fall apart."

Her heart squeezed. The last person she wanted to hurt was Mom. She returned the receiver to its cradle. "Laura will still be here."

"But Laura isn't you."

"I didn't think it mattered." She left him standing in the hall and headed up the stairs. *What did he mean by "Laura isn't you"?* Of course he was referring to Mom's feelings, not his.

At Meg's tap on her parents' door, a wavering voice beckoned. She raised her chin and stepped into the room. "I'm not moving out tonight."

Mom lifted her swollen eyes from the open Bible on her lap. "At least one prayer was answered." She patted the upholstered ottoman in front of her chair. "Come."

While Meg took the seat, Mom blew her nose into a scallop-edged hanky. "Your father said you're writing articles without Oscar's knowledge. That concerns both of us."

Meg closed her eyes. An ache spread through her chest. She'd let her mother down. "I've been writing most of the articles since Mr. Zimmer was hospitalized, and he thinks Lester is responsible for the stories."

"Why not use Lester?" Mom flipped through her Bible.

"Because he isn't a good writer."

"Doesn't Oscar know that?"

Meg shook her head. "I've been editing Lester's articles behind Mr. Zimmer's back for months."

Mom tipped her head. "Editing? Or rewriting?"

"Rewriting, mostly." She caught her mother's gaze in her own, and her stomach twisted. A sob escaped her throat. "I knew it was the same as lying and told Lester a couple of weeks ago that it had to stop. Then Mr. Zimmer got sick and Jack needed me to get the paper out on time."

"How is it Jack was aware you could write well?"

"He overheard Lester and me talking a few weeks ago and asked about it. I told him I'd already decided to stop the practice. But with Mr. Zimmer ill, there's no one else to write articles." She wiped her wet cheeks with the back of her hand.

"Do you think you're giving Jack a good Christian example?" She glanced at the open Bible. "Listen to what the Word says—"

"I don't need to hear Scripture." Meg flew to her feet. "I already know I'm not a good example."

Mom gripped Meg's hand as though it were a lifeline. "You've always been the daughter I didn't have to worry about straying from the Lord. Now it seems. . ." She tightened her grasp. "God loves you and wants only His best for you."

Meg yanked her hand away and went to the door. "I'm sorry, Mom. I love you and don't want to hurt you, but I have no choice." She left the room and marched down the hall.

Laura appeared in her bedroom doorway before Meg reached her room, and Meg braced herself for a snide remark.

"It's all my fault, isn't it?" Laura blinked.

Meg stared at her sister. "I'll admit, it will be nice not to hear your bratty remarks, but it's not because of you."

A tear trailed down Laura's cheek. "The economy was the reason Dad pulled you out of college. He said he felt terrible doing it since your grades were improving. I'm sorry."

Meg's emotions clawed at her insides as relief and anger battled for attention. She wanted to hug her sister, but the scars were too raw. "I don't understand why you lied, Laura, but thanks for setting me straight. Look on the bright side. I'll soon be gone and you'll have the house and Mom and Dad all to yourself."

She headed toward her room. What had she become? Laura had just confessed her lie and said she was sorry. Still Meg left her with a biting remark. Forgiveness wasn't going to come easy.

Chapter Twenty-Eight

....

On Wednesday night, Jack pulled up to the curb alongside the high school. He glanced over at Meg. She'd done something different with her hair. What, he had no idea, but he liked it. "You were a million miles away over supper. I know the Utopia isn't the best eatery in town, but seeing as we didn't have much time—"

"It doesn't have anything to do with where we ate." The same tightness he'd seen around her eyes and mouth since the morning remained. "I have a lot to consider and barely had time to think, with all my assignments."

He'd dumped a lot of work on her that day, but with Thelma tending to her elderly mother, what choice did he have? Or was she stewing over his bad attitude from last Friday? He'd decided by Saturday that it wasn't his problem and thought things were better since Sunday. "Is it anything to do with my bad mood last Friday?"

She shrugged. "No."

A long silence fell between them.

"My parents know that Mr. Zimmer thinks Lester has been writing the articles this month. They didn't say they would tell him, but knowing my father. . ."

He gave her shoulder a slight squeeze. "But, remember, Oscar knows you're helping with the articles."

"Yeah, the minor stuff, but not the major stories."

Jack drew in a breath and exhaled. "If your father had called Oscar, I'd have heard. No doubt he doesn't want to upset him while he's sick any more than we do." *He probably treats his men friends better than his own daughter.*

In the dusky light, her gaze flicked back and forth over his face. "If not my dad, who's to stop one of the subs or Thelma? They agree it's for the good of the paper and that in his condition it's best he not know. But if one person slips. . ." She lowered her eyelids. Moisture on her long lashes glinted in the streetlight. "I'd rather he know the full truth now. It's not right."

"But we haven't lied."

"Omitting facts is as much a lie as telling them."

Jack's gut twisted. He hadn't thought about it that way. Many of the Proverbs in the Bible said dishonesty in any situation was wrong. "You're right. Oscar needs to know the whole truth. I'll talk to him soon. Did your father mention anything about the Fred Newman business?"

"He presumed the story was going to run when I asked for my education money." She sniffed and took a handkerchief from her coat pocket. "He asked me to leave and then changed his tune because Mom was upset. Not him, mind you, just Mom." Her lower lip quivered.

Jack slid his arm across her shoulders and tugged her close, loving the lilac scent that came with her. He pressed her face into his shoulder. Dangerous territory, but the woman was distressed. "He probably meant it for both of them. Sometimes it's hard for men to express their feelings." If she only knew how true that was.

"He had no trouble expressing himself when he told me to leave." She turned, causing her cast to dig into his ribs, but he wasn't moving for anything.

Jack brought his hand to her chin and lifted her face until they looked eye to eye. He longed to feel her lips against his and imagined their softness.

She stiffened.

He pulled back. "What's wrong?"

"Nothing."

Was she thinking about Matthew? If the guy was waiting out there in California for her to arrive so they could marry, would she snuggle with another man? He needed to know the truth—now. "There's something I want to ask—"

She straightened. "We've got to get inside." She slid over and grabbed her belongings.

He yanked the keys from the ignition and opened his door. Sometimes he wished he'd never heard of California.

* * * * *

Meg entered the auditorium ahead of Jack and scanned the seats. There were probably dozens of places to sit, but who could think after what happened in the car? She'd wanted him to kiss her in the worst way. But she couldn't. She might not like Ginny all that much, but she refused to cooperate with Jack's two-timing ways. Good thing she stayed strong and resisted temptation.

"What about there?" Jack pointed to a pair of seats in the next-to-last row.

Meg nodded, and he guided her with his hand burning a spot on her back like a branding iron. They squeezed past a couple sitting on the end and dropped into their seats.

Meg pulled out her notebook and pencil while Jack did the same, his left arm brushing hers. A trail of goose bumps snaked up her arm. She cast him a sideways glance. He'd shed his coat and hat, tucking the fedora under his seat. Her gaze went to his lips. Lips that moments ago had been so close, she'd felt his breath. He probably was a good kisser. Not that she'd shared kisses with enough men to know what was good or bad.

She faced the front. Movement flashed off to the side, and she turned.

Fred Newman shuffled down the far aisle and took a seat several rows ahead, his eyes riveted in front of him. On the stage, Dad stared at Fred, his mouth cemented in a tight line. Dad shook his head and sat at a table with several others as the committee chairman's call to order quieted the crowd.

The chairman gave a prolonged welcome then introduced the architect and building contractor. Both men rambled on about facts most people already knew. Meg doodled on her notepad. The contractor sat to polite applause, and tension filled the air.

The chairman came to the podium. "And now for the reason most of you are here. Louis Alden, our contest chairman, will make a very important announcement."

"They better not say they're sticking with Northport again," a man behind Meg muttered.

Across the way, Fred moved to the edge of his seat, his jaw working like a cow chewing her cud.

At the lectern, Dad cleared his throat. "Good evening, ladies and gentlemen." He grinned and scanned the crowd. "We have a name I think everyone will approve of."

Someone applauded and then others followed, the sound building like a wave.

Dad sent an intense stare in Fred's direction before looking at his notes. "We had an overwhelming ninety-eight entries, but only one stood out. The dictionary describes the chosen name as a coastal resort area, and that description aptly describes the building and its surroundings. With its exquisite bathhouse facilities and beautiful ballroom, there is no more appropriate name than the one chosen for our fine-looking structure.

"In a few months, the summer sun will shine down on our beautiful new recreation building, which will henceforth be called. . ."

He let his gaze travel the span of the auditorium.

"The Riviera."

Everyone took a collective breath while Meg whispered the name and liked the sound.

Dad held up an envelope. "This contains the twenty-five-dollar prize won by Mrs. Hobart Smith for her excellent submission. Is Mrs. Smith. . . ?"

Meg gasped. Murmurs broke out in pockets around the large room. Dad asked again for Mrs. Smith to come forward.

Meg surveyed the seats. Had Violette been warned not to come?

"Someone from the committee will contact Mrs. Smith tomorrow." Dad peered at Fred Newman.

Fred nodded his head, gave a slight salute, then sauntered out of the auditorium.

Jack bent his head toward Meg. "Why is everyone so stirred up? I think it's a wonderful name."

"Mrs. Smith is Violette Fenner."

His eyes widened. "The same lady who won the first contest?"

"Bingo."

On stage, the chairman called a man to the podium to discuss budget numbers.

"Gus is waiting to set up the Linotype. Let's go."

Meg did double time to keep up with Jack's long stride. By the time they reached his car, he'd rattled off the points they needed to make in the announcement. The piece would sit above the fold with the headline "It's the Riviera." The paragraph would say that the winning name was submitted by Mrs. Smith and not mention she was the previous prizewinner. And would Meg find the *Webster's* and look up the word's description?

* * * * *

Gus set a green-tinted Coke bottle on his worktable and flashed a grin as Meg and Jack stepped into the office. "So what's the good word?"

"The Riviera," Jack and Meg answered in unison. They looked at each other and laughed.

Gus repeated the name. "I like it. Sounds classy."

"I agree." Meg headed for a bookcase while Jack rolled a sheet of paper into his typewriter.

"So who won the contest?" Gus ambled toward Composing.

Meg caught Jack's eye. "A Mrs. Hobart Smith. She wasn't even there."

Gus chortled. "For twenty-five smackers, I'd show up. She must not need the money."

Meg one-armed the dictionary to her desk and flipped to the *R*'s. "I found the word, Jack." Then her face heated and she glanced at Gus, relieved that he was busy with the Linotype and likely hadn't noticed how she'd used Jack's first name. "Mr. Wallace, let me know when you want me to read the description."

He looked up from his typing, and she almost dissolved at his crooked grin. "You can begin now, Miss Alden."

She glanced at the page. How had she ended up in the *T*'s? She flipped back and landed in the *Q*'s. "I had it a minute ago. Sorry." *Did he just chuckle?* "It's not funny," she mouthed, finding the page.

"You're cute when you get flustered."

He'd whispered the words across the expanse between their desks, but she peeked at Gus anyway. The man had his back to them.

"Ready when you are."

She read the description of "riviera" as her dad had earlier.

Jack stopped typing. "Thanks. Got it."

She slammed the book shut. "I'll go ahead and walk home."

He looked over at her, his eyes telegraphing concern. "It's black as pitch out there. I'll run you home."

"I'll be okay. Lake Geneva isn't Chicago."

He typed a few more words then ripped the paper out of the machine. "Article's done." He stood and called over his shoulder as he passed her, "Don't you dare leave. That's an order."

Meg saluted him and giggled. She hadn't had this much fun in a long while.

Like an unwanted guest, a wave of realization washed over her. In a few weeks she'd board a westbound train, out of Jack's life forever. But Ginny would still figure strongly in his world, and even if she and Jack didn't end up together, Chicago was full of attractive women who would love a man like him.

Jack returned from Composing, gathered up his hat and coat from where he'd tossed them on Lester's desk, then took Meg by the arm and led her toward the outside. "Night, Gus."

In the car, Meg pressed herself against the door.

Jack put the vehicle in motion. "If you sit any farther away, you'll be on the running board. You okay?"

Meg straightened. "I'm just tired."

Silence hung between them until Jack made a U-turn in front of her house and pulled up to the curb. He faced her and stretched his arm across the back of the seat. "Before I walk you to the door, I need to apologize for almost taking advantage of the situation and making a move to kiss you earlier. I had no right to do that given your plans for California."

"How does my moving affect whether you kiss me or not?"

"Because you and Matthew. . ."

The man wasn't making sense. "Matthew could care less who I kiss. He's living in Minneapolis and engaged to be married."

Jack slumped against the seat. "Then who is Mattie?"

"Mattie?" Meg frowned. "My girlfriend who used to work at the paper. She lives in Santa Monica."

"Mattie is a woman? I thought. . .well, when I heard your old boy-friend's name was Matthew. . ."

His words weren't making sense. "Mattie's real name is Matilda, but don't ever tell her I told you that. She hates it."

"She's a woman."

Meg gave a nervous laugh. "Last I checked. Her husband was on the crew building that big dam on the Colorado River. He was killed last year."

Even in the dark she could see his face clear enough to know that he was grinning. "Then you're not planning to get married?"

"Married? Hopefully someday, but not soon. Jack, this conversation is confusing me."

"Me too. Maybe someday I'll explain." He opened his door and climbed out.

Meg chuckled. Whatever gave him the idea she was engaged? He sure sounded relieved that she was still unattached. Not that it changed any-thing. She was still moving, and he still had Ginny.

Jack held her arm as they strolled to the door. She wished someone had remembered to turn on the porch light so she could see what was likely his red face. They took the two steps to the tiny porch and faced each other.

He shifted his weight from one foot to the other. "I feel like an idiot. You kept saying 'Mattie,' and I thought it was your pet name for Matthew."

She giggled. "I'm glad you finally asked. But I don't remember ever telling you Matthew's name."

"You didn't. Let's just say I heard it from someone else who shall remain nameless."

She crossed her arms. "I can only think of two women who would tell you that. Either Helen or Emily. But I'm glad you were straightened out before you bought me a wedding gift."

"Me too. Very much," he whispered then bent his head. "Since you're not taken, I'd like to finish what I started before the meeting."

Stomach tingling, she stood on her toes and tilted her chin.

The outside light flicked on, and they stepped apart.

Jack chucked her under her chin. "Best we just say good night."

She reached for the door handle. "Right. See you tomorrow."

"Night, Meg. Sleep tight."

Her chin still tingling from his gentle touch, she waited until his taillights disappeared around the corner and then let go of a sigh. She stepped inside and shut the door.

"I suppose you two have a story ready to break in the morning."

She faced her father. "Just a short announcement that the new name is the Riviera chosen by Mrs. Smith." She stepped past him. "Not a single word about Mrs. Smith being the former Miss Fenner."

He grabbed her arm. "Mrs. Smith is Violette Fenner?"

She studied his widened eyes, and relief washed over her. *He didn't know*. "I really thought you knew. Can you tell me the truth about Fred now?"

He released her arm. "There's nothing to tell." He turned and headed toward the kitchen.

Chapter Twenty-Nine

. . . .

"If you plan to attend Good Friday services this afternoon, I hope you'll consider changing clothes." Mom peered over her coffee cup and fastened her brown eyes on Meg.

The Rice Krispies she'd swallowed lodged halfway down, feeling like a lump of dough. Meg looked down at her yellow print dress. She'd always loved Easter weekend, but what was she to do when God seemed to have deserted her? She raised her head. "I may have to work."

"Why? You've always had Good Friday afternoon off." The lines around Mom's mouth tightened. "I don't like this, Meg."

"The paper is closed from noon till three like always, but I can't afford to take the time off if I'm to get my research done." Her words sounded hollow to her ears. She pushed her bowl away. "I can't finish this."

"I'll eat it, but I won't let you go to work on an empty stomach. You can munch on toast while you walk." Mom went to the counter and took two slices of bread from the bread box. She popped them into the toaster then turned. "What's going on, Meg? You haven't been yourself since Jack started at the paper."

Meg shrugged. "It has nothing to do with Jack. Like I said before, when I read the Bible, it seems dry and lifeless. When I pray, God doesn't answer."

Mom studied her with watery eyes, and an ache filled Meg's chest. She jumped up and quickstepped across the room, wrapping her arms around her mother. "The research can wait. I'll meet you at church."

Mom returned the hug. "I hope you're doing this to please God, not me. Scripture tells us He's the same yesterday, today, and forever."

Meg looked her mother in the eyes. "I know what the Bible says,

213

but when I trusted Him to give me the desires of my heart, He didn't come through."

The toast popped up, and Mom spread butter and jam on the slices. She wrapped them in waxed paper and handed them to Meg. "Maybe your desires need changing."

Meg turned away. "I'll see you at church."

Wearing her three-year-old navy suit and carrying her toast, which by now was cold, Meg headed down Main Street. Wasn't it God who gave her the ability to write and the desire to be a reporter? Why would He do that just to block the opportunities for her success? She'd attend church, but her heart wouldn't be in it. She unwrapped the toast and forced it down. To not do so would be wasteful.

* * * * *

Meg studied her notes from the previous day's interview with Violette Smith. The two-time winner said she hadn't expected to win but was grateful because of the money. Violette doubted they would attend the grand opening since they didn't dance, and that was the end of that. No feature article like Meg had hoped. She checked her watch. Almost eleven thirty. She'd come back after church and rough up the beginnings of the news article summarizing the contest outcome.

Her telephone rang, and she reached for the receiver. Probably Mom, making sure she was still planning on attending the service.

"This is Fred Newman. I'm ready to talk."

Her heart racing, she lowered her voice. "When?"

"Two o'clock at my house."

"Today's Good Friday."

"So? Haven't been to church since I buried my wife and son."

Fred had been married? Had his family died in an accident? No wonder he was so crotchety. "I can't be there until after three."

"Too late."

She'd promised Mom, but this was important. "If I can find a ride, I'll come." A stabbing pain penetrated her conscience.

He harrumphed. "I don't suppose you'll get a lift with everyone in church. Meet me by the statue in Flat Iron Park at two."

Tension eased out of her shoulders. The Flat Iron Park statue was only a couple blocks' walk. "I can come at three-thirty," she said, her voice firm.

"Two o'clock or nothing."

Meg winced. Her morning conversation with Mom echoed in her ears. She should decline. Maybe she could attend the service at noon and slip out at one thirty. "Okay. I'll see you then."

She hung up as Jack ambled over. "What time do you plan to leave for the service?"

She stared into his ardent face. His excitement over church when hers had ebbed continually challenged her, but surely he'd understand. "Soon, but I'll have to slip out early." She grinned. "Guess who called?"

He cocked his head. "Who? Mattie? The *Examiner*?"

Meg glanced around the nearly empty office. Only Emily remained. She lowered her voice. "Fred Newman wants to meet at Flat Iron Park at two. He's ready to talk."

"On Good Friday?"

"He said he doesn't care because he doesn't go to church."

"Maybe if he went, he'd change his attitude." Jack's jaw muscle throbbed against his cheek. "Couldn't you reschedule?"

"I tried, but he said it was two o'clock or nothing."

He crossed his arms. "He's baiting you. Don't go."

Meg flew to her feet and pressed her fist on her desk, leaning on her arm. "And miss what might be a break in our story? I'm surprised you'd say that, newsman that you are."

"And newsman that I am, I recognize a trap when I see one." His voice reverberated in the air.

"I don't believe you." She matched his raised voice and then some.

"I'm ordering you not to go. I'll see you at church." Eyes sparking, Jack turned and strode to his office.

Meg glared at his closed door as heat crept up her neck. How dare he shout orders at her. She glanced at Emily and caught the girl's wide-eyed stare before she turned away.

Meg cleaned off her desk then stared once more at Jack's closed door. She heaved a sigh then walked to the entrance. "I'm leaving, Emily. Have a happy Easter."

The girl opened her mouth as if to say something but then shut it. She glanced out the window. "Are you walking to church?"

"Yes. Why?"

"It looks like rain. If you wait until my father comes, we can give you a ride."

Meg stepped to the window. A thin layer of haze covered what had been blue sky earlier. "I don't see any dark clouds."

"Over toward the west it looks threatening."

Meg forced a smile. "I won't melt."

* * * * *

When Meg walked up to the church, Mom and Laura were waiting at the door, Mom in a dark skirt and white blouse and Laura in a brown dress.

Her mother glanced around. "I thought Jack might be with you."

"He's still working. Let's go in."

Mom gave her a curious look but fell in step behind Laura. Meg followed and settled next to her mother. She opened her Bible then twisted around. Her gaze found Jack sitting several rows back. Their gazes locked, and he scowled.

She turned away. The rat must have taken a longer route to avoid her. Maybe Fred *was* baiting her, but what if he wasn't and she missed out on hearing the truth? The organist began the prelude, and she bowed her head.

Lord, please show me whether I should leave or stay.

Dad arrived as the congregation was standing to sing the first hymn. Before he could step in, Meg slipped into the aisle and gestured for him to sit next to Mom. He gave her a puzzled look but followed her lead.

Three hymns, a short meditation, and two more hymns later, Meg gathered her purse. If God had responded to her earlier prayer, He must have spoken so softly she didn't hear it. She nudged Dad. "I need to leave. I'll see you at home."

His brows knit together as the lines around his mouth creased. "Are you sick?"

She shook her head and hurried down the aisle, her eyes focused straight ahead. With one look at Jack, her legs might give out before she could reach the double doors that opened into the narthex. Meg slipped inside and let the door close softly. No one had followed. Tamping down hurt feelings, she opened the church's outside door, peeked out, and shut it before the rain could blow in. Emily should take up weather forecasting. Now what?

Voices drifted in from the sanctuary and heaviness settled over her shoulders. The congregation was reading the crucifixion scene in unison. Words she almost knew by heart. Should she slip back inside? But if she learned the truth from Fred and it didn't implicate her father, she could clear his name.

The Lost and Found box caught her attention. She spotted a black umbrella and dashed over to grab it.

* * * * *

Meg tossed the inside-out umbrella into a park trash can. A wind gust had taken it out back at the school yard. She hunched over, praying that her spring coat had kept her cast dry. She glanced over at the whitecaps on the lake then toward the far end of the park. The Three Graces statue beckoned, looking as cold and alone as Meg felt. Did Fred wait on the other side? Or was he sitting in that truck parked farther down? She placed her foot on the grass, and her right heel sank into the ground. She tugged it back out, drew in a breath, and took another step, careful to land on the ball of her foot. Icy water seeped into her shoe.

Meg continued across the grass, making sure to step on the balls of her feet. She slogged onto the cement apron that surrounded the three toga-clad stone ladies then pushed her water-soaked hair out of her eyes and surveyed her surroundings. Not a squirrel in sight, or a bird. Even the parked truck was gone. Well, she'd find a spot out of the wind and wait.

She rounded the base to the second of its three sides and stopped to read the words etched into the stone: *In Memory of Good Friends at Lake Geneva*. She continued to the third side, where a list of women's names had been carved into the base. How had she forgotten that the statue had been donated in celebration of women being granted the right to vote? Those women, long deceased, had been part of the suffrage movement. Meg ran her fingertips over the names and whispered, "Thank you." If they could succeed with the right to vote, surely she could do her part for journalism.

She lifted her gaze to the three sculptured ladies, ignoring the pounding rain slapping her face. "I'm afraid I lost this one, ladies. I guess Jack was right."

"Right about what?"

Chapter Thirty

....

Meg spun around and gasped. "What are you doing here?"

"Looking for you."

Warmth washed over her, replacing the chill that had attached itself to her bones. *Jack came for me.* She drew in a breath, but it caught somewhere in her throat.

His eyes twinkled as his smile lit up the gloom. "You'd better get under here before you get any wetter."

Meg scurried under his huge black umbrella and ran her gaze over his handsome face. "Why aren't you in church?"

"When the rain started pelting the windows like a tommy-gun attack, I decided I needed to find you." His eyes softened. "Guess who I met at the door with the same intention?"

"Who?"

"Your father."

She figured looking for her was the last thing Dad would do. But then, she'd never expected Jack to come either. Especially after their argument.

"I didn't think it wise for your father to find you talking to Fred if he showed up. I told him I had a hunch where you'd gone, and he agreed that I should search for you." He looked about. "Fred didn't come?"

She expelled a breath. "No. And don't you dare say 'I told you so.'"

"It's tempting, but I won't."

He wrapped his arm around her and drew her against his chest. His citrusy scent tickled her nose, and his heart thumped beneath her ear, steady and strong. He'd come and nothing else mattered. Not Fred Newman. Not even that her hair must be frizzed into tiny coils.

She nestled closer and shut her eyes. Would he have come looking for her if he didn't care? But helping was part of his nature. She shouldn't take it seriously.

"I'm sorry I lost my temper this morning."

An apology? She snuggled closer and tipped her face up to meet Jack's gaze. "I deserved it. You were right."

"It doesn't matter. I'm sorry for embarrassing you in front of Emily."

"And I shouldn't have shouted back."

His lips spread into a crooked smile while he pushed a lock of damp hair off her face. "Do you know how irresistible you are, soaking wet?" He traced a finger around her mouth then lowered the umbrella until it enveloped them like a cocoon.

"Not really." She lifted her chin until she felt his mint-scented breath caressing her mouth. His lips brushed hers, and a surge of warmth spread through her body. She wrapped her free arm around him as their hungry mouths found each other. The kiss deepened, his lips so soft against hers. Tingles swirled in her stomach, the pitter-patter on the umbrella drowning out all sounds except her heart's tattoo against her breastbone. How silly it was to fight.

A sudden chill trailed down her back. She had to be careful. She broke the kiss and eased away. "I should get home and into dry clothes."

"I know, but it's nice and dry under here. Let's stay just a minute longer." Jack looked at her through half-closed eyes. "I've wanted to kiss you for so long, Meg." He kissed the tip of her nose then trailed kisses back to her mouth.

She quivered as a tiny moan escaped her throat.

He broke the kiss and held her tightly against his chest.

She didn't want to move, but what if Fred was standing there watching them? Or anyone, for that matter. She tilted her head back and whispered, "What if word gets out that we were necking in Flat Iron Park on Good Friday?" Using her thumb, she wiped a lipstick smudge from the corner of his mouth.

His smile dissolved. "You're right. Let's get you home."

All at once, she didn't want to say good-bye. "I'll change and then you can bring me back to work." She smoothed her wet jacket.

"I told everyone not to bother returning after three. I'll go to the office and wait in case anyone comes or calls. Meanwhile, here's one more for the road." Like nails to a magnet their lips came together in one long, delicious kiss.

A minute later, he took her arm and guided her across the grass toward his car. No need to worry about her heels sinking in, because she floated at least a foot off the ground.

* * * * *

Meg sank into the lilac-scented bubbles. She'd squeezed out the last of her favorite bubble bath and intended to breathe in every bit of its soothing aroma.

Resting her casted arm on top of the armrest Dad had built, she closed her eyes and pressed her fingertips to her lips. Less than an hour ago, Jack had pulled her under the umbrella and into the most romantic kiss imagined. Forget those dreamy movie scenes Helen always went on about. Her hero had come for her through the driving rain and then drawn her into his warm, dry cocoon and kissed her deeply. Giggling, she sank into the sudsy water, nearly dunking her casted arm.

She reached for her washcloth then pressed the warm cloth to her lips, reaching to relive the first moment their lips met and all defenses drained out of her. Was she falling in love with Jack? Was he falling for her? She wanted to ask, but shouldn't he be the one to say something first? By the time he walked her to the door and planted a soft kiss on her forehead, she'd come to her senses. She wasn't his type, not like Ginny or any of those debutantes in Chicago. Maybe she was good for a fling while he bided his time in Lake Geneva, but not for life.

A tap on the door broke into her thoughts. "Meg, it's Mom. Can I come in?"

The family was home. She braced herself for the barrage of questions. "Come in."

Mom stepped into the room and settled on the commode, smoothing her apron over her skirt. "Where did you go this afternoon?"

"I had an appointment with a source." Meg kept her eyes on a chipped wall tile straight ahead.

"In the middle of Good Friday?"

"The person doesn't attend church. It was the only time he could meet."

"Where did you go?"

"Flat Iron Park."

"In the pouring rain, without an umbrella. Meg, I—"

She faced her mom, who sat stone still, her hands clasped in her lap. "I borrowed one from the Lost and Found at church, but the wind blew it inside out."

"Did you get the needed information?"

Meg swished her free hand through the water. "He never showed." She palmed tears out of her eyes, ignoring the sting from the bubbles. "The man made a mockery of me. I'm sorry for upsetting you."

"Am I allowed to ask who the source is?"

Meg huffed, sending bubbles into the air. "Fred Newman."

Mom stiffened and crossed her arms. "I wouldn't trust that snake farther than I could toss him."

A jolt coursed through Meg. Mom didn't talk that way about anyone. "Why do you say that?"

"I have my reasons." The tautness left Mom's face, and she let her hands slide into her lap. "Things aren't always as they seem." Her brown eyes searched Meg's face. "Wanting to be a reporter is fine, but not when it obsesses you and tears your family apart."

Meg scooped up a handful of bubbles and studied them. "I planned on attending the whole service, but when he called this morning, I had to agree. I'm trying to clear Dad's name, not besmirch it. I don't know why, when it's obvious Dad doesn't care about what I want."

Mom's jaw dropped. "Of course he cares about what you want. How can you say that?"

She flicked a soap bubble into the air. "If he did, he wouldn't try to block me from pursuing my dream, insisting that I work for him instead, doing something I detest."

Mom came to the side of the tub and fell to her knees. She wrapped her arms around Meg. "He's always been awkward at showing his love for both you girls, but he was only trying to protect you. Don't forget, he stopped insisting you work for him."

Meg gave in to her tears and let them come. "Protect me how?"

Mom sat back, her long knit sleeves dripping water. "The night he said he wanted you to be his secretary, he told me he doesn't want you to fail. Your father feels duty-bound to guard you from more disappointment. I tried to assure him that God is your Protector, but he said that as your father, it was his responsibility." A hint of a smile crossed her lips. "So I interfered in a practical way by fixing the ketchup soup and getting my job at the library."

A lump rose in Meg's throat. She'd been so immersed in her internal and outward battles with Dad, she'd not thought of how much Mom had sacrificed for her. "You've done a lot for me, and I've been unappreciative. Forgive me, Mom. I'm so sorry."

Mom squeezed the fingertips that poked out of Meg's cast. "That's what mothers do, dear daughter. You'll learn that for yourself someday."

Meg huffed. "*If* I ever get married and have children."

"Oh you will. In fact, I would be surprised if Jack isn't the man God has for you, and I will be very pleased if he is. He's mature, considerate, kind, and he has a growing faith in God."

Meg stared at her mother. "Does he?"

"Jack has gone to church every Sunday since he began joining us for services, even while running the paper. He's still searching, but I have a feeling that God is going to take hold of his heart. And when He does, look out."

Meg had to agree, and warmth filled her stomach at the thought of Jack's growing interest in God.

She had to change the subject off Jack. "I still don't understand why God isn't answering my prayers about a reporting job."

Mom let out a loud breath. "Maybe it's because you place conditions on your prayers, saying, 'I'll trust You, God, if You allow me to get a promotion.'"

"There's nothing to be promoted to."

"With his father in the sanitarium, I'm assuming Jack will move on to the *Beacon* when Oscar recovers. Then what will happen to his position?"

Meg huffed. "I've been asking for a reporter position since long before Jack arrived. I thought God would change Mr. Zimmer's mind like He changed Pharaoh's heart. But it's not going to happen." She looked at Mom. "I wish I had a faith like yours. You continue to trust God no matter what life throws at you."

"You're letting your will push against God's, instead of submitting to Him and seeing where He takes you. Remember the cross, Meg, and what the Lord did for you there. Nothing you are allowed to suffer can ever compare. Nothing."

"I know what He did for me, but if I don't at least try to get ahead by moving out West, I'll never have peace." She grabbed her washcloth. "Is it okay if I wear a dressing gown to dinner?"

Mom stood. "I asked Laura to call Jack and invite him to supper. It's the least we can do after he left the service to find you." She winked. "I suggest you put on something pretty." She reached into her apron pocket and extracted a white envelope. "This came today. I admit, I was tempted to hide it, but that wouldn't be right." She propped the business-sized envelope on a tiny shelf that hung above the commode.

The door closed behind Mom, and Meg scrambled out of the tub. The envelope taunted her with the name *Los Angeles Examiner* printed in bold letters on the return address. She wrapped a towel around herself and stared at the imprint. In some ways it was easier not knowing for sure whether the answer was yes or no, because then she could keep the hope alive. But the moment of truth had come. She opened the envelope and unfolded the single sheet of paper, skimming the first paragraph and moving on to the next.

Mattie speaks highly of your typing abilities and keenness for
hard work. I would be pleased to hold the position if you arrive in
Los Angeles no later than June 15.

Good news, except for two things. Dad had to agree to give her the money, and she was falling for Jack.

* * * * *

By the time Meg flitted downstairs wearing a black skirt and a soft gray sweater, Jack was in the living room with Dad, listening to the news. She waved at him and continued into the kitchen. "Am I too late to help?"

Mom turned from arranging sandwiches on a large platter, their traditional Good Friday supper. "Not so fast. What did the letter say?"

"Mattie's boss is holding a position if I can be there by June fifteenth." Her wavering voice hardly sounded excited.

Mom's forced smile dissolved. "Since you plan to leave on June first, you'll be there. You can ladle soup into the tureen. Laura is filling the water glasses."

Meg moved to the stockpot and scooped up a ladleful of soup. "If Dad gives me my school fund, I'll be there." She released the fragrant soup into the tureen. "That's a big *if*."

"You know how he always balks at first but then comes around. Meg, I've been thinking about our conversation."

Meg paused the ladle in midair.

"Has something happened between you and Jack that you're not talking about?"

Meg's cheeks heated. "Why?" She slid the dipper into the pot and filled it.

"The way he charged into that rainstorm to find you—a man doesn't do something like that unless he cares deeply for the woman. And the way you seemed to be on the defensive earlier when I suggested that Jack would be a good man for you. . ." Mom grinned. "Are you sure you want to move?"

Meg let the soup fall into the tureen. "Jack has lots of women friends. Besides, it can't be more than friendship since, despite his coming to church, he hasn't professed the faith. And we both know it takes more than church attendance to make a person right with God."

A vision of her visiting from California several years down the road drifted into Meg's thoughts. She'd stop by the *Beacon* to say hello to Jack and Ginny, who would be married, and Ginny would be the *Beacon*'s first woman reporter. An ache stabbed at Meg's heart. "But even if we married, I'd still have to move." Meg set the ladle down and headed toward the dining room door. She needed some distance.

"Chicago's a whole lot closer than California. But I only want—" The closing door cut off the rest of Mom's words.

Meg regarded the dining room table as the image of Jack working at the *Beacon* reentered her thoughts. This time *she* sat at a typewriter in the place of Ginny, pounding out her latest article then moving a hand to her rounded belly—

"Something smells good."

Meg faced Jack, feeling as if he'd read her crazy daydreams. "Mom's onion soup. Our tradition on Good Friday."

He ran his eyes over her, approval written on his face. "You look nice."

"At least dry and not like a drowned rabbit." She looked away, lest her gaze linger on those eyes, his boyish smile, and those tender lips that had kissed her. Was Mom right about his feelings for her? She forced her thoughts back to reality.

He came closer. "A most appealing drowned rabbit."

His gaze settled on her mouth. Was he going to kiss her right there in the dining room? Her thoughts went to the letter now stuffed in her lingerie drawer. "I heard from Mr. Gibbons at the *Examiner*."

His face fell, and he averted his gaze. "And?"

"He says that on Mattie's recommendation alone, he'll hold the typist job if I can be there by June fifteenth."

He jammed his hands into his pockets, went to the window, and stared out. "Looks like you're on your way."

Was that a catch in his voice? "Yes, if my dad allows me my college fund."

The door to the kitchen flew open, and Mom came through. "Jack, can you carry the soup to the table?"

"Sure." He turned and followed Mom into the kitchen.

Meg stared at the still-swinging door. Her mother was right. There was something between her and Jack, and Jack and Ginny, and Jack and whomever's broken heart he'd left behind. Time to move before hers lay shattered on the new ballroom floor.

Chapter Thirty-One

....

Strolling through Elm Park with the lake as blue as the sky and Meg by his side was usually enough to cause Jack to feel that all was right with the world. But right then, what he really wanted was to sit, and all the benches were taken. Since they'd attended the sunrise Easter service and the rest of the Aldens were at the second service, this was the only time he'd have alone with Meg.

Earlier they'd enjoyed a pancake breakfast in the fellowship hall with the men of the church, including Mr. Alden, doing the cooking. Jack shifted his Bible to his right hand as they trekked down the shore path. "Let's keep walking. Maybe we'll find an empty bench toward the Riviera."

She rewarded him with a smile. "I love the new name." She picked up her pace to match Jack's and peered down the shore toward the building. "Doesn't it look magnificent? I can't wait for the grand opening. The ballroom is going to be beautiful."

"It's a swell name. You really are attached to the place, aren't you?"

She appeared pensive as they walked with only their muffled footfalls and a bobwhite calling to its mate to disturb the silence. Despite her frown, she looked adorable with her wide-brimmed straw hat festooned with pink flowers resting on her dark curls. His gaze fell to her red lips, and memories of their kiss under the umbrella tumbled into his mind. Of her soft lips that seemed to not want to stop kissing him. The feelings were mutual. He pulled his gaze away. Never thought an umbrella would be so handy for more than keeping dry.

"What are you smiling at?"

Jack started and cast her a sideways glance. "A very pleasant memory, but forget that for now. I could turn the question around and ask why the frown. You seem preoccupied this morning."

"I was just wishing the black cloud of my father's and Fred Newman's connected past would disappear. Mom mentioned something—"

Jack stopped and faced her. "Miss Alden, this is an order. If this is related to work, there's plenty of time tomorrow to sort out the situation. No work talk today." He started walking again. "Let's grab that bench up ahead before anyone else gets it. There's something else I want to discuss."

* * * * *

Seated in the shade, Meg buttoned her jacket against the chill, wishing that whatever Jack wanted to talk about could wait. He probably wanted to make sure she didn't read too much into their kisses on Friday afternoon.

A short distance away, the Riviera stood like a newly crowned king surveying its domain. Soon it would be a beehive of activity. She'd been happy to see that old dance hall come down with its unpleasant memories and had anticipated spending good times in the beautiful new ballroom. Now, here she was, planning to move thousands of miles away, never to enjoy it. Overhead a cloud blocked the sun, and her mind went to her father. As much as she felt misunderstood by Dad, she didn't want to move away while on bad terms with him.

"Isn't this a glorious day?"

She crossed her arms. "I guess so."

Jack jumped to his feet and boxer-punched the air, his navy-and-gold patterned tie flying in the breeze. "I feel as if I could take on the world and win."

She huffed a laugh. Cheerful people were bad enough to tolerate when one didn't share their mood, but today Jack was downright obnoxious. How could he have so much energy after all those pancakes? "I've been thinking, Jack. Maybe I should leave the mystery of my dad and Fred Newman with you and be done with it."

"Hey, remember?" Jack sat and stretched his arm across the back of the bench, cupping her shoulder with his fingers. "No thinking about work."

She faced him. "How can I forget the rumor when my father's glare is a constant reminder?"

"He didn't glare at you during breakfast."

"Yes, he did. Sometimes it's subtle."

"Sometimes it's imagined."

She tossed him a disparaging look.

"Didn't he agree to give you your education fund?"

She nodded. "Yes. After Mom's interference yesterday."

"And wasn't he ready to drive around in Friday's storm, looking for you?"

Her heart squeezed.

Jack flipped through his Bible, and the pages made a crinkling sound. "Something happened today during the sermon. As I read the passage Reverend quoted, I understood the words in a way I hadn't before. Then when I waited outside while you put the ham in the oven, I read a different section and the same thing happened."

Excitement bubbled in Meg's chest, and as if on cue, the sun broke through the clouds. "Do you remember what you were thinking about beforehand?"

"Yeah. How full of pride and selfishness I've been, and how Jesus suffered my punishment for me. I prayed to God, apologizing for my sins, and a peace came over me. I knew He'd forgiven me."

"You've been saved, Jack."

His eyes widened. "Saved?"

She blinked and grinned. "It's a word for becoming a Christian. I'm surprised you didn't go forward when Reverend Hellman asked people to do so."

"I thought about it, but when no one else got up, I didn't. Does that mean I'm not a Christian?"

Meg hated herself for the tinge of regret she felt. Despite how upset she'd been with God, she could never marry a man who didn't share her faith, and that had helped to keep her from entertaining much thought of a future with Jack, no matter how delicious his kisses were.

"Did you hear my question?"

She turned. "You don't need to say or do anything in public to make your faith authentic."

"Good. When were you. . .um, saved? Were you as excited as me?"

Meg's thoughts drifted to the day her fourth-grade Sunday school teacher explained how the Lord had died on the cross for her sins, giving her a way to heaven. That night, Mom had led her through a prayer to commit her life to Him.

She smiled. "When I was nine. I was too excited to sleep, and I felt like I was floating." Meg shrugged as a wistful feeling washed over her. *Like how I felt on Friday night after kissing you.* What was it she'd heard Reverend Hellman say? The order of priority was God first, then spouse and family, then work. Somehow she'd managed to reverse the order.

Jack squeezed her shoulder. "This is the best day. It's Easter, I've become part of God's family, and I have my girl with me."

Meg's pulse raced. "I'm your girl?"

Jack's smile dissolved. "Of course you are. Do you think I go around kissing women like that all the time in front of God and everyone? Granted, we were under the umbrella and no one else was dumb enough to be out in that storm, but I would have kissed you no matter what."

"I thought. . .well, what about Ginny?"

His brows raised. "Ginny? You think Ginny and I are. . . ?"

"Why wouldn't I think that? You nearly held a celebration party when she showed up, found her a job, and have been with her a lot. She's beautiful and polished and—"

Jack's lips suddenly connected with hers, soft, tender. In a flash he sat back, a grin splitting his face. "Only way I knew to stop all that meaningless chatter. Ginny and I go way back. We worked on the college paper together, and she got into trouble because girls were only allowed to work behind the scenes, not report the stories. But Ginny thumbed her nose and slipped a news article into an edition. She was booted off the paper immediately. I went to her defense and nearly got the same treatment. It was only because of a sympathetic professor that I wasn't. Ginny and I went our separate ways after graduation, but we've always kept in touch as best we could. Ginny is like a second sister to me."

Meg bit her lower lip. "You don't look like brother and sister, always hugging each other."

He moved closer to her. "I'm a hugger. My sister and I hug. My mom and I hug. My good friends and I hug." He drew her nearer. "And my girlfriend and I hug, if she lets me."

The sun had gone behind another cloud, but warmth surrounded Meg like a perfect summer day. "I like hugs too." She glanced in both directions. "Although I'm not sure I want the world to see so much affection."

He laughed. "Nor do I. Trust me, if we were alone, I'd be hugging you to pieces right now. And throwing in a kiss or two." He brought his mouth close to her ear. "Too bad we don't have an umbrella today."

Meg giggled. "We'll just have to take walks in the rain." She faced him and their gazes met. She could drown in those deep blue eyes. "I'd love to be your girl, Jack."

He reached across and squeezed the fingertips of her left hand, sending tingles up her casted arm. "Ever since the first day I was at the paper, I've wanted to hear that."

Meg forced herself to take her eyes off him and stared out at the lake. "We have to remember, though, I'm to move soon. . .but we can enjoy the time until I do."

She felt his arm, still resting across her shoulders, tense.

"You may not have to move so far away to get past writing society news. There are other ways of writing for a newspaper."

"Like what?"

"Have you ever thought about being a columnist?"

"Don't columnists have to be based at a big paper? I'm not sure what I'd write about."

"Can't say, off the top of my head. I'm only suggesting that you not limit yourself to one direction. Writing a column could lead to reporting opportunities later, and with wire services these days, you don't have to live in the big cities to do the job." He pulled out his watch and flipped it open. "If we start walking now, by the time we get to your place, your family should be home."

They strolled up to the house just as the family car rolled down the street and pulled into the driveway. Mom waved them over, and Jack carried in the table decorations from the pancake breakfast while Meg followed with a bundle of tablecloths. She went down the twisting narrow steps to the cellar to leave the dirty linens then returned to a kitchen already saturated with the smell of baking ham. The men's voices drifted in from the living room, and she stepped into the hallway.

"Jack, that's wonderful," Dad's voice boomed.

"If your wife hadn't invited me to church, I'd probably still be wallowing around, trying to find my purpose."

"God does have a calling for each of us."

Meg smiled. At least Dad's acrimonious attitude toward Jack had softened.

"Meg and I had an interesting discussion a few minutes ago, and I suggested. . ."

The voices lowered, and Meg inched closer to the arched opening.

"Meg, are you eavesdropping?"

With her voice projection, Laura was a good choice for the lead in the play. Meg faced her sister. "Just passing through. Keep your voice down."

"Looked like eavesdropping to me."

"Meg, is that you? Come in here," Dad called out.

Hoping the heat in her face wasn't visible, Meg stepped into the room. The men sat in the matching wingback chairs that flanked the fireplace.

"Jack's been telling me the good news about his decision at church this morning." Dad's eyes twinkled. "It sounds like you've taken

Reverend Hellman's challenge to heart, Jack. The final sermon is to be on Mother's Day. Usually at the end of a series, the preacher asks for short testimonies on how the sermons have helped us. You game?"

Jack scratched his head. "And tell everyone what happened this morning?"

"Yes, but if you don't feel comfortable, you don't have to."

"I've got time to think about it. Mom will still be in Colorado, so I won't be with her this year for Mother's Day. I'm sure I'll be at church."

"What about you, Meg?" Dad regarded her.

Meg studied the tiny buckles on her shoes. Dad might as well have said what he meant. Had she surrendered to God this crazy idea of moving to California? Had she resigned herself to God's will for her life as far as being a reporter was concerned? She raised her eyes to meet her father's penetrating stare. "I'm still praying about it."

"Are you going to tell your father about what we discussed?" Jack asked.

She stiffened. Did he expect her to say that she'd agreed to be his girl? "I'm not sure what—"

Jack's eyes widened. "About a possible column?"

Dad's gray brows arched like a pair of croquet wickets.

"I haven't given it much thought." Unless she counted the million ideas that swarmed her mind the whole walk home, none of which sounded plausible now.

"What is this about, Meg?"

She shrugged. "Just an idea. I have to admit, it sounds appealing."

"I think column writing is splendid," Dad said. "Much better than news stories."

Dad was encouraging her? She moved to the davenport and sat. "I've wanted to be a reporter for so long, I'm just not—"

"Meg is a wonderful writer, and a column would be great experience." Jack moved to the edge of his seat and rested his elbows on his knees. "Maybe someday when the field opens up to women, she can become a reporter."

"How would she start?" Dad patted his pocket as though looking for his pipe.

"She'd begin by writing one for the *News-Trib*, and then after it. . ."

Meg stood and strolled into the kitchen. Mom bent in front of the open oven door, humming a tune known only to her.

"Whatever help you need, I'm at your service." Meg opened the icebox and took out a pitcher of water.

Her mother slid the ham into the oven and straightened. "I'll never turn down assistance, but I thought you were visiting with your father and Jack."

"I was, but they don't need my input."

"What are they discussing?"

Meg slammed the icebox door. "Me."

Chapter Thirty-Two

....

On Monday morning, Meg set out along Warren Street as memories of yesterday flooded her mind. Joy over Jack's coming to faith in God had made it a very special Easter morning. And she loved the idea of him calling her his girl, but at the same time, he'd had lots of girlfriends and had apparently moved on. She had to see it for what it was, not for what she wanted.

Meanwhile, she would enjoy him until June 1 rolled around. She smiled, remembering a time yesterday afternoon when Laura went upstairs to do homework and her parents went outside to greet a neighbor. Within seconds Jack had pulled her into the living room in front of the fire, where they shared a long kiss that had chills running down her spine and into her toes. He'd just whispered, "That's to show you what I meant earlier," when the back door slammed and they moved apart so quickly that she nearly fell off her high heels. Later, when she walked him to his car, they laughed over the episode before he gave her a quick peck to dream on. The man had a way of sweeping a girl off her feet, and she needed to be careful.

She reached Main Street. Across the road, the lake glistened under the morning sun. Meg always loved the park, but especially so on summer mornings when she woke early and brought her Bible to the water's edge. Now she hardly cracked her Bible most mornings.

Maybe the change of scenery in California would draw God close again. And out there she wouldn't have to wait until summer to spend time with Him outdoors. Helen had mentioned orange trees in their backyard, but would they even have a yard, given their tiny budgets? Would the warm breezes all winter long be enough to replace the warmth Jack brought to her heart?

Meg turned east toward the office. The Riviera came into view. At least she'd have a chance to dance in the ballroom with Jack before she left.

A horn beeped as Jack pulled up his Ford to the opposite curb. He rolled down the window. "Morning. Want a ride?"

Her pulse increased, and she returned his smile. Accepting would give them a chance to talk before work, find out how serious he was about the columnist idea. She hustled across the road before the next car sped by.

He reached across the seat and opened the passenger door.

She climbed in, admiring how his lightweight summer suit eased over his broad shoulders as though it were made for him. It probably had been. "Good morning."

Jack grinned and ran his gaze over her in an appreciative way. "You look nice today. Sleep well?"

Her face heated, and she studied her lap.

"I love how you blush when I say things like that."

"It was hard to fall asleep. I couldn't stop thinking about writing a column." *Or you.* "I'd like to try writing one this week."

A hush fell between them. "I'll have to talk to Oscar first."

The bubble of expectation popped, and Meg slumped against the seat. "I thought you meant I could give it a try—while I'm still here."

He gave her a quick side glance. "I did, but a column isn't a one-time thing. You may have to think about delaying the move if it takes off." He hesitated. "In the meantime, can you try to reschedule the missed appointment with Fred? If Lester can't drive you out to Fred's place, I'll do it."

How could he change the subject so fast? Would he do that if he really wanted her to delay the move? All the more reason to do all she could to be ready for California. "If I had a driver's license, I wouldn't have to bother others to take me places."

Jack pulled into a parking place next to the office and turned off the engine. "Then you'd need a car."

Meg frowned. It would be nice to have a driver's license before she moved. "Guess I need driving lessons before I can worry about a car."

He leaned against the car door, his eyes twinkling. "Have you ever driven?"

"Once." She laughed. "I tried backing Dad's car out of the driveway. It jerked into the street and then the engine died."

He laughed and opened his door. "It's all in how you work the clutch."

As he rounded the car, Meg visualized marching into the house and showing Dad her new license. Wouldn't he be surprised?

Jack opened the door, and she climbed out. She caught his gaze with her own as she stood. "Will you teach me how to drive?"

Chapter Thirty-Three
....

Midmorning, Meg finally reached Fred after several tries. "Since you missed our meeting on Friday, I'd like to come to your place today."

He hauled in a loud breath. "I figured you wouldn't meet me in the rain, so I didn't bother. Today's my busy day."

Irritation nipped at her determination to remain calm. "What day isn't so busy? Tomorrow?" She drummed her fingers on her desk through the silence. "You still there?"

"You need to come now. I have field work to do."

"Wait a second." She put the phone down and scurried to Jack's door. "Fred is free to talk if I come right away. Lester's not here."

"Give me five minutes."

* * * * *

Meg observed Jack's movements from the moment he slid behind the wheel. Forget driving—just getting the car started seemed complicated.

Put in the key. Flip a switch. Turn a thingamajig. Pull out a knob. Put in the clutch at the same time you're pressing something with your heel, and then press a button. Maybe she didn't need a license after all.

By the time they'd rounded the lake to the south shore, Meg's focus had shifted to Fred. She wanted to give him a piece of her mind, but she couldn't let him manipulate her feelings. She had to treat him with kindness. How does one treat a snake with kindness?

Jack turned on Zenda Road, and a mile later, they approached Fred's property. He stood by his mailbox wearing his trademark overalls with a paint bucket in one hand and a brush in the other. Jack jousted the car into the driveway's all-too-familiar ruts and stopped beside Fred. Meg cranked down her window. "Hi, Fred, shall we talk here while you paint?"

The farmer bent down and peered into the car, his hard stare on Jack. "Thought you said you were coming alone."

She turned away from his alcohol-and-tobacco breath, swallowing bile. "You know I don't drive." She pressed her lips together. She wouldn't let him get to her this time.

Fred gave Jack a curt nod. "You part of this discussion?"

"I don't have to be."

Fred stepped back. "You'll hear what I tell her anyway. I'll meet ya both at the house."

Meg and Jack waited on Fred's front porch. She fixed her eyes on the barn, which needed paint more than the mailbox. A warm breeze carried a stench worse than Fred's breath into her nostrils. She scrunched her nose. "I wonder if farmers ever get used to the smells."

"Probably. Here he comes now."

Fred lumbered across the yard and climbed the two steps to the porch. "It's a warm day. We can sit here."

Meg glanced over her shoulder at a pair of rusting metal chairs. "I can stand."

Fred scowled. "I'll fetch you a towel to sit on." He turned to Jack. "I'll bring out an extra chair for you if you tell me your name, young fella."

Jack stuck out his hand. "Sorry for my impoliteness. Jack Wallace. I'm a reporter at the *News-Trib*. I'll lean against the railing."

Fred ignored his hand. "Fine by me, but you might get your britches dirty."

"It's only dirt."

The older man stepped inside and returned quickly, carrying a dish towel. He spread it over a chair and peered at Meg. "Go ahead and sit, missy."

Meg settled onto the seat and opened her notebook while Fred shoe-horned his ample behind into the other chair. He pushed his cap farther back on his brow. "Let's get this over with."

She caught his eye. "It's my understanding that some time ago you were stopped by a policeman."

Fred tugged a pack of Lucky Strikes from his pocket and shook out a cigarette. "Off-duty policeman. Big difference." He stuck the unlit smoke in his mouth then plucked a kitchen match from his shirt pocket and struck it. Lighting the cigarette, he extinguished the flame. "He should have been mindin' his own business."

"What year was it?"

"Eleven years ago this September."

"Why were you pulled over?"

His right eye twitched. "You already seem to know."

"I've heard a rumor. You can tell the truth."

"I went by Bill O'Brien's to borrow some tools, and he offered me a drink from his still. I wasn't about to say no. It ended up being a couple of drinks.

"I took Center Street home to avoid going through downtown, and the next I know, Henry Booker is honking and motioning me from his Model T to pull over. He tells me I was weaving and orders me to breathe on him so's he can smell my breath. Then he says I'm drunk and need to go before a judge."

Meg glanced at Jack then back at Fred. "Were you drunk?"

He drew on his cigarette until it seemed he'd suck the entire thing into his lungs all at once. "I had a few drinks. Never heard of anyone being stopped for that before. I decided I wasn't going to be the first, so I climbed out of the truck and took a swing at Henry." He smiled as he rubbed his fisted left hand. "Knocked him flat to the ground." Smoke trailed out through Fred's mouth and nose.

"Then your daddy pulls up. Said he saw me hit Henry. By that time, Henry was sputtering to Lou how I shouldn't be on the road. I thought your daddy was gonna save my hide when he said he'd take care of things." He shook his head. "Was I wrong."

Meg scribbled on the pad. "What did my father do?"

"He had me get into his car. I thought he was taking me home, but we went to the jail. He told Sheriff Mason I needed to dry out but didn't want it on my record, seeing as I'd lost my wife and boy a few years before." He drew in a long breath as his eyes glazed over. "The sheriff put me in a cell in the cellar." He winced. "I swear there were rats and snakes down there."

Meg cringed. At least she and Fred agreed on something.

"I was let out three days later." His face reddened. "We'd had lots of rain that year and I was late getting in my corn. Those three days, we'd had a frost, and I lost half my crop. If it weren't for my neighbors, my herd would've died." He crossed his arms and narrowed his eyes at Meg. "Go ahead and print the story. Let's see what happens when people find out that the esteemed Louis Alden didn't book me the proper way."

Resisting the urge to give Fred a piece of her mind for not recognizing her father's compassion toward him, she said, "I'm sure my father wasn't aware of the crop situation."

"Then he should have asked someone. Now I need to get my planting done." He tossed his cigarette onto the grass then waved a hand as big as a catcher's mitt. "Get off my property now. Both of ya."

Meg closed her notebook. "Thanks for your time."

Back in the car, Jack slid behind the wheel and looked at Meg. "Casts a different light on your dad, doesn't it?"

She faced him. "It just doesn't sound like Dad to take a risk like that. He is generous with his pro bono work, but—"

"You've got only half the story. Maybe when you tell him about this, he'll explain his side." He began the process of starting the car.

Memories of the last exchange she had with Dad about Fred played in her mind like a bad movie. "I just hope his side clears him of wrongdoing. I'm scared, Jack."

Jack put the car in gear and steered the vehicle over the ruts. They reached the pavement, and he pointed the car toward town. "How old were you when this occurred?"

"Thirteen or fourteen."

"Do you recall anything strange happening then?"

"No. But at that age, I was having difficulty with school. Everything else went unnoticed."

"What kind of difficulty?"

"I kept getting distracted. I still have the same problem, except for when I'm writing."

"Maybe because writing is your calling. My cousin is a professor at a teacher's college, and she told me educators are realizing that people have different ways of learning. Students who have a hard time paying attention need to learn tactics to assist the learning process."

Meg sat up straight. "You mean there are others like me?"

"Sounds like it."

Jack turned on a side road and stopped. He faced her, his gaze meeting her own. "It's time for your first driving lesson."

Chapter Thirty-Four
....

Meg sat in stunned silence while Jack got out of the car and circled around the front to the passenger side. Her car door opened, and she stared into his mirth-filled eyes then ran her gaze over the dashboard buttons and dials down to the floor. How did one keep her foot on that tiny gas pedal? It looked like a spoon. "I can't drive with my arm in a sling."

He grinned. "You'll have enough use of your left hand to hold the wheel while you shift. We'll stay on this deserted road." He nudged her shoulder. "Slide over."

An hour later, after a few fits and starts where Meg let up on the clutch too fast and killed the motor, she got the car moving and smoothly shifted the gears until they cruised down the road. Grinning, Meg pressed in the clutch at the same time as she braked, and the car halted without one sputter. She laughed. "I did it."

Jack slid over and wrapped her in a hug. "I knew you could." He leaned back, and their gazes caught and held.

"I don't see anyone around for miles." A playful grin lit his face.

Meg lifted her chin. "Neither do I." She closed her eyes.

Soft as a whisper his lips feathered hers, and she let his kiss take her into an otherworldly bliss she didn't want to end. The kiss lingered until they broke for air.

"We've got to stop meeting like this." Jack's lips continued to brush against hers as he spoke, sending a warm fuzzy feeling into her stomach.

Meg giggled and kissed him back. "I never knew driving lessons could be so nice."

"Or investigating a story." He placed a kiss on her nose then opened his door. "Time to go to the office."

While he rounded the car, she slid over. After hearing Fred's explanation, she had no choice but to confront her father as soon as possible. She might be on her way to California before she had a chance to write her first column or have that dance with Jack in the new ballroom.

* * * * *

Meg forced her last bite of apple pie into her mouth and then rubbed her damp right palm on her skirt. Ever since arriving home from work, she'd wanted to discuss Fred's story with Dad, but she decided to wait until after dinner.

Across the table, her father finished up his last forkful of pie and washed it down with a swallow of coffee.

"Dad, can we talk privately?" She hated how unnatural her voice sounded.

He scowled. "If it's about that Newman fiasco, I'm done discussing it."

"It's not—"

"Then let's go." He looked at Laura. "Be sure to help your mother with the dishes."

Laura pulled a face. "But I have to study for an English test."

"If we work together, we'll have it done in a half hour." Mom picked up Meg's plate and stacked it on top of hers then reached for Laura's. "You get the glasses and silver."

Meg followed Dad into his study, and he shut the door.

"I hope you want to tell me you're canning that story." His chair creaked as he sat.

Meg dropped into the chair across from him and smoothed her navy skirt over her knees. "I had a chat with Fred Newman."

Dad's eyes suddenly grew wide and fiery, and he slammed the desk with a palm. Papers flew onto the floor. "This *is* about the Newman business. You said it wasn't."

"I started to say it's not a rehashing, but you cut me off."

"You're committing libel, you know."

Heat filled her abdomen, and she forced herself to not fly out of the room. "We're not in court."

"We will be if you print your story." He folded his arms across his chest.

How had they come to this place? And where was the compassionate man Fred unwittingly portrayed?

A sharp knock split the air. "Louis, are you two okay?"

"We're fine, Margaret. Just having a little chat," Dad said with a lowered voice. He glared at Meg. "I'll listen to what Fred told you. But I do not want you printing anything about this."

Meg took her notebook from her skirt pocket. "I want to make sure I state it correctly." She flipped the cover open and recounted Fred's perspective of the incident.

"Fred lost most of his crops to frost and would have lost his livestock if it weren't for his neighbors." She closed the notebook. "Please tell me your side."

Dad's jaw muscle pulsed as his gaze flicked around the room. "It's all true."

Meg's heart raced. *Lord, what am I to do?*

He selected a pipe from a stand next to the humidor and turned it over in his hand. "How much do you know about Fred?"

Meg shrugged. "I see him around town, is all."

"He hasn't always been bad-tempered. He used to attend our church and was an elder."

For as long as Meg had known Fred, she'd avoided him, never curious about what made him ornery. Last week she learned he'd been married. Then he'd mentioned that his wife and son had died. Now Dad said he used to be a leader in their church. What else would she learn?

"Fred married right after high school. When their son was drafted during the Great War, he just about busted his buttons. Made the boy wear his uniform around town before he shipped out. The boy died in battle eight months after leaving, and Fred started railing against anyone with a German last name. That's when he started hitting the sauce.

"About a year after their son's death, Fred and his wife were driving back to their farm after a family gathering. I gather he'd spent most of the afternoon in his cousin's barn around the still." Dad paused and swallowed hard. "Fred passed a slow car on a hill. Said he never saw the car coming from the other direction until it was too late. His wife died in the crash."

Meg gasped and her hand flew to her mouth. "Oh my goodness. How terrible."

Dad nodded. His eyes glistened with moisture. "There's more. . . . The couple in the other car died too."

Meg groaned. She'd been so unfair to Fred, saying unkind things about him, joking with others about his crotchety attitude. . . . "And he's had to live with that for years."

"The police wanted to charge him with reckless driving and illegal drinking. I felt sorry for him and defended his case. Got it down to a stiff fine and a promise to stop drinking."

An ache pressed against her heart. God cared about Fred despite his attitude, and so should she. "I feel awful for not being more understanding, but what does this have to do with what happened when you jailed him? If he was guilty of breaking his promise, then. . ."

Dad tamped tobacco into his pipe and lit it. "Your mother's going to have a conniption for my lighting up inside." He paused. "I think for some, alcohol is very addictive. People go to it to numb a pain they're experiencing, and long after the pain is gone, they can't stop drinking."

Was that why Fred had stopped in his barn before their interview? Maybe he wanted a nip before he faced Meg's questions? "I don't know much about drunkenness since, outside of Fred, I don't know anyone who drinks."

"You think you don't. Many hide it since we're under Prohibition. Fred concealed his habit for a while, but when he came to church smelling like a distillery several times in a row, he was asked to step down from his elder position." Dad rested his pipe in a glass ashtray. "He never came back to church. The reverend visited him once or twice but was chased away. I worried we'd find Fred dead, having had an accident with his farm equipment. When I came upon Henry lying on the road that night with Fred weaving back and forth next to him, I had to stop."

"But why the secrecy? You did a benevolent thing."

Dad placed his elbows on the desk and looked Meg in the eyes. "What I did was illegal. As an officer of the court, I could lose my license. I'd saved Fred from a jail record before, and I didn't want that to change. I thought that getting him into a cell would dry him out and make him think twice the next time. The intention was to hold him there overnight, but he was still in bad shape the next day, so we kept him there another night, which evolved into three because he had the shakes so bad." He stared at his clasped hands.

"He still drinks. I've smelled it on him."

"Sadly, yes."

"Thanks for telling me."

Dad nodded at the notepad. "You didn't write anything. You sure you have the facts straight?"

"There's no story to write."

Chapter Thirty-Five

....

Jack's car wasn't parked in its usual spot the next morning, and Meg breathed a sigh of relief. Her father had told the truth, but what good would it do to run the story? It would only cause trouble for Dad. He hadn't done it to break the law. He'd merely been trying to help a man who desperately needed assistance.

She entered the office and passed Emily without stopping. At her desk, a note from Jack sat under her paperweight.

> *Meg, I'm meeting the mayor for breakfast. Oscar is coming in this afternoon for a couple of hours. Let's try to wrap up your story this morning when I get in. Jack*

She crumpled the paper and threw it into the waste can. The decision was made, and she wasn't changing her mind.

* * * * *

Jack waited for Meg to take a seat across from him. He couldn't wait to tell her all the wonderful details of the grand opening celebration the mayor had shared over their toast and eggs.

He grinned, enjoying the way her blue dress draped over her shapely legs. She had no idea how attractive she was, a trait he found most appealing. She returned his smile, but it didn't reach her eyes. She must have had a bear of a time with her father last night. Hopefully she had the article done. He'd already composed the headline: *Cover-Up Exposed—Local Man Jailed Off the Record.*

She crossed her ankles and gave him a vacant stare as her tight smile dissolved.

"Meg, are you okay?" Dumb question. Of course she wasn't.

She nodded.

After an awkward moment, he said, "I take it you spoke to your dad?"

"Yes."

"Then the story is ready?"

As though someone lit a match, fire filled her eyes. "I can't write it, Jack." She straightened and jutted out her chin. "I won't betray my father."

"What did he say?"

"I'm sorry. I can't tell you."

His abdominal muscles tightened. Weren't they in this together? The newsman in him wanted to shake sense into her. But his heart twisted at the pain in her eyes. The newsman won the battle. "Where's your fighting spirit? If you learned answers—"

"You'll have to write the article if you want it printed."

"I can't, without knowing what you learned."

Meg's face blanched. "You'll have to ask my dad." Her eyes shifted from Jack to the floor and back to him. "I'm sorry. If you prefer me to resign now, I will."

What kind of ogre did she think he was? He looked her in the eyes. "Of course I don't want you to leave the paper. In fact, I was hoping you'd change your mind about leaving town at all." He ran his gaze over her face. "Since we're seeing each other now."

She blinked. "You were?"

He ached to comfort her with a hug. But it was best not to in the office. "Yeah. I thought that since we're a couple now, you would change your mind, or at least delay making plans until we see where this is going."

She stared at her lap. "I already promised Helen I'd move with her if I got the money from my dad. I can't turn my back on her now. Not without good reason."

His heart felt as if it'd just been pierced with a saber. Wasn't *he* enough of a good reason?

She stood. "I'll have the King article you assigned yesterday done in a half hour." She turned on her heel and marched to the door.

The door closed, and Jack exhaled. Was it only a few minutes ago he felt like he was king of the world? He was finally right with God, his dad seemed to be improving, and he had a girl he adored. But maybe Meg didn't care as much for him as he thought.

* * * * *

Jack dusted Oscar's desktop with his handkerchief and set the folder containing the week's articles on the shiny surface. A dull ache pressed against his conscience. He felt more like a kid preparing to confess sneaking out after dark than a man telling his boss that they'd kept the truth hidden to protect his health.

A chorus of "Welcome backs" drifted from the outer office. Jack hustled into the newsroom. A much thinner Oscar stood next to the switchboard as the ladies fussed over him. The same shock of white hair crowned his head and he wore the same glasses, but his suit appeared to be at least four sizes too big. Had he returned too soon?

Oscar waved at Jack. "There's the man who's been keeping the ship afloat. I'd better check on his work."

"Mr. Wallace has been doing a great job, Mr. Zimmer." Emily bounced on her toes. "Miss Alden too."

Meg's face paled, and she took a step back from the others.

Jack hurried across the room and shook Oscar's hand. He had to straighten out this mess as soon as possible. "They've all pulled their weight around here, Oscar. I waited for you to set up this week's front page."

Zimmer nodded. "We can't keep Composing waiting. I'll only be here a few hours."

"The doctor said no more than two hours, Dad."

Jack smiled at Lester where he stood a few feet back from the huddle. "Les, good of you to bring your dad."

Lester scowled. "Seems that's all I'm good for anymore."

Ignoring Oscar's curious expression, Jack led his boss across the room. "I think you'll be pleased with the stories we're running this week."

Jack waited for Oscar to sit in his desk chair then pulled a chair around next to him.

Oscar picked up Meg's story on Wayne King. "Sure you want this above the fold? If it were grand-opening week, I'd say fine, but that's several weeks away. Isn't there any hard news?"

Jack's thoughts raced. "Nothing worthy of the front page. I had something else, but the lead dried up. I stuck the King piece in to fill the space."

"Was it the story you were chasing over at the sheriff's office?"

"Yeah. Without the source, it didn't have legs."

"Probably just as well." Oscar scanned the King article. "Well-written. Did my boy do this?"

Jack's mouth turned dry. "Not that one."

Oscar set the story on top of the other articles and closed the file. "I was afraid you'd say that. Go ahead and give the guys the folder."

Jack dashed to Composing. Already, the guys would work longer than usual, even for a Wednesday. He returned to Oscar's office. Zimmer had removed his jacket and rolled up his sleeves. Jack pulled his chair back around so they could face each other.

Oscar ran a hand through his hair, the effort failing to rearrange his cowlick. "How's your father?"

"He's responding well to the mountain air. Mom is planning on attending the Riviera's grand opening. They both wanted to come until Dad became ill."

"Any idea when he'll return home?"

Jack shook his head.

Oscar removed his glasses and polished the lenses with his handkerchief. "Did you say the managing editor has taken over the *Beacon*?"

Jack nodded. "You heard right."

"I appreciate your faithfulness to the *News-Trib*, Jack, but if you prefer to return to the *Beacon* early. . ."

A heaviness pressed on Jack's neck and shoulders. He should head down to Chicago, but Dad had been emphatic that Snow be given a chance. He'd have to go eventually. . .for Kate. But he enjoyed what he was doing at the *News-Trib*. "I'll think about it after you're back full-time."

Oscar grinned and returned his spectacles to his nose, looping the sidepieces over his ears. "That's a relief. As soon as I spoke, I thought I'd dug my own grave. Who could run the paper as well as you?"

Jack squirmed. "I'm sure you'd find someone. Oscar, there is something I need to talk to you about."

The phone jangled and Oscar grabbed it. "Zimmer." He grinned. "Yes, in the flesh, but only for a short time." He covered the mouthpiece with his hand. "This is going to take a while. I'll call you back in later."

Chapter Thirty-Six

....

That evening, after the waitress at the Geneva Grill brought their coffees, Helen leaned forward on her elbows, her platinum waves falling forward to frame her face. She looked at Meg. "I'm glad you called today. Beatrice is visiting, and I had to give her and Mom time without me to work out their plans for after I'm gone."

For the first time, Helen's voice lacked the usual enthusiasm whenever she talked about moving. Meg frowned. Maybe her friend wasn't as much on board as she had been. She dismissed the thought. "I'm glad too. Today was quite a day."

Helen sat back. "I'm almost afraid to ask what happened."

She stuffed down the temptation to blurt out everything going on with Dad and Fred. Helen would never consider herself a gossip, but more than once she'd told Meg things she'd heard from her customers. Meg had to be careful. "I can't say."

"Is it about you and Jack?"

The waitress reappeared, platters of sandwiches and chips balanced on her arm. While she placed their orders on the table, Meg pondered Helen's question. "It's work-related."

Helen added mustard to her sandwich. "Did Jack spend Easter with you?"

"We went to the sunrise service."

Helen lifted her cup to her upturned lips. "That sounds interesting. Sure it's not about that good-looking man?"

"I'm sure. Mr. Zimmer came in for a while today." Meg stirred sugar into her coffee.

"He's strong enough already?"

"He appeared frail and wasn't there more than an hour."

"He's lucky to be alive." Helen took a bite out of her sandwich and returned it to her plate. A dollop of mustard clung to a corner of her lip.

Meg lifted the bread on her chicken sandwich and wrinkled her nose at the sparse dollop of mayo. "Thanks to Jack, the bad situation resolved itself."

Helen wiped her mouth. "It *does* have something to do with him."

Meg took a small bite of her sandwich. She ached to tell Helen about Jack kissing her in the park, asking her to be his girl, and how she practically floated through the weekend. But she didn't want to cause Helen to worry that she was going to back out of moving. "Indirectly, Jack is involved. It's something I shouldn't be talking about outside of the office."

Helen shook her head. "You're confusing me, but I guess you still haven't given yourself a chance to see if there's something between you and Jack."

"We like each other, but I'm sure that as soon as Mr. Zimmer is healthy again, he'll move back to the *Beacon*, what with his dad being sick." She lifted her coffee cup in a salute. "And we'll be on our way to California."

Helen relaxed against her chair. "Last week I was making a list of what I need to take with me, and a nagging doubt at the back of my mind kept saying, *What if Meg and Jack get together and she won't want to move?* I kept telling myself I'd be happy for you and I'd be fine setting out alone. That maybe Mattie would still let me stay with her for a while even though I don't know her like you do."

Meg blinked at her tears. Who'd been more committed to her than Helen? Friends since grammar school, she'd let Helen cry on her shoulder when her boyfriend left her high and dry after graduation. And when Matthew ditched Meg, who was there to hold her up? Helen, of course. For years she'd heard her friend go on about her dream to move to Hollywood. Meg couldn't back out now. She'd never live with herself. She reached across the table and grabbed Helen's hand. "Dad gave me the money on Saturday. Book those train tickets. We're going."

Helen bit her lower lip, leaving a speck of lipstick on her tooth. "Thanks, dear friend. You know, you're so lucky to have a father. Yours may have resisted giving you that money, but at least he was there to give it to you. Think of how he saved it for you all these years despite this depression. You have no idea how blessed you are." She palmed away a tear.

A surge of guilt washed over Meg, and she looked away. Helen's dad had deserted her and her mom when Helen was about three. Meg realized she had taken Dad's provision for her, Laura, and Mom for granted. "I'm sorry, Helen, for not thinking. If you knew how often I've envied you for not having to deal with a father like mine. . ."

Helen signaled for more coffee. "I guess the grass on the other side is always greener, as they say. Let's call it even and talk about the move."

* * * * *

Two weeks later, Meg sat on her bed and stared at the playbill from the high school senior class play. Having finally gotten her cast off yesterday afternoon, she begged off attending the play that had all but disrupted the family routine for weeks. Instead, she spent the time doing the exercises the doctor had prescribed to get her arm back to normal. . .and trying not to think about leaving Jack.

It hadn't taken long for their coworkers to realize that she and Jack were dating. Of course, none of them knew she planned to move away, so as far as they were concerned it was only a matter of time until he proposed to her. Sadly, despite his claiming that he wanted her to stay to see how things went between them, he still hadn't expressed a word of how he felt about her. Just as well, because without his saying those three little words, it was much easier to fulfill her promise to Helen.

She turned to the cast acknowledgments inside the trifold playbill. When Mom had handed it to her last night after she and Dad got home, she said, "Thought you'd like to see Laura's acknowledgments. She thanks you for the example of courage and tenacity she needed when she was asked to take over the lead with only four weeks' notice."

Meg had skimmed the paragraph. Then, blinking at tears, she'd laid it down. "She was probably asked to say something nice."

"Maybe, but she didn't have to say those exact words."

Now, nearly twenty-four hours later, she reread Laura's words. She'd had no idea Laura felt that way. Ever since she could remember, they'd gone at each other like they were the world's worst enemies. Now Meg was going to be living thousands of miles away. By the time she returned for a visit, Laura would likely be out of college and married or teaching school. Strangers, despite being raised in the same family. Were the few weeks she had left in Lake Geneva enough to mend years of hurt?

God, I still struggle. Help me.

She ached to call Jack and talk about it, but he'd said he needed to spend time at home that afternoon, and even though he was her boyfriend, she'd never be the one to call him unless it was an emergency.

* * * * *

The next morning Meg left for work early, the letter of resignation that she'd rewritten several times tucked between her coin purse and her ever-present notebook in her handbag. By the time Jack called her last night after supper to see how her afternoon had gone, everything she'd thought she wanted to talk about escaped her memory. All that mattered was hearing his voice, like always.

She got to the office and pulled the long, slender skeleton key she'd carried for years out of her purse. How pleased she'd felt the day Mr. Zimmer gave it to her. Giving it back to him would feel like she was giving up an appendage.

Across the newsroom, light spilled out of Mr. Zimmer's office. He wasn't scheduled to come in until afternoon, and Jack hadn't mentioned coming in this early. Maybe he couldn't sleep either. She ambled to the open door. "Good morning, Ja—Oh! Mr. Zimmer."

Oscar Zimmer glanced up from the stack of mail he was sorting. "Morning, Meg. I see I'm not the only early bird today. Thought I'd come in now. Mornings are my best time."

He'd put on some weight, but was it too soon to have him back? "Well, I hope you don't overdo."

He held up two fingers in a salute. "Scout's honor. I have strict orders from the missus to come home the moment I feel weary."

"Good. I'd better get to work myself."

"Why are you here so early?"

"Just am." Behind her, the morning stillness seemed to shout at her, "*Do it now!*" "Do you have a minute?"

He pushed the stack of mail to the side. "No time like the present."

"I'll be right back." Meg stepped out of his office for a moment, so she could retrieve the letter from her handbag and collect her thoughts. As she approached Mr. Zimmer's door, she paused, suddenly feeling drained of her determination. Once she handed over the letter, there wouldn't be any turning back. She took a deep breath and stepped into the office.

He squirmed as deep furrows appeared on his brow. "Must be serious, if you're closing the door."

"It is." She took a seat, wishing away the tremble in her hand. "I'm turning in my resignation, effective May thirty-first. After the *News-Trib* night at the Riviera." She set the letter on his desk and pushed it toward him.

He ignored the envelope and removed his glasses. "I thought you loved working here." He pulled a handkerchief from his back pocket and blew his nose.

"I do, but I'm moving to California. Mattie Nordman's boss is holding a typing pool position for me at the *Examiner*."

"I've thought about Mattie often. Glad she's still in the news business." He returned his glasses to his nose. "I'd hoped you'd tire of nagging me about a reporter job and be happy with the status quo. Especially since you and Jack have come to be close friends. But I guess you got a taste of newswriting while I was sick."

"Actually, I'd already realized I needed to go to where change is happening, before you took ill."

He looked her in the eyes. "What if you never make it to reporter? Not everyone is so liberal to hire a woman."

"I can't not write. I have to believe I'll become one eventually."

"You've been writing here—for quite a long time now."

Her mouth went dry, and she stared at her lap. He'd known all along. "I wanted to tell you about rewriting Lester's articles. I didn't mean for it to get so involved, but he wanted to please you, and before I knew it, I was rewriting whole paragraphs." She looked up through blurry eyes at his compassionate face. "I'm so sorry, Mr. Zimmer."

"I was referring to the society news. But the truth is, I recognized your voice in those pieces long before I got sick. Time I admitted that Lester doesn't have a voice when it comes to writing. In fact, his writing stinks."

She fished a hankie out of her pocket and dabbed her eyes. "Why didn't you tell us you knew?"

"Because confession is good for the soul. I was hoping to force it out of Lester when I assigned him the layout the first day I got sick, but he never said a word."

Meg gazed at the floor. "I can leave today rather than the thirty-first."

"Some would say I should agree to that but, I'm not other people." He held up the envelope and studied the sealed flap. "Sometimes we try to make things happen before their time. You've got tenacity, Miss Alden, like Jack's friend Ginny. I probably should have told you about the Burlington job, but I held back."

Meg swallowed the fist-sized lump in her throat. "You did the right thing in sending her."

"Your family must be upset about you moving so far away. You didn't want Chicago?"

"I'm going with Helen McArdle. She hopes to find work styling hair at a movie studio. I hate leaving my family and Lake Geneva—and Jack—but without moving I'll never—"

He opened a desk drawer and interrupted her. "For now I'm going to leave your letter here. If between now and June first you change your mind, I'll tear it up."

She didn't deserve his patience. Meg stood as her chest welled. "Thank you." She wanted to say more, but if she didn't get out of there, she'd slobber all over his desk.

Her boss stood. "Before I forget. . . Lester said he'd like to learn the Linotype. It's a good place for him. He's going to work with the guys back there and learn the trade."

Meg didn't move. If Lester were to work in Composing, who would that leave to report the news but Jack? Unless. . .

"I've contacted a retired reporter over in Delavan. Gerald Purvis starts tomorrow. He'll stay until a new reporter is hired."

She pressed her lips together. Mr. Zimmer might as well have chiseled it in the sidewalk out front. *No Women Reporters Allowed.*

Meg thanked him for his time and stepped into the outer office. Jack glanced up with a questioning expression. She plopped into her chair and turned toward the water-splattered window. When had it started raining? She looked at Jack.

Without a word, he wheeled his chair over. "You okay?"

She nodded, loving him for his concern.

"Before I go in with Oscar, is there anything you want to talk about?"

She turned and slipped a stack of want-ad forms from a drawer. "I told him about rewriting Lester's articles. He already knew and was waiting for me to confess. I also gave him my resignation. My last day is May thirty-first."

His face dissolved into a frown. "You really did it."

She faced him. "Did you think I was kidding?"

He shook his head. "Not really."

"He said I can change my mind anytime. Why is he being so nice to me?"

"I told you he was fond of you."

"He also said Lester will be moving to Composing."

"Composing might be a good place for him. That means there's an opening for a reporter."

She sucked in her lower lip. "He hired a retired newsman from Delavan to pick up the slack."

Jack pursed his lips and stared out the window. "I'm sorry, Meg. I'd hoped he'd softened after seeing how well you've done these past weeks. You know, that's what I would have done." He brought his attention back. The sudden sadness in his eyes jolted her. "I thought I'd ask Ginny if she'd like to come to church on Mother's Day. Her mother is in Florida, and she'll spend the day alone."

Meg forced a smile. "That's a good idea. I'm sorry I won't be at the service. I told Mom I'd buy a big beef roast and make Mother's Day dinner for her. I'll stay home to cook that morning." Never had she been so happy not to go to church. As much as Jack insisted that he and Ginny were only friends, the woman still got on Meg's nerves.

Chapter Thirty-Seven
....

Meg lay in bed listening to the chug of Dad's car motor as he pulled out of the driveway. She hadn't missed a Sunday at church in weeks. But the moment she suggested that she would buy the meat and fix dinner for the whole family on Mother's Day, Mom couldn't stop grinning, and Meg knew she'd hit the jackpot.

The day couldn't have worked out better since Jack had invited Ginny to the service. After the way Ginny had mocked Jack and Meg for attending church, Meg doubted the woman would even show up. But she knew that if Ginny did come, Mom would no doubt invite her home for dinner. Meg winced at the thought and climbed out of bed. She'd think about that if and when she had no choice.

* * * * *

By the time Meg heard a car motor outside the house, she had the finished roast beef resting on the kitchen counter and was mashing the potatoes.

Mom stepped through the back door first. "My, it smells good in here." She came up to Meg and hugged her from behind. "Thanks for cooking, dear. The service was wonderful, and Jack surprised us by sharing his testimony when Reverend Hellman invited the congregation to speak. He mentioned you as the reason he ever came to our church. It was very touching."

Meg's heart squeezed as guilt pressed against her chest. She should have been there. But if Ginny showed up, it was good for her to hear his story. "I've hardly been a good witness. It was God who worked on Jack's heart, not me."

Mom slipped out of her spring coat. "As it should be. But if you hadn't brought him here to the house that Sunday afternoon, we might never have had the opportunity to invite him to church." Mom plucked out her hat pins as she walked toward the hall. "Jack should be along shortly. He was chatting with someone."

"Ginny, no doubt," Meg called after her mother's disappearing form. She lifted the pot of mashed potatoes and began dropping the white mounds into a serving bowl.

"Who's Ginny?" Mom was back in the kitchen.

"The friend from college he invited to attend the service. A tall, willowy woman."

Mom shook her head. "We were the only people there with Jack."

The back door opened, and Dad and Laura stepped through. "Meg, Jack looked so lonely without you there. But Betsy Horner is in for the weekend from Chicago." Laura sashayed across the room, exaggerating Betsy's walk.

"Laura Alden, stop making fun. You know Betsy's changed since she came to God last year." Mom looked at Meg. "She had a handsome young man with her. He and Jack seemed to hit it off when they talked after the service."

"Well, I didn't see a ring on Betsy's finger. Mark my works, sis, you'd better be careful with Betsy in town." Laura scooted out of the room before Meg could throw the dish towel at her.

"Don't pay her any mind, Meg. I don't know what's gotten into her."

"And that's why I don't take those comments she made about me in the playbill seriously." Meg went to the stove and turned down the flame under the green beans. "The vegetables are ready. All I need to do is to dish them up, and Dad can carve the roast."

The front doorbell rang and Jack's voice called out. "Can I come in? Hope I'm not too late for dinner."

Meg felt a grin filling her face. "We're in the kitchen."

Jack walked into the kitchen and made a beeline for Meg. He gave her a side hug. "Missed you this morning."

"Mom said you shared your testimony after the sermon. I'm sorry I missed it."

"Ginny never showed up." His face slackened. "She needs God, Meg."

"I know. But maybe you aren't the one to lead her to Him."

He wandered over to the meat. "Now this looks like a man's meal. I'm *almost* glad you stayed home."

A vision of cooking for Jack every night rolled into Meg's thoughts. She had to put on the brakes. This would likely be the one and only meal she'd ever cook for him.

Jack picked up the bowl of potatoes. "I'll take these to the table."

Throughout the meal, Meg basked in the comments of how good everything tasted, especially when the words came from Jack. The meal was for Mom, but was it wrong to enjoy his comments too?

After the apple pie Meg had made the day before, Mom ordered Laura to do the dishes. As usual the teenager pulled a pout, but Dad reminded her that it was Mother's Day and it was the least she could do.

Mom smiled at Meg. "And you have the rest of the day off, Meg. Why don't you and Jack do whatever you'd like?"

"Great idea, Mrs. Alden." Jack looked at Meg. "It's a beautiful day. Up for a ride? I know a great place to sit and look at the lake."

* * * * *

Jack slid behind the wheel and looked at Meg already seated next to him. "I'm glad we have a few minutes to talk. The pier at home was put in this week and it's a beautiful day. You willing?"

She answered with one of her heart-stopping smiles. "Sounds swell. Being next to the water after cooking all morning suits me fine."

He started the motor and drove to Main Street. After Jack had the car headed west up Dummer's Hill, he glanced over at Meg. "Seems like a long time since I drove you out to my house and we sat on the porch swing."

"It does, but in reality it's only been a little over a month."

He swallowed against the lump in his throat. "A lot has happened in those weeks, though."

She didn't answer. It was just as well. It was in his mind to convince her to not move, but he didn't want to bring that up until they were at the dock. Elgin Club Road came up and he turned off the state highway. Mottled sunrays splashed over the road ahead, the overarching tree branches giving shade that would be most welcome when spring turned to summer. He braked as they descended the long hill toward the lake and made the sharp turn toward his house. A minute later he came to a stop on the parking apron. "Are you thirsty? Shall I get us a couple of ginger ales before we sit on the pier?"

Meg shook her head. "I'm fine for now."

He helped her out of the car and held her hand as they walked alongside the house and out onto the front lawn. Ahead, the lake appeared as blue as the sky. In the distance, off toward the small village of Fontana at the western end of the lake, a lone sailboat bobbed along. He looked over at Meg, loving how her blue print skirt lifted slightly in the breeze and gave him a peek at her shapely legs. He also loved her simplicity, her unawareness of how beautiful she was. She usually wore only a little bit of lipstick, which he'd happily volunteer to remove with a few kisses. But first things first.

They came to the bench at the end of the dock and sat. "Dad had the bench installed a few years ago, facing west for the purpose of watching the sun set each night. We're a little too early for tonight's show."

Meg smiled for the first time since they'd arrived. "I sometimes walk over to Elm Park to watch the sunset from there."

And I'd love to have you stay the summer so I can show you the view from here every night.

He circled his arm around her narrow waist and nudged her into the crook of his arm. "You fit perfectly, like you belong here."

She answered with a "Hmm" and rested her head on his shoulder. "Everything is perfect right now."

He reached over and crooked his index finger under her chin to turn her head until he could easily cover her mouth with his own. Her lips slightly parted, sweet and tender. He let himself fall under her spell, grateful for the lack of an audience. Pulling back, he smiled at her half-shuttered eyes and loved how her long lashes fluttered when she looked up at him. "It's not often we have this place all to ourselves. Just you, me, and the lake. I can't wait to have you see what it's like when everyone moves in for the summer. Kids running around, neighbors enjoying each other. . ."

She eased back, and creases formed between her eyes. "But, Jack, I won't be here for the summer. You know I turned in my notice."

The warm feeling that had filled his chest since they started kissing dissolved. "Oh, I know, but Oscar said he wasn't accepting it until you truly walked out the door for the last time."

"Not exactly how he put it. He said I could change my mind anytime and he'd tear it up."

He leaned in and kissed her. "Same thing in my book."

"But I've not changed my mind." She sat back and crossed her arms.

He pushed one of her waves behind her ear. "You've still got three weeks left to rethink things. I don't want you to move, Meg. We're just getting started."

She turned and ran her gaze over his face. "What's getting started?"

He stared out at the lake. He was falling for her, but he wanted to be sure before he told her he loved her. What if she postponed her plans and their feelings faded? He would have caused her to lose out on her job opportunity. But at the same time, the thought of not having Meg in his life had his stomach turning.

"I can't let Helen down, Jack. This has been her dream since we were teenagers. . .and if I say I'm not going, I'm afraid she won't go."

He wasn't giving up that easy. "What if you go long enough to help Helen settle in and then come back?"

A corner of her mouth twitched. "I doubt Mr. Zimmer will keep my job while I decide whether I like it there. But even if he did, what would I come back to? By then you'll be at the *Beacon*."

Jack ran his free hand through his hair. She was slipping away from him. He'd tried his best, and she stood her ground. He'd have to leave it to God. He stood and pushed down the hurt. "Stay here a minute. I've got something to give you. It's in the house."

* * * * *

Meg sat stone-still, listening to Jack's footfalls fade as he walked toward the house. A door slammed, and she reached into her skirt pocket for her hankie and dabbed her eyes. She was falling hard, and the thought of not seeing him almost every day as she had for nearly two months was killing her.

Jack sounded like he didn't want to leave Lake Geneva any more than she did now that they'd met. She bit her lower lip. If God's timing was so perfect and it was His will she meet Jack, wouldn't He have had them meet when they had time to develop a relationship?

A door slammed, and Meg looked to the shore. Jack came down the cement steps and crossed the lawn toward the dock with a thick book under each arm.

He sat beside her. "I thought you could use these." He laid one of the books on her lap.

She ran her hand over its blue cover. "A journalism text?"

"It has a whole section on column writing." He reached over and flipped it open to a bookmarked page.

She ran her gaze over the opening paragraphs. A wad formed in her throat. Helen would think her daffy to consider such a gift romantic, but it meant more to her than a dozen bottles of perfume. He understood her. "Jack, this is wonderful—but don't you need these?"

"I have others." He took the book and set it on the bench before handing her the other one. "This is about newspaper publishing. Of course, you already know some about things, but it explains how the big papers operate."

She flipped through the pages, hungry to read more. "I don't know what to say."

"Just say thank you and start reading them." He stood. "We'd better get back to the house. Your dad mentioned that he wanted to play a round of Landlord's."

Chapter Thirty-Eight

. . . .

Meg had little time to read Jack's books until the next evening after dinner. She settled on her bed and flipped through the pages of the first book he'd shown her. Seeing his familiar handwriting scribbled in the margins here and there made it seem as though he'd given her a little part of him to take to California. Was she crazy to not stay as he asked?

"Hey, roommate, what are you doing here in your bedroom on such a beautiful evening?"

Meg glanced up. Helen stood in the bedroom doorway wearing a pair of sport trousers and a perky blouse. Meg closed the book and scooted up against the headboard. "Reading about column writing."

"I thought you wanted to be a reporter." Helen stepped into the room.

"Jack suggested I think about being a columnist as another way to write for a paper."

Helen sat on the foot of the bed, her flowery scent filling the air. "Meaning the *News-Trib*?"

"Mr. Zimmer agreed this morning to a trial piece for the last two weeks I'm here as long as it is something for women—but I want to come up with an angle that reaches men and women. Start with one paper, and hopefully it will eventually get sent out through a syndicate to other dailies. Maybe while I'm working the typing pool at the *Examiner*, I can play around with different column ideas." She paused, switching topics. "How was your Mother's Day yesterday?"

A shadow seemed to cross Helen's features. "Not very good. Mom's arthritis started acting up again. I'd planned to treat her to a movie, but we stayed home. She was a bit better this morning, though. I came by to see if you wanted to catch the movie tonight." Helen picked up the book and read the writing on the face page. "Jack gave you these?"

"Wasn't he thoughtful?"

Her friend closed the textbook. "Maybe he's making a silent bid for you to not move by suggesting you write a column from here."

Meg laughed. "Mr. Zimmer is only letting me have a stab at it because Jack convinced him that doing so will help me when I move. Nothing will change if I stay. Mr. Zimmer will soon be back to running the paper full-time, Jack will move on to the *Beacon*, and I'll be at the *Examiner*." She focused on the unopened book as a dull ache flooded her chest. "The perfect arrangement."

"I was thinking of you and Jack, not your career. He's mad about you, Meg. Can't you see it?"

She averted her gaze to the window and blinked.

"Hey, are you crying? Look at me."

Meg shook her head. "Only tears of happiness to be moving away and finally doing something on my own." She palmed a tear off her cheek.

"My Aunt Fanny. What's going on?"

Meg faced her. "Helen, I'm so confused. Jack acts like he wants me to stay, but he won't say how he feels. And even if he did say he's falling for me, how can I believe he'll feel that way in a month or two? How can I give up my dream for him if there's no guarantee he won't jilt me like Matthew did?"

Helen tipped her head. "Forget Matthew. It's clear Jack is nothing like that big old—" She paused. "Never mind, I'd best keep my thoughts about *him* to myself. But I can guarantee Jack has it bad for you. Would he spend most of his free time with you if he didn't?"

Meg shrugged and pulled her handkerchief from her pocket. "I know Jack's not like Matthew. But for some reason, I'm less afraid to move to California than I am to freely enjoy Jack's company." Meg blew her nose. "Maybe my fears aren't overblown. He has half the women in town eating out of his hand, even the waitresses."

"Well, that's not exactly true, but I doubt he's kissing anyone else he knows."

Meg jerked her head up, her cheeks heating. "I never told you he kissed me."

Helen crossed her arms. "Didn't have to. Emily said she saw you two kissing in Elm Park on Easter Sunday."

"She never told me she was there, the little stinker."

Helen leaned in and whispered, "I bet that's not the only time he's kissed you, either."

Meg closed her eyes to the memory of Jack's soft and tender lips pressed against hers, the strength of his arms around her, the almost perfect way she fit into his arms.

"By the goofy smile on your face, you must be enjoying the kisses too. Why are you holding out on me?"

Meg shrugged. "I didn't want you to think I was going to change my mind about going."

Helen's brow shot up. "What if he asks you to stay?"

Meg hesitated. "He kind of did yesterday. He wants us to enjoy the summer together and see where it goes. But chances are, he's going to have to move back to Chicago and work at the *Beacon* since his dad is so sick." Meg looked at Helen. "If I stayed, I'd betray my promise to you and for no good reason." She went to her closet and opened it. "I've already organized my things, and next week I'm purchasing a new suitcase at Bucknall's." She indicated the clothes pushed to one side that she wasn't taking. "I can't wait to see the ocean and palm trees. Spend winters not bundled up and freezing to death." Her eyes stung, and she faced the closet.

"Then why are you still crying?"

Meg crumpled onto the floor as a sob escaped her throat. "I don't know what to do. For months I nursed the hurt after Matthew and I broke up and then prayed for someone to come along who was better than him. And nothing happened. When Mr. Bowman left the *News-Trib*, I thought God was giving me a chance to be a reporter, but Jack came along. Isn't it ironic that I end up falling for the man who stole my job?"

"Seems to me God answered your prayer."

Meg looked up and blinked. "How?"

"He sent you just the kind of man you asked for. That's His answer."

"And I'm afraid to take the risk." Meg took several gulps of air and palmed the tears away from her face. "I got comfortable being alone and thought I was over Matthew. I guess his ghost is still hanging around, reminding me of the hurt he caused. Making me question myself, doubt that anyone could ever really love me or stick by me."

"That's just silly. You are absolutely wonderful, and Jack knows it. He would never jilt you like that." Helen picked up Meg's Bible from the nightstand and then sighed deeply. "Truth be told, Meg, I'm having second thoughts about leaving when we planned. If Mom's health continues to go downhill. . .well, we'll have to play it by ear. No need to cancel yet." She flipped through the pages and stopped to read for a moment. "Can I borrow this?"

Was she hearing things? Helen actually wanted a Bible? Meg stood. "Better you have one that isn't written in. I'll freshen up so we can leave for the movies. I think I need some diversion. We'll ask Mom for a spare copy of the Bible on our way out. She'd love to give it to you."

* * * * *

The walk to the movies was quiet. They'd stopped first at Helen's to drop off her new Bible and then continued, each in her own thoughts. Meg knew why she was quiet, but why Helen? Was she thinking about God, or was she disappointed that Meg had met someone?

Meg doubted the second idea. Helen had her choice of suitors— if she wanted one. She'd had dates here and there, but she'd never become involved in a serious relationship since high school. Meg suspected that Helen was as fearful as she was of getting hurt again, even if Helen never admitted it.

They turned onto Main Street, and the theater marquee's bright lights came into view.

"Isn't that Jack?" Helen sped up.

Meg peered down the sidewalk, feeling as though they'd staged this scene before. Except that last time, Jack was alone. Tonight he wasn't.

By the time they arrived at the ticket booth, they could see through the glass door that Jack and his strawberry-blond companion stood at the refreshment counter. He kept his arm draped casually over her shoulders and said something to make her laugh—the same thing he'd often done with Meg. The woman responded, and he offered her the same lopsided grin he'd given Meg many times.

Meg clenched her teeth as a burning sensation filled her chest. It seemed he'd quickly gotten over the thought of being apart from her. After all that talk about missing her—and to think, just yesterday they'd kissed! Well, it wouldn't happen again. Ever.

"Got the tickets." Helen came up beside her.

Meg stepped back. "I've changed my mind."

Helen raised a blond brow. "Why?" She followed the direction of Meg's gaze and her jaw dropped. "Oh," she whispered. "She's quite lovely. The scoundrel!" She gripped Meg's arm and squeezed. "I'm sorry. I take back what I said about him not hurting you."

Meg rolled her eyes, the tears threatening to spill again. "Better I find out now, before making a drastic decision."

Helen pulled her toward Franzoni's. "Come on. We'll go drown your sorrows in a couple of sodas. Forget the movie."

"We already bought our tickets. We have no soda money, remember?"

"Maybe the ticket guy will give us our money back."

Meg yanked her arm from Helen's grip. "No. I'm not going to let him dictate how I spend my evening. The theater is big enough for both of us." She marched toward the theater entrance and flung it open as Jack and his date slipped through the doors on the right side of the auditorium.

After Helen bought popcorn, Meg followed her to a pair of seats at the left side of the theater. On the screen, the newsreel was showing scenes from the World's Fair in Chicago. Meg surveyed the auditorium until her gaze fell on the couple sitting on the far aisle. The flickering light from the screen reflected off their upturned faces.

The blond said something, and he brought his mouth to her ear to answer. Meg could nearly feel his breath in her own ear as she watched. Tears pressed at the back of her eyes as she swallowed a lump. She pulled her gaze away and forced her attention to the screen. *A Bedtime Story*'s first scene beckoned her into its movie world, but the drama across the way drew her like a magnet. Was he holding her hand like he had last week when they'd sat almost in the same seats?

And where had the beauty come from? Meg knew all the single women who lived in Lake Geneva. She must be from the shore. More his type anyway. Meg's stomach burned hot, and the munching sounds from Helen enjoying her popcorn was about to drive her crazy. She nudged Helen. "I'm going to leave. This place is too small for the three of us after all."

Helen nodded. "You want me to come with you?"

Meg shook her head. "Stay. I'll talk to you tomorrow."

She slipped into the lobby and Laura came down the stairs off to her left, her usual pouty mouth set in a grimace.

Meg approached her. "What are you doing here?"

Laura shrugged. "I came with a boy from the play, but he was more interested in me than in the picture, if you know what I mean."

A wave of concern washed over Meg. "Glad I didn't know. Sounds like you handled it okay. Want to walk home together?"

Laura tipped her head. "Not stopping for sodas with Helen like you usually do?"

"Nope. I'm trying to avoid seeing a certain someone and his date, if you know what I mean."

Laura's mouth fell open. "Jack is cheating on you?"

Meg clenched her teeth. "You could say that. And if I meet up with them, I'll likely say something I'll be sorry for later."

"Then we'd better get out of here."

Outside, Meg led the way toward Main Street.

"Hey, sis, I know you're upset, but do we have to walk so fast?"

Meg slowed her pace. "Sorry."

Laura caught up to her. "For a minute I thought you were trying to outwalk me on purpose."

"Why would I do that?" Meg made the turn in front of Cobb Hardware.

"Because—because you've never liked me."

Meg stopped in her tracks. "That's not. . ." She clamped her mouth shut. "Oh, Laura. You're right. I haven't liked you very much lately. But I've always loved you. And, honestly, I never thought you liked *me*."

Laura uttered a sardonic laugh. "Ironic, isn't it?"

Guilt pressed against Meg's chest. Maybe this accidental meeting wasn't so coincidental. Maybe God had allowed it to happen. She glanced at her sister. "You wrote such nice things about me in the playbill, but I don't deserve them. I haven't been much of an example. I'm sorry I've treated you so badly."

Laura studied her feet as she walked. "I meant them, and I didn't want you to move without our making up." She grabbed Meg's arm and squeezed it. "I know you're the one Mom and Dad love best. All I ever hear is concern over you. First over your school difficulties, then over your obsession about being a reporter and moving. I thought while you were at college I'd get some relief, but then they worried about your grades and Matthew. They didn't like him at all. They like Jack a lot, but after tonight. . ."

Meg's breath hitched. "Funny, since you were born I've felt they loved you better."

Silence fell between them, thick and heavy.

"It couldn't have been since I was born, because I didn't join the family until I was six months old." Laura drew a deep breath. "I know I'm adopted."

Meg's mouth fell open, and she stared at her sister. "How long have you known?"

"Since third grade, when I realized I didn't look like any of you. Then I noticed other differences. A couple of years ago, Sarah Jennings told me she'd known she was adopted since kindergarten, and it got me to thinking.

"The next time everyone was out, I snuck into Dad's study and found a file with my papers." She sniffed and wiped her cheek with her palm. "I don't know why they're keeping it a secret, but I can't tell them I know. Can you imagine what would happen if Dad found out I snooped through his office? I also learned some things about my parents' deaths I'm sure he doesn't want known."

"What things?"

"I'd rather you find out yourself. If Dad learns I snooped, I'll be grounded until I'm fifty."

Meg could almost pinpoint the time Laura had learned the truth about her adoption—the same time she began acting like an entitled brat. She drew her sister into her arms and hugged the sobbing girl. "I don't know why they're keeping it from you either. I've wanted to tell you, but Dad and I are at odds enough. . . ." Meg sniffed. "We're a sorry mess. Let me get my handkerchief out of my purse. We can share it."

She released her sister then handed the laced-edged hankie to Laura. "We'll keep this to ourselves until God shows you the proper time to tell them."

Laura dropped the handkerchief into Meg's open purse. "We've wasted a lot of time. And now you're moving away."

Heaviness pressed Meg's heart. Maybe once she made a place for herself as a reporter, she could move home and, like Ginny, find a similar job nearby. That's what she'd shoot for. She had to. There was so much lost time to make up.

Chapter Thirty-Nine
....

Only a lamp burned in the living room when Meg opened the front door. "Looks like Mom and Dad went upstairs early." She gave her sister a hug and whispered, "One good thing came out of my seeing Jack there with that blond and your date not behaving. We got to talk." She drew Laura into a hug. "Love you, little sister."

"Love you too, sis." Laura offered her a small smile. "See you in the morning."

Meg slipped off her heels and padded to the kitchen. A light shone from beneath Dad's door. Instead of going to the icebox as she'd intended, she walked to the sink and stared out the window at the darkened backyard.

God, I don't know what is going on. First Jack shows up at the movies with a gorgeous date, and then I end up making up with Laura. At the same time one relationship seems to have ended, another has been repaired. Is that coincidence?

On impulse, Meg crossed the room and tapped on her father's door. "It's Meg, Dad. Can I come in?"

"Enter."

Dad sat hunched over his desk, reading a law book. He peeled off his glasses and sat back to look at her. "I thought you and Helen were at the movies."

"We were, but I left early. Laura was leaving at the same time, and we walked home together."

He frowned. "I can't remember when the two of you did anything together unless you had to."

"Pretty sad, isn't it? It got me to thinking about when Laura first joined the family. I had a rough time of it."

"Yes, you did. We didn't have much time to warn you about a new sister. Things happened so fast."

Meg frowned. She had to choose her words carefully. "I've been wondering about how it all happened. I was so young at the time. You said our getting her was a surprise. . .but didn't you have to have your names on a list at an adoption agency?"

He stiffened. "It was private. No agency." He closed the law book. "Are you still digging up dirt on Fred Newman?"

Meg straightened. "What does he have to do with Laura's adoption?"

Dad shook his head. "Nothing." He stood and jammed his hands into his pockets. Jingling his coins, he walked to the window then spun around to face Meg. "It's time you knew the truth, Meg. But not one word to your sister."

Meg's thoughts darted around in her mind. Was Fred Laura's father? No. That didn't fit. Grandfather? But he had only one son, who'd died in the war.

"Promise? Not one word to Laura."

Meg's gaze went to her father's intense face. "Promise. But whatever it is, isn't she old enough to know?"

"After she graduates from high school, she'll know." Her father retook his seat. "The people Fred hit in the accident were Laura's parents. I told you they died. . .but I didn't tell you they had a baby who lived. Laura is the baby who survived the crash." He slumped against the chair.

Meg gasped and felt the blood drain from her face. Had she heard right? She stared at Dad, willing herself to speak, but nothing came out.

"The couple had no other family," Dad continued in a hoarse voice. "Laura would have gone to an orphanage. I told your mother about the blond baby girl who was orphaned by the crash, and without hesitation she said we should adopt her. You see, we hadn't been able to. . . We hadn't intended for you to be an only child, but until the accident, God hadn't blessed us that way.

"We felt terrible about not preparing you, but we didn't want to promise you a sister and have the adoption fall through. I'm so sorry, Meg." He dug into his pocket, pulled out a handkerchief, and blew his nose. "When you had such a hard time adjusting to Laura, we blamed ourselves." Dad looked down at his handkerchief. "I've always felt guilty for how you struggled in school. And when that blasted teacher of yours said you wouldn't amount to anything, right in front of you, I wanted to demand she be fired. You mother insisted I calm down. I knew that rotten woman had been wrong and prayed her remark hadn't caused you harm." He looked up, searching Meg's face. "All I've wanted is to help you, protect you, encourage you to be all God wants you to be."

Meg wiped her eyes. "Mom tried to tell me that's why you insisted I work for you. But I didn't believe her."

"You've become so engrossed with wanting a reporter job, and I knew Oscar would never allow it. I was trying to spare you the disappointment." He shook his head. "Your mother set me straight on that one too. I'm sorry, Meg. I forget you're a grown woman now. I need to sit back and let God work your life out according to His plan."

Meg nodded. "As do I. I've felt so far from Him these past months. When I ask Him what to do, He doesn't answer me."

Dad leaned forward and leveled bloodshot eyes on her. "If you keep your distance from Him, how are you going to hear Him? Remember, He spoke to Elisha in a whisper." He reached across the desk and took Meg's hands in his. "I don't know what's going on between you and Jack, but he's a fine young man, and I can see that he cares for you a lot. Don't throw away God's plan for you just to chase a dream of your own making."

She yearned to tell Dad that, after tonight, she thought Jack could jump in the lake, but she held her tongue. He'd find out soon enough about the two-timer. "I'll pray about it." She stood and came around the desk, arms open. He stood and drew her into a hug.

"I'm going upstairs now to work things out with God. Thanks, Daddy. I love you."

Chapter Forty

....

When Meg reached the top of the stairs and saw Laura's light glowing beneath her door, she fought the urge to knock and tell her that she knew everything. But she'd promised Dad she wouldn't say a word, and besides, she had unfinished business with God to take care of.

She slipped on her nightgown then climbed into bed and lifted the Bible from where Helen had left it on the nightstand. Hugging the book to her chest, she closed her eyes. "God, I've no right to come before You without saying I'm really sorry for not trusting You. I've been very wrong and selfish about a lot of things. Please help me get back into Your Word and learn to fully trust You for my life."

She flipped open the Bible and found Proverbs 3:5–6. She hadn't studied the passage since that long ago Sunday when Jack happened upon her in the park. She read the words. *"Trust in the Lord with all thine heart; and lean not unto thine own understanding. In all thy ways acknowledge him, and he shall direct thy paths."*

For as long as Meg could remember, she thought her father believed her old teacher's words. The way he had tried to block her desire to advance in newswriting seemed to prove it. How wonderful to know she was wrong. And after Jack told her what his college professor said about other people having similar struggles, she'd realized it wasn't her fault—it was the way she was made.

She flipped to Psalm 139 and read the familiar words to herself. God had made her exactly as He wanted her to be, fearfully and wonderfully made. Made to write, for sure, but how and where? Even Mr. Zimmer had softened lately. Helen's words from earlier in the evening echoed in her thoughts. Had God really answered her prayers by sending Jack into her life? Before he came, the only writing she'd done was on the sly, but now she didn't have to hide it. She pressed her palm to her chest. "I'm so sorry, Lord."

She threw the covers off and knelt beside her bed. "Father, forgive me for not trusting You or depending on You. You do know what's best for me. All the time I thought You weren't answering my prayers, You were. I've been so selfish.

"I admit that I was very jealous tonight. Help me to not jump to conclusions about the girl he was with until I know the truth. If Jack and I are meant to be together, I'll let You work it out. I do love him, Lord. I only hope I love him enough to let him go, if You say it's not to be."

She finished her prayer and crawled under the covers. Tomorrow couldn't come soon enough. Since it was deadline day, she'd probably have to wait until evening for a private conversation with Jack. She closed her eyes. By this time tomorrow night she'd either be the happiest she'd been in a long while or the saddest. But either way she'd be at peace for the first time in ages.

Chapter Forty-One

....

Meg stepped through the office door a little past seven the next morning and stared at Jack's clean desktop. Usually on deadline day he was there by six thirty. Maybe he was in Mr. Zimmer's office doing the layout. She scurried across the room, her heels click-clacking on the wood floor, and peeked into Mr. Zimmer's office.

Her boss looked up and blinked. "Miss Alden, don't tell me you've come early to give me another letter. I've still got the other one right here and don't need another unless it's to say you've changed your mind."

Her heart squeezed at his words. How many times had Jack said that Mr. Zimmer loved her like a daughter? "No letter, but I was looking for Jack."

A grin split his face. "I keep hoping he'll convince you to stay even when I can't. Didn't he tell you he's taking a couple days off? How could I say no after all the hours he's put in, keeping this rag afloat? You too. I know you worked hard, same as him. Purvis starts today, so we can handle it."

Meg's thoughts darted into a world of doubt. Why hadn't he told her he was taking a couple of days off? Was Jack with that girl? "Jack worked far harder than me. I guess he forgot to mention his plans for today. What I wanted can wait."

"Well, in the meantime, I could use some help while I get Mr. Purvis started. Do you mind doing some fillers to put in 'Town Talk'?"

She stepped into his office. "I'd be happy to." She took the folder he held out.

"Good. Get them to Composing after they're proofed. We'll get this paper out on time without Jack. He deserves some time off."

Meg frowned. Waiting a couple of days wouldn't be easy, but with her new attitude, she'd manage to take each day as it came and trust God.

* * * * *

On Thursday morning Jack arrived at the office, excited to finally see Meg. He hadn't caught a glimpse of her since that day on his pier. He should have called her when he found he wasn't going to be in the office, but after their last discussion, he'd thought putting some distance between them might be helpful.

His eyes went straight to her desk, and his heart skipped a beat. Dark wavy curls, cherry-red lips, tan suit concealing the curves he found so appealing. . . He approached and came to a halt in front of her desk. "Morning, Meg."

She looked up. "Hi, Jack."

"Sorry I kind of disappeared on you for a few days. Unexpected company." He waited for her to ask who his company was, but she didn't. "There's an exclusive unveiling of the Riviera ballroom this morning for the press and city council. Care to go with me?"

She glanced away, and he followed the trail of her gaze to Mr. Purvis, the fill-in reporter. His sleeves rolled up, revealing hairy forearms, and his jaw looking like he forgot to shave that morning, the man seemed as if he'd be more at home reporting on the doings in the Bowery. "What about him?" Meg asked. "He's the reporter."

The man could care less about the Riviera. He'd said so himself during his interview last week. "He doesn't have your background knowledge. Besides, it will add strength to the piece you're going to do about the event."

"What piece? I—"

Jack held up a hand to stop her. "Oscar approved it. Nothing on the sly. Your angle is the society side, but it can be more than a report of who came with whom."

"Mr. Zimmer approved?"

He loved telling her good news. "As long as yours is from a society point of view." He glanced at the clock. "We need to leave at ten fifteen." He ambled back to Oscar's office, which was his for the morning, and closed the door behind him.

Instead of sitting, he wandered to the window and looked out at the new mortuary being readied across the alley. Oscar would have an interesting view when funerals began over there. He supposed he deserved the lackluster greeting from Meg, given they were a couple and he'd not shared his plans with her. But if she missed him at all, wouldn't she at least have something to say about his lack of communication?

Was it time to begin thinking seriously about moving on to the *Beacon*? The problem was that by doing so, he'd push Mr. Snow out of the way. Was running the paper something Snow aspired to? Had his hopes soared at being given the opportunity? Jack turned and stepped over to the desk. Why did everything have to be so complicated?

* * * * *

Two hours later, Jack smiled at how Meg matched his stride as they set off down Main Street. He enjoyed how her hat rested on the back of her head with her brown curls spilling out around it. It suited her. "Still making arrangements for your big move?"

"Yes, but we're playing things by ear as to the exact date. Helen's mom's health has worsened. Helen's worried about her, but her mother insists we go and follow our dreams. She does have a friend moving in to take Helen's place in the shop, so she won't be alone."

Jack's spirits lifted. Not that he'd wish a woman bad health, but if it delayed Meg's departure even a couple of weeks, he wouldn't mind. It might help him get back into her good graces.

Meg lifted her eyes to meet his. "I guess this is where trusting God has to prove itself, doesn't it?"

He gave a half smile. "You're right about that." Sometimes he wished he could do something to help God along, like call that guy at the *Examiner* and strongly suggest he give Meg's job to someone else.

They turned south at the intersection and continued down the east side of Broad. Meg stopped when they came to the Geneva Hotel. "Doesn't the Riviera look stunning?"

Across the road, the sand-colored building with its terra-cotta-tiled roof looked as if it had always been there. The architect had outdone himself. *Stunning* wasn't the word. Maybe *magnificent*. He couldn't even remember the building it replaced, so insignificant it must have been.

They crossed over, and Meg picked up her pace as though she were a child racing to get the last piece of candy.

The closer they came, the more Jack's insides trembled at the excitement of finally seeing the interior. Of course, half of his enthusiasm was because of Meg's joy. She'd not said much about attending dances at the old building. Had she and Matthew spent time there? Was she a good dancer? He hoped to find out come Monday night.

They arrived at the same cement steps he and Meg had raced up that long-ago Sunday. At the top of the staircase, a red-and-green-striped awning had been added to shield ticket buyers from the elements. Men's voices drifted toward them from behind, so he turned. Mayor Taggart and several aldermen approached.

The mayor grinned. "Glad to see the *News-Trib* here. I know you'll write glowing reports about this place." He kept his eyes on Jack, ignoring Meg.

"We both will." Jack stuck out his hand. "Good to see you again, Mayor. You know Meg Alden, one of our writers?" He pressed the small of Meg's back with his palm.

The man focused on Meg for the first time. "Yes. Of course." He turned to his companions. "Shall we go on in?" He gestured for Jack and Meg to lead the way.

Jack's mouth fell open as he stepped inside and let his gaze rove from the white columns surrounding the dance floor to the promenade behind them. Other than the green-tinted walls that coordinated with the blue-green-and-tan tiles in the promenade floor, everything else was in shades of white or cream. He expected a line of chorus girls from a Busby Berkeley movie set to parade onto the floor at any moment.

"Isn't it gorgeous?" Meg gave a twirl as she wandered to the center of the parquet dance floor, her skirt whirling out and giving a glimpse of lace before it resettled around her legs. She paused beneath the mirror ball that hung dead center from the tiled ceiling. It twinkled in the sunlight that streamed through the roof's clerestory windows. He fought the urge to join Meg for a spin around the floor. Not exactly the proper decorum for a newsman, even in a small town.

She wandered to one of the black table-and-chairs on the promenade and ran a hand over a chair back.

Jack joined her. "I had no idea it would be this marvelous. The windows let in wonderful light. Too bad the effect will be lost at night."

"But think how the lights will play off the mirror ball. It's going to twinkle like the stars." Meg sighed. "Guess we'd better take some notes."

They simultaneously pulled out notebooks and burst out laughing. Meg's eyes twinkled as much as the mirror ball. Her point of view would be so much better than his. Too bad he couldn't step out of the project altogether. "I have an idea. I'll write from the male point of view, and you take the lady's."

"That's perfect," they said together, and Meg giggled.

"What's so funny?" Meg's father strolled up, an uncharacteristic wide grin broadening his face.

"Dad, when did you get here?" She scooted up to him and hooked her hand through his arm. *Whoa*. What had happened since he'd last seen them?

Mr. Alden patted Meg's hand. "A minute ago. I hope that whatever is so funny has nothing to do with the decorating."

"Not at all, sir." Jack stepped forward and offered his hand. "We both said the same thing about an article for this beautiful place."

Mr. Alden's eyes lit up. "Did you see the terrace at the south wall? Great place for dancers to cool off and view the lake."

Following his suggestion, they headed toward an arched door next to an expanse of windows and stepped onto the veranda. Jack strolled to the waist-high wall. The lake shimmered in the morning sun, while a private yacht bobbed at the white dock below.

Meg joined him. "I don't know if I can find enough words to describe this place."

He leaned an arm on the wall, careful to not get his sleeve entangled with the wrought-iron trim, and fixed his gaze on her eyes. Who cared about lake views with beauty right beside him? "You will. I can't help but notice that your father seems so..." He scrambled for the right word and came up empty.

"Changed? He's been like that since Laura and I buried our hatchet. Jack, the tension has left our home. He and I talked about a lot of things. And I had a long talk with God and realized how wrong I've been not to trust Him. In fact, I wanted to tell you—"

"Meg, Jack, you'd better get in here." Mr. Alden stood at the door leading inside.

"Coming, Dad." Her face a wonderful shade of pink, Meg pushed off from the ledge. "Shall we go inside?"

He followed her to the door. Odd... She seemed to be embarrassed about something. But what? They stepped into the ballroom. A cluster of people stood around the man hired to manage the facility.

"We expect Mr. King and his orchestra to arrive at the Geneva Hotel about midmorning on Monday," the tall bald man said. "The mayor will greet them, and after they've checked in, they'll come across the street here to practice."

"How will they get from the train depot to the hotel?" a reporter from Janesville asked.

"The orchestra has its own tour bus. They won't be taking the train." He scanned the crowd. "Any more questions?"

"What other bands have you booked for the summer?" Jack held his pencil over his pad.

"Several, including Tommy Dorsey in July. The full schedule will be released within the next two weeks."

Meg stood on tiptoe and whispered to Jack, "I can't wait to hear Tommy—"

"You won't be here."

"Oh. That's right." She stuffed her pad into her handbag and gave him a tight smile.

The meeting drew to a quick close. After saying good-bye to Meg's father, they took the back stairs to the lower level and strolled through the first-floor concourse running from the front of the building to the back, where it opened out onto the docks. Behind one counter, a workman scrubbed a griddle. Two other men installed a popcorn machine at the counter next to him.

"I almost hate to go back to the office. Is there any chance we could get lunch somewhere?" she said as they walked.

Jack jammed his hands into his pockets. "Isn't it kind of early for lunch?"

She shrugged. "I suppose so, but we haven't talked in several days."

"I know. But I have to leave. Mom's coming in from Colorado on the train, and I have to meet her."

Her eyes widened. "She's coming for sure, for the grand opening? Maybe after she settles in at the house, you and I could chat a bit."

He lifted his fedora and ran a hand over his hair. "I'm meeting her in Chicago at that train station. We're going to spend the weekend at our house in Lake Forest. We have lots to discuss regarding my dad and the *Beacon*. If I get a chance, I'll give you a call and we can talk on the phone."

They'd arrived in front of the office, and he paused by his car, taking her hand. He hated seeing the disappointment that had registered on her face ever since he'd mentioned heading into Chicago. He wanted to throw caution to the wind and kiss her right there, but he had to think of her reputation. On an empty pier with no one around was one thing, but on Main Street? He gave her hand a squeeze and let go. "See you Monday."

She smiled up at him. "I can't wait to meet your mom. Please give her my best." She turned and walked toward the door. He took a step in her direction. One brotherly kiss on the cheek wouldn't hurt. Movement in the window caught his eye. He waved at Emily, and she ducked out of sight. Jack turned and got into his car. He waved at Meg then watched her step inside. Something was bothering her. He could only hope it wasn't him.

Chapter Forty-Two
....

Meg glanced over her shoulder. "Come on, Helen. I need to be in the ballroom before the crowds arrive." Her friend had stopped to study a coming-attraction poster on the Geneva Theatre's wall. Helen's scarlet-red halter dress, a copy of a Jean Harlow frock from a recent movie, fit her like a second skin. Other than Harlow herself, Meg couldn't imagine anyone else wearing the dress.

Helen laughed. "We're a half hour ahead of when Jack asked you to arrive and only five minutes away." She twirled toward Meg, her white-gold hair glistening in the late afternoon sun. Her skirt's sheer fabric swished and lifted above her ankles to give a hint of her slender legs. Legs Meg would trade her more muscular ones for any day.

They stopped at the intersection to wait for the light, and Helen looked Meg over with a satisfied smile. "I'm glad I convinced you to order that dress. It looks like it was tailor-made."

Meg fingered the ruffled trim of her chiffon print frock then lifted an edge of the skirt and let the breeze catch it. She'd hesitated to order the dress since, even from Sears Roebuck, it cost almost a week's pay. But she had to admit, she loved how pretty it made her feel. Would the gown knock Jack's socks off like Helen said? What would it matter? She'd only talked to him once since last Saturday, when he called from Lake Forest to say that he and his mom were having a good visit and he wouldn't be coming back to town until Monday morning, the day of the grand opening. Well, tonight she would keep her dance card open only for him and get him alone as soon as possible.

A car passed in front of them, and Helen stepped back from the curb. "Meg, can we talk a minute before we go in?"

Meg faced Helen, startled to see worry lines creasing her friend's forehead.

"I'm not saying I'm backing out of our plans," Helen said. "But I keep thinking, What if something terrible happens to Mom and we're way out there on the West Coast? This whole week, every time I've cut someone's hair, I've been reminded I'll never cut the woman's hair again." She stared at her feet. "I'm not saying I'm not going. . .but I've been reading the Bible your mom gave me, and it's becoming clear I need to put my mom first. She's raised me alone, taught me all she knows about hair, and will leave the shop to me someday. How can I run out on her?"

Meg bit her lower lip. "You're forgetting you let me off the hook a couple of weeks ago, and the agreement works both ways. I've been praying for God's clear direction myself."

Helen wrapped Meg in a hug. "Thank you."

Meg took her hand. "Let's just let each day take care of itself and see what God has planned for us." She squeezed Helen's hand. "Shall we go?"

They crossed and arrived at the staircase leading to the ballroom. A couple rushed past them, all but running up the concrete steps. The woman's taffeta dress crinkled as she moved. Meg took a deep breath before pulling her notepad from her purse. "Wait, Helen, while I write down my first impressions." She jotted short words and phrases in a kind of shorthand she'd developed. *Soft warm breeze. . .wispy clouds in the sunset reflected in the water. . .ladies in elegant finery. . .hair swept onto their heads in a tangle of curls. . .men in lightweight linen suits with boater hats. . .air electric.*

Tomorrow she'd turn them into full phrases. She stuffed the pencil and notebook in her beaded handbag and waited while Helen bought her ticket. Then Meg gave the ticket taker her press pass, and they stepped through the glass doors.

Next to her, Helen squealed. "Are you sure we aren't on a movie set? You told me it was beautiful, but I never expected this."

Meg grinned. "It does look like Hollywood." She raised her eyes to the ceiling, which had turned almost orange from the reflected sunset outside the windows. White chiffon streamers attached to the center ceiling above the mirror ball floated down to where they were anchored to the column bases.

Laughter and chattering voices from early arrivals mixed with the orchestra's soft warm-up tones. Meg drew out her pencil and noted several dignitaries who had just arrived. More people filtered in, gathering in groups, oohing and ahhing or getting punch at the concession counter.

She strolled from group to group, getting quotes and noting their impressions. As dusk fell, the soft interior lights cast a glow, giving the room a magical feel. Meg wandered to the east windows. Lights twinkled from the Luzern Hotel where it sat on a rise across from Flat Iron Park. She turned and scanned the crowd. People from the lakeshore like the Wrigleys and Sydney Smith, the famous "Andy Gump" cartoonist, mingled with residents from town and surrounding farms. She spotted Mrs. Branigan and waved.

She surveyed the room, but she knew without searching for him—everyone was there except for Jack. Had he had an accident? Had his dad taken a turn for the worse?

"Meg, look who's here."

She turned.

Helen hurried up to her with a broad-shouldered man following. His dark, short-cropped hair framed a handsome face that looked vaguely familiar.

Meg tilted her head. "Have we met?"

He laughed and pulled at the sleeve of what looked to be a new suit. "You're the second person who hasn't recognized me. I'm Tom Rutherford. We were in high school together."

Of course. The boyfriend who'd left Helen for the navy. Meg stepped down from the promenade. "Good to see you again, Tom."

He grinned. "I've been in the navy and then lived in Indiana awhile, working for my uncle in his auto-repair business and boxing on the side.

Got so the boxing started taking over my life and I needed to get out of there. I'm working for Lakeside Chevrolet now." He smiled. "Didn't recognize Helen here, with her blond hair and all."

Helen batted her eyelashes. "Tell her what you said when you saw me."

Tom laughed. "You mean that I thought Jean Harlow was in town?"

"Yeah." She looked at Meg. "Isn't that funny?"

Meg started to say, "That's what half the people think when they see her," but thought better of it. She looked toward the entrance. "Well, I'm on the job tonight and need to cover the door. Good to see you again, Tom. Enjoy the evening."

He nodded. "I plan to, now that I've run into Helen."

Already, Helen had seemed to come alive after bumping into her old beau. Meg didn't want to see her friend hurt twice by the same man and hoped Helen would be careful.

Scurrying across the dance floor toward the front of the ballroom, Meg stopped dead center under the mirror ball. Jack stood at the door, tall and erect. Like everything else he wore, his white dinner jacket and tuxedo pants fit him perfectly.

Her heart pounded in her throat as she wended her way toward him. Whatever had detained him didn't matter. Tonight he'd see that she indeed did dance, and he wouldn't leave without her telling him exactly how she felt about him.

She raised her hand to wave as he turned his head and offered his arm to the woman behind him—the same strawberry-blond he'd been with the other night. The woman slipped her dainty hand into the crook of his elbow, and they proceeded across the promenade.

Meg tried to pull her eyes away from the elegant angel-like figure floating on Jack's arm, but her gaze refused to move regardless of the stab of pain pressing at the back of her eyes.

An older woman came behind them, regal in a black crepe gown, its glittery top elegant but understated. Jack whispered something to his date then guided the lady who must be his mother over to the mayor and his wife for introductions.

An ache filled Meg's throat. She squared her shoulders as irritation overrode the hurt. Not only had he come late, but he was acting like a guest. She turned toward a group gathered on the far side of the room and marched their direction. At least one of them was working.

She'd just thanked Mrs. Hammersley, the druggist's wife, for her comments when a booming voice welcomed everyone to the Riviera's grand-opening celebration. Meg turned toward the orchestra. Wayne King stood taller than she expected and was better looking in person than in his publicity pictures. She let out a sigh. If only they had access to camera equipment. A shot of the room, the orchestra, and everyone in their finery would have made a swell splash on the front page. Well, she'd have to work harder to take a picture with words.

The musicians broke out with "Twelfth Street Rag" and people poured onto the dance floor, including Helen and Tom, matching move-for-move with a version of the Lindy Hop. Next to them, Jack and his date whirled around as though they'd danced together for years. It was just as well he brought her. Meg couldn't dance near as well. She stepped up to the promenade to engage the mayor and his wife in conversation then made a note of Mrs. Taggart's rose-tinted frock. Satisfied that she had enough, Meg returned her pad and pencil to her bag as a stir at the entrance erupted.

Hat in hand and wearing a rumpled suit, Mr. Zimmer and his wife stood next to Lester. Had he climbed those stairs? Wasn't it too soon to exert himself like that? Meg zigzagged her way through the throng and came up to her boss. "Mr. Zimmer, I didn't realize you were coming."

He peered at her over the top of his glasses. "And miss the most exciting night in Lake Geneva's history? It's wonderful to see everyone dressed up and having a good time." He scowled. "Did I see you over there taking notes? I agreed to you and Wallace doing that article together, but I expect you to enjoy yourself."

Despite the twinkle in his eyes, Meg's face warmed. Truth was, she'd been so busy gathering comments and staying far away from a certain man and his date that she'd let the first hour of the event fly past her. "I'm enjoying myself."

"By the look on your face, I'd never have guessed it. You'd do better to be out there dancing with Jack than talking to me."

The orchestra segued into a lively tune. "I love this song," Lester said. "Meg, do you want to dance?"

She gulped and forced a smile. "Sure."

On the dance floor, Lester placed his hand at the small of her back and jerked her to the right. She stumbled over his foot and scrambled for her balance.

"I'm not much of a dancer. Sorry."

"No problem, but why don't we just take small steps?"

Over Lester's shoulder, a small crowd formed to watch a couple dance.

"Let's see who they're watching." Meg stepped out of Lester's hold and peeked over a woman's shoulder.

Emily turned. "Meg, I didn't see you here. Aren't they wonderful together? They really know those swing moves."

Jack twirled his date under his arm and lifted her in the air, her gauzy dress floating.

Emily looked at Meg again, her eyes sad. "I really thought you made a perfect couple. I'm sorry for manipulating you two together like I did."

Meg pushed her voice past the lump in her throat. "Not to worry. We were only dating, not getting married to each other."

"I had no idea Wallace was such a swell dancer." Lester had come up beside her. "And he always seems to find a good-looking gal too. Know who she is, Meg?"

"Lester, don't you ever know when to be quiet?" Emily sent him a scowl and turned her shoulder to him.

"What did I say?"

Meg shook her head. "Nothing, Lester. I don't know who she is." Lester was right. Jack always managed to have an attractive woman on his arm. All the more reason not to let him get under her skin. If only her heart would listen. "I see Helen. Talk to you later." Meg dashed across the room. Best to be out of the vicinity before the music ended and she had to face Jack.

"Isn't this the most fantastic night?" Helen squealed her words above the din of laughter and chattering voices as Meg approached her.

"It's wonderful." Meg looked around. "Where's Tom?"

"Getting me some punch. You know, it's like we've never been apart. Do you think God has other plans for both of us, Meg?"

Meg forced a smile. "Maybe." Though her own heart ached, she didn't want to be a killjoy in the face of Helen's newfound happiness. Maybe she'd find herself on a train going West alone. At least she'd know for sure that God's plan for her didn't include Jack.

Chapter Forty-Three
....

"There you are, Meg. Would you like to dance?"

At the sound of the deep, smooth voice, Meg's heart skipped a beat. She turned.

Jack stood a few feet away, a corner of his mouth pulled up into the crooked smile that always sent her heart racing. He ran his eyes over her in a way that seemed like a caress.

She nodded and took his hand. At his touch, tingles shot up her arm. He pulled her toward the dance floor. What was she going to do if it was a fast number? She knew none of those swing steps she'd watched him do. And where was his date? She scanned the crowd. The blond beauty chatted with Jack's mom, not once looking their way. Wouldn't she be concerned about Jack dancing with someone else?

The orchestra began a slow number, and Meg relaxed. Slow, she could do. Jack gathered her into his arms and held her snug against him, guiding her around the perimeter of dancers. Her feet felt light, as if she were floating. He drew her closer until their cheeks met. The scruff of his shaven jaw rubbed against her skin, and more tingles raced up her spine. She tightened her left arm across his back as the crooner's mellow voice sang out the words. Jack sang along.

"I'll be loving you always, with a love that's true always. When the things you've planned need a helping hand, I will understand always."

Meg closed her eyes. Jack nuzzled his mouth closer to her ear and sang the words again. She all but groaned, wishing he really did love her that way. She had to keep her head, guard her heart. It was only a song. He'd come with someone else. The same someone whom he took to the movies.

"You're a wonderful dancer, Meg."

She drew back as his eyes searched her face. "It must be the man who's leading me so well."

He grinned. "Ah, compliments will get you everywhere. Great dance, isn't it? The committee must be very proud. And in case you're concerned, I plan to summarize my impressions when I get home tonight and then bang out my article in the morning."

There he went, reading her mind again. But the truth be told, she'd forgotten she was even angry or hurt. "I was a little concerned. Did you see Mr. Zimmer?"

"I did, but I haven't had a chance to say hello."

She scanned the crowd on the promenade as they danced. "Maybe you'll have one now. He's over there, talking to your date."

Jack stared at her, his brows arched high. "I call my sister a lot of things, but I've never called her my date."

Meg's right foot landed on his left, and she stumbled backward. He caught her and drew her against his chest. "Whoa, girl."

All tension left her shoulders. "She's your sister?"

"I intended to introduce you, but I couldn't find you in this mass of humanity. She surprised me last week by popping in for a few days before heading to Milwaukee to visit a friend. That's why I took those days off." He stepped back and ran his eyes over her frame then caught her gaze in his own, drawing her in like a lion to his prey. "You look beautiful tonight, Meg."

His gently spoken words washed over her like a warm spring rain. Grateful for the dim lighting that hopefully masked her blush, she smiled. "Thanks."

He stepped closer and brushed a lock of hair off her cheek. Tingles filled her stomach. "I'm not just saying that because you're all dressed up. I've thought you beautiful since the first day we met."

"There you are, brother dear." Jack's sister came up and grinned at Meg. "Hi, I'm Kate Weber, Jack's sister. You must be Meg. I've heard so much about you these past few days, I feel like I know you."

....

Feeling really stupid for wasting so much time on being jealous, Meg held out her hand. "And I've heard a lot about you too."

Kate took Meg's hand and gave it a soft squeeze, "I hope it was all good."

The band started a jive song and Kate looked at Jack. "Meg, do you mind if I steal my twin from you for this song? We've not danced together in a long time, and I'm enjoying it."

Meg laughed. "Be my guest. I'll be happy to watch." She stepped away as the dance floor filled. If she and Jack did end up together, she'd have to work on her dance skills.

* * * * *

Jack spun Kate and circled her waist with his left arm as he let her down into a dip to end the song. She straightened, and he hugged her. "Katie girl, you haven't lost your touch. You'll have to come up here this summer so we can perfect our moves."

She pressed a palm to her stomach. "This will probably be my last dance for the next seven months or so. No time like the present to ask how you like the idea of being called Uncle Jack."

Jack's jaw dropped. "Really? I'm going to be an uncle?"

Kate nodded. "Paul and I found out a couple of weeks ago, and I'm waiting until you, Mom, and I are together after the dance to tell Mom. We had so little time between you two arriving and having to leave for the dance. We're absolutely thrilled."

Jack grabbed her and whirled her into a slow dance that had begun a few beats earlier. "That's the best news I've had all day. From now on, only slow songs for you, Katie girl."

She leaned back and grinned. "Don't you want to save the slow ones for Meg? I saw that dreamy look on your face when you two were dancing. You'd better snap her up fast."

"I'm trying, but it seems like everything is against us."

"Like what? That dreamy look wasn't only on your face, Jack. She's crazy about you. I can see it. Mom can see it. In fact, if you don't bring her over to meet our mother, Mom's going to go crazy."

He loved hearing Kate's words, but now that she was expecting, he had no choice but to go to the *Beacon* and save it for her. "I have other priorities before I can settle down, and Meg is thinking about moving to California to chase her dream of being a reporter."

"What priorities?"

He pressed his head to hers and whispered, "Making sure that managing the *Beacon* is there for you as soon as you are ready. I know Dad has Will Snow running things now, but not giving you a chance because you're a woman isn't fair."

She stopped dancing, and he stumbled over her foot. "Would you repeat that, please?"

"You've dreamed of running the *Beacon* ever since we were in high school. I'm going to make sure it's yours whenever you're ready for it. But I have to figure out how to have Dad see the light and let me have the job first."

Kate laughed and shook her head. "Jack, I love you for being so faithful to me, but I haven't dreamed of running the paper since I left for college and met Paul. I'm happy being Paul's wife, and I think motherhood is going to be my full-time job for a long time. You know, Jackie, I get the sense you don't really want the *Beacon* either. As far as I'm concerned, let Snow have the job. Maybe when the time comes, we can still own the business but pay someone else to run it."

Jack spun her around the floor, suddenly feeling as if he could fly. He felt free—except for two things. He needed to find Oscar and Meg. Meg first. "You're right. I don't want it." He grinned. "Do you mind if I find Meg?"

"I never thought you'd ask. I'm heading for the punch."

* * * * *

When Meg saw Jack and Kate continue dancing, she turned away and chatted with a lady she knew from the bank. It felt good to not worry about Jack and Kate—or Jack and Ginny for that matter. She probably wouldn't be seeing Ginny for a while anyway; Meg had heard she'd gotten a reporting job at the *Chicago Tribune*. Meg was happy for her.

An arm came around her from behind, and Jack pulled her into his arms as the orchestra began another slow dance. "Glad I found you. May I have another dance with the beautiful lady in my arms?"

She giggled. "Do I have any choice?"

"Not if I have anything to do with it. But you'd better behave. . .I see your parents." He turned until she had a view. "Let's work our way over and say hello." He artfully moved his feet until they came up beside the older couple.

"Well, Margaret, look who's here." Dad flashed a grin as he bounced to the beat. "So what do you think, Meggie? Does the Riviera meet your expectations?"

Meg laughed. He hadn't called her *Meggie* since she was small. "More so, Dad. It's breathtaking."

The couples danced their separate ways, and a few minutes later the music ended. Jack kept his hand on Meg's waist and looked at her expectantly. Was she to stay with him the rest of the evening? He'd said he'd write down his impressions later at home. No reason why she couldn't do the same.

Jack took her hand. "Let's go see my mom and Kate."

Meg let Jack lead her across the room, loving how he kept his hand tight around hers. They came up to his sister and mother. "Mom, here's someone I want you to meet. This is Meg."

Mrs. Wallace greeted Meg with a warm smile. "It's nice to meet you, Meg. Jack has told me so much about you. I hope you can visit at the house while I'm here."

Jack grinned. "We have to work on our article tomorrow, but maybe I can bring her out for dinner tomorrow night." He looked at Meg. "Okay with you?"

Meg nodded. "Of course. I'd like that."

"Come on, let's get another dance in." Jack tugged her toward the parquet dance floor, as "Dream a Little Dream of Me" filled the air. "We'll be back in a bit, Mom."

With some people having left, they had plenty of room, and Jack widened his steps. Meg leaned back and grinned, her eyes twinkling. "You're a wonderful dancer."

"Thanks to Kate and me being forced to take dancing lessons." He twirled her under his arm and drew her in, bringing their cheeks together. She followed him like they'd always been partners. He brought his mouth close to her ear and sang the lyrics like the time before. *"Stars shining bright above you, night breezes seem to whisper, 'I love you,' birds singing in the sycamore trees, dream a little dream of me."*

Jack leaned back and caught her gaze then snuggled her close and whispered, "I'm really going to miss you if you go to California." The singer began crooning again, and Jack did too, tightening his arm around her.

When the music wound down, he kept hold of her hand. "Let's test out that terrace and see if it's as nice as we thought."

Still tingling all over from Jack's crooning in her ear, sounding as though he meant every line, Meg let him lead her across the dance floor past the orchestra. Her knees wobbled, and she grabbed his arm. He slowed and smiled down at her before circling her waist with his arm, pulling her snug against him.

She didn't want to say good-bye to this man. Ever. Could she take the risk without an immediate commitment from him?

He held the door, and she went through first. A couple standing in the shadows stepped away from an embrace, and the woman giggled.

Jack took her hand and led her to the far end of the terrace. They stopped next to the wall. "Look at the water and how it reflects the moon. Isn't it just as we imagined?" He settled an arm around her shoulder.

As if God had hung His own mirror ball, a full moon beamed in the sky. Meg snuggled into the crook of Jack's arm, and he pulled her closer and wrapped her in a hug. She pressed her face against his chest and reached around his torso. Never had she felt so safe and content.

"Those words I was singing in there before. . .I meant them for you, Meg."

She stopped breathing and leaned back. He bent down and placed a kiss on the tip of her nose. "I love you, Meg. Don't go to California."

Without waiting for her to answer, he lowered his head and kissed her. Softly, tenderly.

Finally, the words she wanted to hear. "Oh, Jack, I love you too. I'm sorry I've been so mistrustful of you."

He pressed his fingertips over her mouth. "Sweetheart, I will never hurt you like Matthew did. You're the only girl for me—the woman I believe God has for me. But if you need time to try your wings in California, go. I'll be right here, waiting and running the *News-Trib*."

She blinked. What was he saying? "You? Running the *News-Trib*? Why? I don't understand."

"This afternoon, Oscar asked me if I wanted to buy the paper. He's had a lot of time to think while recuperating, and he realizes it's time to hang up his hat and get out of the paper business. To leave it to the next generation."

"But how can you own the paper here and run the *Beacon* for your dad?"

"I'm not going to run the *Beacon*. We hope Mr. Snow will be there a long time while Kate and I get on with our lives. Working here for the past several months, I've realized that running a small paper is more to my liking. Dad knew that, and he and Oscar worked out the plan for me to work here for a year in the hopes that I'd realize what Dad already knew. Of course, when they both got sick, things became a little confused for a while."

Meg just stared at him.

"All this time, I'd thought Kate wanted to run Dad's paper, so I turned Oscar down. But he wouldn't let me say no just yet." He turned to her and took her face in his hands. "I'm going to go in there in a minute and tell Oscar the deal is on. I'm staying here in Lake Geneva."

Meg covered her mouth with her hand. How could she ever leave now?

"I'd best do this right." Jack dropped to one knee and took hold of Meg's hand.

Her heart pounded against her chest, and she gripped his hand tightly.

"Meg Alden, I love you with all my heart. Will you marry me?"

"Yes. Yes. Yes!"

Jack popped to his feet and grinned. "You do realize that by saying yes, there's no way you're moving anywhere. . .unless I go with you."

She giggled. "I wouldn't dream of leaving."

He bent slightly and brought his lips to hers. A delicious sensation filled every pore of her body. She brought her hand to his neck and the kiss deepened. She loved this man, had for weeks, and he loved her.

The kiss broke, and he whispered, "I hadn't planned on proposing tonight, so I don't have a ring. But you'll get one very soon. How does a late-summer wedding sound? Maybe right here in the ballroom. With Reverend Hellman officiating, of course."

"Like a dream come true."

The strains of "Always" drifted from the ballroom, and they began to dance. He crooned into her ear, "I'll be loving you always, Meg Alden." He stopped and hugged her. "Soon to be Meg Wallace, reporter extraordinaire."

She giggled. "Correction. Wife, mother, and columnist extraordinaire."

Author's Note

....

Pamela and her mother at Lake Geneva

Ever since I began writing stories for publication, I have dreamed of writing a novel set in my hometown of Lake Geneva. What better setting could there be than a beautiful Wisconsin lake and a small town with a colorful history? When opportunity came to write this story, I headed to the Lake Geneva Public Library and spent hours parked in front of a microfilm machine reading nearly every article spanning the years of 1932 and 1933, when the Riviera was built. I not only learned about the stages of construction of the *Riv*, as we locals like to call it, but also discovered the hearts of the people who lived there at that time—many of whose descendants came to be my classmates.

What I didn't expect to find was a piece of my heart that had been missing since I moved away. Growing up, I took Lake Geneva for granted. Through my research and writing of Meg and Jack's story, I came to love my hometown as never before. I am so grateful I had the opportunity to grow up in such a place. Like Meg, I thought I needed to leave to chase my dreams. Now it's been in returning that one of my biggest dreams has come true.

About the Author

....

 PAMELA S. MEYERS grew up in Lake Geneva, Wisconsin, where she learned to swim in the shadow of the Riviera, attempted figure-eights on the lake's frozen waters in winter, and basked on its sunny beach as a teen.

She began telling stories as a child while playing with her collection of paper dolls and the occupants of her dollhouse. Pamela's tagline, "Take a Sentimental Journey," aptly describes her stories, which she sets in small towns mostly in her native Wisconsin. She is the author of two published novels and busy working on her third. She has also published articles in dozens of magazines and contributed to a nonfiction compilation.

Pamela makes her home in the Chicago suburbs where, when she isn't dreaming up new stories, she is involved as a women's life group leader. She's also served as an interpreter for the deaf community and in an outreach ministry. Read more at PamelaSMeyers.com.

POST CARD
CARTE POSTALE
Love Finds You

**Want a peek into local American life—past and present?
The *Love Finds You*™ series published by Summerside Press
features real towns and combines travel, romance,
and faith in one irresistible package!**

The novels in the series—uniquely titled after American towns with romantic or intriguing names—inspire romance and fun. Each fictional story draws on the compelling history or the unique character of a real place. Stories center on romances kindled in small towns, old loves lost and found again on the high plains, and new loves discovered at exciting vacation getaways. Summerside Press plans to publish at least one novel set in each of the fifty states. Be sure to catch them all!

Now Available

Love Finds You in Miracle, Kentucky
by Andrea Boeshaar
ISBN: 978-1-934770-37-5

*Love Finds You in
Snowball, Arkansas*
by Sandra D. Bricker
ISBN: 978-1-934770-45-0

Love Finds You in Romeo, Colorado
by Gwen Ford Faulkenberry
ISBN: 978-1-934770-46-7

*Love Finds You in
Valentine, Nebraska*
by Irene Brand
ISBN: 978-1-934770-38-2

Love Finds You in Humble, Texas
by Anita Higman
ISBN: 978-1-934770-61-0

*Love Finds You in
Last Chance, California*
by Miralee Ferrell
ISBN: 978-1-934770-39-9

*Love Finds You in
Maiden, North Carolina*
by Tamela Hancock Murray
ISBN: 978-1-934770-65-8

*Love Finds You in
Paradise, Pennsylvania*
by Loree Lough
ISBN: 978-1-934770-66-5

*Love Finds You in
Treasure Island, Florida*
by Debby Mayne
ISBN: 978-1-934770-80-1

Love Finds You in Liberty, Indiana
by Melanie Dobson
ISBN: 978-1-934770-74-0

Love Finds You in Revenge, Ohio
by Lisa Harris
ISBN: 978-1-934770-81-8

Love Finds You in Poetry, Texas
by Janice Hanna
ISBN: 978-1-935416-16-6

Love Finds You in
Martha's Vineyard, Massachusetts
by Melody Carlson
ISBN: 978-1-60936-110-5

Love Finds You in
Prince Edward Island, Canada
by Susan Page Davis
ISBN: 978-1-60936-109-9

Love Finds You in Groom, Texas
by Janice Hanna
ISBN: 978-1-60936-006-1

Love Finds You in Amana, Iowa
by Melanie Dobson
ISBN: 978-1-60936-135-8

Love Finds You in
Lancaster County, Pennsylvania
by Annalisa Daughety
ISBN: 97-8-160936-212-6

Love Finds You in Branson, Missouri
by Gwen Ford Faulkenberry
ISBN: 978-1-60936-191-4

Love Finds You in
Sundance, Wyoming
by Miralee Ferrell
ISBN: 978-1-60936-277-5

Love Finds You on
Christmas Morning
by Debby Mayne and Trish Perry
ISBN: 978-1-60936-193-8

Love Finds You in
Sunset Beach, Hawaii
by Robin Jones Gunn
ISBN: 978-1-60936-028-3

Love Finds You in
Nazareth, Pennsylvania
by Melanie Dobson
ISBN: 97-8-160936-194-5

Love Finds You in
Annapolis, Maryland
by Roseanna M. White
ISBN: 978-1-60936-313-0

Love Finds You in
Folly Beach, South Carolina
by Loree Lough
ISBN: 97-8-160936-214-0

Love Finds You in
New Orleans, Louisiana
by Christa Allan
ISBN: 978-1-60936-591-2

Love Finds You in
Wildrose, North Dakota
by Tracey Bateman
ISBN: 978-1-60936-592-9

Love Finds You in Daisy, Oklahoma
by Janice Hanna
ISBN: 978-1-60936-593-6

Love Finds You in Sunflower, Kansas
by Pamela Tracy
ISBN: 978-1-60936-594-3

Love Finds You in Mackinac
Island, Michigan
by Melanie Dobson
ISBN: 978-1-60936-640-7

Love Finds You
at Home for Christmas
by Annalisa Daughety and
Gwen Ford Faulkenberry
ISBN: 978-1-60936-687-2

Love Finds You in Glacier Bay, Alaska
by Tricia Goyer and Ocieanna Fleiss
ISBN: 978-1-60936-569-1

COMING SOON

Love Finds You in the
City at Christmas
by Ruth Logan Herne
and Anna Schmidt
ISBN: 978-0-8249-3436-1

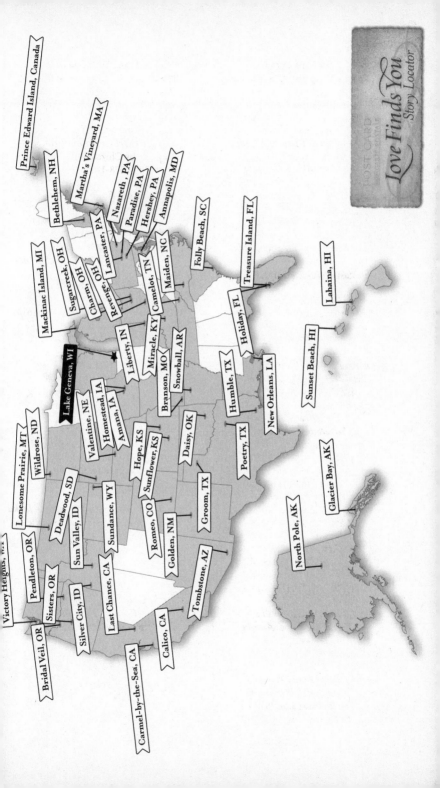